A low roar of ignition shook the shuttlecraft.

Sulu kept his eyes on his gauges as he fired the thrusters to halt the *Kepler*'s spin and then steered into the strongest headwind. The sudden reversals and competing forces of momentum and acceleration tossed Spock and the rest of the landing party around like rag dolls. Only their seats' harnesses kept them from bouncing around inside the shuttle like dice on a craps table.

Good thing we added harnesses.

He had just brought the shuttle's attitude back to level when the impulse engine kicked back on, greatly reducing the effects of turbulence on the hull. He disengaged the emergency thrusters to save hydrox fuel, and then he spared a moment to look back at his shaken passengers. "Everybody okay?"

Ilucci looked nauseated but gave him a thumbs-up. "Five by five, sir."

Apparently in shock, Chekov said, "Define *okay*."

Sulu made a special effort to look over his shoulder at Doctor Babitz, who was sitting directly behind him. The slender woman was hanging on to her harness's straps for dear life as tears rolled from her squeezed-shut eyes. Worried, Sulu called out, "Doc? You okay?"

Babitz shook her head *no* and kept her jaw clenched.

Sulu poured on the speed and sent the *Kepler* screaming through a stormhead like a duranium bullet. "Hang on, Doc, we're almost there. You're gonna make it, I promise."

She reacted with a cross between a sob and a hysterical laugh of despair. "Don't say that. The hope of dying is the only thing keeping me alive."

The Star Trek: Vanguard Saga

STAR TREK™

THE ORIGINAL SERIES

HARM'S WAY

David Mack

Based upon *Star Trek*
created by
Gene Roddenberry

GALLERY BOOKS

New York   London   Toronto   Sydney   New Delhi · Kolasi III

G

Gallery Books
An Imprint of Simon & Schuster, Inc.
1230 Avenue of the Americas
New York, NY 10020

First Gallery Books trade paperback edition December 2022

GALLERY BOOKS and colophon are registered trademarks of Simon & Schuster, Inc.

For information about special discounts for bulk purchases, please contact Simon & Schuster Special Sales at 1-866-506-1949 or business@simonandschuster.com.

The Simon & Schuster Speakers Bureau can bring authors to your live event. For more information or to book an event, contact the Simon & Schuster Speakers Bureau at 1-866-248-3049 or visit our website at www.simonspeakers.com.

Interior design by Kathryn Kenney-Peterson

Manufactured in the United States of America

10   9   8   7   6   5   4   3   2   1

Library of Congress Cataloging-in-Publication Data is available.

ISBN 978-1-6680-0866-9
ISBN 978-1-6680-0867-6 (ebook)

For my editors,
because you asked for this.

Historian's Note

The events of this story occur in July 2267, roughly one month after Spock returns to Vulcan for his *pon farr* (TOS: "Amok Time") and shortly after the *Enterprise* crew destroys the planet-killer (TOS: "The Doomsday Machine").

It has been one year and eight months since the *Enterprise*'s first unexpected detour to Starbase 47 (*Star Trek: Vanguard* novel *Harbinger*).

Fear is a reaction. Courage is a decision.

1

Searing bursts of white, then violet afterimages—that was all Doctor Mozhan Rashid saw of the jungle as she ran from the shadows. During the day the equatorial forests of Kolasi III were lush tableaus of green beneath a leaden dome of clouds, but by night there was only pitch darkness punctuated by moments when ribbons of lightning bent across the sky. Rains warm yet endless had long ago made the jungle's floor a sea of mud and moss, and every square kilometer teemed with life and stank of death.

Was she still heading south? She had no idea. Every direction felt the same in the dark. The trail was close, she was sure of it. She just had to keep moving, keep running—

She tripped on a root and sprawled face-first into a tree's trunk, hard enough to fill her head with crimson flashes of pain. Her cheek throbbed with a deep ache and stung with prickly heat as she pushed herself away from the tree and kept running. Escape was all that mattered now. Before the serpents of smoke and shadow found her again.

Nettled vines caught her sodden jacket and trousers, both of which ripped loudly in several places as Rashid tore herself free with a violent twist.

The ground sloped downward, catching Rashid by surprise. She slid down a muddy grade in the dark and caromed off large stones and tree trunks for what felt like nearly a minute. At the bottom of the incline she plunged headfirst into a shallow, muddy creek. She was submerged for only a few seconds, but that proved more than long enough for her to become a host to half a dozen leeches of varying sizes. She staggered out of the creek and with primal shouts of disgust swatted the smallest ones from her forearms and neck, but the big ones on her legs she had to pinch behind their heads to force them to open their jaws and let go. She flung them away into the night, hurling each one with a grunt of effort and revulsion.

Mere words could never express how deeply Rashid hated this jungle.

Thunder shook the ground, and the sky blazed with electric fury. Around the doctor, the jungle seemed to radiate malign intent. It echoed with the howls of savage appetites, and when lightning set the clouds ablaze, a thousand keen eyes shimmered in the darkness.

She forced herself back into motion. The electrical storm granted her only momentary glimpses of her surroundings, cast in the harshest hues and deepest shadows, but it was enough to help her find the ragged swath cut by her mentor's ship, the *S.S. Heyerdahl*. The Ardanan research vessel was decades old but had been well maintained—until Verdo lost control of it inside the brutal ion storm that encircled Kolasi III's equator and tropical latitudes. Its crash landing had been a spectacular display of both incompetence and good fortune: none of its three passengers had been hurt, but the ship would likely never fly again.

If only I'd died then. I could've been spared these horrors. . . .

And, of course, the rain. This damned endless rain. The perpetual, omnipresent, relentless rain. It shifted in direction, waxed and waned in its intensity, rose and fell in temperature . . . but it never stopped. Rashid's first day in this forest had been enough to make her fear she would never again know how it felt to be dry. Now, after three weeks in this festering armpit of a jungle, she no longer dared to dream of freedom from the damp.

There was no time now for dreams.

Another retina-burning parade of lightning crossed the sky overhead, and at the edges of her peripheral vision, Rashid thought she saw smoky coils undulating between the trees and through the lush greenery blanketing the forest floor. She spun toward the moving shadows, only to find them gone—or perhaps never there.

The ribbon lightning faded, and then all Rashid perceived was the darkness.

She was tempted to use a small palm light she had retrieved from the *Heyerdahl*'s emergency kit after the crash a few weeks ago, but she feared it would only make her more of a target for whatever was lurking beyond her sight.

Just have to keep moving. Almost there.

The next volley of lightning revealed the outline of the *Heyerdahl*'s crumpled hull a few dozen meters ahead, at the end of the scar its crash had cut through the jungle.

Finally!

Rashid quickened her pace and sprinted the last several meters to the small ship. Its portside hatch was still open, and several centimeters of rainwater had pooled on the deck inside the spacecraft. Tendrils of creeping vines and several varieties of moss had colonized its outer hull. The Kolasi jungle was nothing if not tenacious.

Inside the ship, strips of amber-hued emergency lights along the top and bottom of each bulkhead panel switched on as Rashid entered. She took a moment to savor the absence of rain falling on her. She didn't care that she was sopping wet from head to heels. It was a blessing to be relieved, however briefly, of the patter of precipitation on her shoulders, back, and head.

Then she remembered why she had come, and how little time she had.

Most of the *Heyerdahl*'s accessible interior space resided on a single deck. At the forward end was the cockpit. Crew bunks, a food dispenser, and two refresher compartments flanked the main corridor in the forward section. Aft of the crew's accommodations were the research lab and the sickbay. Most of the ship's engineering functions had been automated and confined to a single compartment aft of the laboratory, and inorganic cargo had been stored in compartments beneath the main deck.

Rashid went directly to the cockpit, which housed the ship's communications system. The cockpit's transparent-aluminum viewport was fractured dramatically from corner to corner, upper port-side to bottom starboard. Rainwater trickled in through the fracture, spilled over the main console, and collected on the deck, ankle-deep and tepid.

Driven by equal measures of hope and desperation, Rashid poked at the comm panel's controls. The system was slow to respond. It was drawing power from the emergency reserve batteries, which were down to twenty percent. Would that be enough power to get a signal through the planet's storm belt? She tried to do the calculations in her head but gave up.

Even if someone gets my message, will anyone really risk coming here to help us?

There was only one way to find out.

She keyed up the ship's automated Mayday, set it to broadcast on repeat, and tuned the ship's antenna for a narrow-band transmission toward the Federation. Then she set the transmission's power level to maximum and pressed the TRANSMIT key.

A serpent of smoke and shadow crashed through the forward viewport. Jagged bits of transparent aluminum exploded into the cockpit ahead of the monster, a storm of glasslike shrapnel that hit Rashid like a hurricane and all but flayed her to death.

She landed hard on her back. Her wet clothes had been torn to pieces, and she with them. Countless needles and shards of transparent aluminum poked from every part of her ravaged body, and it felt to her like twice as many more lay embedded inside of her. She felt light-headed as the rainwater puddled around her was warmed by her spilling blood.

The tentacle of black vapor hovered above her, as if to study her, or perhaps to revel in the agony of her last breaths as her lungs filled with blood, suffocating her.

From the console above her, an automated voice repeated a simple message: *"Mayday, Mayday. This is the Ardanan science vessel* Heyerdahl. *Mayday, Mayday. This is the—"*

The smoke-serpent drew itself back from the console and then lunged forward, thrusting its entire mass through the comms console. With a single blow, it reduced the panel to a sparking mess of broken circuit boards and tangled optronic cables. Then the creature reared up and crashed through the cockpit's overhead, splitting it open with such power that the duranium panels were left splayed in all directions, like the petals of a flower in bloom.

Its goal apparently achieved, the monster retreated into the night with an atonal, keening roar that echoed and reechoed across the jungle.

Lying on the cockpit deck, awash in muddy water and her own blood, the last thing Rashid felt as she succumbed to her own endless night was the patter of rain on her face.

2

Captain's Log, Stardate 3795.4

The Enterprise *is paused in interstellar space for a much-needed rendezvous with Starfleet refueling tanker* Jamnagar, *which is replenishing our ship's supply of antideuterium and delivering a consignment of fresh dilithium crystals for our warp reactor.*

"Computer, end recording. File log entry."

Captain James T. Kirk leaned back from the small desk in his quarters. He had far more on his mind this morning than the *Enterprise*'s routine operations, but his other concerns were matters better suited to a personal log than to the ship's official record.

So where to start? A personal log? He reached toward the log recorder controls, only to reconsider before switching the device on. A dozen thoughts twisted through his troubled mind, eluding him as he tried to focus. What was this? Confusion? Guilt? Regret?

Maybe I just need a cup of coffee.

A glance at the ship's chrono confirmed it was just after 0700. Plenty of time to grab a bite in the officers' mess before heading up to the bridge.

Kirk left his quarters to find everything business-as-usual on deck three. A pair of Chief Engineer Scott's red-jumpsuited technicians were busy running diagnostics and making repairs to a duotronic cable relay inside a Jefferies tube. On his way to the turbolift, Kirk noticed the overnight deck officer, Lieutenant Willa Roscoe, checking to make certain that the doors to restricted areas of the ship were locked in accordance with regulations.

If Kirk was surprised by anything, it was that Scott didn't have more of his people working double shifts to catch up on needed repairs. It had been less than a week since the *Enterprise* and its crew had survived a brutal encounter with an extragalactic alien "doomsday weapon"—a planet-killing machine that had assumed a direct heading toward some of the most densely populated star systems in the United Federation of Planets.

Though the mission to stop the planet-killer had been successful, that victory had come at a terrible cost. The monstrosity had claimed the life of Kirk's friend Commodore Matt Decker, and Decker's command, the *U.S.S. Constellation*, which had been a *Constitution*-class starship like the *Enterprise*. Compared to those losses, which included more than four hundred members of Decker's crew, the extensive damage and few dozen casualties the *Enterprise* suffered under Decker's temporary and ill-advised command might have seemed minor, but when it came to his ship and crew Kirk felt every wound and mourned every loss.

Is that why I can't stop thinking about it? Am I grieving for Decker, or am I raging at him for getting so many of my people killed and my ship pummeled?

Questions without clear answers. No matter how many times Kirk pondered them he found neither closure nor comfort.

He remained distracted by melancholy as he entered the officers' mess and made his way to the food synthesizers. At an open slot he inserted his meal card, which, like those of all Starfleet personnel, was programmed to create meals he would enjoy that would also satisfy his nutritional needs, in portion sizes appropriate to his recorded physical activity profile. This morning he had a choice of three options for breakfast. He chose meal number one: three scrambled eggs, wheat toast with butter and jam, a fruit cup, and a mug of hot black coffee.

Semimusical machinations whirred behind the food slot's closed panel. When it slid upward to reveal Kirk's morning meal on a tray, he savored the mingled aromas of eggs, toast, and coffee. To him, that would always smell like a good morning waiting to be met.

He carried his breakfast to an open seat at a nearby table. As usual, most of the junior officers made a point of giving the captain his space. Living together for months or even years in the close confines of a starship taught people to respect others' boundaries. In that circumstance, sitting apart from someone wasn't a sign of disfavor but a gesture of respect for their privacy.

As appetizing as his breakfast had seemed just a minute earlier, once Kirk sat down he found himself poking at the eggs and thinking they felt rubbery. The fruit cup tasted off, and the toast had gone cold more quickly than he'd expected. All in all, a disappointment.

At least the coffee's still good. Thank heaven for that.

He sipped his java and thought once more about Commodore Decker—*Matt*. Kirk had nearly been forced to sacrifice himself in order to pilot the limping husk of the *Starship Constellation* inside the planet-killer and then trigger its self-destruct package, to cripple the alien machine from the inside. Thanks to the planet-killer's neutronium outer hull, a suicide run had been deemed the only viable tactic for stopping it before it reached the Rigel colonies. But the *Constellation* had been Decker's ship, and if anyone should have been there to pilot her to a noble ending, it should have been him. But Decker had snapped; he had succumbed to crushing guilt and threw away his life by flying a defenseless shuttle into the planet-killer.

So it had fallen to Kirk to guide the *Constellation* to its end, to trigger the self-destruct sequence that would turn it into a weapon against the unthinkable.

All to stop the mindless destruction of a technological nightmare that Kirk still could not believe any rational, advanced civilization would ever want to build. Who would make such a pitiless horror? Worse, who would unleash such a thing without some means of halting its rampage? The only solace he found in the matter was Spock's conclusion, based on several factors, that the planet-killer had originated somewhere beyond the Milky Way galaxy. Perhaps in one of the Magellanic Cloud galaxies, or the Sagittarius Dwarf Elliptical, or perhaps even from somewhere in the great void of intergalactic space.

At least none of our neighbors in this galaxy have built anything like that. He sipped his coffee as his inner pessimist added, *Yet.*

The recorded subspace message downloaded to the terminal in Commander Spock's quarters while he finished getting dressed. He was due on the bridge for first watch within the hour, but he was confident he still had sufficient time to procure some fruit and tea for breakfast.

A soft ping from the desk console informed him that the message was ready for playback. He pulled on his blue uniform tunic and smoothed its front, then pressed the PLAY button.

The face of his mother, Amanda Grayson, appeared on the small screen mounted to his desk. She appeared to be healthy and in good spirits, and she wore traditional Vulcan garb, as was expected of the wife of one of his homeworld's most prominent diplomats.

"Hello, Spock." Amanda started to smile but quickly reined in that human affectation. *"I apologize for not having contacted you sooner, but your father's schedule keeps us quite busy."*

Behind her Spock noted a plain terra cotta–hued bulkhead, a common feature aboard most modern Vulcan civilian vessels, and he presumed that she and his father, Sarek, must presently be traveling in connection with Sarek's role as a Federation ambassador emeritus.

"As always, I'm precluded from saying where we've been, where we are, or where we're going. Though I'm sure you could find that out if you really wanted to."

She was correct, of course. As the first officer of a capital vessel in Starfleet, Spock had a high enough security clearance to obtain such information whenever it was needed. Though why he would want or need to abuse such a privilege to assuage a curiosity he did not feel with regard to his parents' whereabouts, he could not imagine.

"In case you haven't heard, your half-brother Sybok is still alive. Or at least he was, as of several weeks ago, when he and a dozen of his acolytes were expelled from Toroth Prime. Rumor has it he invoked your father's name to escape charges of mass brainwashing."

Spock appreciated the irony of Sybok trading on their father's political status for favor, when he was likely the only person in the galaxy Sarek held in a deeper degree of contempt than that which he reserved for Spock.

Amanda's tone acquired an edge. *"Now, lest you think I've used up all my criticism on your sibling, I have a grievance of consequence with you, as well. I know your father and I can be difficult to reach at times, especially when he's traveling on official Federation business, but that's no excuse for failing to invite us home to Vulcan for your wedding, young man."*

A man with lesser control of his involuntary emotional responses might have flushed with anger or embarrassment at being rebuked in such a manner by his mother. Spock said nothing. To argue with a recording would be most illogical. He merely arched one eyebrow by the slightest measure and waited for Amanda's message to continue.

"As I understand it, you returned to Vulcan last month because you'd finally experienced your first pon farr. *Is that correct? I*

imagine that must have come as quite a surprise after all those medical opinions we heard in ShiKahr when you were young."

Her reminiscence led Spock to confront an unpleasant memory from his first several years in Starfleet after receiving his commission. He had felt great embarrassment about not experiencing his first real *pon farr* in his early twenties, as most Vulcan men did. At the time Sarek had tried to console him by saying Spock should be grateful to avoid the indignity of a crude biological assault on his logical Vulcan mind. He had wanted Spock to believe that his body's rejection of the *pon farr* was a blessing. As Spock had grown older, he had hoped the human half of his ancestry might spare him the exquisite agonies of the blood fever, or *plak tow.*

His mother's countenance softened. *"As I'm sure you've already surmised, I'm not really upset with you, Spock. Sarek and I both understand why you might have wanted to keep the news of your* pon farr *private, after all these years. And considering the deplorable behavior of T'Pring, and how close her scheme came to ending in tragedy for everyone involved, I think it perhaps was for the best that Sarek and I were off-world. Had we been present to witness what she did, I think your father might have momentarily found his logic to be . . . uncertain."*

Spock paused the message's playback.

He appreciated Amanda's talent for understatement. T'Pring, to whom Spock had been betrothed in a childhood ceremony decades earlier, apparently had harbored the same dashed hope as he had, that he would never experience *pon farr* or return to claim her as his mate. In her case it was because she had, in the time since they had last seen each other, found a new mate, Stonn. Consequently, she had invoked the *koon-ut-kal-if-fee,* or "marriage challenge by combat," to permanently end her bond with Spock. In what Spock had to grudgingly admit was a masterstroke of logical cunning, she had designated not Stonn but Spock's closest friend and commanding officer, James Kirk, as her champion in the *kal-if-fee.*

To claim his mate, Spock would have to kill his captain.

If he had won the challenge, he would have left Vulcan to be court-martialed, and T'Pring would have been free to be with Stonn. If Spock had died, Kirk would not have claimed her, and again she would have been free to resume her relationship with Stonn.

Her logic had been cold and unassailable.

Lost in the throes of the *plak tow*, Spock had been unable to stop himself from fulfilling his species' biological imperative. Thankfully, a clever deception by Doctor McCoy had enabled Kirk to be legally dead for nearly two minutes but still able to be revived after being transported back to the *Enterprise*.

Believing his opponent in the *kal-if-fee* slain, Spock had been set free of the *plak tow* and the urges of *pon farr*. Expecting to face a court-martial for his actions, he had released T'Pring from their pledge and bade her and his homeworld farewell, for what he presumed might be the last time. Only after his own return to the *Enterprise* did he learn that Kirk was alive.

He remembered shouting "Jim!" with greater relief and joy than he had ever felt before. It had been only a momentary lapse in his control of his emotions, but Kirk had seen it, as had McCoy and Nurse Chapel. Spock's elation had turned to self-consciousness and embarrassment, both of which he had struggled to conceal behind a mask of detachment.

It intrigued Spock to imagine Sarek's emotional discipline lapsing in the face of T'Pring's treachery. Despite Amanda's assertion, he doubted Sarek would ever allow that to happen.

My father prizes his control far too much to ever succumb to base emotions.

But can I say the same?

Self-doubt plagued Spock, as if he were yoked beneath a terrible weight. His missions aboard the *Enterprise*, first under Captain Christopher Pike and now beside Captain Kirk, had subjected his mind to a great many unexpected invasions, violations, and traumas. How many times had his emotional control been tested and found wanting? How many more times might it happen again? What if he lost control of his dark side? The fusion of his Vulcan and human physiology had gifted him with a brain structure and neurochemistry that was truly unique. As savage as Vulcan emotions could be, Spock knew from years of introspection, meditation, and psychic training that the human components of his psyche were possibly even more violent, more dangerous, and more powerful than any Vulcan could imagine.

What if the darkness inside me someday takes control?

It was a possibility that filled Spock with trepidation. Until recently he might have dismissed such concerns as hypochondria. But until a month earlier he also had thought himself immune to the fires of the *plak tow* and the barbaric compulsions of *pon farr*. After everything he had endured from powers outside himself that had sought to control his mind, it had been primal forces from deep inside him that had reduced him to little more than a bloodthirsty animal.

Might such impulses continue to lurk in the shadows of my mind? How can I ask my shipmates to trust me when I am unsure whether I can trust myself?

He pressed PLAY to hear the rest of Amanda's message.

"At any rate, Spock, your father and I heard how you and your shipmates resolved the matter, and we commend you all. You turned what might have been a tragedy into a victory"—she permitted herself a fleeting ghost of a smile—*"but that's always been your forte, hasn't it?"* A bittersweet sadness crossed her face like a passing cloud. *"I love you, Spock. So until we meet again"*—she raised her right hand to offer the Vulcan salute—*"Live long and prosper, my son."*

Her image was replaced by blue laurels and stars on a field of white, the emblem of the United Federation of Planets, and then the screen went black and reverted to standby mode.

Live long and prosper, Mother. For both our sakes I will find a way to be the man you believe I am . . . whether Father believes me capable of such a feat or not.

Free time was a rarity aboard a starship, and the phenomenon known as the long lunch was rarer still. Determined not to waste a second of it, Lieutenant Hikaru Sulu and Ensign Pavel Chekov had rushed through their meals in the officers' mess and then hurried down to the rec room to continue their epic match of three-dimensional chess. The gold-shirted young men had started the match the evening before but had been compelled to leave it unfinished when they'd realized they had barely reached the middle game shortly after 0100. Luckily for them, Petty Officer Chong, who was one of three noncoms who supervised the use of the rec room, agreed to make sure their game pieces would remain undisturbed until they completed their match.

Watching his young opponent from across the table, Sulu grinned. "Ready to resign?"

Chekov squinted at one level of the board and then another. "Never." His heavy Russian accent and youthful timbre provided a dramatic contrast to Sulu's rich baritone and flat American delivery. "I've got you right where I want you."

"You *want* me to be two moves from putting your king in check?"

Sulu's gentle verbal jab drew chuckles from the small crowd of the crew who had gathered to watch them face off in a game most of the crew associated with Spock or even Captain Kirk. Side talk and whispered wagers circled the table like a lazy breeze.

After several more seconds of procrastination, Chekov gently rotated the platform on which the three-level board was mounted. Perhaps he thought that looking at the game from a different angle might somehow change the rules or the relative positions of the pieces. Sulu was happy to let the ensign take all the time he wanted. It wasn't going to change the outcome; he was sure he had left the young Russian no viable route to a counterattack.

Of course, that's what I thought the last time I played Spock, and he wiped the floor with me. Then again, who am I kidding? Chekov is no Spock. If it weren't for his bowl cut's crazy bangs, I'd probably see creases forming in his forehead right now.

Chekov reached toward one game piece but stopped shy of touching it. Grimacing in frustration, he reached instead toward a different piece only to hesitate once more.

Sulu widened his grin. "There's no shame in conceding."

The mere suggestion seemed to offend Chekov. "Of course there is shame. There is *always* shame in losing." He withdrew his hand from the pieces and curled it into a fist. "Would you consider calling it a draw?"

"I would not."

Glowering at the board, Chekov muttered a string of Russian curses. After a heavy sigh, he said, "I will resign if you will tell me how you beat me."

"Fair enough. You telegraphed your intentions from the start, by opening with the King's Indian attack. You pressed a reckless attack during the middle game, even after I'd weakened your flank with an Aldabren exchange. When you committed to a Kriskov gambit, I knew you had to be desperate—no one uses a Kriskov gambit after both their rooks are gone. I neutered your late-game attack with an el-Mitra exchange, and from there it was just a mop-up job."

With a tap of his index finger, Chekov knocked over his king on the middle board, signaling his surrender. "I hate you."

"Don't hate the player, Ensign, hate the game."

The small crowd of spectators drifted away, some arranging for payment of wagers won or lost, others critiquing Sulu's and

Chekov's respective strategies with all the confidence that comes from knowing the ending of the game and not having had to play any part of it.

Chekov glared as he shook his head at Sulu, but then he offered him his hand in congratulation. "Well played, Hikaru."

Sulu shook his friend's hand. "Thanks, Pavel. And seriously, you played a great game. It wouldn't have lasted"—he looked over his shoulder to check the chrono on the bulkhead—"over six hours if you hadn't. So I'm not kidding when I say, 'You made me work for it.' "

"Kind of you to say. But next time I will not be so merciful."

"Hang on. You're not implying you *let* me win, are you?"

"I would never say such a thing. . . . But chess *was* invented in Russia."

"I'm pretty sure it was invented in India."

"But *perfected* in Russia."

"No, *adapted* in southern Europe."

"And *then* perfected in Russia."

"I'm reasonably sure Russia had nothing to do with the creation of the game. Though I'll grant there's a long tradition of excellence in chess within the Russian culture."

Chekov regarded him with a weary stare. "You can't just let me have this?"

"If I do, Pavel, where does it end? I've heard you give credit for just about everything in human history to Russia. Next you'll be telling me *jazz* was invented in Russia."

"It was." Somehow, Chekov had spoken those words without a trace of irony.

"You see, this is what I'm talking about." Sulu stood from the table, and Chekov rose from his chair and followed him toward the rec room's exit. "Name one good thing from Earth that you think *wasn't* invented in Russia."

The question gave Chekov a moment of pause. His pale expression brightened as he replied, "Haggis!"

"I said a *good* thing."

"That's not fair. Have you ever *had* haggis?"

Sulu stared in disbelief at Chekov. "Have *you*?"

The rec room's door slid open before they reached it, and Doctor Leonard McCoy, the ship's chief surgeon, strode in, looked around, and seemed to deflate. "I missed it, didn't I?"

"Our match?" Chekov asked. "*Da.*"

Sulu nudged Chekov's elbow and prompted him under his breath, "*Yes.*"

"That is what I said," Chekov replied in a tense whisper.

McCoy folded his hands behind his back and shuffled his feet. "Damn. I had a few bets riding on this one. Mind telling me who won?"

Sulu cracked a prideful smile. "Who do you think, Doc?"

"So *not* the 'Moscow Mule' here?" He frowned in disappointment, then grumbled half to himself, "That'll teach me to back the underdog."

An electronic boatswain's whistle shrilled from the room's overhead speaker, and it was followed by Spock's voice. "*Attention, all decks: refueling operations have been completed. Stand by to decouple from the tanker* Jamnagar. *Senior officers, report to duty stations.*"

"That's our cue," Sulu said. The three officers headed for the door.

Leading the way, McCoy asked over his shoulder, "When's your rematch?"

Sulu smiled. "Soon."

Chekov scowled. "When hell freezes over."

Kirk scrawled his signature across the bottom of the data slate, confirming he had approved the transfer of antideuterium and dilithium from the *Jamnagar*, and then he handed the slate back to Yeoman Martha Landon. The tall young officer in an operations division red minidress wore her strawberry-blonde hair in a complicated style: it had been swept back from her brow and gathered in an elegant braided crown on the back of her head, from which spilled a long fall of more loosely braided golden tresses. It was an eye-catching style, judging by the attention Landon had garnered from her fellow officers during her recent visits to the *Enterprise*'s bridge.

Only one of those officers, however, seemed to command her attention. More than once when handing a data slate and stylus back to Yeoman Landon, Kirk had noted that she appeared to be distracted. On this occasion he was quick enough to catch the angle of her eye line and trace it back to the object of her interest: the ship's boyish navigator, Ensign Pavel Chekov.

That surprised Kirk, though only slightly.

I would have sworn she'd been looking at Spock. Though I guess Mister Chekov would be a more age-appropriate romantic interest for Landon. To each their own, I suppose.

"Thank you, Yeoman," Kirk said a bit louder than normal, to help break Chekov's inexplicable spell over the woman.

Landon blinked and recovered her composure. "Aye, sir."

She put away the stylus, tucked the data slate under her left arm, and headed for the turbolift. She paused to collect a data card from communications officer Lieutenant Nyota Uhura, whose flawless brown skin and elegantly coiffed crown of sable hair stood in bold contrast to Landon's fawn complexion and flaxen hair.

From the forward dual console, Chekov tried to steal a furtive look at the departing yeoman, only to find himself looking into the steely, knowing eyes of his captain.

Not one to waste an opportunity to put ensigns through their paces, Kirk said, "Mister Chekov, have you finished your scan of the adjoining sectors?"

To the young man's credit, he answered with cool professionalism, "Aye, Captain. No threat vessels or navigational hazards detected. The *Jamnagar*'s path home is clear."

Kirk glanced at Spock, who confirmed Chekov's report with a nod. "Very well. Lieutenant Uhura, please inform *Jamnagar* actual that she's cleared to depart."

Uhura lifted her right hand to the transceiver she wore in one ear. "Aye, sir. Relaying message now." As she transmitted the message, another channel flashed on her console. She switched over to the second comm circuit, listened for a moment, and then looked at Kirk. "Captain, we're receiving a live subspace communication from the office of Admiral Fitzpatrick at Starfleet Command, on a priority channel. Urgent."

Kirk swiveled his command chair forward. "On-screen, Lieutenant."

The image of the departing fuel tanker was replaced by a closely framed shot of Vice Admiral Theodore Fitzpatrick. He wore a gold command tunic adorned by a special insignia used only by the Admiralty. His ruddy, weathered face had jowls that were starting to sag, and his head was topped by a thinning layer of hair that once had been blond but now was turning silver. He wore the expression of a man who had long ago forgotten what it meant to be happy or content.

"Kirk! How's your ship? I heard you took a bit of a beating last week."

"Yes, sir. Our repairs are mostly complete, or at least as far along as they can be without a stop at a starbase." The *Enterprise*'s battle with the planet-killer had happened only five days earlier, but Kirk saw nothing to be gained by correcting an admiral on so minor a point.

If Fitzpatrick actually gave a damn about the content of Kirk's answer, he didn't show it. *"Splendid. I have new orders for you and your crew. A search-and-rescue mission."*

"Search-and-rescue, sir?" Kirk did his best to stay informed of events in any sector to which he was assigned. He hadn't heard of any Starfleet ships or personnel going missing recently, but clandestine operations went wrong all the time.

"*Affirmative, Captain. A civilian scientist, one Doctor Johron Verdo, a Zee-Magnees Prize–winning xenobiologist from Ardana.*"

Spock looked up from the sciences console to interject, "I've read Doctor Verdo's paper on recombinant xenogenetics. His work has been nothing less than revolutionary."

Kirk nodded at that factoid and then returned his attention to the admiral. "What, exactly, were the circumstances of Doctor Verdo's disappearance?"

"*He left three weeks ago on a private research expedition with two of his senior associates: Doctor Mozhan Rashid of Mars, and Lofarras th'Sailash of Andoria. They were supposed to check in after reaching their destination, but according to Verdo's people on Ardana, that message never came. Twenty-one hours ago, a brief and very weak distress signal was sent from Verdo's ship, the S.S. Heyerdahl. Attempts to establish two-way contact failed, but the signal's origin was confirmed as the equatorial region of planet Kolasi III.*

"*I want you to take the Enterprise to Kolasi III, mount a search-and-rescue operation for Doctor Verdo and his assistants, and recover as much of their research and data as possible.*"

It was not Kirk's nature to refuse direct orders, but something about this mission felt off. "Admiral, with all respect, wouldn't a civilian agency be better suited to this mission? I fail to see why three missing civilians merit the diversion of a capital starship."

His pushback prompted a grim nod from Fitzpatrick. "*Normally, I'd agree, Kirk. But there are complicating factors that elevate this matter to one concerning Federation security.*"

"Such as?"

Fitzpatrick's face went from stern to exhausted, as if he had been hiding his fatigue. "*First, the missing Doctor Verdo is the brother-in-law of Ardana's representative on the Federation Council. Since she's one of the more influential members of the security committee, we're taking heat directly from the president's office to find this man.*

"Second, Kolasi III is a primitive Class-M world with a small pre-warp humanoid civilization—and it's located inside the newly established Federation-Klingon Neutral Zone. So we've got both Prime Directive issues and treaty-violation problems to contend with. Not exactly the kind of thing I'd want to leave in the hands of amateurs.

"Obviously, proceed with discretion inside the Neutral Zone. But if the use of force becomes the only way to rescue Doctor Verdo and his people, and to save his research, do whatever you need to do and let the diplomats sort out the rest. Is that clear, Kirk?"

"Perfectly, sir."

"Then I suggest you get moving. Fitzpatrick out." The admiral closed the channel, and the image on the main viewscreen reverted to the serenity of a wide-open vista of stars.

If only we could take a moment to enjoy this view, Kirk lamented.

"Helm, set course for Kolasi III, warp seven. Mister Spock, compile a mission dossier and gather all senior personnel in the briefing room in one hour. We have lives to save, and the clock is ticking."

3

Alone in the interstellar darkness more than four hundred light-years from Andoria, on the border of the frontier sectors known collectively to the Federation as the Taurus Reach, stood Starfleet's Starbase 47, better known to its denizens and visitors as Starbase Vanguard. The Watchtower-class space station was home to more than two thousand personnel and presently served as the home port and base of operations for three Starfleet starships: the heavy cruiser *Endeavour*, the frigate *Buenos Aires*, and the scout ship *Sagittarius*.

To one side of Vanguard lay the vast territory of the Klingon Empire, a colossal threat waiting for its moment to strike. On the opposite side sprawled the secretive domain of the Tholian Assembly. Where the Klingons could be relied upon to compete with Starfleet for access to the secrets of the Taurus Reach, the Tholians had made it their priority to prevent anyone from unraveling those ancient mysteries—by any means necessary.

The office of the Starfleet Intelligence liaison resided deep inside the station's domelike command tower. It comprised a few small suites and a handful of private offices, all of them hardened against external surveillance or intrusion, and it was served by several encrypted hard-line uplinks to the station's subspace communications array.

Like so many other expenditures made in the service of an interstellar-intelligence apparatus, it was redundant in the extreme. In fact, most of the office space assigned to the Starfleet Intelligence liaison had gone unoccupied since the station had first opened for service two years prior. From then until a few months earlier, these sparsely furnished accommodations had been all but the personal fiefdom of a single woman: Lieutenant Commander T'Prynn of Vulcan.

Then had come a series of calamities aboard the station, all of them fallout or collateral damage from intelligence operations gone sideways, culminating in the greatest shock of all: T'Prynn's public psychological meltdown, followed by her collapse into a catatonic state.

The fall of that domino had in turn toppled several more, leading the station's former commanding officer, Commodore Diego Reyes, to expose the details of classified Starfleet operations to the civilian media. In short order, Reyes had been arrested and shipped off to a penal colony—a journey he apparently never finished, thanks to a pirate attack on his transport ship. T'Prynn, meanwhile, had been taken off the station by Doctor M'Benga, so that she could be treated on Vulcan by specialists in telepathically induced deep psychic trauma.

M'Benga had since returned to duty; his patient had not. Now a fugitive from Starfleet military justice, T'Prynn was at large somewhere in the galaxy. Consequently, her former billet, which had fallen to Lieutenant Commander Serrosel ch'Nayla on what he had been told was a strictly interim basis, had in fact become ch'Nayla's permanent assignment.

It was a series of events ch'Nayla had greatly come to resent.

I should never have accepted promotion. I was happy in the field. Now my whole life is reading reports and filing paperwork. I trained to be a spy, not a damned clerk.

It was a soothing daydream, but ch'Nayla knew it had never been a possibility. Within the ranks of Starfleet Intelligence, declining a promotion was unheard of. Doing so was a sign of dissatisfaction, the kind that could earn one a transfer to monitor a comm relay on a lifeless ball of ice at the end of the galaxy, or even an involuntary dishonorable discharge.

The Andorian *chan* was spending yet another night alone in the liaison's office, reviewing a seemingly endless trove of work product derived from signals intelligence, known in the trade as SigInt. Tonight's virtual haystack consisted of random snippets of subspace comm chatter intercepted between foreign ships and commands, as well as the occasional tidbit of civilian comm chatter snagged from monitored government frequencies. If one was lucky, any given morsel might come complete with an AI-generated transcript. When one was unlucky, the absence of a transcript meant listening to entire clips, one after another, and generating those transcripts manually. Nothing in ch'Nayla's Starfleet medical profile suggested he was at risk for narcolepsy, but on a night of nonstop transcription he would have sworn otherwise.

Then a rarity crossed his screen: a file from Starfleet Command. A bulletin about a prominent missing person, an Ardanan scientist named Doctor Johron Verdo. For some reason, Vanguard's system had red-flagged this report specifically for ch'Nayla's attention. Setting aside all other open projects, ch'Nayla dug into Verdo's dossier.

What's so important about you, *Doctor?*

By the second paragraph, ch'Nayla had his answer. Doctor Verdo had served as an expert scientific consultant to Operation Vanguard, the classified program that was the real reason for Starbase 47's very existence and for Starfleet's risky, aggressive push to claim the Taurus Reach as its own. The Ardanan xenogeneticist's work had served as the foundation for several initiatives being pursued by the team in the Vault, the top-secret Starfleet research laboratory hidden deep inside the core of Starbase Vanguard.

The more ch'Nayla read about Verdo, the more concerned he became. Verdo had been permitted early access to unredacted raw scans of the insanely complex alien DNA string known as the Shedai meta-genome. Though Verdo had not been told what it actually was or where it had been found, his follow-up questions had made it clear that he understood both the opportunities and the dangers it represented, and he was desperate to know more. Judging him a security risk, Starfleet had refused his application to join the Vault team.

Now the man was listed as missing along with two of his most experienced colleagues on Kolasi III—a world on the periphery of the Taurus Reach, one not yet explored but on the short list for a clandestine planetary survey. Clandestine because the planet lay inside the Klingon-Federation Neutral Zone established by the recent Treaty of Organia.

Making matters worse, Verdo had a relative on the Federation Council.

It was enough to make ch'Nayla want to resign his commission on the spot. He couldn't have cooked up a bigger potential mess if he had tried. Most troubling of all were the questions he knew would be asked once he brought this report to the attention of his superiors—questions for which he presently had no good answers.

Is Verdo still on the planet? Does he want to defect to the Klingons? Do the Klingons know he's there? If he finds the Shedai meta-genome, what will he do with it? Is he dangerous?

He added those queries to several others and tasked his AI daemon to perform a deep-level data scrape of every bit of accessible information, public and private, domestic and foreign, open or classified, all in the service of generating a virtual model of the missing scientist, one that could predict his actions before his disappearance provoked the entire quadrant into war.

Then he forwarded the entire misbegotten mess to Admiral Nogura, the Starfleet flag officer presently in command of Operation Vanguard, accompanied by a single unequivocal recommendation: WE NEED TO FIND JOHRON VERDO, RFN.

Blood, sweat, and hot metal—those were the scents that told Captain Kang, son of K'naiah, that he was where he belonged: aboard a Klingon warship.

He strode through the corridors of the *I.K.S. SuvwI'*, a *D'ama*-class battle cruiser. She was one of the older vessels in the fleet, but she and her crew had proved themselves in battle many times over. Great songs were sung of her victories, and tales were told around roaring fires of foes who had learned to fear her name. Kang was proud to call her his own, and to lead the 297 elite warriors, engineers, and scientists who served aboard her.

He passed the crew's mess and caught the high-pitched squeaks of fresh *gagh*, followed by the tantalizing aromas of *pipius* claw and a *rokeg* blood pie. It was enough to make him regret having skipped breakfast that morning, but not tempting enough to make him stop.

If only I had the time.

Near the forward end of the corridor, a handful of soldiers stood in a cluster at the bottom of a gangway. One barked order from Kang—"Make a hole!"—put all their backs to bulkheads. Each of them held their chin high as he marched past and clambered swiftly up the ladder.

From the gangway it was just a few long strides to the command deck, which was bathed in soothing crimson light. Warp-stretched starlight filled the main viewscreen. The senior members of Kang's command crew were all at their posts. As on most Klingon starships, the majority of critical duty stations were arranged in a shallow arc at the front of the cramped space, while the captain's chair sat behind them, elevated on a dais. Sometimes Kang questioned the wisdom of having an elevated seat in a compartment with a low overhead, but he appreciated the fact that the combination served to make the captain loom large, as was right and proper.

His first officer, Commander D'Gol, vacated the center chair
as soon as he noted Kang's arrival. "Captain."

"D'Gol. You said I have a comm from High Command?"

"Yes, sir. It was coded for your eyes only. I routed it to your
ready room."

"Good. As you were."

The lanky warrior returned to the command chair as Kang
headed aft, past the science and communications stations, and
into his ready room. It was small, but it served Kang's needs. He
sat down behind his desk, and his computer terminal powered
up as it registered his presence.

"Computer, open message from High Command."

A gruffly masculine but clearly synthetic voice replied, *"Au-
thorization code required."*

"Kang *cha' vagh Qob Hegh beH tajVaq.*"

"Authorized."

New orders from General Garthog appeared on Kang's
screen. They were, as Kang had come to expect from the general, terse: PROCEED AT HIGH WARP TO KOLASI III. FIND MISSING
SCIENTIST. RECOVER CLASSIFIED ALIEN GENOME IF POSSIBLE.

Kang shook his head in disappointment. *Why is there always
a missing scientist? And why don't we ever let them stay missing?*
He didn't worry about the absence of the scientist's name in the
communiqué. Garthog preferred to keep his comms brief and
bury the meat of his messages inside encrypted dossiers sent as
attachments. It was a tedious habit, but Garthog was a general,
which meant his idiosyncrasies had to be indulged without
comment.

Well, without *public* comment.

For a moment Kang felt inclined to brush off this latest as-
signment as being beneath him—until he saw the warning
Garthog had appended to his orders: EXPECT TO ENCOUNTER
FEDERATION *STARSHIP ENTERPRISE.* GOOD HUNTING.

The very mention of *that ship* filled Kang with the thrill of the hunt.

Kirk, you old devil! Cross my path again, will you?

It had been almost two years since Kang had last encountered the increasingly infamous Starfleet captain. Freshly promoted to his first command, the *I.K.S. Doj*, at roughly the same time that Kirk was elevated to his command of the *Enterprise*, Kang had thought himself fortunate to be the one to intercept the *Enterprise* after it illegally entered Klingon space, on a direct heading for Qo'noS, the Klingon homeworld. To his chagrin, however, he soon learned that Kirk's ship had been hijacked by Klingon renegades, and that the young Starfleet officer and his crew were not, in fact, to blame for the incursion.

And Kirk, damn him—even though he had willingly remained Kang's prisoner, he had appealed to Kang's honor, asking for a chance to reclaim his ship and, with it, his own honor. Though Kang had offered Kirk no assistance, he struck a bargain that he never expected Kirk to fulfill: if Kirk could retake control of the *Enterprise* in one hour and deliver the Klingon fugitives to him so they could face Klingon justice, Kang would let Kirk have his ship back.

To Kang's lasting surprise, Kirk did exactly that.

Nearly two years later, Kang still had no idea how Kirk did it.

Maybe this time I will get a chance to ask him, face-to-face once more.

He decrypted the files from the communiqué and copied them onto a data card, which he took with him as he returned to the command deck.

As expected, all eyes were upon him as he emerged from his ready room. New orders were often cause for excitement. He hoped this time would be no different.

Kang reclaimed his command chair from D'Gol, and then he handed the man the data card. "We're going hunting. A missing lab rat or something. But more important, we might get a chance to face off with Kirk and the *Enterprise*. Have the crew battle-ready by the time we get to Kolasi III, and put together a landing party to find the lab rat."

"Yes, Captain."

D'Gol backed away from the dais, and then he turned and set about issuing orders to the gunners, engineers, and other officers, in preparation for a chance to bring glory to their names.

A discreet, silent notice blinked on Kang's tactical console. It was a signal from his science officer, Lieutenant Mara—who, as it happened, was also his wife. They had taken care not to spark resentment among the other officers by doing anything that would suggest she wielded undue authority simply by virtue of her status as Kang's mate. At the same time, he knew that to sideline her too forcefully would aggrieve his true love. So they had devised a system by which they could covertly let each other know when they wanted or needed to speak.

Kang waited half a minute, and then he swiveled his command chair aft, stood, and descended to the deck. He moved aft to Mara's post, the science console. In a confidential register he said, "Speak, my love."

She replied with equal discretion, "I've reviewed the survey file for Kolasi III. The planet's equatorial and tropical latitudes are encompassed by a powerful electric storm that will make it too dangerous to use transporters there—and the mission profile indicates our missing scientist is likely in that region."

"What do you recommend?"

"Our strike team should go planetside by shuttle."

"Agreed. Anything else?"

He could tell by the way Mara averted her eyes from his that she was reluctant to speak her mind, though he wasn't sure why. "What else concerns you? Speak freely."

"Besides the fact that Kolasi III is located inside the new Neutral Zone, it's also technically inside the Gonmog Sector.

That region has seen a recent sharp increase in reports of lost or missing vessels. There's no telling what Starfleet might have stirred up out there. Perhaps we should exercise a measure of caution—for once."

It was all Kang could do to keep his reaction to a low chortle and not a roaring laugh. "Mara, really? Are we to start marking our star charts of the Gonmog Sector with 'Here there be monsters'?" She narrowed her eyes into a cold glare that made clear she did not find him funny, at all. He reined in his mirth. "Forgive me, my love. I meant no insult. But I beg you—pay less mind to *ghojmok*'s tales of ghost ships and creatures of legend, and focus on the strike team's loadout for the search mission." With a mischievous gleam in his eye he added, "The only monster we'll need to slay at Kolasi III will be *James T. Kirk*."

4

A search-and-rescue mission was not what Kirk had expected to be doing when he had woken up that morning, but serving in Starfleet had taught him to accommodate the unexpected. Pushing the Federation's frontier a bit farther into interstellar space had been his hope, but what he wanted was ultimately irrelevant. The mission always came first, whatever it turned out to be, and it was as subject to change as every other detail of life that Kirk and his crew took for granted while living aboard a starship. It was a risk that came with the uniform.

Walking from his quarters to the nearest turbolift, Kirk felt the subtle but steady pulse of the ship's warp drive resonating through its spaceframe and bulkheads. Even the deck plates under his feet hummed with potential as the starship hurtled at high warp toward Kolasi III.

He noticed fewer personnel than usual passing him in the corridor, and then he recalled that most of the ship's complement were already at their primary or secondary duty stations. *Maybe I should sound yellow alert more often. I like having the corridors to myself for a change.*

The door to Spock's quarters slid open ahead of Kirk's approach. Spock emerged, a data slate tucked under his left arm. With balletic ease he fell into step beside Kirk. "Captain."

"Running late, Spock? That's not like you."

The half-Vulcan man ignored Kirk's mild verbal jab. "I was

compiling data relevant to our mission. I found significantly more than I had expected."

His statement intrigued Kirk. "What did you find?"

They stopped in front of the turbolift. Spock handed his data slate to Kirk and then pushed the call button for the lift. "I uncovered a report from Starfleet Intelligence that proves the missing Doctor Verdo had prominent ties to Operation Vanguard."

Mild alarm snuck into Kirk's voice: "Vanguard? Are you sure?"

"I am quite certain."

The turbolift doors parted. Spock stepped into the lift car and gripped the throttle control as Kirk followed him inside. As the doors closed, Spock gave the control a half turn as he said for the computer, "Deck six." With a low purr of electromagnetic propulsion but almost no sense of movement, the lift car began its gentle descent, its speed kept in check by Spock.

Kirk perused the information on the slate. Not only did Verdo have professional relationships with several scientists who were presently assigned to Operation Vanguard's research unit, there was evidence that Starfleet had consulted Verdo. Recalling the secretive machinations of Vanguard's senior personnel, Kirk found himself suddenly ill at ease. "How much do you think he knows about Vanguard's true mission?"

"Difficult to say. However, Doctor Verdo is an expert in xenobiology and genomic medicine—two fields that would be essential to Vanguard's principal objective."

It was clear to Kirk that Spock was taking care not to say certain things out loud—in particular, he was avoiding any mention of the ancient precursor species known as the Shedai, or of their mysterious meta-genome, a genetically encoded information string they had seeded into the primordial soup of dozens of worlds throughout the vast region known as the Taurus Reach.

Kirk handed the slate back to Spock. "The last time we got involved in Vanguard's business, we were too late to do any good."

"I presume you refer to the colony at Ravanar IV?"

"The smoking crater that used to be a secret Starfleet listening post, yes."

"I would hardly consider that mission analogous to our present assignment."

"Maybe we should, Spock. What if Vanguard's precious alien genome is the reason Verdo went to Kolasi III? Its mere presence provoked the Tholians into bombing that lab and risking a war with the Federation." The turbolift slowed and came to a halt. Its doors opened, and Kirk led Spock out onto deck six, and then down the corridor to the briefing room. "I mean, think about it, Spock. If we're not careful, we could end up in a war that'll make Starfleet's last conflict look like a playground scuffle."

"Then it would seem a policy of extreme caution is in order."

"At the very least."

A look of concern accentuated the fine creases that lined Spock's brow. "If I might offer a suggestion, Captain? In the interest of prudence."

"I'm listening."

"Given the classified nature of all matters affiliated with Operation Vanguard, and the potentially incendiary nature of a mission into the Neutral Zone, perhaps we should contact Admiral Nogura on Starbase 47."

Kirk halted outside the briefing room's door and faced Spock, who stopped with him. "What are you saying, Spock? You think we ought to hand off the search for Verdo to Nogura and his people? On what grounds?"

Spock lowered his voice for the sake of discretion. "If Doctor Verdo is associated with Operation Vanguard, the admiral and his team will have a vested interest in his safe return. And if, as I suspect, Doctor Verdo's research on Kolasi III is connected to the Shedai meta-genome, Admiral Nogura will wish to ensure it remains secret."

"All true, Spock. But also one hundred percent speculative. We don't *know* for a fact that Doctor Verdo was working on behalf of Operation Vanguard when he disappeared, or that the purpose of his journey to Kolasi III was connected to Vanguard's mission objectives in any way. All we know for certain right now is that he and two of his colleagues have been reported missing, a distress signal indicates their last-known location is in the tropical jungle of Kolasi III, and we have orders in hand from Starfleet Command to risk breaching the Neutral Zone in order to effect a search-and-rescue mission. Until we know otherwise, this is *our* mission. *We'll* get it done. Is that clear, Mister Spock?"

"Perfectly, Captain."

"Good." Kirk turned toward the briefing room, whose door opened ahead of him. "Let's get this show on the road."

Chekov looked up as the briefing room door slid open. He and the other officers seated at the briefing table—McCoy, Uhura, Sulu, and chief engineer Lieutenant Commander Montgomery Scott—all started to stand as Captain Kirk and Commander Spock entered.

Kirk moved to the open seat at the head of the table. "As you were."

Chekov and his shipmates settled back into their chairs as Spock took the open seat to Kirk's right. Kirk folded his hands atop the table and regarded his senior officers. "By now you all know we're heading to Kolasi, a star system inside the Klingon Neutral Zone. It is *imperative* that we avoid any direct conflict that could jeopardize our fragile truce with the Klingons. This need for restraint applies to both the *Enterprise* and its landing party." The captain looked at Chekov. "Ensign: What is your threat assessment for this sector?"

Keenly aware that he was on the spot, Chekov straightened his posture, and then he inserted a data card into the slot on the table in front of him. Star charts and Klingon starship specs appeared on different screens of the three-sided viewer mounted in the middle of the table. "The Kolasi system is not part of the Klingons' regular patrol route in this sector. But they have several vessels deployed from Zeta Cancri that might pose a danger to our mission. Most notably, the *I.K.S. SuvwI'*, a D4-type Klingon battle cruiser." Punching in commands from the panel at his seat, Chekov highlighted some of the Klingon ship's specifications. "The *SuvwI'* has a crew of approximately three hundred, and carries four shuttlecraft. She has two disruptor cannons and four torpedo launchers—two forward, two aft. Her deflector screens are almost as strong as ours, and she can easily match our speed at warp and impulse. The latest report from Starfleet Intelligence says her current commanding officer is Captain Kang."

At the mention of Kang's name, Kirk's focus sharpened noticeably. Chekov had no idea what history Captain Kirk shared with Kang, but it was clear he knew who Kang was.

The captain recovered his composure and looked at his first officer. "Mister Spock, your findings about our destination."

Spock inserted a data card into an open slot and began his briefing as images of a lush green world appeared on the table's viewer. "Kolasi III is a Class-M world with a mass equivalent to that of Earth, gravity of zero point eight nine Earth standard, and an axial tilt of sixteen point two degrees. It has one small moon, which possesses a strong magnetic field, just like the planet itself. It used to have a second, much smaller moon, which broke apart several million years ago; its remains now constitute a dense, colorful, and highly ionized ring of rock and ice around the planet's equator. Eighty-one percent of the planet's surface is covered by water. Its oceans are saline, but only mildly so. It has a single continental land mass, the bulk of which lies along the planet's equator and is contained within its tropical latitudes. It is inhabited by a primitive humanoid species, so the Prime Directive is in effect."

He keyed in a command, shifting the images on screen to meteorological reports. "The tropical and equatorial regions of the planet experience persistent cloud cover and heavy precipitation, by way of a powerful electrical storm. The power of these storm cells, combined with the planet's extremely energetic and erratic magnetic field, make the use of transporters unsafe. All travel to and from the surface will need to be done by shuttlecraft."

Sulu spoke up without waiting to be called upon. "That's only the start of the fun. The same factors that scramble our transporters can also knock out a shuttlecraft's impulse systems and navigational controls. We can harden a shuttle's systems against some of these effects, but not all of them. Which means we'll need to make some serious modifications to one of our shuttles, to guarantee it can survive the trip down and have enough power to get back to orbit."

Scott nodded at Kirk to catch his eye. "I'm on top of it, sir. My boys are stripping down the *Kepler* as we speak, putting in new electromagnetic cladding, and beefing up its thrusters. It won't win any beauty pageants, but it'll get you there and back."

"Good work, Scotty." Kirk looked next at Uhura. "Lieutenant, review who it is we're going there to find."

Uhura keyed up her own data card for the table's viewer. An image of a plain-looking middle-aged humanoid man appeared on its screens. "This is Doctor Johron Verdo, noted xenobiologist from Ardana. Fifty-nine years of age, no known medical or psychological issues. His rescue is our principal objective. Also considered of vital importance are his two colleagues who are believed to have joined him on this mission." The image of a human woman with light-brown skin and black hair replaced Verdo's picture on the viewer. "This is Doctor Mozhan Rashid, human, from Mars. Specialist in genomic medicine." The last image to appear was that of an Andorian *thaan* with boldly angular facial features. "This is Doctor Lofarras th'Sailash of

Andoria. Xenocultural specialist." Uhura called up an image of a small civilian vessel on the viewer. "The *Heyerdahl* is a private research ship built on Ardana. It's owned by Doctor Verdo and was the source of the brief distress signal detected by Starfleet."

Uhura switched off the viewer, and Kirk leaned forward. "We're about eight hours from making orbit of Kolasi III. Mister Spock, you'll command the landing party. Mister Sulu will be your pilot, and I want you to take Mister Chekov, Doctor McCoy, and three security personnel as your search team."

McCoy frowned and shook his head. "Why do I always win a seat on this ride?"

Ignoring the surgeon's complaint, Kirk added, "Until we reach Kolasi III, Mister Scott and Mister Sulu will continue working on their modifications of the shuttlecraft *Kepler*, to help make sure it can stand up to whatever that planet's permanent storm system can dish out.

"As for the rest of you, try to get some sleep. Based on the few maps we have of the planet's surface, you should expect to need to cover a lot of ground on foot after you land."

"A long march in the rain," Chekov deadpanned. "Just what I've always wanted."

More of the shuttlecraft *Kepler*'s key components lay strewn about the *Enterprise*'s hangar deck than were still attached to the shuttle's spaceframe. Sulu had watched a team of young enlisted mechanics take the craft apart under Scott's direction. Now he watched them scratch their heads while he and Scott deliberated exactly how to put the *Kepler* back together, and what changes to make along the way. So far, Sulu was at a loss. He sighed. "What a mess."

Scott was undaunted. "Have to break eggs to make an omelet, Mister Sulu."

"Is that what this is?"

"Not yet. But give me time, lad. We're just gettin' warmed up."

They circled the stripped-down shuttlecraft. Sulu stayed a pace or two behind Scott and tried to see the possibilities that the chief engineer insisted were here, waiting to be found. But all Sulu could think about were the odors of overheated metal and industrial solvents, the aching fatigue in his limbs, and the steady low rumble in his gut that reminded him he had missed his usual dinner break because of this emergent crisis.

If Scott harbored any similar distractions, he kept them well hidden. He pointed at the nose of the shuttle and said to one of the mechanics, "Hideki, get me some ablative carbon mesh from reactor supply. If it's good enough to hold in the heat of an impulse core, it should do nicely as a thermal shield for the *Kepler*." A few steps more, and Scott paused again. He aimed a curious look at Sulu. "Could you still fly it if I yanked out half its inertial dampers?"

Sulu gave Scott a reproachful sidelong smirk. "*Please.* I once pulled ten gees making an Immelmann turn at half impulse. I can handle a bumpy ride."

"Good, that'll let me fit two extra tanks of hydrox."

A memory from flight training nagged at Sulu. "Isn't hydrox unstable?"

"No more than any other binary liquid fuel." Scott regarded Sulu with mild worry. "Are you having second thoughts, lad?"

"No," Sulu said, sounding a bit more defensive than he had meant to. "But do we really need to pack that much hydrox onto the shuttle?"

"Afraid so." Scott picked up his data slate from a nearby rolling tool cart. He called up a page of data, and then he handed the slate to Sulu. "Look at these interference patterns. That's a disaster waitin' to happen. What if one o' them hits the *Kepler* while it's headin' for orbit?"

As both a trained flight control officer and a physicist, Sulu understood Scott's concern. "It would knock out the primary controls and the impulse coil for up to a minute, maybe more." Masking his newfound dread, he handed back the slate. "We'd drop like a rock."

"That you would." Scott pointed at more of the shuttle's exposed inner workings. "I can insulate the fly-by-wire system if we pull some of the redundant comm circuits, but the impulse core? Not a millimeter to spare on any side. No way to shield it, so we have to make sure you can fly without it, at least for a couple of minutes."

"Will that be enough?"

Scott shrugged. "I guess we'll find out."

Sulu gestured at the various bits and pieces scattered around the hangar's deck: circuit boards, cabling, and assorted tiny devices whose functions were not immediately evident. "What about the rest of this? Is any of it going back in?"

"Likely not. Had to pull most of it to bring down the overall mass."

"Let me guess: Part of making sure we can reach orbit on thrusters alone?"

"Aye. But don't go losin' sleep over it. I only pulled out backup systems."

This time Sulu didn't bother trying to hide his alarm. "Is *that* all?" He pointed at a boxlike object next to the tool cart. "Tell me that's not the small-arms locker."

"That was the *aft* arms locker. We left the main locker in place, by the hatch."

"How generous. I'm surprised you didn't rip the seats from the passenger compartment."

"Don't think we didn't consider it, laddie."

"And I suppose that heap of fiber over there *isn't* the shuttle's insulation?"

Scott's usually sanguine manner betrayed the first signs of irritation. "We had to replace it with a duranium-fiber–laced foam that can do the same job at a fraction of the mass, *and* protect you and the rest of the landing party from the sixty to seventy lightning strikes Mister Spock estimates will hit the *Kepler* on its way down—and again on its way back up."

That statistic gave Sulu a moment's pause. "Did you say *sixty to seventy* lightning strikes will hit us? Each way?"

"Aye, lad. Are you seeing a method to my madness yet?"

Sulu nodded. "I think so." He moved closer to the gutted shuttlecraft and examined the systems still in place. "Can we add an emergency parachute system? In case the thrusters fail?"

"Not without losing your sensor package, which would leave you flyin' on full manual, with no instruments. No offense, Mister Sulu—I know you're one hell of a pilot—but even *you* don't want to take a risk like *that*."

He was right, though Sulu was loath to admit it. All the same, Sulu was determined to make the *Kepler* as safe as it could be. "Can we at least get a few extra cross supports, to better distribute any impact force? And some five-point padded harnesses for the seats?"

"Consider it done. Anything else on your wish list? We do have nearly *five* hours until deployment. Might as well work a miracle or two."

Sulu stepped inside the skeletal shuttle and settled into the pilot's chair. "I have to fly this shoebox into an electric maelstrom, go looking for a scientist in a jungle where it never stops raining, avoid corrupting a primitive, Prime Directive–protected indigenous culture, and then somehow get this hunk of junk back into orbit without getting vaporized by the Klingons. I guess if I were making wishes, I'd ask you to make the *Kepler* invulnerable, invincible, and invisible."

"In five hours I can give you less fragile, mildly intimidating, and vaguely nondescript."

"Sold. But, seriously, I need this thing to be able to take a hit."

"I can make that happen, trust me." Scott gave Sulu a reassuring pat on the back. "Go grab some shut-eye, lad. I've got this from here."

The mere mention of sleep was enough to make Sulu drowsy. He set one hand on the engineer's shoulder. "Thank you, Mister Scott."

Sulu headed for the hangar's exit. His steps felt heavy, and his mind seemed already to be drifting toward dreams, in anticipation of finally getting some much-needed time in his bunk.

As Sulu neared the door to the corridor, Scott asked his mechanics a question that instantly snapped Sulu back to full, paranoid consciousness.

"Does it really *need* the hatch?"

───────────────

The endless storm that encircled the equator and tropical latitudes of Kolasi III was every bit as alarming as Starfleet's advance reports had made it sound. Its swirling clouds of black and gray pulsed with constant flashes of sickly green lightning that made Kirk think of a witch's cauldron churning with forces dark and terrible. Watching it roil on the bridge's main viewscreen, Kirk felt a sense of foreboding. *Am I really sending my people down into that?*

It had been almost fifteen minutes since the *Enterprise* had entered orbit, and Kirk felt edgy. He wanted to get the mission underway as soon as possible, not just for the benefit of the missing scientists, but also to improve the chances that the landing party might be able to complete its mission and return before the *I.K.S. Suvwl'* arrived to complicate matters. At the same time, looking at the nightmarish tempest wrapped around the planet, he couldn't help but have reservations about deploying a shuttlecraft into its primordial violence.

That's not what's eating at me, and I know it.

Counting down the minutes until the launch of the shuttlecraft *Kepler*, Kirk admitted to himself that the root of his misgiving was that he wouldn't be leading the landing party. Doing so had become second nature to him in the short time since he had assumed command of the *Enterprise*. Never mind that it flew in the face of Starfleet regulations, which insisted that the proper place for a commanding officer was on the bridge of their ship. Kirk wanted to be in the thick of things. In the mix. In charge. Always.

But not this time.

Why did I put Spock in charge instead of going myself? And why now?

He examined that question over and over in his mind, considering all the reasons why he might have second-guessed himself. It wasn't the first time he had placed Spock in charge of a landing party, nor would it be the last. From a tactical perspective, it had made sense. Operations of any kind inside the Neutral Zone were fraught with risk, not just to life and limb but to the fragile political equilibrium of two great interstellar powers. If the Klingons inserted themselves into this situation, the potential repercussions could affect not just the outcome of this mission, but the fates of millions of people across local space. It would take a seasoned officer not only to extricate the landing party ahead of any Klingon reprisals but also to do so in a way that wouldn't lead to war. That wasn't a burden Kirk could expect anyone else to bear, not even someone as experienced and capable as Spock.

Managing this kind of military and political crisis was a duty for a captain.

Still, Kirk's conscience plagued him. *That's not it. Not really.*

When he put aside the official rationale and looked inside himself for the truth, he saw the face of Matt Decker: that haggard countenance, those eyes marked by the sight of horrors beyond imagination, the unmistakable aura of grief and guilt that had surrounded him. But when everything had been at stake, Decker betrayed his oath. Stole a shuttle. Threw his life away.

Why? Did he think death would wash away his sins? What twisted moral calculus led him to think the waste of one more good life would atone for the loss of four hundred others?

Is that why I let Spock lead the landing party? Do I feel guilty for all the times I put my ego ahead of the good of my ship and my crew?

His somber rumination was interrupted by Lieutenant Uhura. "Captain? Commander Spock reports the shuttlecraft *Kepler* is starting its preflight check. He says they'll be ready to launch in three minutes."

Kirk swiveled his chair just far enough to acknowledge Uhura's report with a nod. "Thank you, Lieutenant." As he let his chair return to its normal forward-facing position, he realized that Uhura's was the only familiar face on the bridge this morning. With Spock, Sulu, and Chekov all assigned to the landing party, their posts on the bridge were crewed by relief officers whom Kirk barely knew.

At the helm sat Lieutenant Julie Benson, a woman who had joined Starfleet in her thirties rather than in her youth, as so many had done. She had pale skin, light blue eyes, and dirty blonde hair pulled back in a utilitarian ponytail. Unlike many of the *Enterprise*'s female personnel, Benson eschewed the mini-dress uniform, preferring instead the classic duty uniform of black trousers and a gold command division tunic.

Occupying the navigator's seat at the forward dual console was Lieutenant Aaron Waltke. The thirtyish human man's light brown hair was thinning and his hairline receding, but his neatly trimmed beard gave him a distinguished bearing that suited his calm, genial nature.

Standing at the sciences console was Ensign Bantu Nanjiani. Fresh out of the Academy, the young Pakistani man was all nerves and enthusiasm, a combination that manifested in his tendency to speak at warp speed and—judging by the coffee stain on his blue tunic—a propensity for clumsiness.

The ship's chrono counted down the minutes and seconds until the *Kepler*'s launch.

Kirk considered summoning Lieutenant Commander Scott to the bridge to serve as his acting first officer, but he quashed that impulse.

Right now, Scotty's exactly where he needs to be—making sure that shuttle launches safely. Just like I'm exactly where I need to be: in this chair. In command.

An alert beeped on the navigator's console. Waltke silenced it and made a quick check of his instruments. "Sensor contact: bearing one-three-one mark twelve. A small ship, but fast"—he looked over his shoulder at Kirk—"and coming right at us, Captain."

Kirk's pulse quickened. "Raise shields and arm all weapons. Order the *Kepler* to hold."

Nanjiani damned near tripped over his chair in his rush to peer down into the hooded sensor display. Kirk watched without criticism as the ensign spent a few seconds fumbling with the controls for the sensors. Then Nanjiani said in a rapid-fire string, "Sensor contact confirmed, Captain! A small ship maybe a bird-of-prey approaching at high warp still trying to identify it but it's moving *really* fast, I mean just *so* fast, sir—"

"Relax, Ensign. Take your time."

"Yessir, still scanning it's still on a direct heading coming right at us—"

Waltke interjected, "Captain, the incoming vessel is too small to be a *B'rel*-class bird-of-prey. Also, her energy signature registers as Starfleet."

"Starfleet?" Confusion and irritation competed for control of Kirk's expression. "Mister Nanjiani, get me a visual on that ship, full magnification."

"Aye, sir, working on it now, realigning visual—"

"Spare me the running commentary, Ensign."

Abashed, Nanjiani put his face to the sensor hood and kept it there while he worked. Seconds later, an image appeared on the main viewscreen: a Starfleet vessel, a tiny *Archer*-class scout ship. Kirk recalled that *Archer*-class ships usually had crews of only fourteen persons, and their typical mission profile was to push far past the boundaries of known space, out into the frontier, as far and as fast as they could go.

So what the hell is a scout ship doing in the Klingon Neutral Zone?

Nanjiani looked up from the sensor hood. "Ship identified, Captain. It's the *U.S.S. Sagittarius*, based out of—"

"Starbase Vanguard," Kirk said, finishing Nanjiani's sentence. "Mister Waltke, cancel yellow alert and drop the shields. Lieutenant Benson, weapons back to standby." As the relief officers restored the ship to normal operating status, Kirk turned his chair once again to look back at Uhura. "Lieutenant, hail Captain Nassir on the *Sagittarius*, and tell him I want to know what the *hell* he's doing here."

5

On the scale of things Captain Adelard Nassir would have been happy to avoid for the rest of his life, being harangued by Captain James T. Kirk of the *Enterprise* ranked somewhere just below a near-fatal bout of Rigelian dysentery and just above being used to incubate a brood of Denebian slime devils. It didn't help Nassir's mood that Kirk was so many things Nassir most pointedly was not: young, suave, athletic, and entrusted with command of a capital starship.

Kirk's face filled the viewscreen on the bridge of the *Sagittarius*. The compartment was so cramped in every dimension that it made Kirk's enlarged face appear far more imposing than it really was. Nassir was sure he could count the human man's eyebrow hairs as Kirk bellowed, *"I just want to know what you and your ship are doing in this system!"*

Nassir spread his arms, palms upraised, in a conciliatory gesture. "As I've already said, Captain, I'm not at liberty to share that information at this time." Cool air from the overhead ventilation ducts kissed the sweat from the crown of Nassir's bald head. It reminded him of the soothing autumn breezes he had so loved during his youth on Delta IV—unlike Kirk's repetitive tirade, which for Nassir evoked the septennial firestorms of Bersallis III.

"At the very least," Kirk continued, *"show me the courtesy of telling me what your orders are."* The human seemed at least to

be trying to rein in his temper. He was failing, but Nassir gave him credit for making the effort. *"And don't tell me they're—"*

"Classified? I'm afraid so, Captain."

Veins along Kirk's temples and jaw began to throb with great intensity. Nassir wondered how long it had been since Kirk's last physical exam. *What a terrible shame, to suffer from high blood pressure at his age. He needs to learn to relax.*

"On whose authority are you in this system? At least tell me that."

"What's that? You want me to set myself up for an Article 32 hearing and a general court-martial? No, thank you." Around him, Nassir heard his bridge officers doing their best not to laugh as he made sport of tweaking Kirk's infamous temper.

The young captain, however, was clearly losing patience with Nassir's aloof repartee. *"Captain, I know your ship is part of Starbase 47's action group. Since you're here, and this planet technically falls within the boundaries of the Taurus Reach, I have to assume your presence has something to do with Operation Vanguard. Would that something happen to be a missing Ardanan scientist by the name of Doctor Johron Verdo?"*

Nassir glanced at his first officer, Commander Clark Terrell. The human man stood in front of one of the starboard duty stations. Tall, lean, and muscular, Terrell had the physique of a fighter, the mind of a scientist, and the soul of a poet. His sepia-brown skin was a shade lighter than his umber-brown eyes, and he wore his crown of tightly curled black hair short and neat. When he noticed Nassir's inquisitive look, all he could offer in reply was a shrug.

Nassir looked Kirk in the eye and said with all the sincerity he could muster, "I'm sorry, Captain, but I can neither confirm nor deny the existence of any initiative known as 'Operation Vanguard,' nor the association of any individual with such a program."

"You do *know this is a secure channel, yes?"*

"The strength of our comm encryption isn't really the issue—but I suspect you already know that. Do you have any other questions I can fail to answer for you?"

Kirk's frustration darkened into anger, and for a moment Nassir really had to wonder whether Kirk was the sort of man who would order his crew to fire on a fellow Starfleet vessel.

I certainly hope we don't need to find out.

Another muffled snort of laughter arose behind Nassir. Based on its direction alone, he knew it had come from tactical officer Lieutenant Faro Dastin, one of the ship's recent transfers, a replacement for Lieutenant Commander Bridget McLellan, who had accepted a transfer to a new assignment no one could speak of, which meant she was now with Starfleet Intelligence.

Dastin, a charming, dark-haired Trill man in his thirties, pressed the side of his fist against his mouth to stifle any further sounds of amusement. Nassir could only hope that the other troublemaker of his bridge crew—Martian-born human science officer Lieutenant Vanessa Theriault—could hold her mirth in check until he finished this conversation with Kirk. For good measure, Nassir shot a look of preemptive warning at the petite but spirited young redhead, who pursed her lips and mimed locking them with a key that she then tossed away.

I will never understand how she graduated from Starfleet Academy.

On the viewscreen, Kirk appeared to have mastered his anger. Once more he was calm and professional. *"Captain, regardless of what our respective orders and agendas might be, neither of us should proceed with our mission until we know more about each other's assignments. If we both push ahead lacking such knowledge, we could quickly find ourselves at cross purposes, interfering in each other's operations. And, as I'm sure you know, that kind of mistake can get people killed out here. Would you agree with that?"*

"With every word of it, Captain. It's in our mutual best interest to avoid potentially fatal miscommunications. Unfortunately, I lack the authority to share the information you need. So what say we kick this upstairs and let the brass hash it out?"

"Sounds good to me." Kirk nodded at someone off-screen. *"We'll contact Admiral Fitzpatrick at Starfleet Command and bring him up to speed. And if you wouldn't mind, tell Admiral Nogura that I said 'Hello.' "*

Nassir felt his confidence abandon him in a rush that left his back awash in cold sweat. "You know Admiral Nogura?"

"He's an old friend of my parents—and he sponsored my application to the Academy." Kirk waved away his quasi-familial connection to the admiral as if it were nothing and put on a smug expression. *"At any rate, just tell the Old Man that Jimmy T sends his best. Kirk out."*

Kirk closed the channel, and the viewscreen reverted to an image of the *Enterprise* looming like some sort of mythical colossus above the *Sagittarius*.

Nassir clenched his jaw. *Of course Kirk knows Nogura.* He anticipated what likely would come of this clash of flag-officer titans, and he sighed. *We never catch a break, do we?*

More than one person through the years had described the temper of Admiral Heihachiro Nogura as "volcanic." It was an apt metaphor. Nogura was the sort of person whose anger dwelled deep beneath his surface. His countenance had often been called stonelike, his voice like a tiger's purr filtered through fresh-broken gravel. Had he been the sort of man who indulged in such pastimes as playing cards, he might have proved a formidable opponent across a poker table. If he was known for one quality in particular, it was his cool and steady demeanor.

Which made his rare eruptions of raw fury all the more intimidating.

Today his deep-throated roar shook the bulkheads of his

office on the operations level of the command dome of Starbase Vanguard. "And you just thought it would be a good idea to send a goddamned *Constitution*-class heavy cruiser into *my* theater of operations, on a search-and-rescue for three *civilians*? Without even giving me the courtesy of a heads-up? Where the hell did you learn fleet ops, Ted? Was your textbook the kind you color with crayons?"

Glowering on the other end of the real-time subspace comm was Vice Admiral Fitzpatrick, whose pasty face was turning scarlet with rage and embarrassment. *"These aren't just any three civilians, Chiro. They're three of the—"*

"Don't call me 'Chiro,' you feckless wonder. And I know damned well who you're looking for. Odds are my team and I knew about them *long* before you did. And if you or any of those cretins you call a staff had the brains the universe gave an amoeba, you might have dug deep enough into Verdo's file to figure out why he took a research team into the Taurus Reach!"

Fitzpatrick started shaking, as if he might cry or soil himself at any moment. *"It's not our fault their files were redacted. We had no way of knowing he was affiliated with Vanguard."*

"But it *is* your fault that two Starfleet ships were sent to the same star system in the Neutral Zone at the same damned time. One ship in the Neutral Zone can claim it suffered a navigational malfunction, or was hijacked, or got spit through some kind of anomaly. Give the Klingons *some* pretext to hang a hat on and let our people leave without starting a war. But *two* ships in the same system? Good luck explaining *that*, you beef-witted twit."

Fitzpatrick sat up and lifted his chin in a fair simulacrum of pride. *"I've had just about enough out of you! Might I remind you that I outrank you, Rear Admiral Nogura?"*

That was the trigger that elevated Nogura's rant from a normal eruption to a Krakatoa-level event. "Did you just try to *pull rank* on me? My ears must be deceiving me, because I *know* that can't be right. Even *you*, toadying weasel that you are, wouldn't be *that* foolish."

"*Heihachiro, I—*"

"Shut up, I'm not done yet. You've been around long enough to know the measure of authority is more than the stripes on your cuff or the fruit salad on your chest. It's about respect, a quality with which I imagine you have very little experience.

"In case you didn't get the memo, *Ted*, with the exceptions of the Starfleet C-in-C and designated members of the civilian government of the United Federation of Planets, I answer to absolutely *no one* on matters pertaining to Operation Vanguard, or on any mission that transpires within my sphere of authority, which encompasses every last cubic meter of the Taurus Reach. There's a battalion's worth of admirals at Starfleet Command who technically outrank me—but except for you, not one dumb enough to *pull rank* on me."

"*I wasn't pulling rank, I was just asking for the same degree of respect that—*"

"What makes you think you've *earned* my respect? What have you ever done that merits even an ounce of my regard?"

"*You know as well as I do that you salute the rank, not the man.*"

"We're in Starfleet, you prattling vonce. We don't salute at all. So I ask you again: What the hell have you ever done that deserves even a passing display of esteem? Enlighten me."

The demand left Fitzpatrick flustered and stammering. "*I was a flag officer when you were still a midshipman! While you were earning your stripes, I was writing the book, the literal book, on Starfleet regulations and—*"

"I've read that book, Ted. It's not exactly a page-turner."

"*You insolent sonofa—*"

"Save it for someone who's scared of you—but I'm guessing that's a short list. Maybe a couple of first-year cadets and a very small dog you like to kick when you take walks along the

Presidio." Nogura inserted a red data card into the slot beside his desk's computer terminal. As he continued, he transmitted a file on the encrypted subspace channel's data subfrequency. "I'm sending you a copy of my new orders for the *Enterprise*, because unlike you, I have enough common courtesy to tell others in the chain of command what the hell I'm doing."

Fitzpatrick was perplexed. "*What are you talking about? What new orders?*"

There was no point couching the matter in euphemisms, Nogura reasoned. "I'm officially invoking my authority under the command charter for Operation Vanguard, and assuming oversight of the *Starship Enterprise* for the duration of its mission to Kolasi III. My team and I will coordinate with Captain Kirk and his crew from this point forward, and any results or findings produced by this mission are hereby classified top secret."

Enraged almost to the point of tears, the vice admiral pounded his fist on his desk. "*You can't just take the* Enterprise *out from under my command!*"

"I just did."

Fitzpatrick squinted at Nogura, as if he were trying to perceive him from a great distance, or through a thick fog. "*Who in blazes do you think you* are, *Nogura?*"

"Who am I? I'm the one telling you how it *is*. Men like you have held us back for too long. Our rivals move quickly. We need to be faster. Smarter. We need to be ready to do what they think we *can't* do, or *won't* do. It's a time for men of action, Ted. A time for men like me."

"*You want action, Nogura? I'll give you a goddamned court-martial.*"

"No you won't. You don't have the stones for it. You're a swaggering phony, Ted, and you always have been. You've never commanded anything larger than a goddamned bathtub, and you've never been farther from home than the quad at Starfleet

Academy. You're a paper pusher, a career bureaucrat, a politi-
cian playing Starfleet dress-up. If you really want to do Starfleet
a favor, hand in your resignation and leave fleet ops to those
who know what they're doing. If you're quick about it, you can
muster out and be back in San Francisco for a long three-gimlet
lunch at L'enclume before anyone gives a damn you're gone.
Now, if you'll excuse me, I have to go finish straightening out
your latest mess. Nogura out."

As he closed the channel, Nogura savored the gutted, dumb-
struck look on Fitzpatrick's jowly, dough-colored face. *Fitz has
been throwing his useless weight around long enough. It was time
someone put his unearned pride into check.*

As a younger man, Nogura might have felt a twinge of guilt
for having taken the older man's knees out from under him with
such spite, but those days were gone.

Sorry, Ted, but karma's a bitch.

6

"I've gone to more than my usual amount of effort to make this possible, so I'm counting on both you and your crews to play nice. Is that understood?"

Kirk nodded at the image of Admiral Nogura on the briefing room table's three-sided viewer. "Perfectly, Admiral." To Kirk, Nogura's swarthy complexion, close-cropped black beard, thick eyebrows, and crew-cut dark hair made him look more than a little like a Klingon.

Captain Nassir leaned toward Kirk to share his angle on the viewer. "Crystal clear, sir." Only now, up close, did Kirk appreciate how trim the Deltan's physique was. Kirk guessed the man might weigh just over half of what he himself did.

Nogura acknowledged their replies with a throaty sound halfway between a grunt and a cough. "You both have reputations for being—how shall I put this? Unconventional. Please do me a favor and don't try to outdo each other in that department."

"Noted," Kirk said, trusting in brevity to keep him from saying the wrong thing.

"Wouldn't dream of it, sir," Nassir added.

"I don't believe either of you, but it's too late to do anything about that now. You were both given the same mission briefing, so you know what you're doing and what you're up against. I want you two to send down a mixed landing party. Pool your resources and find a way to make your shared presence an advantage—

you're going to need it. Sensor outposts along the Neutral Zone have confirmed the Klingon battle cruiser I.K.S. SuvwI' is en route to the Kolasi system at high warp. Expect them to make orbit in the next hour. I presume I don't need to tell either of you where your ships should be by then?"

"Somewhere else," Nassir replied.

"Gold star, Sagittarius. Now get to work. Nogura out." The Starfleet emblem replaced his image momentarily, and then the viewscreen dimmed as it reverted to standby mode.

Free of the admiral's gaze, Kirk and Nassir faced the officers they had assembled in the *Enterprise*'s briefing room. On Kirk's side of the table sat Spock and Doctor McCoy. Seated on Nassir's side of the table were his science officer, Lieutenant Vanessa Theriault, and his chief medical officer, Doctor Lisa Babitz.

Eager to get the mission back on track, Kirk took the initiative. "Where do we stand with regard to basic mission details, Captain? Are we still sending our shuttlecraft, or do you plan to land the *Sagittarius*?"

Nassir shook his head, visibly disappointed. "I'd hoped to land my ship and deploy my landing party using our motorized surface vehicles, to reduce their time spent on foot. But now that we've seen the planet's storm belt, it's clear that we can't land the *Sagittarius* on Kolasi III. Our impulse system would be just as vulnerable to its ionic storm as the one on your shuttle, but our greater mass would make reaching orbit on thrusters alone impossible."

From behind thoughtfully steepled fingers, Spock replied, "That was my conclusion as well, Captain." He shifted his focus to Doctor Babitz. "Doctor, I've been made to understand that you are one of Starfleet's leading experts on the Shedai. Is that correct?"

The tall blonde physician looked slightly embarrassed. "Not exactly, Commander. I'm an expert with regard to the Shedai meta-genome and its applications to genomic medicine.

If you're looking for an expert in the Shedai as individuals or as a culture"—she tilted her head left toward her younger shipmate—"Lieutenant Theriault is the person you'll want to consult."

Theriault flashed a broad smile and waved at Spock. "Hiya."

Spock arched an eyebrow at the young woman's effusive greeting, and then he continued as if it hadn't happened. "I'm sure both forms of expertise are equally useful in the proper context. However, given the nature of Doctor Verdo's research into the Shedai meta-genome, I suspect, Doctor, that your specialty will be more likely to prove relevant to our objectives."

Theriault interjected, "Can I jump in here?" Kirk nodded his approval, and she continued. "I've studied the terrain and surface conditions of the Kolasi jungle. I think it's worth noting that it has many similarities to the conditions we recorded last year on the Shedai's homeworld of Jinoteur, including average temperature, humidity, and general topography. If ever there was a setting that was ripe for a Shedai reawakening, this would be the place . . . I'm just sayin'."

"Thank you, Lieutenant," Kirk said. "Forewarned is forearmed, especially when it comes to the Shedai." He turned his attention to Nassir. "Captain, there are seven seats aboard a Class-F shuttle. I would like to recommend my first officer, Mister Spock, for command of the landing party, and my helm officer Mister Sulu as its pilot. Have you given any thought to which members of your crew you'd like to send to the surface?"

Behind Nassir, Kirk noticed Doctor Babitz crossing her fingers and muttering some kind of prayer under her breath. Nassir seemed oblivious of his chief medical officer's desperate whispered entreaty as he said, "My first choice, of course, is to send Doctor Babitz."

She abruptly ceased her prayers. "*Dammit.* Now I *know* there's no God."

McCoy gave her a sympathetic half smile. "I know how you feel."

Kirk let the complaints pass without remark. "The landing party will need a jungle guide. Are any of your people qualified?"

"Senior Chief Petty Officer Razka. A Saurian. He'll feel right at home."

"Excellent. If you don't object, I'd like to send Ensign Pavel Chekov as the landing party's science officer."

The Deltan captain turned to face Theriault. "How do *you* feel about that?"

Theriault looked surprised to have been asked. "If someone else wants to risk getting up close and personal with one of those nightmares, I am more than happy to stay on the ship. Sir."

Satisfied, Nassir looked back at Kirk. "No objections. With your consent, I'd like to send my chief engineer. I've never seen anyone better than him at improvised repairs, and if the trip down and back is as bad as you say it'll be, I think you'll want him along for the ride."

"Done."

Theriault muttered, "Master Chief's gonna throw a fit when he hears this."

"Let him," Nassir said. "He needs the exercise."

"Last but not least," Kirk said, "I'm sending Ensign Tingmao Singh, one of my security officers, to watch everyone's backs."

Nassir held up a hand as if to say, *not so fast.* "I do have one more request, Captain. My ship's complement is only fourteen people, so sending even three of them on a landing party leaves key stations empty. In an emergency, every post on my ship could become critical. Any chance you could spare a few bodies from your crew of four-hundred-plus to lend a hand?"

Kirk had to smile at Nassir's gentle verbal jab. "Consider it done, Captain. We'll make sure you have all the help you need."

"Much obliged."

"In the meantime, we need to get our landing party under

the storm before the Klingons show up, and then find ourselves a place to hide. Mister Spock, assemble your new landing party on the hangar deck and prep the *Kepler* for immediate launch. Dismissed."

Master Chief Petty Officer Mike "Mad Man" Ilucci nearly tripped while scrambling out of his green jumpsuit duty uniform and into the camouflage jumpsuit and poncho he had just been told to put on before reporting to the *Enterprise*'s shuttle-bay for a mission he didn't understand.

Whose bright idea was it to send me on the landing party to Hell? And what happened to my left boot? It was just here! It— Oh, there it is.

He tugged his boots on as fast as he was able, grabbed his lightest field repair kit from under his rack, and plodded out the door of the quarters he shared on the *Sagittarius* with lead scout Lieutenant Sorak, medical technician Ensign Nguyen Tan Bao, and Tactical Officer Dastin. Their cabin was on the starboard side of the main deck, right next to the ship's only lifeboat.

It's true what they say about real estate—it's all location, location, location.

Toting his kit over his shoulder, he headed aft, away from the hubbub on the bridge. *With any luck I can get around to the airlock and off this boat before—*

A beefy hand reached down through the ladderway and grabbed Ilucci's shoulder. He knew before he looked up that he'd been stopped by senior engineer's mate Petty Officer First Class Salagho Threx. The huge, hirsute Denobulan was the only member of the crew with arms long enough to have reached Ilucci from the engineering deck. "Master Chief! Can you come up a second?"

"I'm running late, Threx. You'll have to sort it—"

"Your replacement's being a major tool. If you don't straighten him out, I will—but I doubt he'll survive." The edge in Threx's voice made it clear he wasn't joking.

Ilucci dropped his kit and climbed the ladder to the engineering deck. *Why does everybody suddenly need something from me the second I'm late to be someplace else?*

He was only halfway off the ladder when his entire cadre of tool-pushers descended on him, all talking over one another. It was a litany of strident complaints unlike anything Ilucci had heard since basic training. Meanwhile, standing behind the engineers with crossed arms and a sour look on his too-handsome face was an officer from the *Enterprise*: a tall, broad-shouldered, square-jawed, brown-haired fellow wearing operations-division red.

Ilucci let out a shrill whistle piercing enough to scratch duranium. The choir of protest ceased, and blessed quiet filled the engineering deck. "What's the problem here? And make it fast, I need to be somewhere ten minutes ago."

Petty Officer Second Class Karen Cahow erased the pout from her face and stripped all the anger from her tone. "Lieutenant DeSalle insists on trying to run our engine room the way he and Mister Scott run the *Enterprise's*"—the tomboyish young woman fought the urge to turn a pointed stare at DeSalle—"without any regard for *our* way of doing things."

I don't have time for this.

He faced the youngest member of his team. "Is this true?"

Terrified at being put on the spot, Crewman Torvin trembled like a small animal fighting the urge to piss all over the deck. The young Tiburonian's prodigious and ultrasensitive ears brightened by a half shade of scarlet as he said, "It's true, Master Chief. He's all *by-the-book*."

A quick look at Threx. "You on the same page, big guy?"

"Damned straight, Master Chief."

"Okay then. All of you . . . *shut up* and do whatever DeSalle tells you! In case you've forgotten the basics of our chain of command, Mister DeSalle is a commissioned officer, and you grease-stained tool-pushers *aren't*! So unless you feel like spending the rest of this mission in the *Enterprise*'s brig and the rest of your hitches in a Martian stockade, *snap-to*!"

All three engineers reacted reflexively, instantaneously standing at attention.

"That's more like it." Ilucci showed DeSalle a crooked half-smile of contrition. "Sorry about that, Lieutenant. They'll remember their manners soon enough, I promise."

DeSalle nodded. "Thanks, Master Chief. I'll owe you one."

Ilucci slid down the ladder to the main deck, scooped up his kit, and continued heading toward the portside hatch. As he passed the open doorway to sickbay, Tan Bao called out to him, "Come back in one piece, Master Chief!"

"That's the idea, brother."

A man whose voice he didn't recognize remarked in a near monotone, "Odd. You and Master Chief Ilucci do not look at all like brothers."

All he heard Tan Bao say in reply was, "Is 'M'Benga' a Vulcan name, Doc?"

Just when I thought this ship couldn't get any weirder.

Ilucci reached the port side of the main deck and found the airlock hatchway blocked by two women. Standing on the *Sagittarius*'s side of the hatch was Ensign Taryl, an emerald-skinned Orion wearing a *Sagittarius* standard-issue olive-drab utility jumpsuit. On the *Enterprise*'s side was a tall, athletic human wearing a red minidress uniform and carrying a tricorder on a strap. Her rich brown skin was made lustrous by its warm undertones, and she wore her long, straight black hair in a simple ponytail draped over the front of her right shoulder.

"Sorry, Ensign Jamal," Taryl said, "but I can't let you come aboard until I see a properly authorized copy of your transfer orders."

Jamal wasn't amused, but she wasn't angry. "Fine." She lifted her tricorder, called up some data on its readout, and showed it to Taryl. "There you go."

Taryl scowled. "That's just a time-and-temperature reading."

"Tsk. You got me. But in my defense, who'd expect an Orion to be able to read?"

The situation seemed a few choice words away from turning into a fistfight when both women suddenly broke into delighted laughter and embraced.

"Damn, I've missed you, Zahra!"

"Great to see you, too, Taryl."

Ilucci cleared his throat. "Excuse me, sirs? Not that your reunion isn't touching, but if you could please do it someplace other than the airlock?"

Taryl grinned away any awkwardness of the moment. "Sorry, Master Chief." She retreated from the hatchway and led Jamal inside the *Sagittarius*, clearing the way.

Stepping through the airlock and into the *Enterprise*, Ilucci rolled his eyes. *Three minutes to walk fifteen meters of corridor. Someone call Guinness, that's a new* Sagittarius *record.*

Why do we always cut these things so close? Kirk watched the ship's chrono creep inexorably forward, ticking away his remaining moments with relentless precision. The *Sagittarius* was still docked to the airlock on the port side of the *Enterprise*'s saucer. It was a precarious connection. The *Sagittarius* was linked to the *Enterprise* while facing aft, toward the warp nacelles. While the two vessels remained joined by a pressurized connection, neither would be able to maneuver. As long as their connection persisted, the *Enterprise* was effectively dead in space—a condition that made Kirk more anxious than anything else going on.

He heard the turbolift door open and looked over his shoulder. Lieutenant Commander Scott stepped out of the lift. Kirk had summoned him to fulfill his duty as the ship's second officer, to take over for the absent Spock. "Mister Scott! Glad you could join us."

"Came as soon as I could, sir."

"Can your engineers handle a few hours without you?"

"I'm sure they'll muddle through, sir."

"Let's hope so. How long until we can separate from the *Sagittarius*?"

"Any time, sir. Though I—"

An alert shrilled from the sensor console. Nanjiani hurried to mute the alert and check the hooded display. "Captain, long-range sensors have confirmed the Klingon battle cruiser *I.K.S. SuvwI'* is nearing the edge of the Kolasi system. Estimated time to orbit is thirty-four minutes, and just nineteen minutes until they have us inside their maximum sensor range."

"Noted, Lieutenant." Kirk used his chair's armrest controls to open a channel to the shuttlecraft *Kepler*. "Mister Spock, we have confirmation that a Klingon battle cruiser is nineteen minutes from sensor range and thirty-four minutes from orbit. What's your status?"

Spock replied over the ship's internal comm, *"We are fixing a malfunction in the rewired flight controls, Captain. As soon as that's done, we'll be ready to launch."*

"Give me a time estimate, Spock. How long?"

"Approximately twenty-five minutes."

"Do whatever you can to shorten that, Spock."

"Acknowledged."

Kirk thumbed the internal comm channel closed, and then he looked at Scott. "You were saying, Mister Scott?"

The chief engineer picked up their conversation from the moment it had been interrupted, a skill that Kirk had learned to appreciate during the few years he had so far served with him. "Having the *Sagittarius* linked with our airlock presents us with a unique opportunity, sir."

"Explain."

"*Sagittarius* carries a half dozen probes, all of which are launched using a standard-issue torpedo launcher. That little ship was made for speed and stealth, not for standing toe-to-toe in a firefight. But if we end up in a bind, I'd feel better knowing she could deal out a few good hits."

"You're suggesting we swap her probes for photon torpedoes?"

"Aye, sir. That's a sting the Klingons might not see coming."

"How long to get it done? Time *is* a factor, Scotty."

"Ten minutes. Fifteen, tops. But only if we start now."

Kirk considered the risks and the rewards and made a decision. "Do it, and make it fast. We and the *Sagittarius* both need to get free so we can maneuver."

"Aye, sir. Already on it." Scott stepped away to the bridge's engineering duty station to coordinate the last-second trade of probes for torpedoes.

Time's passage seemed to accelerate as the moment of confrontation drew near. Kirk felt almost thankful for the interruption of a yeoman handing him a data slate containing a standard shift report for his approval. He scribbled his signature on the bottom of the page and handed the slate back to the yeoman, who left the bridge without speaking a word.

Kirk turned his chair so he could see Uhura. "Lieutenant, is there any way we could jam the Klingons' frequencies inside this system but not have it traceable to us?"

"Most Starfleet jamming frequencies are known to the Klingons. But I have an idea." Uhura experimented with mixing and matching different approaches into a new response. Watching her work was like observing the impeccable timing and elegant dexterity of an orchestra's conductor. After a few moments, she continued, "I might be able to use the magnetic fields of Kolasi III and its moon to create a subspatial resonance field. Properly modulated, it should turn the planet's orbital space into a noise generator on all Klingon comms. But to use it, we would need to keep the *Enterprise* out and fully visible to the Klingon battle cruiser."

"No good, Lieutenant. We're trying to isolate them, not goad them."

"Aye, sir. I'll keep looking."

"Thank you, Lieutenant. Carry on." Kirk once again faced the main viewscreen. He stole a look at the chrono, whose digital display continued advancing toward the inevitable. Powerless to slow the passage of time, Kirk decided to speed the actions of his crew. "Mister Scott, tell your people to finish moving those torpedoes on the double."

Commander Clark Terrell stood at the front of a line of his ship's personnel that extended from the *Sagittarius*'s airlock to the ladderway that led up to its engineering deck, bellowing encouragement. "Move it, people! Let's go!"

At the end of the line, beneath the ladderway, was Salagho Threx. The brawny Denobulan was the only one who could handle receiving the weight of an entire Class 6 probe as engineers Torvin and Cahow lowered it to him using a complicated system of knotted ropes looped around various pieces of engineering equipment to act as pulleys. Likewise, he was also the only one strong enough to boost incoming photon torpedoes up through the ladderway, to assist Cahow and Torvin in bringing the munitions up to the launcher on the engineering deck.

On the other side of the open airlock, a team of red-shirted *Enterprise* engineers and gold-shirted weapons officers raced to unload an antigrav pallet of six photon torpedoes, relay them over the threshold into the *Sagittarius*, and then replace them on the pallet with the probes transferred off the *Sagittarius*. As Terrell had feared, trying to move torpedoes and probes in both directions at once was not proving possible, and so they had been forced to alternate.

Behind him, his shipmates labored to move the second probe in his direction. From the ladderway Threx passed each probe to Dastin and Sorak, who shifted it to the trio of Taryl, Jamal, and Tan Bao. The wiry scout, lithe medical technician, and svelte security officer were proving to be the weak link in the chain, and Terrell hoped he wouldn't have to replace them, because the only two *Sagittarius* personnel not on the chain—aside from those assigned to the landing party—were the captain and the ship's flight control officer, neither of whom were known for their physical strength.

Tan Bao and Taryl clumsily passed each probe to Theriault and Acting Chief Engineer Vincent DeSalle. In their hands, DeSalle bore the brunt of the weight. After them, it was up to Terrell to finish the last leg with the help of Doctor M'Benga, another of the temporary transfer personnel from the *Enterprise*. He hadn't expected the physician to offer much help, but the man surprised him by bearing more of the probe's weight than Terrell had expected.

Terrell cracked a smile at M'Benga, despite the strain it required while exerting himself. "You're a lot stronger than you look, Doc!"

M'Benga was calm and steady. "Must be the time I spent interning on Vulcan."

"That would do it."

They handed the second of six probes through the open airlock, to the relay team of *Enterprise* officers. Then the officers in red and gold tunics sent the second of six photon torpedoes up the line, into the hands of M'Benga and Terrell, who shuffled with it for a few awkward steps before passing it into the care of DeSalle and Theriault.

Once the ordnance left Terrell's hands, there was nothing for him to do but keep track of the time it took his people to move it up to the engineering deck and begin moving the next probe out. The numbers were not encouraging. Based on the latest report from the *Enterprise*'s bridge, a Klingon cruiser would be on top of them in less than twenty-five minutes.

At this rate we'll still be trading probes and torpedoes when they arrive.

Terrell took a fresh look at the work flow his team had set up, and at once he saw where it had gone wrong. They all had become fixated on making the relay work like a bucket brigade in both directions, because the antigrav pallet was unable to cross the elevated thresholds of the airlock passageway. But only half of the process needed to work like a relay.

The logjam was the need to shift the probes off the *Sagittarius*'s engineering deck one at a time, because the ship had not been designed to load or unload them manually via the airlock, but through a pair of topside cargo doors. The *Enterprise* team had no such restriction. They had loaded six torpedoes onto an antigrav pallet and delivered them right to the airlock.

Terrell captured his crew's attention with a short, shrill whistle. "Listen up! Change of plan! Keep moving that torpedo down the line. As soon as you hand it off, get up here, pronto!"

Theriault and DeSalle shifted the torpedo into the custody of Jamal, Taryl, and Tan Bao, and then the science officer and chief engineer hurried to Terrell and M'Benga's side. Theriault was winded but still sounded excited. "What's the plan, Commander?"

"Bring the remaining torpedoes from the *Enterprise* over the threshold and stack them here, along the inner bulkhead. We'll move them up to the launcher later. Right now, we just need to get them aboard, and then get the probes out." He called through the airlock passageway to the *Enterprise* officers, "Sound good to you?"

"Sounds like a plan, Commander! Ready when you are."

"Let's go! Double-time! Move, move, move!"

Moving items in just one direction, over a much shorter distance, seemed to change the entire process. More hands per meter made for lighter work, and by the time Threx and his colleagues had moved the second torpedo up the ladderway to the engineering deck, Terrell and the rest of the crew had started moving the last torpedo through the airlock.

Terrell pumped his fist in the air out of sheer excitement. "That's it! That's what I'm talking about!" He checked the chrono. Did some math in his head.

That's better. It'll still be close, but we'll get it done.

"All right, back on the line! Get those last four probes moving! Shake a leg, folks."

If only someone could figure out a safe way to transport antimatter.

It wasn't possible to use a cargo transporter to move either the probes or the torpedoes because it wasn't safe to use a transporter on munitions whose warheads contained small packets of antimatter, or on long-range research and reconnaissance probes whose miniaturized warp propulsion units were powered by antimatter. The electromagnetic fields needed to keep antimatter stable and secure were so delicate and precise that even the seemingly infinitesimal interruption they might experience at the quantum level during a transporter cycle was enough to disrupt the containment field and unleash nightmarish blasts of chaotically released energy.

With all the torpedoes safely delivered, two of the *Enterprise* officers came aboard the *Sagittarius* to help move the last four probes. With minutes left to spare, the *Enterprise* personnel carried the last one off the *Sagittarius*, and then they sealed the *Enterprise*'s side of the airlock passageway. Terrell closed the airlock's outer hatch, and then its inner hatch on the *Sagittarius*.

He stepped over to a companel on the corridor's inner bulkhead and opened a channel to the bridge. "Captain, airlock secure. Ready to detach from *Enterprise*."

Nassir answered over the comm, *"Acknowledged. All decks, stand by to detach in ninety seconds. Bridge out."*

The comm channel closed with a soft *click*. Terrell projected his voice so that it would carry down the corridor and up the ladderway to the engineers. "We still have four torpedoes that need to be secured! All hands, get down here and get these fish moving."

He was rewarded by the percussion of running footfalls on duranium deck plates. Threx and the others arrived within seconds and scrambled to grab up the torpedoes.

Theriault regarded the torpedoes with a strange look as she and DeSalle struggled to heft one from the deck. "It's so weird seeing these things on the *Sagittarius*," she said.

DeSalle took the bait. "Why?"

"Well, we usually only carry one at a time."

Terrell interjected, "That's true. And after we fired ours last year, we never got around to requisitioning another."

That made DeSalle's eyes go wide. "Are you serious? Why not?"

Taryl grinned. "Look at this ship, man!" The Orion woman gestured at the vessel around them. "This bird wasn't made to fight—she was made to fly!"

DeSalle shook his head, but it was M'Benga who replied, "That might be true, Ensign—but if this ship goes head-to-head with the Klingons, it had best be ready to do *both*."

7

As usual, there was nothing but bad news. Admiral Nogura slogged through his daily labor of reading all the latest reports from Starfleet Intelligence and Starfleet Command. The best he could hope for most days was a repetition of previous reports, with no change worth noting. It seemed that any time new information became available, it was never good news for Starfleet, Operation Vanguard, or the galaxy in general.

Today he found himself besieged by accounts of recent Klingon fleet movements. The Federation's most implacable rival was expanding its empire in every direction that it could without running into Federation territory or violating the Neutral Zone.

He couldn't blame the crafty bastards for wanting to avoid the Neutral Zone. *Hell, even the Romulans would wait until the paint was dry on the damned sign before trespassing.*

Regardless, the rate at which the Klingons were annexing star systems and sometimes entire sectors alarmed Nogura. No matter how many times some fresh-from-the-Academy wunderkind analyst from Starfleet Intelligence told him that the Klingons were overextending themselves and that this would soon lead them to a dire reckoning, perhaps in the form of an environmental catastrophe, he knew better. Expansion had not yet weakened the Klingons' hold on their empire. Each star system in which they planted their trefoil flag yielded raw materials, slave labor, and a larger buffer zone around their core systems.

Maybe the eggheads are right, and the Klingon Empire will implode under its own weight in the next fifty years. But if we don't get off our collective ass, they very well might have us boxed in within ten years, and keep us that way for the next ninety.

He picked up his mug, hoping to soothe his jangled nerves with some java. Naturally, his mug was empty except for an ochre stain in its bottom. *Well, that's just great.*

Nogura reached toward his desk's companel to open a channel to his yeoman, Ensign Toby Greenfield. Before he touched a single thing, his comm buzzed. He let it repeat a few times before he opened the channel. "Nogura."

From the other side came the voice of Ensign Greenfield. *"Sir, Lieutenant Commander ch'Nayla says he needs to see you right away."*

"I presume he's standing outside my office door?"

"He is, sir."

"Fine. Hand him a black coffee, tell him to give it to me, and send him in."

"Aye, sir."

Seconds later the door of Nogura's office slid open. The Andorian *chan* was carrying a data card and, as Nogura had instructed, a black coffee. The Starfleet Intelligence liaison was smart and experienced enough to know to give Nogura his coffee first, even before saying, "Thank you for seeing me on short notice, sir."

"I think you mean 'no damned notice at all,' Mister ch'Nayla." He sipped the coffee and frowned at the discovery that it was lukewarm. "What do I need to know now?"

"The latest sitrep from Kolasi III," ch'Nayla said, handing his red data card to Nogura. "It's not looking good, sir."

"Nothing ever does." Nogura put the data card into one of the open slots on his desk. Sensor data and log reports from the *Enterprise* and the *Sagittarius* appeared on his terminals. "There's a lot here, ch'Nayla. Bottom-line it for me."

"The shuttlecraft carrying the mixed landing party is almost ready to launch, but the Klingons are racing in like their asses are on fire. My people give the landing party a fifty-fifty chance of getting to cover under the planet's tropical storm belt before the Klingons arrive."

"Which is what we expected."

"And signal intercepts decoded in the last half hour suggest the captain of the *SuvwI'* has orders to send down a shuttle with his own landing party. They also appear to be looking for our missing scientist, which means they know what's happening in connection with Operation Vanguard almost as soon as we do. If they capture Doctor Verdo or his research, the situation on the surface might go sideways a lot faster than we expected."

Nogura set his mug off to the side of his desk. "In that case, I need my yeoman to bring me a new cup of coffee—one that's hot this time." He reached toward the intercom button, and just before he touched it, his office door opened and Yeoman Greenfield entered carrying a mug of steaming-hot black coffee. "Sorry, Admiral. I just realized our food slot's on the fritz. I've got engineering coming up to fix it now." The diminutive, brown-haired woman set the fresh coffee down in front of Nogura with one hand, removed the tepid java with the other, and was already halfway out of his office before Nogura had time to say "thank you."

A damned marvel, that woman is. If I had ten of her, I could conquer the galaxy.

He savored a sip of hot coffee, then asked ch'Nayla, "Where were we?"

"Getting ready to head off an interstellar diplomatic incident."

"As usual." He pressed the button to open his intercom channel to Yeoman Greenfield, whose desk was located immediately outside his office door. "Yeoman, please—"

"*I've invited Ambassador Karumé to join you for a briefing on the Kolasi situation, sir. She's on her way up and should be here in the next five minutes.*"

"Excellent, thank you. Carry on." Nogura closed the channel, feeling both impressed and bewildered that Greenfield had anticipated his need to speak with Vanguard's recently promoted chief diplomatic officer. *How the hell does she do that?* He refocused his attention on ch'Nayla. "As I was saying, we should expect the Klingons to howl with rage on all frequencies once they find out. If we're lucky, Ambassador Karumé might be able to get out in front of the situation and put a better spin on it before the Klingons make us look like the aggressors."

The Andorian looked skeptical. "I hope so. It's too bad Jetanien decided to exile himself to Nimbus III. We could really use his gift for steamrolling the Klingons right now."

Nogura downed another sip of coffee. "True, but don't underestimate Karumé. Jetanien knew how to talk *over* the Klingons, but Karumé knows how to talk *with* them."

"I'll keep that in mind, sir. How long do you think we'll have before the howling starts?"

"Maybe an hour. Depends on who's commanding the *SuvwI'* these days."

"Its current CO is Captain Kang, sir."

"Then expect the howling to start in *half* an hour. Kang's an *efficient* sonofabitch."

It mattered not to Kang that there was no air in space and consequently neither sounds nor scents. The closer his ship came to Kolasi III, the more certain he was that he smelled blood. Its ferric tang teased his tongue. His prey was nearby.

Contact was imminent enough for him to start demanding updates. "Tactical! Report."

Lieutenant Boqor stared with fierce intensity at her sensor

display. "Still no ships on our scanners, Captain. But we are picking up fragments of subspace comms traffic. They could be from ships hiding on the far side of the third planet."

Her report made Qovlar look up from the comms panel. "Signal fragments confirmed, Captain, but they might not be from this system. We might be picking up distant comms traffic because of subspatial lensing effects caused by the singularity ghungHov."

Few things annoyed Kang more than ambiguity. "Well? Which is it?"

Boqor answered before Qovlar could speak. "The signals are local, Captain. If they were artifacts of subspatial lensing, they would exhibit nonlinear distortions in frequency. These do not. There is someone beyond the third planet. I am certain of it."

"Good. All hands: battle stations!"

A single whoop of alarm resounded through the ship. The command deck's comforting ambient crimson glow was replaced by the senses-sharpening glare of white-hot overhead light. Kang's pulse quickened, his breathing deepened. Around him, his crew was alert, eyes wide, nostrils flaring, drinking in the moment. It felt good to be on the hunt.

"Helm, increase speed to three-quarters, take us into orbit on a wide arc."

"Yes, Captain."

Kolasi III grew larger on the forward viewscreen. The *SuvwI'* was approaching from the planet's night side, and as the ship swung away from the planet, its parent star flared bright on the screen. Kang squinted into the glare and smirked. *Your death comes with the dawn, James Kirk. Do you smell it? Do you feel its breath hot upon the nape of your neck?*

He entered commands into the tactical console beside his command chair. His first task was to call up a star chart of the Kolasi system. He had reviewed it earlier when his ship had been tasked with this assignment, but now he studied the chart in detail.

He noted the relative orbital positions of its rocky inner worlds and those of its more gaseous outer planets, and compared their respective orbital periods. He committed to memory the number of each planet's natural satellites, the shapes of their orbits, and the quirks of all their respective polar magnetic fields. He paid attention to the trajectories of comets, large asteroids, and other rogue objects transiting the system, and he compared their paths to the system's prevailing solar wind patterns. Then he assembled all of that information in his imagination, and created a mental model of the Kolasi system.

In his mind's eye he could see it all. Feel it all moving. This was his hunting ground, his savannah, his wilderness. He would make its peculiarities work to his advantage.

Now, where would I hide if I were a typical frightened Starfleet captain? There's little chance even Kirk will dare to face me in the open. He'll run for cover, like all Starfleeters.

At once Kang's eye was drawn to two prominent features of Kolasi III. The first was its equatorial rings. The other was its solitary moon. Both the moon and the rings exhibited high levels of electromagnetic activity of the sort that would blind sensors. He was all but certain that Kirk would take advantage of that fact. But which one would Kirk choose?

The moon offers safer cover, but less mobility. Kirk would want to retain his ability to maneuver, especially if he's worried about recovering a shuttle bearing his landing party.

The rings might be able to hide a starship the size of the Enterprise, *but it would need to run with its shields down. Maneuvering a starship through floating rock and ice without shields would be perilous at best—but I wouldn't put such an unusual tactic past Kirk.*

Kang indulged his imagination for a moment and pictured himself firing a torpedo that blazed through the planet's rings, struck the *Enterprise*, and shattered its fragile saucer into a million blue-gray shards. Dreaming of glory, he envisioned the face of Captain James T. Kirk as the human let go of his last breath while watching fire engulf the bridge of his precious starship.

His reverie was cut short by the chirp of an incoming signal at the comms panel. Kang looked aft as Qovlar turned to tell him, "Captain, subspace comm from High Command."

"*Qu'vatlh!* A broken chrono has better timing." Kang pushed himself up from his command chair and strode aft. "In my ready room."

He kept the rest of his thoughts to himself as he stepped off the bridge. By reflex he locked the ready room door behind him, and then he turned the computer on his desk to face him. The system used a silent biometric scan to confirm Kang's identity, and then the live comm from Klingon High Command appeared on the small viewscreen. For a moment it was just the emblem of the Klingon Empire, but that soon gave way to the battle-scarred face of General Garthog, the gray-maned supreme commander of the Klingon Imperial Fleet.

"*Kang! What is your status?*"

"We're about to orbit Kolasi III."

"*Have you encountered any Federation vessels?*"

"Not yet, General, but confidence is high."

A grim expression creased Garthog's heavy steel-gray brow. "*The High Council has demanded that I remind you of the importance of the Organia Treaty. They want us to avoid any* unnecessary *conflict with Starfleet vessels.*"

Garthog's choice of verbal emphasis sparked Kang's curiosity. "What, precisely, is the difference between necessary and unnecessary conflict?"

"*That will be up to your discretion, Captain. But be warned: the High Council will* not *be kind to anyone who plunges us into another war with the Federation. So choose your battles wisely. That is all.* Qapla'."

"*Qapla'*, General."

The trefoil emblem returned for a moment, and then the

small screen went dark. Kang swiveled the screen back toward the other side of his desk, and then he cursed under his breath.

Why have a government if all it does is deny me my right to glory?

His former good mood now tainted with resentment, Kang left his ready room knowing that without the thrill of the hunt, the bridge of his ship would feel more like its brig.

Mara entered the *SuvwI*'s shuttlebay to find D'Gol loading a few last bundles of wilderness gear into the cargo compartment of the shuttlecraft *QInqul*. As he crammed in each duffel, half a dozen engineers and mechanics scrambled around him to finish the last of the shuttlecraft's preparations. Inside the cockpit she saw the forked-bearded Hartür power up the *QInqul*'s engines and start his preflight checks. Through the sleek craft's open side hatch, Mara saw that the rest of the strike team was already on board and strapping into their seats' safety harnesses for the ride down to the stormy jungle of Kolasi III.

As ordered, Mara had packed light. She had limited her kit to essential gear only: a scanner, a small case for samples, her disruptor pistol, a *d'k tahg*, and the recommended quantity of survival rations and potable water for two days in a jungle environment. Nonetheless, she knew what D'Gol would say when she went to add her pack to the others on the shuttle.

He watched her lob her slender pack into the cargo compartment, and then he shot a derisive look at her. "I said to pack light. Did you bring everything you own?"

"Only what was on your list, D'Gol. But I've heard you have a tendency to mistake small things for big things. Or so the Murag sisters say."

She boarded the shuttlecraft without waiting for D'Gol to respond. He followed her inside, muttering angrily to himself. As usual, she had left him at a loss for a clever retort.

The inside of the *QInqul* was sultry thanks to heat bleeding into the passenger compartment from the barely shielded impulse core. The breath and body odor of Klingons dressed in tactical gear had merged into a familiar and therefore strangely reassuring funk.

Mara nodded at Naq'chI and Keekur, two female warriors seated at the aft end of the compartment. Keekur nodded back, and Naq'chI paused in the sharpening of her *d'k tahg* to lift the dagger in a quick, friendly salute.

Instead of taking her seat in front of spindly Doctor Dolaq, the team's xenocultural specialist, Mara nodded to her right at CheboQ, the medic, and then she detoured into the cockpit.

Hartür looked up and acknowledged Mara's presence with a simple grunt.

She slapped her right hand onto his shoulder, and with her left pointed at one of the gauges. "Hartür? Why is our thruster reserve tank only at ninety percent?"

"Commander's orders. He wants us fast and light."

"Then he's a fool. The planet's tropical storm can knock out impulse systems without warning. We'll need all the thruster power we can get. Tell flight ops to top off that tank."

"Belay that," D'Gol said as he entered the cockpit. He shouldered Mara aside and planted himself in the command seat to Hartür's right. "The loadout is fine. I prepped it myself."

His arrogance made Mara seethe. "Then you did not read my recommendations. If you had, you would not be so careless."

"I read as much of your prattle as I cared to, *science officer*. That's all your kind does: make simple things hard for no good reason."

She chose to ignore the way he had spoken her job title as if it were an insult and restrained herself to what she knew really mattered. "My job is to warn you of dangers *before* you fly us into them. Since you refused to add an extra tank of thruster fuel, the least you could do is make sure our only reserve tank is actually filled."

"The *least* I could do is tell you to shut up and take your seat. But we wouldn't want to make the captain's concubine—"

"*Wife*, you *petaQ*."

He smirked like a Denebian slime devil showing its fangs just before it attacks. "We wouldn't want to make the captain's *wife* angry."

"Stop worrying about *my* feelings and focus on not wasting your team's *lives*."

Mara left the cockpit and took her seat with the others. There was little to gain from arguing with D'Gol. She had dealt with his kind too many times before: insecure, petty, and unable to imagine that she might have ascended through the ranks by virtue of her abilities and not merely by association with her husband. He was a waste of her time.

A warrior can be judged by her enemies. He is unworthy of me.

As she arrived at her seat, CheboQ gave her a knowing smile and said in a discreet voice, "I would also have felt better knowing the reserve tank was full."

When she sat down, Doctor Dolaq leaned forward and kept his voice low, as CheboQ had done. "I'll bet you a flagon of bloodwine that *yIntagh* hasn't read my mission recommendations, either. Nothing like being a subject in a kakistocracy."

Mara heard the squeak of crimping leather as Naq'chI and Keekur shifted anxiously in the back row. Keekur held up a gauntleted fist. "If D'Gol spoke to me with such disrespect, I would geld him like the stupid *targ* he is."

Naq'chI added, "Think bigger. You're the captain's wife, and D'Gol is a *petaQ*. If he won't show you respect, cut his throat and drink his blood while it's still warm."

It felt good to have the support of the others on the strike team, but Mara knew it would be dangerous to let such mutinous chatter go unchallenged. She looked aft at Naq'chI and Keekur. "Thank you for your advice, but that's no way to run a ship."

Keekur looked offended. "It is the Klingon way."

"No, the Klingon way is to remove those who fail to uphold their oath, or who act with dishonor. Just because I disagree with D'Gol, that does not make him faithless or honorless."

Naq'chI sounded shocked. "He called you a *concubine*."

"I know what he said. But killing an experienced, competent senior officer for having poor manners serves no one, Naq'chI. It will not salve my pride. It will not make Kang's command more secure. It will not add to the defense of the Empire. It will not bring honor to him or the one who kills him. It would simply be a waste."

Placated, or perhaps chastised, Naq'chI and Keekur leaned back and settled into their seats. Anticipating a rough journey, Mara secured her own safety harness.

Doctor Dolaq regarded her with clear admiration. "Your argument was well stated, Lieutenant. You have a keenly logical mind. At times you seem almost . . . Vulcan."

She fixed the team's oddball scientist with a playful mock glare. "If you're just going to *insult* me, Doctor, I'm afraid we can't be friends."

8

Swift but precise: that was Spock's mantra as he and Sulu completed the preflight check of all key systems on the shuttlecraft *Kepler*. Sulu had focused on verifying the flight controls and navigational system, while Spock had concentrated on performing safety reviews of the fuel system, impulse core, landing gear, and life-support module. By his best estimate, Spock knew they would be finished with some time to spare, so long as they weren't interrupted.

Behind them, their five passengers, who all wore the same jungle-camouflage jumpsuits and ponchos as Spock and Sulu, spent the last few seconds before launch testing the fidelity of their seats' five-point restraint harnesses.

Captain Kirk's voice belted from the overhead comm: *"Spock! ETA to launch?"*

"Ninety seconds, Captain. Completing final flight check now."

"That's cutting it close, Spock. The Klingons are almost here. If you don't get that shuttle beneath the cloud cover before they make orbit—"

"I am aware of the need for urgency, Captain. Spock out." It was technically a breach of protocol for Spock to close the channel without the captain's consent, but he had served with James Kirk long enough to know that the man was not one to insist upon formalities.

So much for avoiding interruptions.

From outside the ship came the dull *thump* of a cargo panel being closed, and then the heavy *thud* of the portside hatch being sealed. A different voice, a woman's this time, said via the comm, "Kepler, *this is* Enterprise *flight ops. Your gear's been stowed, hatch secured. Deck crew is clearing the shuttlebay. You'll be clear to launch in fifteen seconds.*"

"Acknowledged, flight ops. *Kepler* standing by to launch." Spock closed the channel. "Mister Sulu, for our own safety, we will need to keep the blast shutters raised once we enter the planet's atmosphere. Do you wish to raise the shutters now? Or would you prefer to wait until after we launch?"

"We can raise them now." Sulu made a few adjustments on his console. "I can fly on instruments alone. Might as well spare ourselves the distraction of closing them in-flight."

"Logical." With one touch on the control console, Spock activated the duranium blast shutters that covered the shuttle-craft's three forward viewports. It took a few seconds for the trio of panels to slide up and lock into position. "Blast shutters secured."

"Kepler, Enterprise *flight ops. Shuttlebay is depressurized, outer doors are open. All systems green, you are go for launch. Acknowledge.*"

This time Sulu answered the comm. "Flight ops, *Kepler*. Copy that. Lifting off in three . . . two . . . one." With a pass of his hand over the controls, Sulu gradually powered up the shuttle's underside thrusters, lifting the craft gently from the deck. The *Kepler's* hull resonated with the low purr of well-tuned engines. Another fleeting touch of his fingertips nudged the shuttlecraft forward, giving Spock a mild but not unpleasant sensation of being pushed backward into his chair. It was one of the most graceful lift-offs Spock had experienced during his time in Starfleet, a testament to Sulu's exceptional skill as a pilot.

Sulu kept his eyes on his instrument panel. "Clearing shuttlebay doors in three . . . two . . . one. Clear." Another half g of force told Spock that Sulu had accelerated slightly. "Coming about, bearing one-four-four mark nine. Current speed, three thousand meters per second."

"Take us into the atmosphere, Mister Sulu. Accelerate at your discretion."

"Yes, sir." The purr of the engines rose in pitch and frequency to a steady humming as Sulu increased the *Kepler*'s speed and banked into a shallow dive toward Kolasi III.

From the passenger area behind Spock and Sulu came a pitiable groaning.

Despite the restraint of his five-point safety harness, Spock swiveled his chair and turned his head far enough to see that the source of the sickly noises was Doctor Lisa Babitz. Seated just behind the portside hatch, the lanky blonde physician looked distraught. She pressed her right hand to her abdomen, and used her left hand to cover her mouth as she convulsed in what appeared to be a bout of dry heaves.

"Doctor Babitz, do you need assistance?"

Babitz winced, swallowed hard, and grimaced. "I'm fine. I just never liked riding in shuttles, not even in the best of conditions." A sudden lurch rocked the *Kepler*, to Babitz's apparent dismay. "Which these most certainly *aren't*."

Chekov, who was seated on the starboard side across from Babitz, tried to extend the doctor a comforting hand. "It will be okay, Doctor. Just try to relax."

His advice seemed only to vex her. "How the hell am I supposed to *relax* in this situation?"

"Well, for a start, you could put your arms down."

She looked at Chekov as if she thought him insane. "Put them down? Where?"

"Your chair does have armrests, Doctor."

She rolled her eyes. "These filthy things? Yeah, right. I'm not touching anything in here."

Spock grew concerned about the *Sagittarius*'s chief medical officer's state of mind. "Doctor, what is the root of your concern about the interior of this spacecraft?"

"I wouldn't *have* any concerns if your people had let me disinfect it before they strapped me into this chair like some kind of mental patient."

Her complaint perplexed Security Officer Singh. "Disinfect? Doctor, this entire vessel was just stripped to spaceframe and reassembled from the deck up over the past several hours."

"Yeah, I know—but was it cleaned? Did anybody think to wash this flying bacteria can?"

Master Chief Ilucci, who was seated to starboard directly behind Spock, leaned forward as far as his seat's harness would allow. "Sorry, guys, I guess we should've mentioned this earlier. The doc's a bit of a germophobe."

Chekov's normally cheerful disposition melted into weary disgust. "*Now* they tell us."

The hull of the *Kepler* started to shake—infrequently and mildly at first, and then with greater vigor and more steadily. The overhead lights flickered and the forward control panels stuttered on and off as a steady rumbling of turbulence assailed the tiny craft.

Sulu remained strangely calm as he declared for all to hear, "Well, Doc, if you've enjoyed the first part of our ride, you're gonna *love* what comes next."

Hurricane gales howled like banshees as the shuttlecraft went dark and dropped like a stone for nearly a second. As the lights hiccuped back on, along with main power, everyone except Spock and Sulu wore matching expressions of existential terror.

Despite the groaning of the engines and the shrieking wind, Spock's sensitive Vulcan ears heard Doctor Babitz mumble in fear and despair, "Please, for the love of all that's holy . . . kill me now."

Kirk counted the seconds while he stared at the bridge's main viewscreen. The image of the shuttlecraft *Kepler* shrank rapidly as the tiny craft sped toward the atmosphere of Kolasi III. At the same time, he was keenly aware of the moving icon on the forward console's tactical scanner: the one that represented Kang's swiftly approaching battle cruiser.

He knew the prudent thing to do would be to move the *Enterprise* and the *Sagittarius* to cover now, ahead of the *SuvwI'*'s arrival—but if the *Kepler* met with any kind of delay that led to it being spotted by the Klingons, Kang might well order his gunners to open fire and destroy the shuttlecraft. It was up to Kirk to make sure that didn't happen. Until he was certain the *Kepler* would enter the storm and evade the Klingons' sensors, he had a duty to keep his ship here, ready to intervene, no matter the cost.

Kang won't hesitate to fire on a defenseless Starfleet shuttle, but he'll think twice before squaring off with the Enterprise. *I just hope it doesn't come to that.*

Ensign Waltke turned to look at Kirk. "Captain, the *SuvwI'* is forty-five seconds from visual contact. Should we raise shields?"

"No. They don't have line of sight yet, but they'd read the residual energy from our shields instantly." Kirk looked to starboard, hoping for better news. "Mister Nanjiani. How long until the *Kepler* enters the storm?"

"Twenty-five seconds, Captain."

Helm Officer Benson was unable to hide the dismay in her voice. "Which means if we're lucky, we'll have twenty seconds to make it to cover."

And I chided Spock for cutting it close!

He looked toward Scott, who sat at the engineering station. "Scotty, we'll need to push the impulse engines from dead stop to emergency overdrive. Will they be able to take that?"

"Aye, sir. You have my word."

"All I ever needed. Lieutenant Benson, as soon as Mister Nanjiani confirms the *Kepler* is safe, set course for the planet's moon, maximum impulse, and get us under its southern pole."

"Aye, sir," Benson said, already programming the helm for the emergency run to cover.

Kirk turned his chair to look aft. "Lieutenant Uhura, hail the *Sagittarius* on a secure data channel. Tell Captain Nassir to take his ship behind the moon now. We'll follow directly."

"Transmitting now." Kirk was turning his chair for another look at the tactical display when Uhura added, "Captain, *Sagittarius* replies, 'We leave when you do.' "

Kirk frowned, but the truth was he didn't blame Nassir for not taking the safe way out. Nassir's people were on the *Kepler*, same as Kirk's.

"Ten seconds," Nanjiani announced, shifting his weight nervously, like a young child with an overly full bladder.

"Steady," Kirk said. "Benson, when I say go, push the impulse engines to maximum. Bypass the safeties, put them into overdrive. Keep us at full thrust until we're inside the moon's gravitational field, and then let it slingshot us to cover on the far side."

Benson nodded her understanding as Nanjiani started his final countdown.

"Five . . . four . . . three . . . two . . . one! *Kepler* is out of sensor contact."

Kirk almost launched himself from his chair as he snapped, "Go!"

Accelerating from a dead stop to overdrive full impulse in the blink of an eye was more than the ship's inertial dampers had been built to handle. The drastic burst of speed slammed Kirk back into his command chair almost hard enough to give him whiplash, and it held him there for a few seconds until the ship's delta-v dropped to a level the inertial dampers could match. Kolasi III's airless, reddish moon swelled to fill the viewscreen.

"Ten seconds until the Klingons have line of sight," Nanjiani called out.

"Cut engines!"

Benson shut down the impulse drive, and as Kirk had hoped, the *Enterprise* soared under the moon's southern pole and then, snared by its gravity, followed its upward curve. Meanwhile, the faster and far more agile *Sagittarius* shot past the *Enterprise* in a pale blue-gray blur that quickly vanished beyond the moon's horizon.

Eyes fixed upon the hooded sensor display, Nanjiani declared, "Five . . . four . . . three—and we're clear." He sucked in a deep breath, and then purged his anxiety with a long exhalation.

"Well done, everybody. Lieutenant Benson, slow us down, and then bring us to a stop when we're at our most hidden. Mister Scott, take the ship into low-power mode. Minimize our heat and energy signatures as best you can."

"Rig for silent running. Aye, sir."

Kirk sat back and let his people do their jobs. On the viewscreen, the dark side of Kolasi III's moon was barely visible. That was just as well, he decided. If this side of the moon was in shadow, then so were the *Enterprise* and the *Sagittarius*.

What now would follow, Kirk knew, was going to be the hardest part of any mission for a commanding officer: the waiting. He and his colleagues had done all they could up to this point. The landing party had prepared to the best of the crew's ability, and they had done their part, maneuvering on a fast-approach trajectory into some of the most violent atmospheric conditions Kirk had ever seen. He and the rest of the *Enterprise* and *Sagittarius* crews had stayed in position, defending the shuttlecraft's descent into danger, until the very last moment.

What happened next was, for the most part, out of Kirk's control.

Would the shuttlecraft survive its journey to the planet's surface? What would the landing party encounter after they arrived? Would they all make it back? Or would Kirk soon be writing another heartfelt letter of condolence to a grieving spouse, parent, or child? One that would be delivered in person by a pair of Starfleet officers attired in dress uniforms—the last thing any relative of a member of Starfleet ever wanted to see arrive unannounced on their doorstep.

I've written too many of those damn letters. And I still owe one to Matt Decker's wife, and his son, Will. . . . But what do I tell them? Do I lie about his suicide? Call him a hero?

It likely would be at least several hours before the *Enterprise* would receive any word from the landing party. Kirk hoped that by then he and Mister Scott would think of a plan for bringing the *Kepler* safely back aboard without instigating a new round of armed conflict between the Federation and the Klingon Empire.

Kirk stood and headed for the turbolift. "Mister Scott, you have the conn. If there's any change in the situation, alert me immediately."

"Aye, sir." Scott took Kirk's place in the command chair.

The turbolift doors opened. Kirk stepped inside alone and took hold of the throttle as the doors slid closed. "Deck three." With a pleasing hum the lift car started its descent.

Though Kirk would never leave the bridge of his ship during a crisis, he knew that the *Enterprise* and the *Sagittarius* both were safe for the moment, the fate of the landing party was out of his hands . . . and there was a long-overdue letter it was time for him to write.

———————————

Flying by instruments through a maelstrom was a lot like simulator training, only more chaotic and with a very real possibility of actually dying. Sulu had learned to pilot all sorts of machines—aircraft, spacecraft, even a few submersibles. What he had always enjoyed about flying was the experience of seeing his environment shift around him as he raced through it. Piloting by gauges alone, with the blast shutters up, felt unnatural to him. He struggled to monitor all the readouts at once and then transform that information into a real-time understanding of where his vessel was, where it was going, and how fast it was getting there.

He couldn't admit that to Spock. The first officer had no patience for the doubts or insecurities of others. Sulu was sure that if he had confessed his misgivings about piloting the *Kepler* into the planet's insane tropical storm on instruments alone, Spock would have replaced him with someone else—or possibly even insisted on piloting the shuttlecraft himself.

A sound like a bomb going off rocked the *Kepler* and nearly sent it into a barrel roll before Sulu recovered control. Even as he forced the shuttle back into a shallow descent, his hands trembled from adrenaline overload.

Keep it together. Stay focused. Check your gauges. Watch your scanner—

His last glimpse of the sensor readout before it went dark showed the blue circular icons representing the *Enterprise* and the *Sagittarius* vanishing from the scope, and a triangular red icon denoting the Klingon battle cruiser swinging through a wide arcing turn into orbit above. In the space of a few seconds the landing party's only friends for several light-years disappeared, and their worst enemies took up station over their heads.

Now this feels real. The tactical screen went dark. Sulu forced himself not to worry about it. *That's fine. One less gauge to watch.*

An ear-splitting screech like the cry of a giant steel eagle made Sulu wince. He felt the temperature inside the *Kepler* rise a few degrees and realized they had been struck by lightning.

Tell me the insulation is holding.

So far the gauges seemed to still read true. The interior sensors had picked up an elevated level of ozone in the passenger compartment, but it wasn't high enough to pose a threat. The exterior sensors showed little more than static and garbled readings.

If we lose those, I won't be able to land by instruments. And who knows what'll happen if we lower the blast shutters?

Sulu fought with the sluggish, heavy controls to slow the shuttlecraft's descent. "Mister Spock? We have an exterior sensor malfunction. Can you verify?"

Spock, who looked as placid as if this were a simulation, checked his console. "Confirmed. Main circuit damaged by overload. Automatic uplink to secondary circuit has failed. I will attempt to engage it manually." The first officer flipped some switches and remotely rewired the *Kepler*'s sensor system—a feat Sulu didn't follow but most certainly appreciated as the readouts came back into focus, confirming there was solid ground several dozen kilometers below their position.

Now we just need to get there alive.

They would also need to find a way to get off the planet alive, in spite of the malevolent welcoming committee Kang and his ship were certain to provide—but that was a dilemma for later. Right now, Sulu had to contend with winds blowing at more than five hundred kilometers per hour, peals of thunder that could shake the bulkheads off the *Kepler*'s spaceframe, and lightning bolts that could cut the shuttle clean in half. And he had to do it all blind, with nothing to guide him but numbers on a panel.

It was for the best, he knew that. He had learned the hard way as a youth that in a storm, or a fog bank, or especially the deceptively clear environs of deep space, a human pilot simply could not trust their eyes and ears. It was too easy for human senses to become confused, especially in the air or in the weightlessness of space. A pilot flying by eye would swear they were upright and climbing while pushing their craft into an inverted dive. Their first clue that they had made a mistake would be the moment they hit the ground.

In situations like this, Sulu knew his physical senses could not be trusted. His shuttle's flight instruments, as long as they remained insulated from corrupting damage, would be far more reliable than his own eyes. The gauges knew whether he was flying level or keeping true to his heading, even when he didn't.

Learning to trust the instruments was something many novice pilots found hard to do. Sulu had been one of them. He had grown up thinking of himself as an instinctive pilot. As a child he had flown hang gliders. In his early teens he had graduated to wingsuits. Before he finished high school and applied to the Academy, he had already begun training to fly antique rotary-wing aircraft, or "helicopters," as they had been called.

But his early successes had made him cocky. Overconfident. Only a close brush with calamity during his fly-by-instruments training, and a last-second rescue by his instructor, had taught Sulu to approach his passion with a modicum of humility. To remember that being able to pilot a machine through space and sky did not make him a god, just a very lucky person.

A wave of disorienting energy swept over the shuttle, dimming the lights and scrambling the readouts. Sulu heard the impulse engine cut out, and his stomach leapt into his throat as the *Kepler* plummeted. "Ionic disruption wave! Engaging thrusters!"

The hydrox-fueled thrusters took a second or two to kick in. Before they did the shuttle began whirling in a flat spin, a victim of gravity and hurricane-force winds.

A low roar of ignition shook the shuttlecraft. Sulu kept his eyes on his gauges as he fired the thrusters to halt the *Kepler*'s spin and then steered into the strongest headwind. The sudden reversals and competing forces of momentum and acceleration tossed Spock and the rest of the landing party around like rag dolls. Only their seats' harnesses kept them from bouncing around inside the shuttle like dice on a craps table.

Good thing we added harnesses.

He had just brought the shuttle's attitude back to level when the impulse engine kicked back on, greatly reducing the effects of turbulence on the hull. He disengaged the emergency thrusters to save hydrox fuel, and then he spared a moment to look back at his shaken passengers. "Everybody okay?"

Ilucci looked nauseated but gave him a thumbs-up. "Five by five, sir."

Apparently in shock, Chekov said, "Define *okay*."

Sulu made a special effort to look over his shoulder at Doctor Babitz, who was sitting directly behind him. The slender woman was hanging on to her harness's straps for dear life as tears rolled from her squeezed-shut eyes. Worried, Sulu called out, "Doc? You okay?"

Babitz shook her head *no* and kept her jaw clenched.

Sulu poured on the speed and sent the *Kepler* screaming through a stormhead like a duranium bullet. "Hang on, Doc, we're almost there. You're gonna make it, I promise."

She reacted with a cross between a sob and a hysterical laugh of despair. "Don't say that. The hope of dying is the only thing keeping me alive."

9

"We've assumed orbit of Kolasi III," Larzal reported from the helm, captioning what Kang could already see for himself. She added without looking up, "Sensor contacts clear."

Kang remained wary of a trap. "Boqor, confirm all clear."

His tactical officer, now the acting first officer in D'Gol's absence, stepped over to the main sensor console. She spent a moment making a thorough assessment. "I confirm no ship contacts, Captain. But we do read traces of ionized plasma consistent with output from Starfleet impulse engines. Concentrations suggest a fairly recent presence."

Kirk, you wily targ. *You're close, aren't you?*

Though Kang would have preferred to hunt one of Starfleet's most-celebrated line officers, the mission took priority. He checked his tactical panel. He saw little to no likelihood of an ambush of the *SuvwI'* or its shuttle from this position. "Launch the *QInqul.*"

Boqor relayed Kang's command to the shuttlebay. Seconds later, the shuttlecraft appeared on the main viewscreen, speeding ahead of the *SuvwI'* after deploying from the battle cruiser's forward-facing shuttlebay. The *QInqul* skimmed just above the surface of the planet's rings, on a direct heading for its target on the surface.

Over his shoulder, Kang ordered, "Qovlar. Hail the *QInqul.*"

Qovlar pressed a single button. "Channel open."

"D'Gol! May bravery bring you victory!"

"We will return with honor, my captain."

"You'd best return with more than that. Remember what I told you. Bring back the scientist, the research, or both. And do not let Starfleet have either. Is that clear?"

"It is. We will succeed or die, Captain."

"*Qapla'*, Commander." Kang hesitated before continuing, out of concern for the decorum of the situation. "Lieutenant Mara. Give D'Gol the benefit of your counsel, even when he objects. Make sure he does the *right* thing, not just the *easy* thing."

"I will see it done, my captain."

"Most important of all: remember that the wind does not respect a fool."

"Understood. Qapla', *my captain."*

"*Qapla'*, Mara." Kang looked back at Qovlar while making a slashing motion in front of his throat, to cue her to close the channel. As he watched the *QInqul* dive into the charcoal-colored storm belt that encircled the planet, he brooded over the need to send his mate into action while he stayed behind. *Madmen are resurrecting monsters better left dead, but it's my wife who has to hide the consequences of their ambitions. Fek'lhr take them all.*

He dispelled his gloom with a heavy sigh. There was work to do.

"Boqor, take us to standby alert and keep us there until further notice."

"Yes, sir." The wild-eyed woman triggered the alert, which activated with a single siren that blared from all of the ship's internal comm speakers. Then she added, over the still-open channel, "This is the XO. All decks to standby alert." Task complete, she closed the channel and moved to stand beside Kang's command chair. "Orders, Captain?"

He lowered his voice to speak confidentially with Boqor. "We have been told by the High Command to expect interference from Starfleet, most likely the *Enterprise*. I suspect Kirk has already sent a team to the surface. If he has, he will not abandon them. He and his ship will still be somewhere in this system. Most likely, they are close—very close."

Boqor nodded. "If so, they most likely are behind the third planet's moon."

"Yes—but they might also be hiding inside the planet's rings."

"That would be a hazardous choice, though I can see the advantages." Boqor stole a look at Kang's tactical display. "Shall we break orbit and make a fast swing around the moon to flush them out? Or at least confirm where they are not?"

"No." He saw that his answer surprised Boqor, and he concluded that an explanation was appropriate. "We've been ordered by the High Command to avoid any unnecessary direct contact with any Federation vessel, be it Starfleet or civilian. Leaving our assigned station to seek out a direct engagement with the enemy would do us more harm in the long run."

"I see." She looked away and thought for a moment. "How should we proceed?"

"Assuming Kirk and his ship are here—and I can sense they are—we should do what we can to baffle them. Keep them off-balance. Push them into making a mistake that reveals them to us. In that circumstance, we would be free to engage."

Boqor nodded at Kang's tactical panel. "With your permission?"

"Granted."

She called up the *SuvwI'*'s sensor logs from past missions. "We tend to run our sensor sweeps at regular intervals, and in patterns approved by the High Command. Kirk and his people will know this about us. We should change our sweeps' patterns and frequency. For instance, interrupt a scan pattern or repeat the previous one without warning."

Kang smiled in approval. "Yes. Kirk loves to use unconventional tactics. Let's see how he likes being on the receiving end of some." He raised his voice. "Larzal, at your discretion, make random adjustments to our orbit. Closer to the planet, farther out. Above the rings, beneath them. Increase or decrease speed without obvious rationale. Make our movements unpredictable."

"Yes, Captain. Adjusting orbital patterns now."

"Excellent. Boqor, update our sensor protocols as discussed. Concentrate your scans on the planet's moon and its rings, with occasional looks at the planet's polar magnetic fields. If Kirk is using any of those to hide his ship, let's make sure he never feels safe revealing himself."

His acting first officer returned to the main sensor console and began resetting its controls. As he watched her work, one more notion sprang from his imagination.

He rotated his chair to look aft, toward the comms officer. "Qovlar, prep a subspace signal buoy. I want it to jam all frequencies except our primary subspace channel, and I want its transceiver set to constant maximum power."

"*Maximum* power?"

"Yes."

"That will drain the buoy's fuel cell and reserve battery in less than sixty hours."

"We'll be done here before then. But if we aren't, we'll just launch another."

"Understood, sir. The signal-jamming buoy will be ready to launch in one minute."

"Good. Let me know when you've confirmed it's active."

Kang turned his chair back toward the main viewscreen. He did not look forward to the interminable wait for the return of his strike team, but he took satisfaction in knowing that he had made the game a shade more interesting here in orbit.

I have you cornered, cowed, and muzzled, Kirk. Your move.

Lisa Babitz had no idea what she had ever done in this life or any other to deserve having been put on an express elevator to

Hell disguised as a Class-F shuttlecraft, but she was guessing it must have been bad. *Really* bad. Kicked-helpless-puppies bad.

Velocity and gravity pulled at her like wild stallions headed in opposite directions. A crash of thunder like the end of the world sent the *Kepler* into a corkscrew roll, followed by what felt like a vertical dive. The overhead lights flickered and then went out, leaving only the dim glow of the pilot's console to illuminate the passenger compartment.

Babitz clutched the cross straps of her seat's five-point harness and wailed in terror. Her dignity was gone, her pride forgotten. Tears streamed down her face and she didn't give a damn who saw it because every fiber of her being told her she was about to die. In agony.

Then came a ripping sound that ended with a whipcrack— and a blast of sparks from one of the starboard-side environmental panels. Fiery motes showered the passengers and ricocheted off the deck and overhead, and back and forth between the bulkheads. A swarm of burning-hot phosphors settled into Babitz's lap and onto her shoulders. Flailing like a maniac, she swatted them away in a panicked frenzy. "Gah! What the hell was *that*?"

Over the apocalyptic din, Spock replied, "Just a lightning strike, Doctor. An overload to a secondary relay. No major damage. All systems nominal."

"*Nominal*, my ass! There's smoke pouring out of the bulkhead!"

Spock's voice took on a firmer quality: "Please, calm yourself, Doctor."

Then Sulu called out, "Hang on, folks! Just a little—"

A wave of ionic distortion washed through the shuttlecraft. The impulse engine went silent for the second time in as many minutes, and once again the *Kepler* was thrown into a flat-spin free fall. Explosive roars buffeted the little craft, and then the hull shrieked as it came alive with creeping tendrils of lightning *inside* the passenger compartment.

"Uh, guys? Is that supposed to happen?"

Spock replied, "Try not to touch it."

"I'm so glad you said that, because silly me, the first thing I—!"

From beneath her seat came the growl of the reserve thrusters firing at full power. Sulu fought to regain control, but the *Kepler* refused to cooperate. It pitched backward and tumbled end over end, slamming all of Babitz's organs against one another like rugby players in a scrum.

She wanted to cry, scream profanities, and beg a God she'd never believed in to spare her life, but she could barely breathe, and the violence of being used by the storm like a bead inside a rattle was pushing a surge of warm bile up her throat, along with the contents of her stomach.

In between rounds of hyperventilation, she caught momentary glimpses of her fellow passengers. Sulu was clutching the helm console for dear life, and Spock's hands were practically crushing his chair's armrests. Ilucci and Chekov were both hating every second of this mess but doing their best to show brave faces to the world. She had no angle from which to view Singh, who was directly behind her, but when she stole a look at Razka she wanted to kill him.

The mother-loving Saurian field scout was *asleep*, his sinewy limbs floating loose and limber like the branches of a willow tree, as if he hadn't a care in the world.

You lizard-faced bastard.

A *boom* rocked the shuttlecraft as an invisible wall of force slammed Babitz back against her seat. It took all her willpower not to let her guts spew like a geyser.

As God is my witness, I will never eat huevos rancheros again.

Sulu regained control of the shuttle and gunned its thrusters for all they were worth. He shouted over the wild chaos, "We're coming in hot! Brace for impact!"

Oh God, he's gonna kill us all.

The rumbling of the thrusters pitched upward into a shriek

as Sulu fought to keep the shuttlecraft's nose up. Tempest winds slammed against the *Kepler*. It shook and juddered so hard that its interior bulkheads started to detach from the spaceframe.

Nothing like Starfleet craftsmanship.

A sudden free-fall drop. Next, a burst of acceleration, followed by a tremor of impact. Then another, and another. The shuttlecraft was bashing its way through something—

The jungle. We're cutting a path through the jungle.

Sulu fired the reverse thrusters in a bid to slow the shuttle, but it continued to scream ahead, crashing through who-knew-what outside. It rolled onto its starboard side as its wild skid continued, and then it tilted back onto its belly.

As if just for spite, another lightning bolt speared the *Kepler* and blasted the already dark overhead lights into a thousand bits of shrapnel that felt to Babitz like tiny horseflies biting her face, arms, legs, and hands.

A *bang* of impact launched Babitz forward against her restraints.

The *Kepler* slid to a grinding stop.

After what had felt like an endless nightmare of turbulence and deafening bedlam, the abrupt halt seemed to Babitz like the descent of utter silence. Then her ears popped as her body acclimated to the planet's surface air pressure, and she became aware of the heavy percussion of raindrops slamming like a never-ending drumroll against the shuttle's outer hull.

Spock flipped a toggle on the forward center console, and the blast shutters retracted downward, revealing the lush, rain-soaked sprawl of the Kolasi jungle. A thick gray mist lingered high overhead in the jungle's turquoise canopy—but that was about all Babitz could discern through the *Kepler*'s rain-slicked viewports.

Then she felt the unstoppable upward surge of something vile from her gut.

She hurriedly freed herself from her seat's harness and

lurched forward to the portside hatch. She was already fumbling with the door's lock release when she heard Spock shout, "Doctor, wait! We need to—"

That was all Babitz heard before she opened the hatch. She flung herself out of the shuttlecraft and into the merciless downpour. Lashed by wind and rain, she tripped over the *Kepler*'s port warp nacelle and tumbled forward like a rock-bottom drunk. She put out her hands to break her fall. They hit the ground—and sank into ten centimeters of soft, warm mud.

Where she promptly vomited, with great volume and violence.

Part of her brain knew she was going to have a first-class freakout over being wrist-deep in microbe-laden alien muck, but that was a problem for *after* she finished projectile-evacuating the contents of her stomach onto an unsuspecting alien world.

It's finally happened: I'm dead, and this is Hell.

Kirk hadn't progressed further than a few words into the letter he had been composing before being summoned back to duty. He stepped out of the turbolift expecting to find the bridge in crisis mode. Instead, all seemed quiet. The junior officers were at their posts, all of them calm and focused, and Scotty sat in the command chair, his eyes on the main viewscreen.

Curious and also mildly annoyed, Kirk approached the command chair.

Scott noted Kirk's arrival with a snap to attention. "Sir." He vacated the chair to make way for Kirk, who remained standing.

"Mister Scott. I presume you called me to the bridge for a *reason*."

"Aye, sir. The Klingons have deployed their own shuttlecraft to the planet's surface. It's following an approach trajectory almost identical to the *Kepler*'s."

"How far behind the *Kepler* are they?"

"Seven minutes, give or take. It was one of their type-three shuttles, so I'm guessing they sent down a landing party the same size as ours."

Kirk folded his arms in front of his chest. "Just as we expected." He fixed Scott with a critical look. "You called me to the bridge for *this*?"

"You did say to alert you of *any* change in the situation, sir."

"Yes, which you could have done over the comm."

"The next part I thought you'd want to hear in person. We left behind a passive sensor probe at the moon's southern pole, so we could keep an eye on Kang's ship. It was working fine and dandy until about two minutes after their shuttle entered the planet's atmosphere. That's when we lost all contact with the probe."

Kirk's irritation turned to alarm. "Was it destroyed?"

"Unknown. Visual scans detect no debris, but that's not much to go on."

"No, it isn't." He glanced at the image of the *Sagittarius* on the main viewscreen. "Maybe one of Captain Nassir's people knows what happened. Lieutenant Uhura, hail the *Sagittarius*."

Uhura keyed commands into her console. After a few seconds, she became visibly concerned. "Captain, I'm unable to open a channel to the *Sagittarius*." She spent a few more seconds working at her panel. "Captain, all Starfleet and Federation civilian frequencies are being jammed. The power of the signal suggests the source is a Klingon subspace signal buoy deployed in orbit around Kolasi III, and that its range of effect is this entire star system."

Scott frowned. "That's why we lost contact with the probe."

Kirk mirrored the chief engineer's expression. "And now we're cut off from both the *Sagittarius* and Starfleet Command." He glowered at the main viewscreen, imagining he could look through the moon to see Kang's ship. *Very clever, Kang. I won't underestimate you again.*

Helm Officer Benson turned her chair so she could face Kirk

and Scott. "Sirs? If we need to restore contact with the *Sagittarius*, why not have them dock with us, like they did before?"

"Don't even think about it, lass. With our comms jammed, our computer can't talk to theirs. Trying to dock two starships without computers is just asking for trouble."

Kirk added, "He's right. At a minimum, we'd be looking at damage to one or both airlocks. Most likely, we'd breach both hulls."

Ensign Waltke looked back from the navigator's post. "Maybe we could pull up alongside them, then look out a viewport and play charades," he joked.

Lacking a better answer, Kirk said, "At this rate, Ensign, we might have to."

Nanjiani looked up from the sensor display. He had a confused look on his face. "Sirs? Why not just beam over to the *Sagittarius*? Or beam some of their people over here?"

The first person to answer him was Waltke. "The same reason we can't dock the ships. Ship-to-ship beaming involves letting the two ships' transporter systems share data. That's not possible while our comm and data frequencies are being jammed."

The science officer shrugged. "So don't beam platform to platform. Transport directly to some other part of the ship."

Scott raised his eyebrows in reproach. "Laddie, the whole reason we're sitting behind this moon is to stay off the Klingons' sensors. A transporter uses a *lot* of energy—enough for them to pick up from half a million kilometers away, moon or no moon. But even if that weren't a concern, how do you think a transporter knows when it's done its job correctly? It needs *sensor data*—the exact kind of data we presently can't get from our probe. What do you think'll happen when a transporter tries to convert a signal back to matter without a control channel?"

The young science officer looked queasy. "I'm guessing it would be bad."

"To say the very *least*, lad."

Uhura looked up from her console and caught Kirk's eye. "Captain, I might have a solution to our comm problem."

"I'm all ears, Lieutenant."

"Starfleet semaphore, sir."

Kirk aimed a befuddled glance at Scott, and then he looked back at Uhura. "I think I'm going to need a bit more, Lieutenant."

She took the transceiver unit out of her ear. "The *Enterprise* and the *Sagittarius* can use the navigation lights on our outer hulls to transmit messages in Starfleet semaphore code. The computer on each ship can translate a spoken or written message and then blink the lights in semaphore code to send it. The receiving ship's visual sensors observe the semaphore code and translate it back into written or verbal messages."

"Yes," Kirk said. "That could work. With the computers doing the translation and controlling the lights, it would be almost as fast as real-time comms."

Scott interjected, "And as long as we stay out of the Klingons' line of sight, they'll have no way to intercept our comms. It would be fast, secure, and silent."

"My thoughts exactly," Uhura said.

Kirk smiled. "Excellent work, Lieutenant. Set it up, and find some way to tell the *Sagittarius* crew what we're doing. I want this operational as soon as possible."

"Aye, sir." Uhura swiveled back toward her console, put her transceiver unit back into her ear, and started programming her modified semaphore system.

Around the bridge, the other officers all returned their attention to their own duties. Kirk cued Scott with a subtle tilt of his head to follow him out of the command well and onto the bridge's encircling upper ring. The two men stepped away from the others to confer in quiet voices beside the main viewscreen.

"Sooner or later, we'll need to deal with the landing party's return. I want to have a plan for their safe recovery ready *before* we need it. So tell me, Mister Scott: How do we get our people back aboard without losing them to Kang or starting a war?"

"I wish I knew, sir. But the truth is . . . this one has me stumped."

"Well, we'd best get *un*-stumped, Mister Scott. Or else our landing party might not get the homecoming they expect *or* deserve."

The *QInqul* pierced the wild storm like a javelin slicing through smoke. From her seat just behind the cockpit, Mara had an unobstructed view through the shuttlecraft's broad, wraparound viewport. Outside, the sky was a weeping bruise, a *be'mawpu's* cauldron of black blood and golden fire, rendered in streaks and smears by sheets of rain that pummeled the *QInqul*.

Like most pilots trained by the Klingon Imperial Fleet, Hartür seemed confident that the proper response to tornado-like wind and massive bursts of lightning and thunder was to fly even faster than if the sky were clear. He was pushing the *QInqul* harder than Mara had ever seen any pilot dare in the midst of a typhoon of this magnitude.

Forks of lightning stabbed at the shuttlecraft, then snared it like creeping ivy.

Inside the shuttle, the overhead lights erupted into sprays of smoking polymer shards, followed by cascades of white-hot sparks that showered the strike team and caromed about the deck between their booted feet. Thunder roared, and a rippling wave of distortion passed through the shuttle in the wink of an eye—and half a second later the cockpit consoles went dark, and the *QInqul* pitched into a nose dive through a churning sea of smoke.

In the cockpit, Hartür cursed in a loud and steady streak while slamming his fists against the helm console, as any good acolyte of percussive maintenance would do. After the fourth or fifth smack of his hand, the controls stuttered back to life and emergency lights on the bulkheads snapped on, flooding the passenger compartment with harsh white light.

Mara squinted against the glare so she could see what they were flying into.

Wide ribbons of sickly chartreuse lightning arced through gaps between cloud banks. Hartür expertly yawed and rolled the *QInqul* around and between the searing bands of storm-light without sacrificing any speed—until another stormstrike knocked the shuttle into a wild corkscrewing roll to port and set the emergency lights into an erratic flicker that rendered the team's manically flailing limbs into a strobed series of frozen moments, each more ridiculous looking than the last. Smoke pungent with the stink of scorched wiring belched up through the deck's ventilation grates and quickly filled the passenger compartment.

A jolt of turbulence slammed Mara's slack jaw shut, crushing the left side of her tongue between her back teeth. She howled in pain, purely out of reflex, and spit a copious mouthful of fresh blood into her own lap.

CheboQ grinned and shouted to her, "Not even on the ground yet, and already you're bleeding! You overachiever!"

She replied with a bloodied smile, "Shut up, you *taHqeq*."

Hartür bellowed from the cockpit, "Brace for landing!"

Through the forward viewport Mara saw the jungle's blue-green canopy rising to meet the swiftly descending shuttlecraft. By the time she was able to discern one tree from another, the *QInqul* was crashing into them, shearing them away like a razor through stubble.

Each impact threw Mara and the others forward against their seats' restraints. Something hit the viewport, and a crack spider-webbed across the solid piece of transparent *bettI'*. Then the *QInqul* hit the ground so hard that its hull rang like a bell. It was still speeding forward, slicing through tree trunks as it glided across a slick sheet of muddy ground.

Hartür ignited the emergency thrusters and fired them in full reverse. The shuttle began to slow, and then it cut through one last stand of skinny saplings and slid out onto open ground—which turned out to be a relatively steep downward slope littered with large, craggy rocks and ending at what Mara belatedly realized was the edge of a cliff overlooking a jungle basin. A valley that happened to lie very far below the cliff's edge. Which did not bode well, not at all.

moQDu'wIj remqu' qeylIS.

The shuttle bounced over a jagged cluster of rocks, and the thrusters sputtered as the *QInqul* skidded down the slope, bouncing and shuddering with each stone it hit along the way.

CheboQ's eyes were wide as he watched the edge rush toward them. "Call me old-fashioned, but I say death by acute deceleration trauma is *not* a good way to die."

From the back, Keekur replied, "Agreed."

The longer the shuttle slid, the faster it went. It would be just seconds now.

With a curse and a bash of the side of his fist on his console, Hartür brought the thrusters back to full power and banked the shuttle to starboard as hard as he could. The *QInqul* swerved and rocketed toward a cluster of massive boulders—

A deafening bang of metal against stone, followed by the crunch of crumbling rock and the shriek of buckling duranium. The interior of the *QInqul* went dark, and the engines cut out, leaving behind an eerie silence. Thick acrid smoke choked the inside of the shuttle, but it began to clear as fresh air and a drizzle of rain entered the cabin through a new fracture in the overhead.

Mara swallowed hard to acclimate her ears to the ambient air pressure. A satisfying *pop*, and then she heard the mad patter of torrential rain on the hull.

She and the rest of the strike team looked around—at the ship, one another, and then the cockpit and its view of the sheer drop beneath the *QInqul*'s nose, just past their savior rocks, which now held them firmly in their grip.

They had come less than a *qam* from certain death, and they all knew it.

The whole team howled with raucous laughter.

"What a ride!" Naq'chI exclaimed with adrenaline-fueled glee.

Keekur replied, "That's what I call a landing!"

Even D'Gol roared joyously at the thrill of cheating death. "Wait until I tell Boqor she missed this! She'll *never* forgive me for not bringing her down here."

They laughed for several seconds more, and then the mirth abated as quickly as it had come. D'Gol freed himself of his seat's restraints and headed for the hatch. "All right. Let's go have a look at this dumb ball of rock."

The rest of the strike team followed D'Gol's example and left the shuttle one at a time behind him. Mara stepped out into the blustering wind and rain and savored the taste of fresh air and the freedom of being anywhere but on a starship. As the storm lashed her with wind and pelted her face with fat drops of rain, she nodded at D'Gol. "Nice planet."

"Who cares?" D'Gol stared back at the narrow canyon the *QInqul*'s crash landing had slashed through the jungle. "Hartür! How far to the target?"

"Don't ask me. I don't even know where we are."

"You're not much use to me alive, are you, Hartür?" D'Gol turned next to Mara. "Can you get us a bearing and range?"

"I think so. Wait a moment." Mara lifted her portable scanner, adjusted its sensing parameters, and did a sweep of the surrounding area. In one pass she gathered a topographical map of the local terrain, a meteorological report and forecast, and several useful bits of tactical data. "Confirmed, I have our target. Range twenty-four point one *qelI'qam*s, relative bearing six-two mark three-one." She sidled closer to D'Gol so she could show him her scanner's readout. "I also have a mix of seven humanoid life-forms with energy signatures that could only be a Starfleet landing party. Range seven point three *qelI'qam*s, relative bearing two-seven-two mark eight-five. And they're on the move—on a direct heading for *our* target."

The commander grumbled several deeply profane curses, and then he faced the rest of the strike team. "Gear up. Starfleet already has boots on the ground, so we need to be fast. Basic kits only, except for Naq'chI and Keekur. Full tactical kits, both of you." He checked the chrono on the front of Mara's scanner, and then he added, "Be ready to move out in ten minutes. We will *not* let Starfleet beat us to our prize."

10

The landing party moved single file through the jungle, taking care with every step not to disturb the native flora or fauna any more than was absolutely necessary for them to pass. On such a primitive world as Kolasi III, the Prime Directive defended more than the sanctity of pre-warp cultures. It was about minimizing the effect of any Starfleet personnel upon the place being visited. Excessive disruption of a delicate ecosystem could, in a relatively brief span of time, prove more disastrous to a fledgling world than any deliberate interference.

Spock recalled once hearing this provision of the Prime Directive likened to a time-travel concept known as "the butterfly effect." A landing party might inflict many isolated injuries upon an alien ecosystem without any of them ever proving consequential, but it was just as likely that a seemingly trivial action could set in motion a series of events over a span of time greater than many humanoids' lifetimes that would ultimately result in tragedy and calamity. The wrong flower crushed under someone's boot . . . the first mutation of a crucial pollinating species swatted dead when it alights on some unsuspecting crewman's cuff . . . muddy footprints that somehow fossilize and millennia later become the basis for this world's inhabitants to ask, "*Are we not alone in the universe?*"

Spock was near the front of the line, just behind field scout Razka. Led by a tricorder signal that was locked onto what

Spock believed was the wreck of Doctor Verdo's lost ship, the Saurian used a wide blade with a laser-sharpened edge to slash a path through the jungle's otherwise impenetrable curtains of vines draped with moss. Unlike the other members of the landing party, Razka had left his Starfleet-issued boots in the shuttle. As a Saurian he moved faster, more comfortably, and with greater balance through jungle terrain on his broad, bare, taloned feet.

Wearing camouflage ponchos over jungle-patterned jumpsuits, the landing party had expected to blend easily into the alien environment. Instead, after just fifteen minutes of exposure to the jungle's constant rain, they all looked like wet, greenish-brown rags.

There was no escaping the rain here. It was heavy, tepid, and relentless. Spock would not have been surprised if he were to learn that the planet's native intelligent humanoid species had no word that meant *dry*, but two dozen nuanced variations on the concept of wetness.

The white noise of rainfall masked the sawing chirps of insects and was punctuated by the steady tempo of Razka's machete hacking through leafy vines and walls of moss. It was up to him to blaze a trail through the Kolasi jungle until such time as the landing party found any sign of existing paths created by the indigenous people. After nearly an hour of trudging through dense foliage and ankle-deep mud, however, the landing party had yet to encounter any such route. So onward they slogged.

Instead of footsteps, the landing party's passage was marked by rudely organic-sounding squelches caused by the mud's refusal to let go of their boots. It was vexing enough to Spock that the mud was severely slowing their progress; he did not appreciate the jokes it had inspired among the less mature members of the team—to wit, Ilucci and Chekov.

The master chief pulled his left foot free of the mud with a rough sound of resistant vacuum. "Excuse me." His next labored step forward yielded the same ugly noise. "Serves me right for having Mexican-Tellarite fusion tacos for lunch."

Chekov yanked his own right foot from the mud with a flatulent rip of air. "Everyone knows Russia makes the hottest tacos." His left foot echoed the sucking noise. "And the burrito was invented in Russia."

"Like hell," Ilucci said, stomping from mudhole to mudhole. "Burritos are *Italian*!"

From the middle of the line, Doctor Babitz snapped and voiced the feelings Spock was fighting to suppress: "Enough! Shut up, both of you! No more dumb jokes! No more lies about who invented Mexican cuisine! It's culturally insensitive! It's juvenile! And it just isn't *funny*!"

Chekov and Ilucci traded guilty looks and then the ensign turned his stare toward the ground in shame. Perhaps hoping to change the subject, Ilucci said without any apparent irony, "I wonder if we'll get a break in the rain anytime soon."

"If you had read your mission briefing, Master Chief," Spock said, "you would know that sensor data gathered over the past several decades indicate that it has been raining at this level of intensity on this region of Kolasi III for approximately the last 378 years, and it is expected to continue precipitating at an equivalent level for at least the next 500 years."

Ilucci absorbed that information with a blank look. "Guess I'll cancel my plan for a picnic, then."

Before Spock could comment on the inanity of even considering this location for an event such as a picnic, the landing party halted as Ensign Singh cried out in alarm from the rear of the line. Spock turned to see that the bulbous lavender head of a gigantic carnivorous plant had locked onto Singh's right arm. The enormous predatory flora was trying to pull Singh off the trail Razka had cut, but it did not seem to be powerful enough to lift her from the ground.

Chekov turned back from the middle of the group and drew

his type-2 phaser. As he raised it to aim at the plant, Spock called out, "Hold your fire!"

Moving at a quick step, Spock made his way to Chekov's side and eyed the setting of the man's weapon. "Your phaser is set to kill, Mister Chekov. It should be set to stun."

"But Mister Spock! That thing is eating—"

"It has merely latched on to Ensign Singh's arm. Most plants of that variety are not capable of instant digestion. And at any rate, we are required by the Prime Directive to do as little damage to this ecosystem as possible."

Spock drew his own phaser, set it for minimum-power stun, and then he walked back to stand beside Singh and aimed at the base of the attacking plant's root. One zap from his phaser proved more than sufficient to shock the plant into releasing its hold on Singh's arm and retracting its bulbous head up into the jungle's canopy.

Satisfied the threat was neutralized, Spock holstered his phaser and beckoned the *Sagittarius*'s physician. "Doctor Babitz? Could you tend to her injury, please?"

Babitz moved to Singh's side and pulled out her medical tricorder. Its oscillating tones were swallowed by the rain's steady susurrus. "No serious tissue damage. How does your arm feel right now?"

Singh flexed her right hand. "A bit numb from the elbow down."

"That'll pass in a few minutes," Babitz said. "The plant's toxins were relatively mild and are already breaking down inside your bloodstream. If you feel any change in your condition, anything at all, let me know. But from what I see here, you should be fine."

"Thanks, Doc."

Spock returned to the front of the single-file formation to find Razka staring into the jungle ahead of them. "Chief? Is everything all right?"

"A question, sir?" Off Spock's nod, Razka continued. "Does your policy of minimal force apply to the trio of reptilian apex predators that have been stalking us for the last one point six kilometers? I'd just like to know before they strike whether I need to set my phaser to stun."

"A reasonable question." Spock closed his eyes and listened for the sounds of running steps, snapping branches, and shaken boughs. "I too heard them following us after we crossed the stream. Based on their current movements, I estimate they have widened their following distance by several meters since I fired my phaser at the carnivorous plant."

Razka nodded once. "Very well. How should we deal with them?"

"Monitor their behavior. If they demonstrate increased boldness, we will treat them as an exigent threat. Otherwise, avoid direct engagement if at all possible."

The Saurian seemed dubious of Spock's assessment, but all he said was, "Aye, sir." And then he pressed ahead, letting his machete lead the way through the jungle.

Inactivity was like poison to Klingon warriors. It sapped their strength and dulled their focus. The scions of Kahless loathed few afflictions as deeply as they hated being *bored*.

Patience was not a virtue of the young in any species that Kang had ever met, but rashness was a special kind of fault among his own kind. It spared neither male nor female, rich nor poor, ignorant nor educated. To be a Klingon was to be a creature of drives and impulses, a servant of urges, desires, and appetites. It was a rarity to find a Klingon who matured beyond those attitudes to achieve true self-discipline.

Based on his decades of experience, Kang was fairly certain his tactical officer Boqor would never be one of those rare individuals.

It had been less than an hour since they had deployed the *QInqul* but already he felt Boqor growing anxious. She prowled the *SuvwI*'s command deck, projecting her impatience like a bonfire radiated heat. She paced from one station to the next, haunting the rest of the command crew. Kang watched her with quiet disapproval. *She's lucky she's among fellow* QuchHa'. *If she did that among the* HemQuch, *one of them would have gutted her by now.*

It was a cruel fact of life that the *HemQuch*, Klingons with traditional ridged skulls and sharper teeth, lorded over their more human-looking, smooth-headed kin, the *QuchHa'*—the descendants of Klingons altered a century earlier by the human-made Augment virus. For the sake of order and discipline, the Imperial Fleet kept the two segregated. So it was that Kang and his crew were all *QuchHa'*, "unhappy ones" forever forced to prove their worth to the Empire.

Boqor finished her latest circuit of the command deck and approached Kang's dais. He looked down at her from his seat of command. "What do you want?"

"You *know* what I want. To take the fight to the enemy."

"We don't know where the enemy is, and we have orders to hold our position."

His answer only fueled Boqor's mounting urge to take action. "Starfleet is *close*, my captain. The *Enterprise*. Kirk. They're within our grasp! To Gre'thor with the High Command. What do they know of honor? Of glory?"

"More than you, whelp."

His insult prompted Boqor to raise her chin, as if she were daring him to strike her, to give her a reason to challenge him. He narrowed his eyes at her. *Foolish child. I would break you like a dry twig under my boot.*

Showing more audacity than sense, she pressed the matter further. "Captain, all we need to do is widen our orbit, or shift to an elliptical pattern, and we could flush Kirk into the open!"

"To what end?"

"His defeat!"

Kang had to chortle at that. "So confident. So certain. Have you faced Kirk before? Have you seen him in action? Have you taken his measure in battle?"

His interrogation took some of the fire out of Boqor's eyes. "No."

"Then you have no idea what you're saying. I have seen Kirk stand alone and overcome odds I thought were impossible. You discount him because he's human. Because he's Starfleet. But most of all because *you* are a fool. I know the man. He's no easy target. He's a *warrior*. It's no coincidence that *Kirk* is an honorable Klingon name, Boqor."

Duly chastised, Boqor chose and spoke her next words with greater care.

"If he is as great a foe as you say, why do you not relish the chance to face him in battle?"

"Oh, but I *do*, Boqor. I have dreamed of testing his mettle ever since my last encounter with him. But this is not the time or the place. The High Command has defined our priorities, and neither Kirk nor his ship are among them. If they confront us, we will deal with them. But they are not the reason we are here. Honor and glory are good things, Boqor—but duty comes first. Our mission matters more than our personal desires. Never forget that."

He watched frustration and shame take their turns in her eyes. She was not going to be able to let go of her impulses without a struggle. "Captain, would it really compromise our mission just to confirm the presence of the *Enterprise*?"

His patience with Boqor was bleeding away faster than he cared to admit. "Boqor, if we abandon our assigned orbit to seek out the *Enterprise*, we might find ourselves far out of position at the moment our shuttlecraft returns from the planet's surface. What if that dereliction of our post enables Starfleet to capture or destroy our strike team? Who would be at fault, Boqor? *We* would." He stifled a low growl of irritation and fixed his eyes on the main viewscreen as a signal to Boqor that he no longer wished to look at her face. "From orbit, we control the space above Kolasi III and will therefore possess a major tactical advantage in the event that Starfleet already has a team on the planet's surface, which I suspect they do. We are fortunate to enjoy a major advantage of position, Boqor, and I will not give it up without a fight. *Do you understand?*"

Boqor lowered her chin ever so slightly, a gesture of submission. "I understand, my captain. I will resume monitoring the sensor readouts." She smartly withdrew without making Kang dismiss her, thereby preserving her apparent authority on the bridge and relieving him of the need to wound her reputation.

Someday, Kang knew, her way of doing things might get her killed. Or it might get her promoted. The Klingon Imperial Fleet was populated by legions of hotheads, even at some of its highest levels of command. But it had been Kang's impression that it was warriors like himself who ascended to the highest levels: the cold-blooded ones, the ruthless strategists and brutal tacticians, the ones who were able to see the long-term rewards that came from self-discipline and pragmatism. That was what it took to become a general. To earn noble status for one's House. For a child of commoners to earn a seat on the High Council. To become *chancellor*.

But those are dreams for another day.

Today, there is only my mission.

———————

The landing party had spread out as it traversed the jungle. It had been partly intentional, to make the group a more difficult target, but it also had been the product of fatigue. In the middle of the single-file column, Chekov was soaked to his weary bones. The rain remained intense and steady. Its irregular but continuing patter atop his poncho's hood felt like a kind of water torture, an inescapable nuisance that preempted his ability to hang on to thoughts of anything else.

A whistle from Razka at the front of the line. Mister Spock held up his fist, signaling the group to halt. Chekov shifted his weight to lean clear of Sulu and Babitz so he could see what was happening. Spock and Razka conferred in hushed voices, and then Razka indicated a direction with a quick chopping motion of one arm. Spock nodded at Razka, who made the suggested direction his new heading and resumed cutting a path through the dense foliage.

After marching along that heading for roughly fifty meters, the landing party emerged into a familiar-looking panorama: a long, straight, narrow canyon hewn through a densely clustered forest of jungle trees. And at one end of that butchered trench lay a derelict starship.

Chekov reached for his tricorder. The bent and mangled vessel lying at the jungle's edge resembled that of the missing Doctor Verdo, but in the short time Chekov had spent serving with Mister Spock he had learned to test his assumptions, to rely on facts rather than suppositions. A few seconds later he had the confirmation he needed. "Mister Spock, this vessel's hull configuration and passive transponder ID match those of Doctor Verdo's ship, the S.S. *Heyerdahl*. Other than jungle plants and insects, I read no life-forms inside."

"Acknowledged, Ensign." With gestures, Spock directed the landing party to fan out and surround the wreck of the small ship. A quick reconnoiter of the area confirmed the vessel was far too badly damaged to still be spaceworthy. Its crash had apparently torn large wounds in its fuselage, and one of its warp nacelles was gone, presumably lost somewhere along the kilometers-long scar carved by its crashdown.

Chekov peered into the distance, following the trail of thousands of trees sheared from their trunks just above their roots and flattened into the muddy ground. He tried to see the end of the wound, but all he found were drifting curtains of rain and lingering veils of mist.

Razka finished a walk around the ship and reported, "No sign of traps outside or native predators within. I think we can move inside, but we should continue to be cautious."

"Sensible," Spock said. "Everyone, resume single file. Chief Razka, lead us in."

The Saurian shouldered open the ship's bent portside hatch and ventured inside the *Heyerdahl*. Spock was the next to enter, followed by Sulu and Doctor Babitz. As Chekov neared the hatchway, he noted that the ship was already being absorbed into the jungle. Thick vines had started to encircle its hull, which was covered in patches of moss, mold, and fungi. A deep layer of mud had infiltrated the ship through the compromised hatchway, and leafy plants had already sprouted from the damp soil inside the *Heyerdahl*'s airlock.

Once the entire landing party was gathered inside the ship's central corridor, Spock issued new orders. "Master Chief Ilucci. Please take Ensign Singh and Mister Sulu aft to inspect the ship's labs and engineering section. Chief Razka, please search the crew's quarters. Doctor Babitz, Mister Chekov, please follow me to the ship's flight deck."

Splitting up the landing party made sense with regard to efficiency, but Chekov still found the idea unsettling. He was unable to articulate what exactly was troubling him, but something about the damage to the *Heyerdahl* felt to him like the consequence of a deliberate attack and not just the random violence of a crash landing. Adding to his unease was a foul odor of death and decay that only grew stronger as they continued forward.

He kept his concerns to himself as he, Spock, and Babitz proceeded to the ship's flight deck. The moment he saw its ruined state, he felt certain his fears had been proved justified.

He stepped up beside Spock and gestured toward the overhead, which had been ripped open in a manner that had parted the mangled hull panels like the spreading arcs of a splash caught in hyper-slow motion. Rain coursed through the shredded overhead, feeding the slow-draining, knee-deep pool of fetid water inside the compartment. "Mister Spock? That is *not* normal crash damage. Whatever did that exerted upward force from *inside* the ship."

"Agreed." He gestured toward a nearby console. "See if there is enough power left in the ship's emergency batteries for you to access its logs. If so, download what you can, prioritizing the most recent entries."

"Aye, sir." Chekov waded across the flight deck toward the command console.

He paused as Doctor Babitz called out, "Stop! Watch your step, Ensign." She held her medical tricorder in her left hand and pointed with her right hand at a part of the deck in front of Chekov. "There's a body under the water half a meter in front of you. A human woman, probably midforties. Based on a preliminary DNA scan, I'd say that's Doctor Mozhan Rashid." She pointed toward a different corner of the flight deck. "And submerged over there, by the life-support console, is the body of an Andorian *thaan*, who I'm fairly certain is Verdo's other colleague, Doctor Lofarras th'Sailash." She tweaked a setting on her tricorder. "Based on the relative levels of decay, I'd say th'Sailash has been dead about two weeks, and Doctor Rashid has been dead less than seventy-two hours." Lowering her tricorder, she added with an expression of supreme disgust, "And *we* are marinating in a soup of their innards."

Chekov struggled not to visualize what Babitz had just described, because he knew if he thought too much about it, he would end up vomiting even more profusely than she had earlier. Instead he kept his mind on his task as he detoured around Rashid's corpse in gingerly steps to reach the command console, where he set about patching his tricorder into the ship's computer.

Spock studied the condition of the flight deck with his keen senses. "Doctor Babitz, can you determine the causes of death for Doctor Verdo's peers?"

"Only in the most general sense. Scans show they both suffered fatal injuries from a blunt-force trauma of tremendous power. As far as what inflicted that trauma, I don't have enough evidence to say. Between the advanced state of decay caused by the local heat and humidity, and the fact that moving water has washed away any trace DNA or other evidence that could identify the killer, there really isn't much left to work with here."

At the command console, Chekov wrapped up his work. He faced Mister Spock, feeling slightly contrite. "Mister Spock, I recovered the last four entries from the log, and the ship's last six hours of sensor data before the emergency battery went dead."

"Good work, Ensign."

"I should note, sir, the computer is damaged. The sensor data might be corrupted."

"I will take that into account when I review it later. Thank you, Ensign."

Doctor Babitz shut off her medical tricorder and slung it back at her side, under her poncho. She looked as if she might vomit again. "Are we done here?"

Spock took another look around. "For now. We should regroup with the others."

As he and Babitz turned to leave the flight deck, Chekov looked up into the pouring rain, mesmerized by the spectacular kinetic damage that had ripped open the overhead. "What kind of monster can do *this* to a starship?"

Babitz's voice was colored by the kind of fear that comes only from experience. "Trust me, Ensign—pray you *never* find out."

11

Making a bonfire in a raging downpour had proved far easier than Mara had expected. All it had taken was a tall stack of properly arranged tree limbs, a knee-deep pit bounded with large rocks to contain the blaze, and two canisters of thruster fuel siphoned from the shuttlecraft. As she basked in the warmth of the towering orange conflagration, however, she had to give most of the credit to the insanely combustible rocket fuel.

The strike team had made more progress than D'Gol had expected by the time night fell. The Kolasi jungle was barely visible by day, thanks to its dense canopy, gray curtains of rain, and migratory clouds of mist. Consequently, there was effectively no period of transition between the murky conditions of daytime and the moonless, starless night. In a matter of minutes, the jungle had gone from dim to pitch-dark, almost without warning.

At least the rain had remained consistent. By all accounts, it had been raining on this world since before Mara's great-grandparents' grandparents had been born, and it would continue to rain on this mudball of a planet long after Mara's grandchildren's grandchildren were dead.

Around her, the rest of the strike team sang songs between feasting on the roasted flesh of some unlucky lizards that had wandered too close to them during their march. Keekur and Naq'chI had slain three of the beasts, ensuring plenty of fresh meat for everyone. And for those who wanted a bit of extra tang in their meal, CheboQ had harvested the succulent buds of several giant carnivorous plants, whose sap had a pleasant numbing effect on the gums.

"We're marinating in mud," Hartür growled while gnawing raw meat from a lizard's femur, "but at least we're eating well. I'm calling this a good night."

D'Gol belched and then replied, "Let's not get carried away. It's not a good night when all we have to drink is tangy sap."

CheboQ opened his field pack and pulled out two large black bottles. "Good thing I brought some bloodwine, then!" He grinned at the others' roars of approval, and then he passed the bottles around. One by one, the members of the strike team treated themselves to long swigs straight from either bottle. Even Doctor Dolaq, the oddball scientist, indulged in a draught.

Fresh meat. Strong drink. Raunchy songs.

Life was good, even in this damned rain.

Yet curiosity nagged at Mara. She knew the strike team's camp was secure. Its perimeter was strung with directional stun-field generators. Anything larger than a small bug that approached their camp site would get a jolt strong enough to fry tiny insects, incapacitate small animals, and aggressively discourage larger creatures. As an added measure, the bottom of the pit they had dug as a temporary latrine had been studded with sharpened sticks. Anything that made it past the stun field only to stumble into that would have a very bad night indeed.

Still, Mara wondered what had become of the Starfleet landing party. She had tracked their movements while directing those of the strike team. But the Starfleeters had pressed on with their march, even after nightfall. How far might they have gone in the last ninety minutes?

She stepped away from the raucous, ribald singing of her shipmates and powered up her scanner. It was a tricky thing to use it only in passive mode, so as not to telegraph its presence to the Starfleeters, should they be scanning the area with their tricorders. Even switching it on was a risk. Any powered device might be detectable in a low-tech environment such as this. Regardless, she needed to know that her team wasn't going to end up as the victims of an ambush as a consequence of their decision to stop for the night and feast.

Adjusting the scanner's settings, she was perplexed by what seemed like chaotic noise on several key frequencies. The signal was impairing some of the scanner's readings enough that Mara wondered if she still should trust its readouts. She spent a few minutes trying to cancel out the interference, to no avail. It wasn't an artificial signal with a predictable pattern. Whatever this was, it was natural in origin, and fairly close—no more than ten or fifteen *qelI'qam*s upriver.

Most strange. Could this be connected to our mission objective? It would be quite a coincidence if it were not. But I will need more information before I alert D'Gol. There is no point informing him of this discovery until I can tell him what it is.

After a few minutes and some frequency adjustments, Mara cleared most of the noise from her scanner's readouts and locked on to the Starfleet landing party. She was still assessing their position and status when she saw D'Gol approaching her, his large frame silhouetted in front of the team's still magnificent bonfire. The commander squatted at her side. "Alone in the dark? Why? The night is young, and there are many songs left to sing."

"Naq'chI couldn't carry a tune if she put it in her pack. And the drunker you fools get, the worse your singing. At this rate, we won't need a stun field around the camp. Anything your singing doesn't scare off will be knocked out by the fumes in your breath."

D'Gol threw his head back and belted out a hearty laugh, and then he gave Mara a friendly slap on her back. "You never fail to speak your mind! I *love* that about you!"

"You *hate* that about me. Which is how I know you're drunk."

He wore a dopey grin as he slurred in reply, "I'm not as think as you drunk I am." He pointed at her scanner. "What are you looking for? More bloodwine?"

"That's the last thing we need. I'm tracking the Starfleeters." She showed him the scanner's readout. "They're about six *qelI'qam*s away, relative bearing eight-seven mark two."

D'Gol squinted at the scanner, clearly because he was having trouble focusing his eyes. "What are they doing right now?"

"They've spent the last hour scaling a cliff next to a waterfall, on the far side of the river that separates us from our target. Taking such a risk was an unexpected choice on their part, but it just saved them a lot of time. Once they all summit the cliff, they will be slightly ahead of us."

"And they'll also be done for the night." The commander hefted one of the bottles of bloodwine and poured the last of its contents down his gullet. After he swallowed, he croaked, "Relax, Mara, we'll still beat them to the prize." He tapped his empty bottle against Mara's scanner, as if they were making a toast. "As for their cliff-scaling expedition? Good for them. Those lazy Starfleeters need more exercise."

One of the drawbacks of being known to have greater-than-average strength in comparison to most humanoids was the expectation that one would volunteer for all the tasks that entailed greater-than-average labor. So it was that Spock and Chief Razka had been the first to climb the treacherously slick cliff beside a broad, muddy waterfall. If time were not so clearly against them, Spock would have insisted the landing party detour north around the obstacle and then double back along an easier path. As it happened, the Klingons had enjoyed a modest lead. That fact had made it imperative that the landing party close the gap by any means possible.

Which, naturally, had meant scaling a rain-washed cliff slippery with moss and slime.

Using mountaineering equipment they had brought from the *Enterprise*, Razka and Spock had scaled most of the nearly two-hundred-meter-tall rock face in just under an hour, pausing at several points during their ascent to place belaying anchors for those who would follow them.

Threading one of the anchors with hydrophobic synthetic-fiber climbing rope, Spock realized that leaving these anchors in the cliff might constitute a minor technical violation of the Prime Directive. *Perhaps it might be best if I do not mention them in my post-mission report.*

He and Razka pulled themselves over the top edge of the cliff and found they were on a patch of rocky ground at the edge of a fresh swath of jungle. Though both Spock and Razka were winded after their arduous climb, they stood and finished securing climbing ropes to the trunks of thick, well-rooted trees along the jungle's edge. Using the mountaineering gear, they set up a simple pulley-based system to amplify their lifting capacity.

Then began their next Herculean labor: pulling the rest of the landing party up the cliff. They each hoisted one landing party member at a time to start. Spock's first assist went to Doctor Babitz, while Razka took responsibility for aiding Sulu's climb. With the pulleys, anchors, and ropes in place, they were able to bring Sulu and Babitz to the top of the cliff in less than ten minutes. The same proved true of Ensign Singh and Mister Chekov.

Master Chief Ilucci, on the other hand, proved more challenging to hoist. Whereas the other male personnel in the landing party each weighed between 75 and 90 kilograms, the master chief was 118 kilograms. It took both Spock and Razka working as a team to haul the *Sagittarius*'s chief engineer up the cliff and over its top to safety.

At the end of that ordeal, when all Spock's limbs wanted to do was let him collapse, it was the master chief who made a point of staggering half a meter closer to the pile of rocks Singh and Chekov had heated with their phasers until the stones glowed orange. As soon as he found the warmest open space beside the radiant rock pile, he collapsed onto it.

Between ragged gasps, Ilucci muttered, "I need more exercise."

No one disagreed with him.

Feeling his own urgent need for rest, Spock delegated the next two essential tasks. "Mister Sulu, Mister Chekov: set up our weather shelter over these heated rocks. Ensign Singh, establish a secure perimeter around our campsite." The three *Enterprise* officers acknowledged their orders with polite nods and set to work. Within a few minutes, Chekov and Sulu had raised a waterproof shelter around the landing party's hot rocks. As soon as it was even partly in place, the abrupt interruption of the rain on Spock's face felt like a peculiar absence.

Outside the shelter, Sulu and Chekov worked in tandem to secure it in place on the rocks using electromagnetically propelled spikes. In between the first and second of the spikes near the shelter's entrance, Sulu paused to stare into the sky. "Pavel, do you see that?"

Chekov tilted his head back to gaze up into the rain. He waited for a flash of lightning to reveal a moving silhouette high overhead. "You mean the big flying monster?"

Awestruck by the sight of the creature, Sulu kept staring. "Yeah, that."

"What about it?"

"Why does it keep circling directly above us?"

"Probably trying to decide if we are food." Chekov, bored with the threat of death from above, resumed his task of securing the shelter. "Let's finish this and get dry."

Sulu looked as if he were in a mild state of shock. "I hope I remember how."

They moved on as Singh returned from the jungle and ducked inside the shelter. "Perimeter secured, Mister Spock. Proximity alerts and ultrasonic repellents in place."

"Thank you, Ensign." Spock peeled off his boots, and then his dripping-wet socks, which he wrung half dry over a small vent at the bottom of the shelter. Then he put his socks and boots beside the warm stones to dry. *If we stay here longer than twenty-four hours, avoiding fungal infection might prove to be a serious challenge.*

Razka was unpacking the group's field rations when Sulu and Chekov returned. "If this shelter is still here in the morning, we're the ones to thank," Sulu said as he put away his tools.

Spock waited until everyone had gathered around the stones and opened their meal. "As I'm sure you've all surmised, we will be making camp here for the night. The Klingon landing team we've detected also appears to have stopped for the moment, on the other side of the river. Though it is unlikely they would attack us during the night, we should remain vigilant. We'll take turns on watch, in two-hour intervals. Chief Razka will take first watch. Ensign Singh, second watch. Mister Chekov, third watch. I will take fourth watch, which will end at dawn when we eat breakfast and then break camp. Questions?" As Spock had hoped, there were none. He knew his team wanted to get dry and get some rest. "Very good. Sleep well."

As the others bedded down, Spock took a moment to use his phaser to reinvigorate the stones' warmth. When he had the lot of them heated to yellow-white intensity, he stopped.

He had finished setting out his own gear to air-dry when he noticed that Doctor Babitz had made her way to sit next to his bedroll. She kept her voice just above a whisper. "Mister Spock? Can you spare me a minute to offer a second opinion?"

"How can I be of help, Doctor?"

She handed him her medical tricorder. "I've been going over the data Chekov recovered from the *Heyerdahl*, and running analyses of partial DNA sequences from degraded samples I found inside the ship. The more I compare the data from the *Heyerdahl*'s memory banks with the traces left behind inside its flight deck, the more worried I become."

Spock scrolled through Babitz's reconstructed gene sequences, and then he compared them to the partial files Chekov had recovered. He saw the similarities at once. "Whatever Doctor Verdo was studying on Ardana, there seem to be stray bits of it in his wrecked ship."

"Exactly. That means his trip here was no coincidence. He came looking for something specific, and I'm afraid he might have found it—and *terrified* to think what he did with it."

Concerned about the sensitive nature of their discussion, Spock reined in his voice to a whisper. "Doctor, are you suggesting that Doctor Verdo came to this planet to find a sample of the Shedai meta-genome?"

"No, I'm stating it outright. The genes Verdo designed were purely theoretical, but they were extrapolated from a known property of the meta-genome: that it's highly adaptable to recombination with the DNA of other life-forms. Sometimes the result is benign. The meta-genome just becomes junk DNA in the new host organism until something comes along that knows how to read it. But if certain parts of it were spliced into active gene sequences in a targeted manner, one might in theory be able to create a new hybrid life-form—one that would be capable of harnessing the perceptions and abilities of the Shedai."

Spock had seen only fleeting images of Shedai, in vids recorded the previous year during their brutal attack on Gamma Tauri IV. A catastrophe so horrifying that it had prompted a joint Starfleet-Klingon orbital bombardment of the planet, a scouring so intense that when it ended, nothing remained of the planet's surface except molten rock and radioactive glass.

Now he had to confront the possibility that a scientist rebuffed by Operation Vanguard had pursued his own quest to harness the powers of those nightmarish beings.

"You say Doctor Verdo explored the possibility of imbuing other life-forms with the abilities of the Shedai. Dare I ask, to what end?"

Her voice trembled with both fear and fury.

"I think he's trying to turn himself into a god."

12

Nearly twelve hours had passed without word from the landing party, turning what had been an already very long day on the bridge into an especially worrisome one. During normal operations, new personnel would take over all key bridge duty stations, including the officer of the watch, every eight hours. When crises arose, however, it wasn't uncommon for the senior personnel to remain at their posts for two or even three consecutive shifts.

None of which came as a surprise to Montgomery Scott. He had been in Starfleet for decades now, long enough to know that multishift duty rotations were a fact of military life. Not just for officers, but for everyone, noncoms and enlisted personnel alike.

Times such as these, though—they took a toll on people. Physically. Mentally. Emotionally. Even the most capable personnel found it difficult to be at their best when forced to operate under sustained pressure, without adequate rest, and often forgetting to eat. Scott had seen strong people break when he least expected it, and he'd seen those he'd expected would fold at the first sign of trouble weather all that could be thrown at them and then ask for more.

Down in engineering, he knew the warning signs. Drifting attention. A by-the-book technician whose work turns suddenly sloppy. Someone who turns manic and tries to be a hero in order to avoid facing the fact that they're harboring a death wish.

On the bridge he found it harder to be sure. But now he was the ship's acting first officer, which made the morale and operational wellness of the ship's crew—including its commanding officer—his chief responsibility. Today, Captain Kirk's state of mind topped his list of concerns.

Scott debated with himself whether to bring his latest issue to the captain's attention or to spare Kirk the tedium of this additional detail. In truth, he knew there really was no question. *If it were up to me, I'd leave this off his plate. But regulations say he needs to be told.*

The captain's stare had taken on a glassy-eyed quality. It happened to just about everyone who spent too many hours watching the main viewer when there was nothing worth seeing. If ever there was a time when Scott might dare to suggest a shift change, this seemed to be it.

But first he had another matter to attend.

He left the engineering station and descended into the bridge's command well to stand to the left of the command chair. "Captain? A brief word?"

Kirk blinked and drew a sharp breath, as if he had just been woken. "Yes, Mister Scott?"

"We have a wee timing issue we need to address."

"Could you be more specific?"

"Aye. For the past several hours, we've been using Kolasi III's moon for cover. Which was all well and good while it kept us close enough for a fast recovery of our shuttle. But the moon is on a fast orbit of the planet, and the longer we stay behind her, the farther we'll get from the recovery point for the shuttle. Another twelve hours and we'll be on the far side of the planet from our landing party."

"I agree that's less than ideal, Mister Scott. But do you know of any other natural body we can use for cover from the Klingons while remaining within operational range of the planet?"

"No, sir. I admit the moon is all we have to work with."

"Then there's nothing to discuss. Maintaining concealment remains our priority."

"Aye, sir. Understood. But that raises the question: What happens if our shuttlecraft returns to orbit and we aren't there to retrieve it?"

"An excellent question, Mister Scott. What *does* happen in that scenario?"

"That'll depend on what measures we take in advance. If we can set a trap, or create an obstacle, that prevents Kang's ship from intercepting, capturing, or destroying the *Kepler*, we might have enough time to retrieve it, even from the other side of the planet."

Kirk cleared his throat. "Scotty, we can't afford to do *anything* the Klingons might interpret as an overtly hostile action. If we do, it might be construed as a violation of the Treaty of Organia—and both Starfleet Command and the Federation Council have made it very clear there will be serious penalties for anyone who breaches that agreement."

"I'm well aware, sir. I'm not suggesting we destroy the *SuvwI'*. I'm just proposing we . . . ding her up a bit."

"Ding her up?"

"Aye. Just a wee bit of damage. Some clever sabotage. Or maybe a diversion that slows her down, delays her response time just enough to let us get our shuttle back."

The captain's expression was one of arch skepticism. "And how exactly do you propose to accomplish this undetectable act of sabotage, Mister Scott?"

"Truth be told, I'm still working on that."

"In other words, you have no idea." Kirk's tone took on an uncharacteristic edge. "This isn't a thought exercise at the Academy, Mister Scott. Seven of our people are down on that planet right now, and they're counting on us to have a plan for bringing them home. So no more problems without solutions, you hear me? Sort this out, or find someone who can."

Scott bristled at the undeserved dressing-down, but buried his anger. "Aye, sir."

"Anything else?"

"Yes, sir. Night's fallen on the landing party's region of the planet. This might be a good time for a shift change, sir."

"Very well. Summon the relief officers." Kirk stood and headed for the turbolift. Without looking back at Scott, he added, "You have the conn."

Scott watched the captain exit the bridge. As the turbolift doors glided shut, there was no longer any doubt left in Scott's mind that something—stress, exhaustion, or a factor of which he was unaware—had shortened the fuse on the captain's temper to the point that the next spark might be the one to blow them all to kingdom come.

Machines I can fix. Hearts and minds don't come with manuals. Time to call in the cavalry.

It wasn't the first time Vincent DeSalle had received orders he didn't understand. Life in Starfleet was all about parsing the sometimes incomprehensible desires of one's superiors. Regardless, the latest directive to show up on his data slate was proving to be a real head-scratcher.

Lieutenant Commander Scott had sent the message from the *Enterprise* via the jury-rigged semaphore system. Captain Kirk wanted a way to impede the Klingons' starship from intercepting the shuttlecraft *Kepler* if and when it returned to orbit. The request was nothing unusual, but the limitations Kirk had imposed upon it were, in DeSalle's opinion, daunting.

"It has to be nonlethal," he said, pacing and reading from the slate.

"Mm-hm," mumbled *Sagittarius* engineer Karen Cahow, who was doing her best not to fall asleep while monitoring the impulse reactor manifold for what seemed like the fiftieth consecutive hour.

DeSalle kept reading aloud. "It has to slow the Klingons' ship, or temporarily disable it, without giving them a reason to blame Starfleet or the Federation." He scrunched his brow at that one. "How the hell are we supposed to do *that*?"

"Beats me, sir. Sounds like you've got a real challenge on your hands."

He thumped the back of the slate against his thigh as he paced behind Cahow. "Come on, think. There must be something we can do."

Cahow drew a deep breath in the hope of jump-starting her brain. "What if we jam their frequencies like they're jamming ours?"

"They'd know it was us." He reread the orders and shook his head. "It's all about plausible deniability. Kirk wants to mess with the Klingons but doesn't want to take the blame."

After a dramatic yawn, Cahow offered, "Maybe we can weaponize the planet's rings."

"I've heard crazier ideas." He set down the data slate and walked over to the engineering deck's main computer interface. "Let's see what those rings are made of." He keyed in a data request and skimmed the results. "Hmm, pretty boring. Silicon. Carbon. Some nickel. Bit of iron. A fair amount of water ice. Assorted trace elements but nothing remarkable. I doubt we could magnetize it, much less weaponize it. But that was a good thought, Cahow."

"All part of the service, Lieutenant."

DeSalle was still cogitating strategies for passively neutralizing the Klingons' ship when a shaggy head followed by broad beefy shoulders appeared climbing up the ladderway. Engineer's Mate Salagho Threx had circles under his eyes as dark as his brambly beard. The muscular Denobulan was roughly the same height as DeSalle, but much bulkier. As he stepped off the ladder onto the engineering deck, he gave Cahow a friendly pat on her shoulder. "Hey, K. You still starin' at that thing?"

"Until it learns to play nice."

"I'll take it from here. Go grab some rack time."

Cahow got up from her seat as if the deck had double normal gravity. "Copy that, boss." As she plodded past Threx toward the ladderway, she leaned in to confide, "Try to stay clear of the LT's flight path. He's in thinking mode."

"Got it." Threx continued past DeSalle and installed himself in front of the master systems display. He reviewed the status of all the ship's critical systems first, as regulations required. While he was verifying the ship's continued observation of low-power mode, he peeked out of the corner of his eye at DeSalle, who noted the Denobulan's attention.

"Is my pacing bothering you, Mister Threx?"

"Would you give a damn if it did, sir?"

"Touché." DeSalle stopped in the middle of the deck and read Scott's description of Kirk's request again. "How do we bog down or distract the Klingon battle cruiser long enough for the *Enterprise* to recover its shuttle, without causing an interstellar incident?"

Intrigued, Threx paused his work and looked at DeSalle. "Are you serious?"

"Like a heart attack. Orders came in from the Big E about a half hour ago."

Threx shook his head and returned to his work on the MSD. "Sounds like they're hazing you." When he noted DeSalle's confused reaction, he added, "Y'know. Like when the chief of the boat sends midshipmen to find dilithium polish, or a left-handed plasma fuser?"

"Hang on—are you telling me dilithium polish isn't real?"

Threx laughed first, and after holding his poker face a few seconds longer, DeSalle laughed with him. "No, I'm pretty sure

Captain Kirk is serious about this. He wants to put the Klingons off-balance but not start a war by doing it."

"Well, how big a distraction is Kirk looking for? I mean, you guys went to all that trouble to load six photon torpedoes onto our boat. Why not just have us swoop in and fire all six at the Klingons? *That* would get their attention, right?"

"Sure it would. It would also get us all killed. We've only got one launcher tube, and without an automated magazine for munitions, we'd have to manually reload after each salvo."

Threx folded his arms. "Noticed that, did you?"

"Of course I did. We'd be dead before we locked in our second shot. As fast as this ship is, in a head-to-head fight with a Klingon D4, we'd get pulverized."

"I couldn't agree more. Which raises a question, sir. Given our ship's tactical limitations, who thought it would be a good idea to weigh us down with six photon torpedoes?"

DeSalle looked at the stack of torpedoes lashed to the forward bulkhead. "If I had to guess? Probably chief engineer Lieutenant Commander Scott."

"Well, it sounds to me like those ain't gonna be a whole lotta use to us."

"No, I suppose they aren't." Just for amusement, DeSalle imagined chucking the whole darn bundle out the engineering deck's top hatch, the way that ancient sailors once pitched dead weight into the sea. Picturing the capsule-shaped munitions floating away, he had an idea.

"As torpedoes, these aren't tactically viable for use by the *Sagittarius*. But tell me, Mister Threx"—DeSalle cracked a mischievous smile—"what if they weren't torpedoes?"

The Denobulan narrowed his eyes with suspicion. "But they *are* torpedoes."

"But imagine they weren't."

"Then what are they? Rocket sleds? Suppositories for a cosmozoan?"

"What if they were *passive gravitic mines*?"

As soon as he heard the idea, Threx pepped up. "Gravitic mines? Yeah. Yeah! It wouldn't take much tinkering at all. Swap out timers for proximity fuses—"

"Rip out the drive system for a graviton cell," DeSalle cut in.

"—and scale down the payload from sixty-four megatons to fifty kilotons, and you'll have a weapon that can give a D4 battle cruiser a punch that'll knock the wind out of her without really drawing blood."

"A weapon like that might be very useful to us, wouldn't it, Mister Threx?"

"I think it would, sir."

"Grab your tools, Mister. We've got some tinkering to do."

Kirk found the silence of his quarters stifling. Alone with his memories and his regrets, he found it difficult to get to sleep tonight. Not that he had really tried. He hadn't even taken off his boots or his uniform tunic. The first thing he had done was sit at his desk. It was mostly a matter of habit. He wasn't expecting any messages, and it was unlikely there had been any developments in the current mission in the handful of minutes since he had left the bridge.

Absent-mindedly, he had flipped pages in one book or another, their titles unimportant, their contents even less so. Again, it was old habits asserting themselves. He just liked the feel of a book in his hands. The smell of old paper and binding leather. The weight of it.

He had considered putting on some music, but faced with so many options he had been unable to choose. *I've made too many decisions today,* he had told himself. *No more.*

Instead he had sprawled atop his narrow bed, his feet crossed at the ankles, his hands folded behind his head. Staring at the overhead, he replayed the last day in his mind. Tried to think

ahead to what tomorrow might bring. But the longer he lay idle
the farther back his mind reached, returning him to events he
wished he could forget. To the moment he was struggling to
leave behind. To the sight of Matt Decker flying headlong into a
demon's maw.

Salvation came in the guise of a quick buzz of his door's visitor
signal. At the sound of it he sat up and propped himself in
place by resting his weight on his elbows. "Come."

The door to his quarters slid open, and Doctor McCoy sauntered
inside. He held two doubles glasses with his left hand and
a bottle of bourbon with his right. "Jim."

"Bones. What's all this? A house call?"

The good doctor ambled toward Kirk. "I prefer to think of it
as a social call, but whatever you want to call it is fine by me."
He set the glasses onto the low shelf behind Kirk's bed, and then
he pulled the cork from the bottle and splashed a few fingers
of golden-brown Kentucky magic into each glass. He handed
one to Kirk, who sat up on the side of his bed as he accepted it,
and took the other glass for himself. Leaning against the wall
that separated Kirk's sleeping area from his desk, McCoy asked,
"How've you been lately?"

"That feels like a loaded question."

"Is it?" McCoy sipped his drink. "You've had a sharper edge
than usual the last couple of weeks. Everything okay?"

"I'm fine, Bones." Kirk could tell McCoy was fishing. Had
he come of his own accord? Or had someone put him up to it?
There was no politic way to ask him that, and Kirk knew McCoy
would always say these visits were his own idea. The doctor had
too much discretion ever to betray concerns expressed to him in
confidence. Which was just one of many reasons he had earned
Kirk's unwavering trust and respect.

They each savored another sip or two of whiskey. In his gentle
Southern way, McCoy asked, "So nothing's been on your mind?"

"Other than the hundred thousand details that make up my

average day as a commanding officer? No, Bones, not a thing. I'm just tired, that's all."

"Fatigue can be a stress multiplier, Jim. If you're really feeling worn out—"

"I'm just tired. And worried about the landing party, and about that Klingon ship that's just sitting out there, waiting for us to show ourselves, because Kang must know we'll have to, sooner or later." Kirk rubbed his itching eyes with his right hand. "It's a lot of balls to juggle."

"No doubt. But I'm also fairly certain you're not telling me the truth, Jim."

"You think I'm keeping something from you?"

"I *know* you are. I know your style of command. How you handle stress. And this isn't it. Something is *off* with you, Jim. Your temper's been short. Even with me and Spock, you've been more distant than usual. Something's eating away at you, I can feel it." McCoy took another sip of his drink. "Letting pain fester is one of the worst things we can do to ourselves. Better to face it head on, no matter how hard we think that'll be."

"You think so? I'm not sure I agree."

"Why don't you try talking about it, and we can see for ourselves?"

"I'm not sure I can, Bones."

McCoy's easy bedside manner turned flinty. "Are you really going to make me say it for you? You've been off your game ever since that business with the planet-killer." The doctor softened his tone. "This is about Matt Decker, isn't it?"

The question alone was enough to make Kirk hang his head in shame and sorrow.

"Yes, Bones. But it's not what you think."

For weeks now Kirk had been running from the truth, hiding from the pain. Now the truth had come looking for him, and there was nowhere left for him to seek refuge.

"What happened to Matt . . . it's every starship captain's worst nightmare. Faced with a killing machine unlike anything any-one in this galaxy had ever seen, he took every reasonable step he could to spare his crew—only to see that damned machine kill them all anyway. I admired him for what he did, and pitied him for how it turned out. But that's not what's been keeping me awake at night. That's not what haunts me."

Kirk set down his drink and stood. He turned his back on McCoy and drifted a few steps away from him into the corner of the room, as if to hide from his friend's reaction to what he had to say. "Decker took control of my ship while I was trapped on his. And he came too damned close to losing my ship and my crew for nothing. I should *hate* him for that, Bones.

"But I can't. I know all too well why he did it. I think about the shipmates I lost on the *Farragut*—good people who died because I was too slow to act when I had the chance. And I ask myself what I wouldn't give to avenge them."

He looked into the mirror he kept in the corner, and saw McCoy looking at his reflection. "What's killing me inside is how *powerless* I felt as Matt flew that shuttle down the planet-killer's throat. It should have been him on the *Constellation*. He should have been the one to pilot his ship into the machine and trigger its self-destruct to fry that thing from the inside. It would have made sense for him to do it. It was his command. The machine had killed his crew. He deserved a chance to avenge them. To make things right. To go down with his ship.

"But he broke. He lost faith in himself. Let his guilt eat him alive. Part of me wishes he had thought of sacrificing himself sooner. If he'd shoved the *Constellation* down that thing's gul-let in the first place like he should have, the *Enterprise* wouldn't have been put at risk at all."

As soon as he had said it, Kirk wished he could take it back. But the truth had been burning inside him for too long. It had needed to come out. "I'm a hypocrite, Bones. Part of me blamed Matt for stranding his crew, instead of letting them meet their fates aboard their ship, the way they deserved. But ten years ago, I made a mistake that cost the lives of two hundred people, but I didn't think that meant I deserved to die. Why do I think my life is worth more than Matt's? Why am I angry that he didn't sacrifice himself sooner? What have I become, Bones?"

McCoy took a step in Kirk's direction, but maintained a respectful distance. "You haven't *become* anything. You're not a monster. But being a starship captain doesn't make you perfect, and wanting to live doesn't make you selfish. It just makes you human.

"I can't speak to what he was thinking when he took that shuttle. Each of us handles grief in our own way. But you can't compare your pain to his, Jim. Eleven years ago, you were a junior officer. Barely a grown man. Decker was a *commodore*. A flag officer responsible for the lives of thousands. A loss like this was bound to hit him harder."

There was wisdom in what McCoy said. But one last dilemma vexed Kirk.

"And what do I tell his family? How do I tell them Matt died for nothing?"

"You don't. You tell them he died fighting to save others. And that he showed us how to beat the planet-killer. He didn't die for *nothing*. He died to show us how to *win*."

Kirk nodded. "A beautiful lie."

McCoy downed the rest of his drink. "Sometimes, Jim . . . a lie is what we need."

13

Awakened at dawn, the landing party had broken camp within an hour and continued its march upriver. Dark green and steeped in shadows, the jungle grew denser with each passing kilometer. It made blazing a trail more difficult, but the thickened canopy reduced the rain's omnipresence from a downpour to a misty drizzle. Less precipitation meant less white noise, making the voices of the wild sound clearer and closer than they had the day before.

Above the treetops, the sky burned with one long stroke of lightning after another. Most of the glare was blocked by the boughs, but still the forest shook beneath calamitous crashes of thunder. Each gut-shaking boom silenced the creatures of the wilderness for a second or two, but their chaotic music soon resumed. The buzzing sawsong of insects, the croaks of amphibious things dwelling in the muck, the hisses and roars of larger fauna that no doubt fancied the landing party as ambulatory appetizers . . . wherever the landing party went, they followed.

Ahead of Spock, Sulu and Chekov spoke in subdued voices.

"Is it just me," Sulu asked, "or is this jungle getting creepier with every step we take?"

"It is not just you. It feels like we are the only people here."

Spock interjected, "Quite the contrary, Mister Chekov. Peer-reviewed research suggests the Kolasians have been here in their current form for nearly a hundred thousand years."

Chekov cast a wary look around. "You would never know it."

Razka signaled the group to halt. Everyone stopped and dropped to one knee while the Saurian scout skulked ahead to ferret out dangers. According to Spock's calculations they were close now to the head of the river, its source point. The air here was leaden, sluggish.

From the point position, Razka beckoned Spock, who crept forward to join the scout. "What have you found, Chief?"

Razka handed Spock a pair of holographic binoculars and pointed upriver. "Bearing dead ahead, two hundred eleven meters. Elevation, twelve meters. Some kind of artificial structure built into what looks like a natural cave system inside a rocky cliff face."

Spock focused the image and surveyed the scene. It was as Razka had described. Many of the openings and features on the face of the cliff were obscured by heavy hanging foliage, while others served as channels for long, misty plumes of water that mingled into a great pool at the cliff's base, where muddy water surged from a large cave mouth.

Something else captured Spock's attention. "Movement, on both sides of the riverbank." He refocused the binoculars. "Members of this planet's indigenous humanoid species. They appear to be bringing a steady procession of assorted goods inside the caves."

Chekov sounded curious. "What kind of goods, Mister Spock?"

"Food. Woven cloths with bright colors. Items of polished stone . . ."

"Tributes," Babitz said. "They're bringing gifts to something inside the cave. Or to something they *believe* is in the cave."

"I see merit in your hypothesis, Doctor, but I consider your conclusion premature."

She cast a look of disbelief at Spock. "All right, what do you think it is?"

"The natives could just as easily be using those caves to store important goods for a coming change in the seasons, or for communal redistribution. We have a responsibility to gather more evidence before we render a judgment."

"I'd be keen to know how the natives built that structure," Singh said. "Engineering an arch that perfect above running water isn't easy with stone-age tools."

Razka said in his rasp of a voice, "Maybe they aren't the ones who built it."

Spock looked back at the rest of the landing party. "These are questions for another time and another mission. Stay on task." He faced Babitz. "Doctor, please scan the riverhead and the caves above it."

"Scanning." She held her medical tricorder close to her torso, perhaps to muffle its high-pitched oscillating whine as it worked. When she finished, she frowned at the results. "Hrm."

"What have you found, Doctor? Were you able to locate Doctor Verdo?"

"No. Those caves are packed with sensor-scrambling mineral compounds. But even with all the interference, one reading came through clear as day." She handed Spock her tricorder.

He brushed the rainwater off its display to see that the tricorder had registered several strong readings for the Shedai meta-genome—and energy readings consistent with a living Shedai, somewhere inside the caves. He passed the tricorder back to Babitz. "Is there any chance you could lock in a precise position for that last reading?"

"Not from out here. Hell, even inside the caves it might be a crapshoot."

It was not the answer Spock had hoped for, but he was determined not to let a setback derail the mission. "We need to find a way inside those caves, one that minimizes the risk of contact with the natives."

Singh leaned forward. "I can use my tricorder to make an

ultrasonic map of the caves and surrounding terrain. If there are other ways in, that might help us find them. And it might give us some idea how large an interior space we might be dealing with."

"An excellent idea, Ensign. Please begin at once." He faced the rest of the team. "While Singh maps the cave system, we should consider creating a diversion that might scare away the natives. If we can make them abandon the caves, we will have a better chance of—"

Spock noticed that the other members of the landing party were no longer looking at him. They were looking at something above and behind him.

A sharp point jabbed Spock between his shoulder blades and nudged him forward. He moved as the push suggested and then slowly turned to see a semicircle of nearly two dozen Kolasians had surrounded the landing party. The front rank of green-skinned, red-eyed humanoids held their spears at shoulder height, ready to throw or lunge. The ranks behind them had taken defensive postures, crouched low, spears braced in the mud to resist a charge.

The leader—or at least the one that Spock presumed was the leader—poked Spock's holstered phaser with the tip of his spear, and then he pointed at the ground.

Other Kolasians repeated the gesture with the other members of the landing party.

"It would seem," Spock said, "that they would like us to drop our weapons." Taking care not to alarm the natives, Spock slowly removed his phaser from his belt using just his thumb and forefinger, and then he dropped it in the mud in front of the leader. The other members of the landing party did the same. Within seconds the natives had confiscated all their small arms. In quick succession, they relieved the landing party of their tricorders, and then their gear packs.

Then the natives corralled the landing party back into a single file and marched them through the jungle, heading upriver toward the ominous excavation.

From behind him in the line, Spock heard Babitz whisper with deadpan irony, "On the bright side, sir, I think we might have found a way inside the caves."

———

Mara gazed through holographic binoculars at the Starfleet landing party on the other side of the river. "What do you think, D'Gol? Should we warn them about— Never mind, they just met the locals." She lowered the binoculars. "So much for the competition."

"They were never competition. At best, a distraction." D'Gol put out his hand, and Mara handed him the holo-binoculars. They both were lying prone beneath a thick cluster of ground-covering fronds, atop a low rise in the landscape—just high enough to offer them a better vantage point on the surrounding terrain than what the Starfleeters had. "You have to admire the Starfleeters' efficiency. I've never seen anyone blunder into a trap and get captured so quickly."

Mara felt compelled to ask sympathy for Fek'lhr, as the saying went. "It's not as if our first scout teams on this planet fared any better."

"They at least had the honor to die rather than surrender."

"Insult the Starfleeters' honor all you want, they're still getting inside that stronghold before we are. Granted, as prisoners, but that still puts them closer to the target than we are."

"True." D'Gol put away the holo-binoculars. "Let's regroup with the others."

They crept backward, shimmying on their bellies, until they were clear of the bush. They stayed low as they stole through curtains of emerald-green foliage, back to where the rest of the strike team crouched in a huddle, awaiting their return.

The first to see them was Hartür. "What happened?"

"They got captured," D'Gol said, dropping into a crouch with the team.

Fistfuls of currency passed from Keekur to Naq'chI, and from CheboQ to Dolaq. Curses denigrating the Starfleeters' ancestry mingled with the smug laughs of the winners.

"I told you," Naq'chI said, needling Keekur as she counted her winnings. "The Chwii are stealthy, cunning, and quick. And they know these jungles better than anybody."

"Including us," Mara reminded her, and the others. "Which presents a challenge."

She let D'Gol continue that thought. "The Starfleeters might be prisoners, but they're also being taken inside the caves. Which means they're closer to the target than we are."

Keekur huffed derisively. "If they're prisoners, what difference does it make?"

D'Gol glowered at her. "You've fought Starfleeters before. They look weak, but they're clever. They might be prisoners *now*, but how long do you think that'll last?" Seeing that Keekur was sufficiently rebuked, D'Gol expunged some of the condescension from his tone. "Mara is right to caution us. We have a decisive advantage in weapons and communications technology, but the Chwii have a massive advantage in numbers. They can simply be in more places than we can, and they can absorb far greater losses. We have to be lucky hundreds of times, they only need to get lucky a few times. Do not get sloppy. If we get careless and let the Chwii outflank us, this mission might end a lot sooner than we expect."

Mara drew her *d'k tahg* and used its tip to draw tactical diagrams in the mud as she and the others talked. "We are here, and this is the ridge behind me. The Chwii are running patrols on both sides of the river, and they have hidden sentries on the riverbank and near key landmarks, here and here. Those are what I've seen. What about the rest of you?"

Keekur drew her own dagger and followed Mara's example.

"There are three direct routes through the jungle to the cave temple on this side of the river, and two more on the far side. The ones on our side intersect here. The ones on the far side never meet. But they're all lined with traps and ambush points. For anyone but the Chwii, those roads are a nightmare."

Hartür let out a low, cynical chortle. "The little bastards learn fast. This is what we get for letting any of these *yIntaghpu'* live after resisting our survey teams."

D'Gol turned a cold stare at Hartür. "They might be *yIntaghpu'*, but if they're dead they can't work. We let the *novpu'* live so they can serve the Empire. Remember that." He turned his focus back to the crude tactical map in the mud. "These trails on the far side of the river—that second one looks like it goes behind the caves. Is that right?"

Naq'chI added to the drawing. "Yes, but it leads over a steep hillcrest and then down into a narrow canyon—a perfect kill box. Whoever walks into that while a hostile force holds the high ground is as good as dead." She wiped her blade clean on the leg of her fatigues and then returned it to its sheath. "Before you ask: yes, the Chwii maintain a force above the canyon."

Doctor Dolaq seemed unable to resist stating the obvious: "We need another way in."

A grim chuckle escaped from CheboQ. "Maybe the Starfleeters had the right idea."

D'Gol closed his hand around the grip of his dagger. "Don't even joke about letting yourself be captured, CheboQ. I've executed better soldiers than you for less."

Mara sensed a need to lower the group's rhetorical temperature. "We all know what honor demands of us. And right now its highest demand is that we complete our mission." Using her blade, she traced the line of the river itself. "They don't guard the main cave mouth. So why don't we try an underwater assault under cover of night?"

The others reacted with obvious skepticism. Keekur was the first to speak. "Your plan would have us fighting the current at its source, while submerged. We didn't bring rebreathers or aqua-filters. I might be able to cut some of the native reeds to use as snorkel tubes, but in that kind of current we'd probably lose them in under thirty seconds."

Naq'chI, predictably, piled on. "We also don't know if the part of the caves that holds the riverhead is connected to the rest of the cave temple complex. If it isn't, we might get inside there only to find we have nowhere to go—assuming we don't drown in the attempt."

"Drowning would be the least of our problems," D'Gol said. "Just because we're at the river's source, that doesn't mean the water here is empty. Aside from the absolute swarms of leeches that would cover every exposed bit of flesh on your body, there are predators in that river even I wouldn't want to wrestle."

A crash of thunder punctuated D'Gol's argument as lightning bent across the sky above the jungle's canopy. In the moment after the thunder, Mara took in the eerie silence that fell over the entire forest. It was not a peaceful quiet; it was the hush of a pitiless force brooding with inscrutable intention. It was the jungle regarding everything alien with a will to vengeance.

But what kept her attention was the fluttering of winged shapes between the boughs high overhead. As raindrops pattered onto her face she smiled, and then she met the stares of the strike team with a renewed confidence.

"We can't evade the Chwii by going low. We'll go high."

———

Marched at spearpoint, the landing party emerged from the jungle at a narrow walkway hewn from the cliff face. It led upward to a cave opening several meters above the river. The rain stung Spock's face as he eyed the towering structure that had been built from, or perhaps fused onto, the cliff. Before he could make any detailed observations, he was prodded into motion up the walkway, and the rest of the landing party was compelled to follow him.

The steady downpour made the stone path slippery. Spock took each step with care, fully cognizant of the hazards lurking in the muddy river. Far from being a viable avenue of escape, it was more likely a shortcut to a swift and painful death by predators or parasites.

The open air above the river offered the only clear view of the sky for several kilometers. Fierce ribbons of lightning bent from one horizon to another. Here the thunder was louder, no longer muffled by the thick wood and foliage of the forest, and the rain fell harder, as if the clouds harbored malicious intent toward those who dwelled beneath them.

Doctor Babitz was directly behind Spock on the pathway. Her voice trembled, either from fear or from the effort required not to slip off the path into the river. "Why do I get the feeling we aren't being invited to a nice brunch? Or to afternoon tea?"

Spock kept his eyes on the path in front of him. "As I presume your question is rhetorical, I will refrain from addressing it with critical commentary."

"How sporting of you." Babitz vented her frustration with an inchoate growl. "How long until we get inside the caves? This rain is driving me up a wall."

"The rain is incidental. It is our captors who compel us to climb this wall."

He couldn't see her, but some aspect of Spock's inherited Vulcan telepathic talent felt Babitz's glare of contempt aimed at his back. When at last she spoke, her voice was as steady as a blade in the hands of a Romulan assassin. "That was a clever mockery of my idiom, Spock. I trust you feel proud of yourself?"

"In general, yes. That particular bit of wordplay, however, was merely adequate, since I can work only with what I am given."

"Have any of your crew ever tried to kill you, Spock?"

"Not to my knowledge."

"Give them time."

The pathway ended at a broad cave opening in the cliff's face. Another squad of armed natives awaited the captive landing party there. Once all the others had reached the entrance, they were once again surrounded and led inside.

A steady, ominous rhythm of drums echoed like a leviathan's pulse from somewhere deep inside the caves, whose passages were lit at regular intervals by torches set into recesses in the wall. The dull orange flames had a bluish tinge near their base. That hue of flame, combined with peculiar odors in its smoke, suggested to Spock that the torches' heads of dried vegetable matter had been soaked in some variety of crude oil, or perhaps an animal tallow of a kind he had never seen before. The torches' light was dull and limited in range, but it let Spock see some details of the walls.

"Mister Chekov. What do you observe about the structures around us?"

Walking through the tunnels, the young Russian examined the walls, floor, and ceiling. "It all looks *new*, Mister Spock." He covertly let his fingertips drag over the wall while walking a few steps. "And very smooth."

A few steps behind Chekov, Master Chief Ilucci brushed his fingertips along the wall, and then he made his own assessment of their surroundings. "No tool marks. No seams. And plenty of crystalline artifacts from a high-heat process. These passages weren't carved or formed naturally. Something *burned* through the inside of this cliff, melted these tunnels into existence— something big, and as hot as a sun."

"How long ago, would you estimate?"

"Best guess? Last week, maybe. From the looks of some of these side passages, I'll bet these tunnels run all through this cliff and beyond."

"Is there any chance the native population did this on their own?"

Ilucci shook his head. "No way. Transforming stone this way requires industrial-scale heat and power. Unless the Kolasians are hiding some fusion reactors we don't know about, there's no way they did any of this—and because of that, I can damned well understand why they'd serve or even worship anybody or anything that *could*."

The more Spock heard, the more certain he became that this mission's nobler elements had been doomed long before it had been engaged. "This world and its indigenous people have experienced a disastrous cultural contamination. One that perhaps renders the Prime Directive moot."

Sulu asked, "Does that help us or hurt us, Mister Spock?"

"I am not yet certain it does either. But I fear the current state of affairs has, at the very least, done irreparable harm to the cultural development of all this world's natives who have had direct contact with the force that made these caves."

The pounding of great drums grew louder as the landing party was brought to the end of a long passage, which opened into a vast interior space.

The chamber was vaguely round, approximately twenty-seven meters in diameter, and its ceiling was at least fifteen meters overhead. A four-meter-diameter circular skylight had been cut—or burned—through the ceiling, revealing Kolasi III's steel-gray sky and letting in a steady shower of rain. Directly beneath the skylight an opening of the same width had been hewn—or again, drilled or perhaps even melted—through the floor.

The guards who had brought the landing party here escorted them to the hole in the floor and then left them at its edge while they fell back, behind their captives. Dozens more Kolasians, many of whom wore ornate regalia and dramatic headdresses adorned with brightly colored feathers, stood in large groups to either side of the landing party. Among them were the drummers, all pounding with steady ferocity, and behind them were several open passageways.

On the far side of the pit from the landing party was a large dais, upon which sat a huge throne, one not suited to any normal humanoid. It looked as if it had been made for a giant.

Spock peeked over the edge of the pit to see a fast-moving rush of dark water surging past underneath. Razka edged past some of the others to steal a look at Spock's side. "We must be close to the riverhead." He gestured at the edges of the pit. "Blood stains. It's a good bet they use this pit for some kind of ritual sacrifice."

Babitz rolled her eyes. "*There's* a detail I wish I didn't know."

Another group of natives entered from a side passage. They carried the landing party's weapons, tricorders, and equipment packs inside a large net of tightly woven mesh, and they chanted in tempo with the beating drums as some of their fellows lifted the lid off what resembled a stone sarcophagus. The troop with the net set it inside the coffinlike structure, and then they made a series of gestures and chants as the lid was set back into place.

"At least we know where our things are," said Ensign Singh. "Now if only we could get these folks to negotiate."

Spock arched an eyebrow. "A difficult proposition, Ensign. Without our communicators we have no universal translators, and none of us is fluent in the natives' language."

The tempo of the drums quickened, and the low chanting of the troop that had brought in the landing party's gear turned into a loud, deep, sinister refrain that resounded off the smooth-as-glass stone walls, ceiling, and floor. A native of exceptional size and musculature pulled a stone lever. Behind the dais a vertical seam appeared on the wall, which parted to reveal a dark chamber, most of which was occluded from view by the throne.

Ilucci tensed. "I don't need a universal translator to tell me that means something *bad*."

Several coils of black vapor snaked out of the dark chamber

and curved around the giant throne. The smoke didn't move randomly, or at the mercy of air currents. It was apparent to Spock that the tendrils of dark mist had wills of their own, or were guided by one that drove them to gather and coalesce in a way he would not have imagined was possible.

As he watched the vapors assume a form colossal and monstrous, one that dominated the cavernous space, Spock resented the non-Vulcan half of his biology, because of the all-too-human terror that he could no longer deny had awoken inside him.

Trying to keep up with Mara is going to get me killed.

Most of the tree limbs were thick enough that Hartür could dart across them, as long as he didn't linger. The ones that weren't thick enough tested his reflexes and his jumping skills. But no matter how hard he pushed himself, he couldn't catch up to Mara.

The limber science officer seemed to have a natural gift for brachiation. She danced and hopped and swung from one section of the jungle's rain-drenched canopy to another without ever slowing her pace. It was as if she were immune to doubt, fear, and gravity.

She was at least three or four steps ahead of him when he abandoned his pride and whistled for her to hold up. Using her momentum, she switched direction and alighted upon a branch close to where it met the trunk, and then she curled one arm around the tree's core while grinning back at Hartür. "Tired already?"

"Tired has nothing to do with it." With effort he heaved himself from one perch to the next and clumsily snagged a handhold at the last second. "Lack of a death wish might."

"Listen to you. 'Death wish.' We're only . . . what? Thirty *qam*s up? This fall wouldn't kill you. Paralyze you, maybe. Liquefy your brain and make you a vegetable. But you'd live."

"Nothing you've just described sounds anything like *living*."

"Typical pilot. Take away your fancy machines and you're nothing but talk."

Hartür hopped quickly over the next two branches on his path and halted one step shy of Mara's position. "What in the name of Fek'lhr are we doing up here, Mara?"

"Looking for the path of least resistance."

"Since when are we afraid to overcome resistance?"

"This isn't about fear, it's about speed and efficiency. Yes, we could siege the temple, but that would take time that would be better spent getting eyes on the target."

A shifting of Hartür's weight set into motion a series of chain reactions that culminated in a clutch of fronds above Hartür's head angling ever so slightly downward—and dousing him in a swift deluge of collected rainwater. He stifled his urge to bellow profanities, but Mara laughed into the crook of her elbow.

He wrung water from his forked beard. "I'm glad my bad luck amuses you."

Mara forced herself back into a semblance of composure. "As if you wouldn't laugh yourself sick if that happened to me."

She was right, but Hartür knew better than to admit it. A serpent as thick as his arm slithered up his tree and began to coil around his wrist. With his free hand he crushed the animal's head with a satisfying *crunch*. "Just tell me we're near the end of this crazy recon."

"We're close." She pointed into the middle distance on their left. "The temple is over there. My plan is to find a path through the canopy that gets us on top of the cliff. Then we infiltrate from above, kill everything that gets in our way, and take out the target."

Hartür knew not to look down, but he did anyway. "You're sure this will work?"

"Of course not. That's why we're on recon." She adjusted her stance to make her next leap. "Ready to keep going? Or do I need to put you down for a nap?"

"Must be nice being the captain's *parmaqqay*."

"It has its moments." She crouched to spring. "Now, if you think you can keep up, I—" She froze, then looked back wide-eyed at Hartür and signaled him with gestures to stay quiet and not move. With care she directed his attention to something moving through the jungle below.

Massive undulating tentacles coursed through the thick ground cover, somehow without disturbing any of the leafy fronds in the process. Hartür squinted and fought to get a good look at the thing through the rain and mist despite the distance.

It looked like a giant serpent made of black vapors.

The abomination traveled without touching the ground, snaking through the jungle like something out of a nightmare. Within seconds it was followed by two more gigantic tentacles of smoke, the three of them moving as if they were cooperating in a search pattern.

No, simpler than that, Hartür realized.

They were hunting.

Peering down at the gaseous monsters as they passed under his tree, he saw that some of the flowering plants the vapors enveloped instantly withered and fell into decay; other, dying blooms seemed to revive at the touch of the dark vapors, while others transmuted into or were perhaps cocooned inside an obsidian-like substance, something jet black and crystalline.

Unintelligible whispers seemed to pass among the creatures, intimations of death and destruction, decay and damnation. Without knowing a word of what was said, Hartür still knew he should be afraid to find out. The creatures' very presence sent a chill of fear up his spine, a sensation unlike any he had ever known.

Whatever they were, they felt like evil incarnate.

As the last of them slithered into the fathomless green depths of the jungle, Hartür noticed that Mara had been calm enough to activate her scanner in a passive mode.

Hartür exhaled a breath he hadn't known he was holding, and his entire body shook. He wanted to cry out, but he could barely raise his voice above a tense whisper. "Mara? Mara!" He waited until she looked him in the eye before he asked, "What in Gre'thor was that?"

"Knowing our masters at High Command and the High Council?" Mara's good mood turned to one of grim concern. "I think we just saw the real reason we were sent here."

Fear is not real. Fear is just a neurochemical reaction to danger.

Spock stood motionless, transfixed by the intertwining spirals of ink-black vapor that were coalescing into a solid form in front of him, the landing party, and their dozens of native captors. It was as if the cavernous chamber had been built for this purpose, to channel all these streams of darkness, each one aglow with an aura of evil perceptible only to those with telepathic or empathic skills. They entered the space from many directions at once, but they all converged in front of the giant throne and bled together, many becoming one.

My fear informs me, it does not control me. I master my fear as I master my mind.

As a gigantic humanoid form took shape before Spock, the natives quickened the tempo of their hypnotic drumming and inchoate chanting. This was not a new or unexpected occurrence for them. Those who bore arms lifted their weapons above their heads with both hands, and then they bent forward, arms still extended, to lay their foreheads and weapons upon the floor. It was no accident, no coincidence that their actions were uniform in nature. Their actions had the look of choreography, of practiced worship.

The smoky giant ceased growing, but its form refused to solidify. It changed its posture to emulate the act of sitting upon the colossal throne, but Spock perceived no shift in its center of gravity, no increase in the apparent physical stress of the noncorporeal giant, even as it placed itself in a seat of *judicium de cathedra*. The skeptical side of Spock wondered what the being thought of itself, or if it was fully sentient at all.

And then it spoke: "KNEEL."

Its voice seemed to come from all directions at once, though Spock had not seen anything on the creature that resembled a mouth. At the same time, he was reasonably sure that the being had not communicated telepathically, because he felt the sonic waves of its voice on his skin.

After several seconds during which the landing party had not obeyed the misty giant's command, its voice became palpably angry. "YOU WILL KNEEL BEFORE ME."

Before he or any of the others had a chance to refuse, one of the natives struck Spock behind his knees with the handle of a spear. The blow was enough to buckle Spock's legs and enable the native to force Spock the rest of the way to his knees on the floor. On either side of him, the rest of the landing party was forced into compliance by the same brute-force method.

This, apparently, was enough to appease the caliginous titan. "I AM THE GODHEAD. THIS WORLD . . . IS MINE." Its neck extended upward and then away from its body in the manner of a massive tentacle, with its featureless face still semisolid at its end. Its prehensile neck of black fog undulated and coiled as its head moved past the landing party, whose members had been lined up before it in a single rank.

The first person it studied was Chief Razka. "COLD-BLOODED. REPTILOID MALE. IDEAL FOR LABOR." The floating Godhead moved on to Ensign Singh. "WARM-BLOODED. HUMANOID FEMALE. FRAGILE. LIMITED UTILITY." The head remained steady as the smoky neck twisted behind it. It halted in front of

Master Chief Ilucci. "WARM-BLOODED. HUMANOID MALE. POOR PHYSICAL SPECIMEN. EXPENDABLE."

Then the semi-disembodied head reached Spock. "WARM-BLOODED. HUMANOID MALE. TELEPATHIC ABILITY. SUPERIOR DURABILITY. A POSSIBLE VESSEL."

Unable to restrain his curiosity, Spock asked, "A vessel for what, precisely?"

Crackling forks of lightning leapt from where the Godhead's eyes should have been. Twin coils of numbing electric shock cocooned Spock's head. Pain like white-hot needles stung his face and neck, and he became aware that the Godhead was trying to probe his mind, to expose the secrets of Spock's memories.

Spock marshaled all he had ever learned about defending his mind from telepathic attack. He raised barriers built of logic, and conjured mazes wrought from paradoxes to trap unwary psionic intruders. Behind his mental barricades he divorced himself from his body's suffering.

Pain is merely a construct of the mind. A primitive impulse to flee harm. If my mind refuses to acknowledge the input of my senses, there is no pain. It becomes an illusion. . . .

Though Spock had sheltered his consciousness inside a telepathic redoubt, he remained aware of what was transpiring around him. Chekov and Singh had both reacted to the Godhead's attack on him by charging to Spock's defense, while Razka and Ilucci both moved to protect Doctor Babitz. Sulu bought them all time by disarming one of the guards, stealing a spear, and forcing their closest native captors to back up a few steps from the landing party.

The Godhead ceased its assault upon Spock to lash out at Chekov and Singh with fearsome jolts of lightning that sent both ensigns sprawling backward across the floor.

Lying on the floor, Spock smelled the ozone that lingered in the air after the Godhead's electrical strikes, and he felt the natives' rising emotions of rage and alarm.

Sulu held his stolen spear with its tip pointed at the natives, while he looked over his shoulder and tried to address the Godhead. "Whoever you are, this violence is unnecessary. We come in peace, on behalf of—"

One bolt of lightning from the Godhead stunned Sulu into silence. Then a second tentacle shot out from the creature's body and ripped the spear from Sulu's hands. Disarmed and dazed, Sulu pitched forward and collapsed.

The serpentine neck lifted the face of the Godhead high above the landing party. "DO NOT SPEAK UNLESS I TELL YOU TO DO SO. THIS IS MY TEMPLE. HERE I AM THE ONLY AUTHORITY, JUST AS ON THIS WORLD I AM THE ONLY GOD. YOU WILL—"

The neck retracted the head toward the body, which tensed. New tentacles of dark mist grew from the giant and spilled through cracks in the floor or climbed through the skylight, for reasons unknown. It seemed apparent to Spock, however, that something beyond the cave temple had captured the Godhead's attention, and whatever it was had registered as a more serious threat than any posed by the landing party.

The majestic shape of the Godhead dissolved into fog as it issued a parting command to its followers. "PUT THESE INTRUDERS IN THE CAGE. WHEN I RETURN, YOU WILL SACRIFICE THEM IN MY NAME, AND BRING ME THEIR BLOOD."

14

As usual, D'Gol preferred the sound of his own voice to that of the voice of reason, and Mara was tiring of his refusal to let reality interfere with his schemes for wanton destruction. Unlike D'Gol, Mara knew there could be advantages to delaying an attack until the right moment.

She and Hartür had returned from their unsuccessful recon to find the rest of the strike team had already regrouped near the riverbank, and that D'Gol was already formulating a battle plan before hearing her report. The only reason she wasn't offended was that he had been developing a plan on the assumption that she and Hartür would succeed in finding a route through the canopy that would facilitate a sneak attack from above. Now that she had revealed there was no such route, his mood had taken a turn for the maniacally self-destructive.

D'Gol sketched a new tactical diagram in the mud with one of his fingertips. "If we can't attack from the jungle canopy, any hope of advantage based on surprise is lost. If time were not a factor, I would favor infiltration of the cave temple, combined with a surgical strike on the target, if only to reduce the number of things that can go wrong in battle. But that's no longer viable. So we need to adapt to the facts on the ground." He finished drawing his new battle plan with a flourish. "Tedious as it might be, I think we'll need to kill every last one of these filthy *novpu'*."

Keekur and Naq'chI traded dubious looks. D'Gol noticed and snapped, "What?"

Naq'chI seemed reluctant to criticize, but she did anyway. "Even with all the gear we brought, taking on that many natives in a stand-up fight would be reckless."

"I never said it would be a stand-up fight." D'Gol pointed out details in his drawing. "Put incendiary charges here to force them to use the major trails for their attacks—and then mine the trails. Turn these intersections and gullies into kill boxes with the automated sentry guns. And we might not be able to use the canopy to sneak inside the temple, but we can use it to stay out of the cross fire while we cook these *Ha'DIbaHpu'*. Any that survive the siege weapons, we pick off from above. Once we thin their ranks enough to get close to the temple, we bombard it, force the target into the open, and blast it to Gre'thor."

"Quite a plan," Hartür said. "As long as our enemy shows no capacity for original thought or any ability to change tactics, it should work out just fine."

Now, Mara decided, was a good time to interject some thoughts. "That's the least of this plan's problems. Keekur, Naq'chI, aren't the Starfleeters inside the temple now?"

Keekur nodded. "Confirmed. They were marched up the front pathway, into the main audience chamber. No sign of them since." She shrugged. "Probably dead by now."

Doctor Dolaq waggled a finger in rebuke. "We don't know that."

That news seemed to trouble CheboQ. "If the Starfleeters are still alive and inside the temple when we hit it with heavy ordnance, that sort of thing can start a war—which is a privilege the politicians like to keep to themselves."

Now several heads in the huddle were nodding. Hartür added, "CheboQ makes a good point. Maybe we should adjust our tactics."

"No!" D'Gol's patience was done. "If the Starfleeters get hurt in our cross fire, that's their own damned fault. If they didn't want to become collateral damage in our mission, they should never have come here."

"Easy enough to say," Dolaq replied, "but that kind of thinking can have serious repercussions if you're wrong."

D'Gol tightened his hand around the grip of his *d'k tahg*. "And there can be serious repercussions for *you*, Doctor, if you don't stop questioning my orders."

Mara narrowed her eyes into a contemptuous glare. "Thank you, D'Gol, for that rousing demonstration of debate skills for which you are so rightly famous." She pulled out her scanner and set it to project a holographic image of the smoky tentacles she and Hartür had seen just a short time before. "Have you forgotten about these things?"

"What about them?"

"You don't recognize them? I do. They're identical to a hostile force that wiped out two colonies last year on Gamma Tauri IV—one a Federation colony, the other one ours.

"Creatures like these were the first wave. What came next were monsters three times our size. Unstoppable killers. Agents of destruction so terrifying that the High Command authorized a joint Starfleet-Klingon bombardment of the planet's surface. One that both sides continued until that entire planet was turned to magma and its atmosphere was burned away."

She turned off her scanner's holographic playback. "If these things are here, neutralizing the target might prove harder than we expected. Against these horrors, we might actually need Starfleet on our side. So, yes, D'Gol, maybe you ought to consider coming up with a plan that doesn't treat them as free targets in a kill zone."

The commander stewed for a moment, and then he used his gloved palm to erase the diagram he had drawn in the mud. "So be it." Piece by piece, he sketched out a new idea. "A hybrid plan. We focus on the most direct approach to the cave temple.

Use incendiaries on its flanks to cut it off from reinforcements. Use the automated guns as our rear guard. And then we make a direct assault on the remaining isolated forces between us and the temple." He looked around, appraising the group's reaction. "Once we get inside, we switch to close-quarters battle tactics, clear the temple room by room, and push onward until we eliminate the target. With a bit of luck, we avoid hurting any precious Starfleeters. Once we frag the target, we get the hell out, fall back to the *QInqul*, and go home."

His plan met with satisfied nods around the huddle—until he came to Doctor Dolaq. The scientist still looked concerned. "What if the Starfleeters are alive inside the temple?"

D'Gol was confused. "What if they are?"

Dolaq searched the group's faces for support and found none. "Do we rescue them?"

Even Mara had to laugh. "Don't be stupid, Doctor. All I said was *don't murder them*. I never said we have to *save* them."

―――――――――――――――

The Godhead had called it a cage, but as soon as Babitz was hurled through a hole in the floor into the vile pit below, she recognized it for what it really was—a dungeon.

She splashed down into tepid, meter-deep water that reeked of excrement and decay. She surfaced flailing her arms and sputtering to expel the foulness from her mouth. No matter how hard she shook, the filthy water felt as if it clung to her skin, as if it were something more viscous. The only light inside the dungeon pit was what spilled down through the hole overhead, and that was dim and gray under the best of circumstances.

Something blocked out the light, Babitz's only warning that the next member of the landing party was being tossed down. She scrambled out of the way just before Sulu hit the water. He surfaced seconds later, coughing hard, and regained his feet.

Okay, he's standing. He's probably fine.

Her eyes adjusted to the gloomy dim, enabling her to see that Spock, Razka, and Singh all were conscious and on their feet.

Sounds of struggle echoed from above, and then someone else was falling in, feetfirst this time. It was Chekov. He hit the water, and his balance faltered as he struck the slimy stone floor, but he kept his feet under him and avoided being submerged. He glared upward at those who had delivered him here and muttered Russian curses at them as he stepped out of the light.

The last member of the landing party to plunge through the opening was Master Chief Ilucci. He let out a whoop of dismay as he fell, only to be silenced by the force of impact as he belly-flopped into the shallow water. Kicking and thrashing, he surfaced with all the grace of a wounded hippopotamus mired in quicksand.

Above him, the natives closed a gate made of jungle bamboo lashed together with vines, and secured into place with a simple loops-and-bars system. It was a primitive barrier, but one more than sufficient to prevent the landing party from making an easy escape.

No matter which direction Babitz looked she didn't see any walls. It was possible they were close but just beyond the edge of their dull and narrow spill of light. It was just as possible that this dungeon stretched on for kilometers underground, receding into the darkness.

Chekov tried to draw a deep breath only to gag on the stench. "My God! This must be what a Klingon chamber pot smells like the morning after a *gagh*-eating contest."

Ilucci side-eyed Chekov. "I *know* that smell, kid. Trust me: this is worse."

Sulu cracked a good-natured smile. "Look on the bright side: we're out of the rain."

That got a hiss from Razka. "Don't let the Godhead hear you say that, or he'll make his minions come down here and urinate on us."

Singh feigned shock. "For *free*? On Argelius you pay double for that."

Babitz's anger turned cold. "Well, we're not on Argelius, Ensign. We're knee-deep in a latrine, marinating in a soup of bacteria even more disgusting than it smells."

"Oh, really, Doc? I hadn't noticed." Singh looked up at the grated opening, which was at least two meters higher than anyone in the party could reach. "How do we get out of here?"

"We make a human pyramid," Babitz said, "with you on the bottom."

"Sorry, Doc. I'm a top."

Ilucci stepped between Singh and Babitz. "Sirs, would you two stop flirting? In case you haven't noticed, we're in *trouble* here."

Fighting the urge to retch, Babitz shot back, "*Are* we, Master Chief? What was your first clue? The godlike alien who almost crushed us like bugs? Or was it the throng of wild-eyed spearmen who could have turned us into shish kebabs?"

The master chief turned his back on Babitz, only to make way for Sulu to rant at her. "You want to be mad about something, Doc? Ask yourself how we got captured in the first place. How did these people sneak up on us when we have tricorders?"

"What are you asking me for?" She pointed at Singh. "Ask our *security* officer."

All eyes turned toward Singh, who raised her hands, palms out. "Oh, hell no. You're not laying this on *me*." She looked Sulu in the eye. "You scanned our route just like I did, sir."

"I scanned to get a fix on the target. Defending us from threats was your assignment."

Spock's voice was deep and loud, and it fell like a hammer: "Enough."

The group fell silent. Babitz wondered if any of the others felt embarrassed and ashamed for stooping to blame-shifting and excuses, or if she was the only one.

Moving from one person to the next, Spock circled the landing party. "It is vital that we all remain aware and alert. Our current priority is to break out of this dungeon. After that, our next objective must be to recover our weapons and equipment, and then to escape this temple. Once free, we can regroup and assess our mistakes, with an eye toward learning from them."

Razka nodded at Spock. "Well said, Commander." The first officer stopped next to Razka, who then paced around the landing party in the opposite direction, leading Babitz to wonder if the two of them had rehearsed this while everyone else had been busy arguing. "The most obvious exit is somewhat out of our reach, so we need to focus on finding another way out. The echoes down here suggest a fairly large open space, but not one so large that we can't search it.

"We will split up. Some of us will be sent to the walls to conduct perimeter searches, looking for doors, gaps in the walls, anything that might help us get out.

"Others will hold hands and walk in search patterns through the open middle of the chamber. Use your senses to feel for drains, edges that might mean hatches, or other openings."

Babitz couldn't suppress her skepticism. "This water is too warm to have a link to a fresh source. If we're lucky, this is just runoff, rainwater that's drained to the lowest level. And the fact that it's collected here suggests this chamber is watertight, which would mean no openings except the one through which we entered. So what if we probe all the walls, and walk a search grid, and wind up back here with nothing more than we have now?"

Spock did not seem concerned by the points she had raised. "In that case, Doctor, we shall have confirmed there are no other paths open to us, be they of lesser resistance or otherwise. However, the search might yield other information that can aid our escape or otherwise further our mission objectives."

"Or it might waste valuable time we could have used devising an escape."

"That is a risk. But until we conduct a search, we cannot know for certain." Spock faced Razka, who came to a halt beside him. "Chief, please assign search tasks at your discretion. Everyone, be thorough, but also be quick. It is imperative that we complete our task and devise a means of escape before the Godhead returns and executes us all."

———————

I am not in the jungle, I am the jungle—alive with a million hungers and countless eyes.

I am not the rain; I am the stormhead. I am the thunder and the lightning.

I have sensation and awareness but no form. Though I can reach out with a hundred hands, I cannot feel. I move on the wind and beneath the sea. I am everywhere at once inside the fungal network of a continent's worth of wet loam, yet I feel trapped. Alone. Lost.

Pests afflict me. Insects with fatal stings. I send my pets to contain them, but my Chwii are weak, ignorant, easily overcome. This threat is beyond their ken.

A cascade of memories overcomes me. I try to hang on to them but like water they slip through my nonexistent hands, eluding my subtle body of imagination and dark energy.

Are they my memories? How can they be? Those are the artifacts of a mortal life. My essence could not have preceded my existence.

I have always been. Always will be. I Am.

And I was. But what was I? I am then and I am now and I am what is to come. Time has revealed its shape to me, its ouroboros of secrets unfurled.

So I project myself into the physical realm, my will like a breath across the top of the river. Strangers lurk in my shadows. Some feel familiar, but names escape me now. Are the strangers my friends or my enemies? How am I to know?

Best if I neutralize them. Remove all doubt. Purge the uncertainty.

I snake through the high boughs . . . reach out with the senses of every base life-form that walks, slithers, or swims in this world's tropical jungle . . . and seek the tiny, arrogant little sparks that have challenged me. That have trespassed on this world I have claimed as my own.

I will find you, little sparks. And when I do . . . I will snuff you out, one and all.

After a brief detour into denial and hysteria, the landing party regained its professionalism. Spock had remained under the opening through which each of them had been thrown, making himself visible to the others no matter where they were in the fetid dungeon, and to help them remain oriented as they went about their various tasks.

Sulu felt his way along what appeared to be the pit's bounding wall. He moved in a clockwise direction, counting his paces in order to arrive at a reasonable estimate of the size of the chamber. Spock had insisted that Sulu count out loud because the lieutenant was otherwise lost in the darkness, and the rest of the landing party had no other way of knowing whether Sulu was still conscious and free of interference.

On either side of Spock, searchers moved in pairs. On his left were Razka and Chekov; on his right were Ilucci and Singh. Each pair held hands with their arms pulled taut in order to make certain the distance between them remained consistent. Moving with care, each duo went from one end of the pit to the other, using Spock as their guide to avoid wandering in circles.

That left Doctor Babitz with Spock beneath the entrance to the pit. The two of them monitored the rest of the team between rounds of comparing notes. Babitz looked up at the crossbeams of the dungeon's hatch meters above their heads. "It's just wood. Don't Vulcans have the strength to snap those things in two?"

"That depends upon the wood, and the Vulcan." Spock pointed at the bars as he continued. "This wood is similar in many ways to bamboo. Most importantly, it is very lightweight but incredibly strong. As such, these bars might as well be made of duranium." He shifted his arm to point at the locking mechanism. "The means by which it has been secured are simple but effective: stone loops hewn from the stone floor, with solid beams run through them. Were I to attempt to force my way through it, I would sooner break my neck than that lock."

Babitz looked up and sighed. "Then I guess it would be premature to talk about how to ambush the guard standing watch in the chamber above."

"Quite. Although that is an obstacle we will eventually need to confront."

"As is the Godhead, apparently."

Spock nodded. "True. Did you find it curious that the Godhead addressed us in what sounded like Federation Standard, using a spoken voice rather than telepathy?"

"Did it?" She considered that. "I guess you're right. But why is that odd?"

"Your shipmate Lieutenant Theriault reported that when the Shedai known as the Apostate first addressed her, it did so by telepathy, switching to spoken words only after she requested it. And yet, I sensed no telepathic aura from the Godhead whatsoever."

"None?" Again the doctor paused to ruminate. "That *is* interesting."

"Why? What does that fact suggest to you, Doctor?"

She looked upward, as if she could peer through the stone to see the Godhead somewhere above them. "It's exactly the kind of deviation from the norm I might expect to see in a Shedai-humanoid hybrid. A creature that exhibits many of the physical characteristics of the Shedai but which lacks the more complex sensory capabilities."

"Intriguing. Does your research suggest such a biological fusion is possible?"

"Possible? Sure. Advisable? Not in a million years. All our past experience with the Shedai suggests their minds evolved to inhabit multiple physical forms at once, sometimes controlling them across great distances. That's not the kind of ability one can just pick up overnight. Over the past century there's been a lot of research into expanding humanoid proprioception, to teach us how to handle extra limbs or mentally control non-human bodies, such as remote-controlled robotic avatars. None of them have gone very well. Most humanoids' brains just aren't wired to coordinate more limbs or process visual information from more eyes than what evolution gave them. So a human, Vulcan, or Ardanan who tried to steal the powers and perceptions of the Shedai would more likely go insane than gain super-human abilities."

"And yet, it seems that Doctor Verdo was intent on pursuing just such an outcome."

Babitz shook her head in dismay. "Which makes no sense to me. I've read Verdo's work. He was brilliant. So what the hell made him think *he* would be the exception to the rule? No expert in genomic medicine I've ever met would even think a person could survive that radical a genetic resequencing, and retain even a shred of their humanity if they did."

Anger and bitterness colored Babitz's words as she continued. "Between you and me, Commander? This was one of my greatest fears when I first read the briefing for this mission. I've seen Verdo's type before: a genius iconoclast, egomaniacal, obsessive, ready to play God at the drop of a hat. So certain that he alone has the answer and everyone else is flailing in the dark. Letting a person like him anywhere near Operation Vanguard was bound to present a temptation too great for him to resist. And I was right. Now look what it's gotten him! And us! Damn that sonofabitch for meddling with things he should've left alone."

From nearby came Sulu's voice in reply: "Just one problem with your theory, Doc." He emerged from the shadows towing a decaying corpse behind him. Much of its flesh had fallen away, and insect larvae feasted on what remained. But the body was still garbed in modern clothing, including a now filthy white lab jacket. Stitched over the coat's left chest pocket was a name in Federation Standard script: Johron Verdo, Ph.D.

Spock raised an eyebrow at Sulu's pungent discovery. "Fascinating. Are we certain this is the body of Doctor Verdo?"

Babitz kneeled next to the corpse and shifted its jacket and shirt aside to look at a length of its left clavicle, which now lay exposed thanks to decay and carrion-feeders. She pointed at a prominent healed fracture in the middle of the bone. "This break in the left clavicle matches the one documented in Verdo's medical file." She pushed up the dead man's right pant leg to show a titanium patella and other pieces grafted into the knee joint. "And so does this knee replacement." She stood and frantically wiped her hands on the front of her jumpsuit as she added, "That's definitely Doctor Verdo. Which means he *can't* be the Godhead."

The rest of the landing party had regrouped around Spock, Babitz, and Sulu, all of them looking on in shock and dismay. Chekov seemed particularly spooked. He pointed at the corpse. "But both of Doctor Verdo's colleagues are also dead. So if *this* is Doctor Verdo"—he looked upward in horror—"who was that in the temple?"

Spock replied, "An excellent question, Mister Chekov. An excellent question, indeed."

15

D'Gol knew by the whooping battle cries shrilling through the jungle that something had gone awry with his plan to storm the cave temple. He had meant to lay siege to the stronghold and force the Chwii to take refuge inside until he was ready to go in and kill them. Instead the whole accursed lot of them was stampeding toward him and his strike team. As far as he knew, the Chwii were not death worshippers. That told him the primitive *novpu'* were clearly more terrified of their demigod inside the temple than they were of getting butchered by his team.

He backpedaled through some foliage to find Keekur and Naq'chI still setting up the siege guns, a process made difficult by the constant rain. "How long until those are ready?"

Keekur scowled in frustration as she worked. "Too long."

Mara emerged from the jungle behind the two warriors. As usual, the captain's wife had a scanner in her hands and a surprised look on her face. "Hostiles incoming."

Hungry for information he could use, D'Gol asked, "How many?"

"A lot. As in, we'll be overrun unless we fall back *now*."

D'Gol was dumbfounded. "How in Fek'lhr's name did they know we were here?"

Mara shrugged her shoulders. "Maybe the smoke serpents? Does it matter?" She glanced at her scanner's display. "Range, two *qell'qams* and closing fast."

The two warriors continued working on the setup of the automated pulse disruptors, because so far D'Gol had not told them to stop. He gauged their progress, their current rate of work, and made the best informed estimate he could as to whether they would have the weapons ready in time to keep the *novpu'* at bay. The truth did not align with his hopes.

"Naq'chI, Keekur: stop what you're doing and camouflage the guns. We need to leave them behind." As the two warriors hastily packed their tools and draped the guns, D'Gol turned and whistled toward the trees, in the direction from which Mara had just come.

Seconds later, Hartür appeared. "Sir?"

"A Chwii horde is heading our way. We'll fall back by pairs and cover one another as we go. Keep the river on your left so they can't flank you from that side. You and Mara get CheboQ and Doctor Dolaq moving. The gunners and I will be right behind you."

"Understood." Hartür slapped his hand onto Mara's shoulder, signaling her to come with him, and the pair retreated through the rain, into the verdant shadows.

The warriors were up and ready to move. Naq'chI backed up beside D'Gol, her disruptor rifle pointed at the approaching din. "How far are we going, Commander?"

"Until they stop chasing us or we find defensible cover."

Keekur fell in on the other side of D'Gol and braced her rifle against her shoulder. "Oh, *good*. I do so enjoy it when we *improvise*."

Spears flew past over the Klingons' heads.

D'Gol readied his own rifle. "They're within throwing distance. Move!" The trio walked carefully backward while keeping their weapons pointed toward the enemy, laying down blindly fired swaths of suppressing fire in a classic rear-guard action. Each salvo they unleashed rewarded them with death cries and howls of agony, the sweetest music D'Gol had ever known.

In less than a minute they were almost on top of the rest of the strike team. D'Gol barked, "Faster! And fan out—widen our killing arc." Seconds later, the entire team was firing, filling the jungle with a flurry of blazing crimson disruptor pulses. From beyond the dense curtains of moss and fronds came the shrieks and groans of dozens of wounded or dying Chwii.

D'Gol was feeling fairly cocky until a spear shot past within a hair's breadth of his face and split the trunk of a tree like a woodsman's axe. Then he remembered: *We each have to be lucky dozens of times. They only need to be lucky once.*

The ululating cries of the Chwii drew closer by the minute, and the jungle was offering the strike team nothing that looked even remotely like hard cover. Now large stones were flying between the boughs to rain down on D'Gol and his compatriots.

One struck Keekur, who shook off the blow even as bright blood streaked down the side of her face. Another caught Doctor Dolaq in his shoulder and nearly knocked the lab rat on his ass. D'Gol would have laughed if only he'd had the time.

A spear tip slashed through CheboQ's fatigues and took a piece of his thigh with it. The medic stumbled but recovered his footing with a quick helping hand from Mara.

Enough of this. I will not see us die by a thousand cuts.

D'Gol switched his weapon from pulsed fire to a steady beam, increased its power setting to maximum, and checked to make sure the rest of his strike team was well behind him.

Then he unleashed a piercingly loud prolonged burst of white-hot disruptor energy in a shallow arc. It slashed through tree trunks, knots of foliage, massive tangles of vines, and more Chwii foot soldiers than he could easily count. Within seconds the jungle was ablaze with small fires, choked with gray smoke, and thick with the charnel odors of cooked flesh and burnt hair.

D'Gol grinned at his handiwork and drew in a deep breath to savor the stench of fiery death he had wrought. *Now that's what I call suppressing fire.*

His victory was as brief as it was ugly. Through the smoke came dozens more Chwii, still charging in pursuit of him and the others, apparently undeterred by the sight of so many of their own butchered and incinerated in the blink of an eye.

Curse these HaDIbaHpu'*! What's it going to take to break them?*

He resumed his retreat, quick-stepping backward through the trees, one eye on his path and the other on the enemy. "Keekur! Naq'chI! Cover me!"

Twin storms of disruptor pulses flew toward the enemy, passing on either side of D'Gol as he continued making up ground to regroup. As soon as he rejoined the gunners on the firing line, he discarded his rifle's depleted power cell and slammed in a fresh one.

Keekur shouted over the screeching of their weapons, "How many so far?"

D'Gol knew she was asking how many of the enemy they had slain. "About a hundred."

"Is that all?" She increased her weapon's power level and pulse frequency, and then she resumed firing with manic glee. "Gotta do better than that if we want to get into Sto-Vo-Kor!"

Adding his disruptor barrage to the gunners', D'Gol recalled that Captain Kang's favorite aphorism was *Four thousand throats can be cut in a single night by a running man.* But D'Gol's favorite mantra was one of a more prosaic bent:

Kill everything and let Fek'lhr take the weak.

The silence that surrounded Spock was heavy with anticipation and expectation. As much as he appreciated the landing party's respectful silence while he concentrated, he found it inconvenient that their chaotic stew of emotions clouded his telepathic perception of the mind of the guard who stood watch over the hatch in the corridor above them.

The native's mind was fairly simple, an array of appetites and urges but little in the way of reflection. Under ideal circumstances, Spock would not have found it especially difficult to plant a simple suggestion into the man's mind, though he would still have found it distasteful.

It struck Spock as curious that those who did not possess empathic or telepathic talents were often quick to urge their use upon others, and the first to protest their use on themselves. As someone who had inherited a significant range of psionic talents from his father, Spock had learned from a young age to be both cautious and circumspect in their use. The temptation to abuse such abilities could be significant, even among Vulcans. So it was that when Doctor Babitz had asked whether Spock, as a half Vulcan, possessed such talents, he had been tempted to deny it, but prevarication was contrary to Spock's nature and his upbringing, so he had confessed that he did in fact have some skills in this secretive discipline.

Now he stood beneath the gated opening through which they had all been pushed, doing his best to impose his will upon an unsuspecting primitive humanoid. It was only the necessity of the tactic that made it remotely tolerable to Spock. A thorough search of the entire flooded dungeon chamber had found no other ways out, no other portals, and no weapons or tools. Even so, Spock had not volunteered the truth about his abilities with the others. Nor would he have, had not Doctor Babitz asked rhetorically, "I don't suppose any of you know how to hypnotize that guard into letting us out, do you?"

Though Spock did not speak the native's language, he was sure he could incept within the man's mind the idea of opening the gate to the pit and lowering its ladder of vines. Spock had, after all, made telepathic contact with a Horta, a nonhumanoid alien that shared almost no points of biological reference with humanoids. This would be only a matter of time and mental focus.

My mind to your mind. My thoughts to your thoughts.

Our thoughts are merging. Our minds . . . are one.

He sensed some instinctual resistance to his telepathic entreaty, but with a few seconds of directed effort he became aware
of sharing the guard's perceptions, some surface thoughts, and
flashes of his memories and his sense of identity, including that
his species called itself Chwii.

It was time to impose the idea. Spock conjured within the
mind of the guard—Sapken was his name, Spock realized—a vision of Sapken's green hands releasing the bolt that secured the
gate over the pit's entrance, and then opening the gate and dropping its vine ladder. Once more Sapken resisted. Rather than use
mental violence, Spock paired the idea of opening the gate to the
pit with a sensation of blissful peace, followed by near euphoria.

There is no reason to use force when persuasion is an option.

This time Sapken responded enthusiastically to Spock's suggestion. He pulled away the rod that held the gate shut, and then
he lifted the gate and dropped its attached ladder of vines down
into the pit.

Ascending the ladder, Spock continued to project into Sapken's mind the idea that the person climbing up to him was a
dear friend, someone he cared about, someone he loved.

Sapken got down on his hands and knees next to the opening
and leaned down over the edge, to peer into the shadows and
see who it was he had set free.

When his red eyes focused on Spock, a cloud of confusion
dispelled his joy.

Then Spock's hand clamped onto a nerve cluster between
Sapken's shoulder and his neck, and the last thing Sapken knew
before his world went black was that he was falling.

At the bottom of the vine ladder, Razka, Ilucci, and Sulu
caught Sapken before he struck the water. They set him down in
a squatting pose that left his drooped-forward head just above
the water, and then they joined the line to climb the ladder, one
at a time, to the corridor.

It took a few minutes for the entire landing party to climb out of the pit. Regrouped in the corridor, they were a sorry-looking mess. Their camouflage garments were all caked in filth, and they each were soaked from head to toe, reeking of excrement and decay.

Sulu kicked muck off his boot. "Good thing I didn't wear my lucky socks today."

Babitz looked at him as if he had grown another head. "You have 'lucky socks'?"

Now it was Sulu's turn to wonder what was wrong with Babitz. "It was a joke."

"Are you *sure*?"

Spock intervened before the pair came to blows. "Mister Sulu, Doctor, I recommend we proceed with haste back to the audience chamber to recover our equipment."

Sulu nodded. "Aye, Mister Spock."

Razka moved to the point position, and the group fell into its established single-file formation. They relied on Razka's superior sense of direction to guide them through the labyrinthine lower levels of the cave temple, through smooth-walled passageways that snaked endlessly in the dark, and finally up a slowly winding passage that returned them to the main audience chamber, with its gigantic throne, blood-stained sacrifice hole above the raging source waters of the river, and open ceiling through which rain continued to shower.

Razka whispered to Spock, "It looks deserted."

"What about the Godhead? Is there any sign of it? Perhaps along the ceiling?"

The Saurian looked again. "Nothing, sir."

"All right. With me—to the sarcophagus." Spock and Razka darted from the passageway, across the audience chamber, to the coffinlike structure in which the Chwii had hidden the landing party's equipment. With their combined strength Razka and Spock hefted the massive stone lid off the sarcophagus and quietly set it aside. Spock was glad to see that the Chwii had not moved the team's gear. He beckoned the others, who gathered around the coffin to retrieve their phasers, tricorders, and packs.

They had just finished when the passages around the chamber echoed with the cadence of marching feet, a sound that quickly grew louder and clearer.

Razka pointed toward a smaller side passage: "This way!" He led the landing party out of the audience chamber in a hurry, and within a few minutes the taste of fresh air served as a clue that they were close to reaching the jungle outside the temple.

As the landing party emerged into the cleansing embrace of a heavy downpour, the jungle resounded with the beating of angry war drums accompanied by high-pitched wailing, followed by angry shrieks of Klingon disruptor fire.

Chekov froze at the sound of nearby battle. "Maybe we were safer in the pit."

Spock asked Razka, "Chief, can you tell what direction that's coming from?"

"Far side of the river, the one we used to get here."

"Then I suggest we head in the opposite direction with all due haste."

Razka led the group into the jungle. "I like the way you think, sir."

16

After too short a night's sleep, all Captain Nassir wanted from his morning was a few minutes alone to enjoy his warm apple fritter and a cup of coffee, light and sweet. The crew of the *Sagittarius* knew not to disturb his precious quiet time before the start of first shift on the bridge.

Unfortunately for Nassir, someone had neglected to impart this information to their temporarily transferred acting chief engineer, who entered the ship's mess with a data slate in his hand and a hopeful look in his eye. "Ah, Captain, there you are!"

"Yes, Mister DeSalle. Here I am." Hoping to signal his unavailability, Nassir took a large bite of his delicious fritter and savored the tart sweetness of its lemon-sugar icing.

To his disappointment, DeSalle sat down across from him. "Engineer's Mate Threx and I were up all night, working on—"

"It's just Threx. I know who he is. I only have fourteen people on this ship."

"Of course, sir, sorry. As I was saying, Threx and I were up all night working—"

"All night? Why weren't you in your rack getting some shut-eye? I can't have you nodding off in the middle of a crisis, Lieutenant. I need you sharp."

Defensive and slightly flustered, DeSalle nodded in agreement. "Of course, sir. That's why I had Doctor M'Benga fix me up with a dose of CFM. But if I could just get back to—"

"I've yet to see a counter-fatigue medicine that can replace a good night's sleep."

"Couldn't agree more, sir. But in this case, it was worth it." DeSalle turned his data slate toward Nassir and nudged it across the table to him.

Nassir made a point of picking up his coffee instead. "Is there a reason I can't look at this on the bridge ten minutes from now?"

"Not to be dramatic, sir, but time is a factor. Can I walk you through the proposal?"

"I don't see how I can possibly stop you."

DeSalle tapped the data slate's display and called up a schematic. "Threx and I agreed that the six photon torpedoes we got from the *Enterprise* yesterday won't really do us much good in open combat against Kang's ship. Which is why we want to convert them into gravitic mines."

Nassir set down his mug of coffee. "Gravitic mines? Why?"

With another tap on the slate, DeSalle summoned an orbital chart of Kolasi III and its moon, over which was superimposed the past several hours' movements of the *I.K.S. SuvwI'*. "Kang and his crew are doing their best to mix up their orbital pattern. But after the first few hours the flight controller got bored. The variations became less abrupt, more regular. Now we have enough data to predict their orbital speed, distance above or below the planet's rings, and probable intercept trajectory should they spot our shuttlecraft returning to orbit."

Another sip of coffee gave Nassir time to study the orbital diagram before he responded. "How reliable are these data sets?"

"Very. We had the ship's computer confirm them, and then we had Lieutenant Commander Sorak vet the computer's numbers. It all checks out, sir."

"All right. Dare I ask what you plan to do with this information?"

Another tap brought up an image of Kolasi III from above its northern pole, one that showed the entirety of the planet's rings. Six points within a small region of the rings were highlighted in red and one in green. DeSalle pointed at the latter dot. "This is the designated rendezvous and recovery point for the shuttlecraft *Kepler*." He highlighted the red dots. "And these are the *SuvwI's* best positions to attack the *Kepler* and impede our recovery ops."

"Let me guess: each one of those advantageous positions is going to become a home to one of your new jury-rigged gravitic mines."

"You catch on quick, sir."

"They didn't make me a captain for my singing voice, Lieutenant." Nassir studied the deployment diagram. After a moment, he realized why it troubled him. "These look close on the map, but in fact they're reasonably far apart. Setting these will take more than one run."

"That was our estimate, as well, sir. Mine and Threx's."

"In case you haven't noticed, Lieutenant, we and the *Enterprise* are currently pinned down behind this moon. And from what I saw of your gravitic-mine adaptations, your new improvised munitions would lack propulsion drives or guidance systems. So how exactly do you propose to deploy your mines into the planet's rings?"

"Hit and run, sir. Get in and out and seed the recovery zone with mines."

"A tricky proposition, given that Kirk's current preferred tactic seems to be 'hide under the blankets until the monster goes away and the problem fixes itself.' I really can't imagine Captain Kirk would endorse anything this dangerous, can you?"

"To the contrary, sir, I see no reason Captain Kirk would object. No part of my and Threx's plan puts the *Enterprise* at risk for even a moment."

Nassir pushed the last mouthful of fritter into his maw and spoke as he chewed, confident that DeSalle would get the gist of his muffled, pastry-garbled speech. "I'd ask how that's possible, but I already know the answer." He swallowed, and then he added, "You mean to use *my* ship for this harebrained suicide mission, don't you?"

"In a word, sir, yes. We have no choice since the adapted torpedoes are already here, on the *Sagittarius*. It just makes sense for us to deploy them."

Nassir downed his last swig of now lukewarm java. "I retract my objection to your plan, Lieutenant. Now that I know we'll be doing all the work and taking all the risk, I'm fairly certain Kirk will *love* it."

"It's an interesting idea, but I can't really say that I love it." Kirk turned a curious look at his acting first officer, who stood on the other side of Lieutenant Uhura at the communications console on the *Enterprise*'s bridge. "What do you think of DeSalle's plan, Mister Scott?"

"I'd be lying if I said I didn't have questions, sir."

"That makes two of us. First, what do you make of their assessment that the torpedoes weren't tactically viable for the *Sagittarius*?"

Scott reacted with a rare moment of humble regret. "That's on me, sir. I forgot the *Archer*-class ships don't have automated torpedo loading. If they fire one at Kang's ship, they'll be dead before they get the second one in the tube."

"Which brings me to my second concern: DeSalle's plan to convert photon torpedoes into gravitic mines. Would that actually work?"

"Aye, sir!" Scott's countenance brightened. "It's a rather clever bit of tinkering."

"I'll take your word for it. I guess the next thing we need to ask ourselves is, 'Is this worth it?' It sounds like they'd be taking a lot of risk for a plan that's far from a sure thing."

"There are no 'sure things' in battle, sir. As for the risk, it's Captain Nassir's boat and crew that'll be on the line, and they sound more than willing."

Kirk folded his arms while he thought through the situation.

"Lieutenant Uhura, ask Captain Nassir how long until the jury-rigged mines are ready to deploy."

Uhura entered the query into the computer, which translated it for transmission as Starfleet semaphore via the ship's navigation lights, and then she waited until a reply appeared on her console. "Captain Nassir says the improvised mines are ready now, sir."

"So far so good. Question for Mister DeSalle: How does the *Sagittarius* plan to monitor the Klingons' changing orbital velocity while they're planting each mine?"

After another brief delay of transmission and reply, Uhura read the response: "Mister DeSalle requests that *Enterprise* act as a spotter while using the moon's polar magnetic field for cover. By having *Enterprise* alert *Sagittarius* to the Klingons' position, *Sagittarius* will be able to take cover or maintain an opposing orbit around Kolasi III."

That earned a tilt of Scott's head and a dubious look on his face. "Workable. But if we poke our head out we'll have to run cold as winter on Andoria to stay off the Klingons' sensors."

"I think we can manage that, Mister Scott." Kirk directed his next question to Uhura. "Lieutenant, how do we alert *Sagittarius* while it's deploying the mines? Can we use the semaphore system without giving ourselves away to the Klingons?"

She shook her head. "No, sir. The lag time and exposure both make the semaphore system untenable for that part of the mission." She flipped some switches and showed Kirk what looked to him like a screen of ultratech mumbo jumbo. "The Klingons are still jamming all frequencies except their primary encrypted channel, so I've found a way to use it to send our signals to *Sagittarius*. We can't speak freely on that channel, but we can use seemingly random low-amplitude squelches of static in prearranged sequences to send *Sagittarius* alerts, coordinates, and basic telemetry, with our computers translating at either end, as they are now."

As always, Kirk was profoundly impressed by Uhura's technical skills and proactive approach to problem-solving. "Well done, Lieutenant. Are we sure the Klingons won't know those static bursts are coming from the *Enterprise*?"

"Positive, sir. We're using natural recurring sequences of cosmic background-radiation static, and keying different portions of it to alphanumeric values, like a replacement cipher. Even if the Klingons notice it, their computers should dismiss it as known static patterns."

"Outstanding." Kirk looked up at Scott. "Are we sure the Klingons won't be able to detect the mines once they're deployed?"

"Not as long as the mines remain in passive mode. In that state, they're purely reactive, triggered by proximity or contact, depending on their program." Scott added with a smile, "And the mineral compounds in the rings should mask them nicely, sir."

"Just what I wanted to hear, Scotty." Kirk looked at the image of Kolasi III on the viewscreen. "Trouble is, we have no way of knowing when or if our landing party is coming back. Bottom-line it for me, Mister Scott: How long will this take?"

Scott delegated the question with a look at Uhura, who relayed it to the *Sagittarius*. Seconds later, she had a reply. "Mister DeSalle says 'A few hours if we're lucky. Longer if we're not.'" She turned an apologetic look at Kirk. "That's all he sent back, sir."

Kirk frowned. *I should know better than to expect real figures from an engineer.* He descended the steps into the command well and stood in front of his chair. "Lieutenant Benson, Ensign Waltke, Ensign Nanjiani, can any of you give me a real estimate of how long it will likely take the *Sagittarius* to deploy all six of its gravitic mines?"

Waltke and Benson traded nervous glances, and then they both shrugged at Kirk.

Nanjiani's voice shook almost as much as his hands. "Actually, sir? I took the liberty of computing an estimate based on a simulation of the Klingons' orbital variations, combined with an approximation of the tactics required by the *Sagittarius* to—"

"Just the *number*, please, Ensign."

"Approximately nine hours, twenty-one minutes, sir. Give or take forty-nine minutes."

"Mister Spock would be proud of you, Ensign. Well done." Kirk swung into his command chair and crossed his right ankle over his left knee. "Mister Nanjiani, recalibrate our visual sensors to shield them from the effects of the moon's polar magnetic field.

"Lieutenant Benson, calculate the optimal position in the polar magnetic field for observing the Klingon ship without betraying our own presence.

"Mister Waltke, coordinate with Mister Scott to prepare the ship for silent running. We need to take as many systems offline as possible, to reduce our thermal and electromagnetic signatures. That's going to include weapons and shields, and I want all residual charges purged from the warp coils, and the impulse reactors dialed down to ten percent capacity.

"Lieutenant Uhura, inform Captain Nassir his plan is a go. As soon as we're in position, we'll give him the signal to start his run."

Everyone around Kirk started turning his words into actions. Moments such as this were what made him feel alive. *This is why I became a captain.*

From the comms station, Uhura announced, "Captain Nassir confirms the *Sagittarius* stands ready to fly on your order, sir."

"Thank you, Lieutenant."

As preparations continued, Lieutenant Commander Scott put himself next to Kirk's command chair. "Engineering is making the switch to silent running, sir. We'll be ready to give *Sagittarius* the go-ahead for launch in fifteen minutes."

"Good work, Scotty." Kirk couldn't help but crack a mischievous smile. "Let's give Captain Kang a surprise he won't soon forget."

17

Moving through rain and shadows, the landing party did its best to quickly put as much distance as possible between itself and the Chwii's cave temple. Back in the relatively open spaces of the jungle, Spock became acutely aware of the presence of wild predators stalking the group, always just out of sight, a constant presence of primitive hunger and aggression.

Still proceeding in single-file formation, the group followed Razka, whose confident trailblazing was making their swift retreat possible. As they passed through a dense cluster of waist-high fronds, the landing party was swarmed by tiny flying insects with painful bites. Running offered no escape. The swarm followed them, feasting on their blood as it did, until Spock switched on his tricorder and set it to emit a steady series of powerful ultrasonic pulses. Within seconds the cloud of parasitic insects scattered into the night, leaving Doctor Babitz to treat the landing party's reddened, swelling bites with hypos of antihistamine.

Off in the distance, shrill screeches of energy weapons being fired at full power rippled through the night. The sounds were muffled by the rain and the jungle but still recognizable. Spock whistled once to signal Razka to stop, and then he raised a fist to halt the rest of the group. Lifting his tricorder he scanned for life signs, in the direction of the sounds of battle. To see the readout clearly, he used his hand to shield it from the rain. "It would appear the Chwii are still pursuing the Klingon strike team on the far bank of the river."

"Better them than us," Chekov muttered.

Razka maintained a more professional demeanor. "Still in the same direction, sir?"

"Affirmative. The Klingons are effecting a tactical retreat downriver."

That seemed to surprise Ensign Singh. "Toward the waterfall?"

Ilucci let slip a derisive snort. "Bold move. Let's see how that goes for them."

Continuing his tricorder scans, Spock noticed something curious on the readout. "Chief Razka, I'm reading a broad clearing roughly one kilometer ahead on our present bearing. It might be a trail we can use to expedite our movement."

Chekov was perplexed. "Movement to where? Where are we going, Mister Spock?"

"At the moment, we are seeking safe ground." He shut off his tricorder and slung it at his side. "Once we find it, we can formulate a new plan of action."

Now it was Sulu who sounded confused. "Plan of action? Shouldn't we get to the shuttle and head back to the *Enterprise*?"

Spock turned a quizzical look at Sulu. "Why would we do that?"

"Because Doctor Verdo's dead, and his ship's a wreck, along with his research. We were sent to bring them back, and they're both gone. So can we go back to the ship?"

"We cannot." Spock faced Babitz. "Doctor, would you care to tell him why?"

Babitz was evidently reluctant to speak, but she did anyway. "The creature we met inside the temple might be part of a species known as the Shedai, or it might be a hybrid of some form of humanoid with a Shedai. Either way, it's Starfleet policy that any active Shedai life-form represents a clear and present danger to Federation security."

Ensign Singh struck a suspicious tone. "First I've ever heard of it."

The doctor looked at Singh with mild irritation. "That's because you're an ensign and Operation Vanguard is an ultraclassified covert operation. One with standing orders to contain the Shedai threat anywhere it's found, and by any means necessary."

Sulu, Chekov, and Singh all looked at Spock with varying degrees of disbelief. Sulu asked, "Is this true, Mister Spock?"

"It is. The captain and I, along with Mister Scott, were read into the program roughly twenty months ago, and it is every bit as serious as Doctor Babitz says. When Starfleet demands we suppress the Shedai threat by any means required, that has been shown to include anything up to and including planetary sterilization by photon torpedo bombardment."

Chekov repeated slowly, in a tone of shock and horror, "Planetary sterilization?"

Singh raised her eyebrows in surprise. "I don't like the sound of that. At all."

"No one does," Babitz said. "Which is why we need to find a more surgical and less apocalyptic way to rid this planet of that thing in the temple."

Spock nodded. "Agreed. Both because it will be to the long-term benefit of this world's native people, and because it would be a major strategic blunder to allow the Klingons to obtain this kind of actionable intelligence about the Shedai meta-genome."

"He's right," Babitz added. "Keeping this away from the Klingons is one of Starfleet's highest priorities right now. No matter what else we do, we can't let them leave this planet with a sample of the meta-genome or a scan of the creature in the temple."

Spock raised his voice just enough to make it clear he was addressing the entire landing party. "As of now, that is our new mission objective. And time remains a factor. Chief Razka?"

"I know, I know—onward." He pointed into the jungle with his machete. "This way."

Hacking and slashing, Razka butchered a path through green walls of foliage and vines. The ground underfoot varied from slick mud salted with rocks to carpets of decaying vegetation. The former offered worse footing, but the latter gave off rancid bursts of gas that smelled like a rotting corpse with every step the landing party took.

As the fumes built up, Chekov gagged. He pushed on until they were past the stink-moss, and then he shot a glare over his shoulder at it. "Just when we were finally getting rid of the dungeon smell." Trudging forward, he grumbled under his breath, "I hate this place."

Razka's blade sliced through a curtain of mossy vines to reveal open space on the other side. The landing party sidestepped one at a time through the gap, into the scouring embrace of a windy downpour. As soon as Spock saw the path through the jungle, he recognized what it must be, and he could tell from the group's reactions that they all did, as well.

Just under seven meters wide. All the trees flattened in the same direction, heading down an incline, with most of those in the center of the trail sheared off near the base of the trunk. Bits of scorched metallic debris littering the length of the scar.

It was the gouge inflicted by the crash-landing of a spacecraft.

Spock ran a fast scan with his tricorder, and pointed down the incline. "I am reading a large metallic object, four kilometers in that direction."

Ilucci cracked a knowing smile. "The Klingons' shuttle."

"I think so, Master Chief." Spock put away his tricorder. "I think that will serve our present needs most adequately. Chief Razka, lead the way."

Harried by spears and stones, the strike team was running. All pretense of an orderly fallback had been abandoned. The team's only goal now was to put as much distance as they could between themselves and the Chwii. Even shooting back had been judged a waste of time. Anything that slowed the strike team's pace was just bringing them another step closer to being overrun.

Mara hurdled over a fallen tree and sprinted past CheboQ, turning the medic into her unwilling living shield. *Forgive me, heroes of Sto-Vo-Kor.*

If any of the strike team lived through this, she knew that the one tasked with writing the after-mission report was very likely to omit this part, or transform it into something less utterly humiliating. That was, after all, the Klingon way.

Thorny vines slashed at Mara's face and arms as she slammed through them, her headlong flight guided only by fleeting glimpses of the river, or of the backs of her comrades ahead of her in the rainy darkness. Slung stones caromed off tree trunks on either side of her, and a spear nicked her shoulder before embedding itself in the ground ahead of her.

She threw herself through a wall of tall leafy things and slammed into D'Gol, who caught her and then pushed her away. "Stop running. We're out of road."

Her eyes adjusted quickly, and she realized they were at the edge of a cliff overlooking a long drop into the lowlands. To their right was the river, surging with froth and fury as it coursed around a boulder and then turned into a waterfall, plunging nearly two hundred *qam*s to a mist-shrouded cluster of sharp rocks.

Along with D'Gol, Keekur and Naq'chI had beaten her here, but now they were all equally trapped. CheboQ and Hartür were the next to emerge from the jungle. In the seconds that passed while Mara, Hartür, and CheboQ gasped to catch their breath, she had to wonder if perhaps they had lost the eccentric Doctor Dolaq—but then he stumbled out of the greenery, looking as if he had been put through a shredder with a load of old knives.

From the jungle, the furious cries of the Chwii grew closer and louder.

D'Gol shook his head. "So much for finding cover."

Large stones and spears struck the last of the trees standing between the strike team and the approaching horde. It would be only moments until the enemy overran this naked position, and the looks on the faces of the strike team confirmed for Mara that they all knew it.

Dolaq tried wading into the river, only to have the current knock him down. Sputtering, he pulled himself ashore. "We aren't fording the river."

CheboQ leaned out over the riverbank and looked back the way the team had come—and when he turned around, he wore an expression of horror. "It's coming. The smoke-serpent."

D'Gol let out a cynical laugh. "Of course it is. The perfect end to a perfect disaster."

Mara stole her own look at the serpent of black vapors that was ripping through the trees alongside the river in its haste to reach the strike team. Then she faced the others. "We've got about a minute before that thing gets here, less before the Chwii are on top of us. Hartür, Naq'chI! The climbing gear!"

The warrior and the pilot froze. Naq'chI shrugged. "What of it?"

"Use the bolt rifles!" She pointed at the massive boulder in the middle of the swollen, muddy river. "Put three anchors with abseil lines into that rock, just under the waterline, right now!" She faced the rest of the team. "We need to buy them every second we can."

D'Gol nodded. "Skirmish line! Here!" He dropped to one knee next to Mara, who snagged Naq'chI's disruptor rifle and fell in beside him. On the other side of D'Gol, Keekur, CheboQ, and Dolaq each took a knee and braced their weapon against their shoulder.

"Aim!" The commander put his eye behind his rifle's targeting sight, and the others on the line did the same. Then came the order: "Fire! And keep firing 'til Fek'lhr takes us all!"

Crimson disruptor pulses lit up the night and tore the jungle to pieces.

Smoke and steam, screeching beam weapons and anguished cries of pain, the stench of burning bodies, the acrid odor of overheating metal. Five warriors with rifles held their ground against five hundred zealots bent on wild violence, even as their weapons overheated in their hands and their emitter crystals fractured under the stress of sustained fire. But to cease fire was to surrender, and to surrender was to die, so into the jaws of death the five went on firing.

Behind Mara, Hartür called out, "Lines secured!"

She and D'Gol both glanced toward the river to confirm that the climbing anchors had been sunk into place, and that the abseil lines were still connected to the three bolt rifles that had fired them. Before Mara could say what she was thinking, D'Gol clearly already knew. Over the din of battle he roared, "Take CheboQ and Dolaq! Hartür, Naq'chI! Get on the line!"

Mara backed off the skirmish line, pivoted around D'Gol, and grabbed CheboQ and Doctor Dolaq. As the three of them scampered toward the river, Naq'chI and Hartür grabbed the rifles from the lab rat and the medic on their way past and took their places on the skirmish line.

The trio stopped at the river's edge. Dolaq started to panic. "Now what?"

Mara used eyelets built into their field uniforms to link herself, Dolaq, and CheboQ to the abseil line of one bolt gun, which she slung around her torso, tightening its strap until it felt like a tourniquet. "Now you hang on. With me!"

She charged into the river, dragging CheboQ and Dolaq with her. Within two steps they plunged into deep, fast-moving water whose brutal current swept them up like leaves—and hurled them over the top of the waterfall.

18

For the briefest moment Mara felt almost weightless, but then came the sickening gut-flop of free fall while immersed in dark, cold, filthy water—

—and then came a spine-cracking jolt of deceleration as she, Dolaq, and CheboQ ran out of slack, before the bolt gun grudgingly paid out a few *qam*s more from its reserve spindle.

Then they dangled, suspended on a filament Mara couldn't even see through the muddy spray, while a crushing weight of water slammed down onto their heads without surcease.

Seconds later, two more bodies plunged through the spray into the violent curtain of falling water, jerking to a halt as their bolt gun reacted: Keekur and Hartür.

Only moments behind them came D'Gol and Naq'chI, a wild tumble stopped by a cruel snap, and then nothing left to do but dangle like a fish on a line.

Mara saw D'Gol open his mouth to shout something to her, but she signaled him with gestures to stay silent, and then she made sure all the others saw the warning as well.

Outside the leaden veil of plunging water, something ominous and black hovered and undulated, slowly twisting and turning . . . *searching*. It was the smoke-serpent looking for the strike team, no doubt wondering whether the Klingons could really have been so crazy as to risk plummeting over a two-hundred-*qam* waterfall in a bid for escape.

It lingered for what felt to Mara like forever, a black tentacle of vapor just weaving back and forth in front of the waterfall. Minute after minute an unbearable torrent of water slammed down onto the strike team, hammering their bodies and knocking their heads and limbs against the moss-slicked rock wall behind them. Even under the steady crush, Mara knew she was bleeding from a fresh wound on her temple, and she could see from the unnatural angles in Keekur's tibia and Naq'chI's ulna that the waterfall had broken them. By now most of them had at least one cracked rib and who knew how many other hidden internal injuries.

They stayed silent and let the waterfall punish them. Not a grunt, not a huff of exertion, not one whispered curse. Just stoic silence, like hooked cuts of meat.

Then the serpent departed in a wild flurry of movement. It sped away downstream and vanished into a cloud bank. From above the strike team there was only the sound of the water. Either the Chwii had suddenly mastered the art of stealth or, more likely, they had given up the hunt and begun the long march back to the cave temple.

Mara exhaled slowly in relief. Every joint and muscle in her body ached, and the abseil line had cut deep gouges into her palms. But that was just pain.

D'Gol took a quick look around and made sure the entire strike team was still alive. Satisfied that no one needed to be cut loose for the good of the group, he gave the signal to head back up, over the waterfall, to shore.

It was going to be a long and excruciating climb for the strike team, each of them pulling their own dead weight up an abseil wire with arm strength alone, while fighting the downward force of the waterfall every *mellqam* of the way.

Defying the weight of the water and the pull of gravity, Mara smiled.

Lucky for us that we are Klingons!

With his nerves wound tighter than a tourniquet, Captain Nassir sat hunched forward in his command chair on the bridge of the *Sagittarius*, waiting for the moment when his tactical officer Lieutenant Faro Dastin would declare—

"*Enterprise* says we're clear!"

Nassir pointed at the image of Kolasi III on the viewscreen. "Go, Sayna!"

At the flight controls of the *Archer*-class scout ship, Lieutenant Celerasayna zh'Firro turned words into action, taking the *Sagittarius* from dead stop to overdrive full impulse in the blink of an eye. Other flight-control officers might have hesitated, but not zh'Firro. Nassir had seen the youthful Andorian *zhen* in action more than enough to know she was as fearless as she was precise, a pilot extraordinaire, an artist whose medium was mass and motion.

Pushing the little ship to its limit was what zh'Firro did best. As she leaned into her console her slender antennae bent slightly forward, and a smile of pure exhilaration lit up her sky-blue face. She lived for speed, daredevil maneuvers, and the thrill of cheating death.

On the viewscreen, the planet's rings seemed to shrink and vanish as zh'Firro adjusted the *Sagittarius*'s angle of approach to be nearly level with the rings' orbital plane. To Nassir it looked almost as if she were piloting them into the edge of a razor.

Then zh'Firro banked the ship to starboard and swung it into an orbital trajectory while placing the vessel beneath the plane of the rings, which now seemed to spread across the top half of the main viewscreen like the dust-strewn surface of an unknown sea. Even when Nassir tried to observe what zh'Firro's hands were doing at the flight controls, her movements were too fast, too ephemeral for him to perceive. She executed two critical course adjustments in a fraction of a second, her work so swift that Nassir could barely tell that it had happened. In her hands, the profession of starship piloting became a fine art.

He was still marveling at the elegance of zh'Firro's technique when she cut the impulse engines and triggered a fast series of stabilizing pulses from the navigational thrusters. In under three seconds she guided the *Sagittarius* into an open pocket of space inside the planet's rings, and then she brought the ship to a graceful stop without disturbing a single chunk of rock or ice with the ship's navigational deflector field. She put her poker face back on as she reported to Nassir, "We're in position, Captain."

Nassir swelled with pride that zh'Firro was his ship's helm officer. *She makes this boat dance like a prima ballerina.* He thumbed open an intraship comm channel using the controls on the arm of his command chair. "Engineering, bridge. Deploy the first mine."

DeSalle's pulse had started racing when he felt the *Sagittarius* leap into motion, its impulse coils straining, its hull juddering under the strain of acceleration. From his post at the master systems display he had thrilled at the spikes in the ship's power levels and velocity. *Man, this bird flies!*

After what had felt like too short a run, the ship came to a halt and the captain's order filtered down from the overhead comm: *"Engineering, bridge. Deploy the first mine."*

He turned from the MSD toward the young Tiburonian enlisted man who stood at the controls for the probe and torpedo launcher. "Torvin, release!"

Torvin pushed one button, and their first jury-rigged gravitic mine was launched with the introduction of a pulse of highly pressurized noble gas inside the tube. Petty Officer Cahow tracked the device's ejection from the ship, while Engineer's Mate Threx monitored data from the device itself. Cahow looked up from her panel to report, "Probe is away and clear."

Threx added, "Probe is on course for deployment point one. Time to target point, eighteen seconds. Sharing telemetry with tactical."

DeSalle opened a reply channel from the MSD. "Bridge, engineering. Probe is away and on course. Stand by for final position adjustments."

Nassir replied, *"Sensor lock confirmed. We'll take it from here."*

———————————

So many moving pieces, so little time. Commander Clark Terrell moved from one bridge station to the next as he tracked the progress of their operation. He paused behind the chair of Lieutenant Dastin. "Easy does it, Faro. Dial down the power on the tractor beam another ten percent, or else you'll jar the mine when you take control. That might be enough to set it off."

"Copy that, sir. Reducing tractor beam power to thirty-five percent. Just a nudge." Faro activated the ship's tractor beam, which gently enveloped the jury-rigged munition in its silvery embrace. "Tractor beam locked, target stable."

Clark leaned in closer. "All right. Like we practiced with the sim."

"I've got it, sir." Faro used the tractor beam to delicately move the gravitic mine inside the chaotic clutter of the rings, into position at the coordinates provided by Lieutenant DeSalle. "Bogey is in place."

"Well done, Faro. Now let's put a little English on it."

The thirtyish Trill man looked up in confusion at Terrell. "Sir?"

"Sorry, old Earth expression. It means impart the requisite degree of backspin."

"Ask and ye shall receive, sir." Executing commands with speed and specificity, Faro triggered three separate microbeams from the tractor beam array, with one of them acting as a repulsor beam, to propel the mine into a molasses-slow tumble-roll that looked random but also helped it maintain its position relative to the myriad hunks of rock and ice that surrounded it.

Task completed, Dastin reclined his chair and let it swivel so he faced Terrell while sporting an impish smile. "Don't say I never gave you nothin'."

"Well done, Lieutenant." Terrell left Dastin and moved back toward the center of the bridge. "Helm, do we have time to fall back to cover before the *SuvwI'* comes around?"

At the helm, zh'Firro checked her readouts and shook her head. "Negative. Tracking data from the *Enterprise* says Kang's ship will be back in range any second."

"Take us forward, full impulse," Terrell said. "Put us on the far side of the planet and the opposite side of the rings from Kang. I want all the cover we can get." He turned toward Lieutenant Sorak, the elderly Vulcan field scout who also served as the ship's second officer. "Alert engineering we need to rig for silent running as soon as we establish an antipodal orbit from the Klingon ship. The less plasma we leave behind for them to detect, the better."

Just then Terrell noticed a sly smile on the captain's face. "Something funny, sir?"

Nassir dismissed the query with a wave of his hand. "Not as such." But then his smirk reasserted itself. "I just can't help but wonder—what will we do if the Klingons decide to invoke their own silent-running protocols? This could all get dicey very quickly."

Terrell sighed. "That's what I love about you, sir. Your boundless optimism."

———————————

At Kirk's request Scott had taken over the sensor hood from Ensign Nanjiani, who sat at the bridge's auxiliary science station while Scott monitored the situation outside the ship.

"*Sagittarius* is underway," Scott said, his attention fixed upon the sensor readout. "She's moving into the Klingons' baffle on the far side of the planet, and matching their speed."

The news came as a relief to Kirk. "Good work, everyone. But we're not out of the woods, yet. Uhura, is there any sign the Klingons know we're using their comm frequency?"

The communications officer shook her head. "None, sir."

"Stay on top of it, Lieutenant. If they're onto us, we'll need to warn the *Sagittarius*."

"Aye, sir."

On the main viewscreen, superimposed on the image of Kolasi III, were icons indicating the relative positions of the *Sagittarius* and the *SuvwI'*, and their projected orbital paths and velocities. The estimated speed for the Klingon ship was an educated guess at best. Kang, who Kirk knew from experience was far smarter than most Klingon starship commanders, was doing all that he could to make his ship's movements hard to anticipate. Tactics such as—

"Klingon ship decelerating!" declared Helm Officer Benson. "Dead slow—correction, holding position above the coordinates for the landing party's mission on the surface."

At comms, Uhura worked with haste while trying to stay calm. "The planet is blocking a clear comm link to the *Sagittarius*, sir. I'm not sure they're reading us."

Kirk got up from his chair and took half a step forward, as if being that tiny bit closer to Kang might reveal the Klingon commander's intentions to him. Staring at the image of the D4 battle cruiser on the viewscreen, he wondered aloud, "What are you up to, Kang?"

Scott sounded worried. "*Sagittarius* is slowing, but not fast enough. Unless they fire braking thrusters in the next eight seconds, they'll slip into the Klingons' sensor range."

Eight seconds. Barely enough time to do anything at all, hardly enough time to make any kind of informed decision. But this was what Starfleet trained its captains to do—make the most of seconds when countless lives were on the line. To know when to act, and when to hold steady.

"Ensign Waltke, load forward torpedo tubes. Do *not* arm torpedoes until I give the order. Prepare to target the Klingon ship manually."

"Aye, sir," Waltke said, entering commands at the forward console. "Torpedoes loaded."

"Hold," Scott called out. "*Sagittarius* has diverted into the rings and fired braking thrusters. She's using a cloud of dust as cover; they're just outside the Klingons' sensor range."

Uhura looked up from the comms console to add, "*Sagittarius* confirms: holding position one hundred twenty-two degrees behind the *SuvwI'*."

Kirk let go of a large held breath. "That was closer than I would have liked."

Lieutenant Benson muted new alerts on the helm console. "The *SuvwI'* is accelerating, sir. She's resuming normal orbital velocity."

"Uhura, alert the *Sagittarius*. Make sure they keep the planet between them and the Klingons. Mister Scott, how long until *Sagittarius* is ready to deploy its next mine?"

Scott looked up from the sensor display and considered that question for a moment. "If all goes to plan, they should have the next one loaded and ready in ten minutes. But it might be another thirty before they have an opportunity for safe launch."

"Is there anything we can do to accelerate that schedule?"

"I'm afraid not, sir. For now we're at the mercy of Captain Kang's tactical whimsy."

"Exactly where I'd rather not be, Scotty."

"That makes two of us, sir." Scott forced a smile onto his face. "But on the bright side? One bogey deployed, only five to go."

Imagining all the havoc Kang could wreak in a fraction of the time it would take to place all of the remaining improvised mines, Kirk frowned. "I'm not sure that qualifies as a 'bright side,' Mister Scott. But we've crossed the Rubicon, so let's not waste time on semantics."

"Understood, sir. As the Bard said in the Scottish play, 'If it were done when 'tis done, then 'twere well it were done quickly.'"

Without awaiting a reply, Scott resumed work at the sensor console, leaving Kirk to return to his command chair and brood over the countless variables of this situation that were utterly beyond his control. Then he reminded himself that control was ever illusory.

I cannot control nature. I cannot control the actions of others. All I can control is how I respond to the actions of others, and to the world around me.

Reflecting on the limitations of free will and responsibility restored a measure of Kirk's calm and gave him the emotional objectivity to ask himself what was really troubling him.

The answer came easily, and as no surprise. *I'm worried about Spock.*

I still feel guilty for not leading the landing party. For putting Spock in danger while I stay on the ship. So many times he and I have taken those risks together, but not this time. There were only so many seats, and—

He stopped himself. *This has nothing to do with how many seats were open. This is about me not wanting to repeat Matt Decker's mistakes. It's about me not wanting to be off the bridge of my ship when she needs me. When my crew needs me.*

It was an unfair comparison. Decker had thought he was doing the right thing when he put his crew ashore. He had thought he was sparing his crew, saving their lives at the cost of his own. But the planet-killer had made a cruel mockery of Decker's noble sacrifice. Instead of a safe haven, the planet had become a soft target after the planet-killer disabled *Constellation.*

I can't blame Matt for wanting to share his crew's fate. But when I think of how close he came to making my crew pay for his guilty conscience . . . I never should have left him alone with my ship and crew. I should've known what he would do.

But how could I have known? How do I know I did the right thing sending Spock with the landing party instead of going my-self? How can I know I'm doing the right thing now, letting Nassir and his crew tempt fate six times in a row, to plant a set of mines that might not even work? What if I've made the wrong choice in each case? What then?

To Kirk's dismay, he knew there was only one answer.

If I've made the wrong choice . . . I'll just have to live with it.

19

Rainfall stronger than a chemistry lab's emergency shower beat down upon the landing party. They stood in a semicircle around the twisted wreck of a small starship they had found at the end of the trail of flattened trees. They had been staring at it in silence for over a minute, and Sulu decided that someone ought to say something, and that it might as well be him.

"I don't know what that is, but it's *not* a Klingon military shuttle."

Ilucci plodded through ankle-deep mud to investigate the vessel's starboard side. "Might not be military, but it's definitely Klingon. These markings are in *pIqaD*, their writing system."

Chekov finished a tricorder scan of the ship. "Based on the density of vegetation colonizing its hull, I would say it has been here for three weeks, maybe four."

The landing party fanned out and surrounded the small ship. Spock regarded its crumpled bow. "A Klingon civilian vessel, crashed in the same manner as the *Heyerdahl*, and in the same general vicinity." He lifted his eyebrows in mild surprise. "Curious."

Along the ship's port side, Chief Razka forced open a bent hatch, which surrendered to his brute force with a piercing shriek of metal grinding against metal. The Saurian leaned inside and swept the interior with a harsh bluish-white palm-light beam. "Mostly dry in here. Minimal signs of jungle intrusion. Power seems to be offline."

Spock shot a look at Chekov, who checked his tricorder before reporting, "No life signs detected inside the vessel, Mister Spock."

Satisfied with the team's reconnaissance of the spacecraft, Spock said, "Proceed with caution, Chief."

"Always, sir." Razka drew his phaser and skulked inside the crash-beaten ship.

Ensign Singh stayed close behind Razka, holding her own phaser steady in front of her. Inside the ship Razka headed aft, while Singh proceeded forward to the command deck.

Spock drew his phaser. "Mister Sulu, stay out here with Doctor Babitz and the master chief until we confirm the ship's interior is secure."

"Aye, sir."

"Mister Chekov, continue scanning with your tricorder and follow me."

"Yes, Mister Spock." Chekov followed close behind Spock as they entered the wreckage of the Klingon civilian vessel—a category of ship that Sulu had never before known existed.

Half a minute later, Sulu's communicator beeped on his hip. He lifted the device and flipped open its antenna grille. "Sulu here."

Spock's voice issued from the communicator. *The ship's interior is clear. Please bring the others inside and meet us on the command deck.*

"Understood." With a flick of his wrist, Sulu closed his communicator. Knowing that Babitz and Ilucci had heard Spock's instructions, he beckoned them toward the ship as he tucked his communicator back into its place on his hip.

Once he and the others were inside, Sulu saw that the ship's interior embodied what he expected of Klingons. It was drab and utilitarian with bare-metal bulkheads and grated deck plates, and its humid air was laced with a pungent funk from stem to stern.

I should just be thankful it doesn't smell like dead bodies.

He led Babitz and Ilucci to the command deck at the ship's bow, which was illuminated by reflected light from Singh's and Spock's palm lights. Much of its forward bulkhead and command console had been destroyed, crushed by the force of the crash landing. Spock and Chekov stood together at a console on the compartment's port bulkhead, while Singh stood off to the other side of the cramped space, keeping watch for trouble.

Chekov held his tricorder in both hands while Spock tinkered with the controls on the console, which stuttered on and off repeatedly. Noting the arrival of fresh faces, Spock looked up expectantly. "Mister Sulu, Master Chief. Are either of you familiar with Klingon power relays?"

Sulu shook his head, but Ilucci said with a half shrug, "I've seen a few."

"Could you assist us, please? We are having trouble maintaining a steady power flow to this console, which we need to access the ship's data banks."

"My pleasure." Ilucci edged his way in front of Chekov, and then he asked Spock, "Can you show me what you've tried so far?"

Spock repeated a sequence of actions on the console's control panel. "I have attempted to correct the irregularity of the power flow by bridging the—"

Ilucci gave the front of the console a swift hard kick. Its master panel lit up, bright and steady. "There ya go. All set."

Dumbfounded, all Spock could say was "Thank you, Master Chief."

Sulu sidled up between Chekov and Spock, who had resumed their efforts to tap into the ship's data banks. "Is the main computer intact?"

"Barely," Chekov said. "I have seen arthritic turtles that run faster than this."

Before Sulu could think up a joke about Russian turtles with which to bother Chekov, Spock said, "The first files are coming through now."

The three of them huddled around Chekov's tricorder as the ensign cycled through the various data files they were recovering from the ship's computer. Most of the written reports were in Klingon script that the tricorder was slow to translate. Then Chekov highlighted a series of documents. "Vid files, Mister Spock. Comm recordings."

"Belonging to whom?"

Chekov scoured the files' metadata. "Doctor Chunvig."

Spock furrowed his brow in concern. "One of the Klingon Empire's leading researchers into xenogenetics and genomic medicine."

That sounded familiar to Sulu. "A peer of Doctor Verdo?"

"More like a bitter rival, Mister Sulu." Spock pointed at the last recording in the system. "Play that back, Mister Chekov."

The ensign opened the recording from the ship's communications system. It appeared as a split screen, with a female *QuchHa'* Klingon on the left—and Doctor Johron Verdo on the right.

The Klingon woman was irate and impatient. *"What do you want, Verdo?"*

"I don't want anything from you, Chunvig. I just want you to listen to reason."

"Why should I trust a word you say? You would do anything to beat me to this."

"I already have, Chunvig, and I'm telling you, it's a disaster waiting to happen."

Chunvig laughed derisively. *"You mean you failed to unlock its secrets!"*

"I know more than you think, Chunvig. I know why you want this sample. But using an RNA splicer to augment yourself with the Shedai meta-genome won't work. Believe me."

"You've always been a coward, Verdo, and a fool. If you had any spine you'd already have bonded with the meta-genome. Instead it will be mine, and once it is, I'll rain down my vengeance on the High Council, the High Command, and all the others who

*tried to tell me the Shedai were just a myth, the meta-genome just
a legend. I'll have my revenge on you all."*

"Chunvig, I'm begging you, please don't do—"

The recording ended, leaving the tricorder's display dark.
Chekov called up the file's metadata and observed, "The conversation was ended by Doctor Chunvig."

Ilucci cleared his throat, drawing the group's attention. He
shot a teasing smirk at Doctor Babitz. "I think you owe the
reputation of Doctor Verdo an apology."

Babitz rolled her eyes. "If we get home alive, I'll send his estate a fruit basket. Mister Spock, it sounds as if Doctor Chunvig
and the Godhead are one and the same. Are any of the files
you've recovered from her work with the meta-genome?"

"Several, it appears."

"If I can have a look at those, I might be able to reverse engineer how she fused her DNA with that of the Shedai. Knowing
that might give us some insight into how to beat her."

"A reasonable presumption. Mister Chekov, send a copy of
Doctor Chunvig's research files to Doctor Babitz's tricorder."

The sound of footsteps from the corridor turned the group's
attention aft, where Chief Razka emerged from the shadows into
the reflected glow of flashlights off the overhead. Spock faced
him and asked, "Are the other sections of the ship secure, Chief?"

"In a manner of speaking," Razka said, somewhat sheepishly.

Only then did Sulu and the others realize that there were
other persons behind Razka, prodding him forward. Sulu
drew his phaser, as did Singh, Spock, and Ilucci. In a matter of
seconds, the landing party found itself face-to-face with seven
armed Klingon military personnel.

The biggest one put his disruptor to the back of Razka's head
and grinned. "I am Commander D'Gol, first officer of the Imperial
battle cruiser *Suvwl'*. And as of now . . . you are all my prisoners."

20

There was only so much stupidity that Mara could take in a single day, and she was well beyond her threshold. "D'Gol, stop being a *yIntagh* and put your weapon down."

He glared at her, manic with bloodlust. "Silence! I am in command!"

"You aren't even in control, never mind command." She stepped in front of his Saurian prisoner so she could look D'Gol in the eye. "You haven't thought this through, have you?"

"Shut up and secure the prisoners!"

"You test my patience, D'Gol. There are seven of them, and seven of us. They have weapons out, as we do, so it seems premature to assume their surrender."

D'Gol started to shake with undirected fury. "They will submit! We are Klingons!"

"Oh, *shut up*. How are we supposed to control seven prisoners? We can't take them with us. They'll slow us down or give us away to the Chwii. Speaking of which, those spear-throwing lunatics are the enemy we have in common, as is that abomination in the temple. So maybe you could remember that only a fool fights in a burning house?"

Mara felt like she was getting through to D'Gol, but she sensed that his pride refused to let him be the first one to back down from a fight. So he just stood there with his disruptor against the Saurian's head, his nostrils flaring, wasting everyone's time.

She stepped to one side so she could address the other members of the strike team. "Weapons down. Holstered or slung. Now. That's an order."

Naq'chI wavered in confusion. "But . . . D'Gol is second-in-command."

"And I am the captain's wife. Who do you think can get you executed faster?"

The rest of the strike team put down their weapons, either slinging them behind their backs or returning sidearms to their holsters. Mara faced the Starfleet team and gestured with her palms toward the floor. "We have common cause. I propose a truce and a parley."

The Vulcan man lowered his phaser, and the rest of the Starfleet team followed his example. That left only D'Gol holding a weapon, to the head of his Saurian prisoner.

Mara leaned close to D'Gol and whispered to him, "Stand down or be *put* down."

D'Gol looked ready to scream, but he lowered his disruptor, holstered it, and then he let his prisoner go. The reptilian biped stepped forward and turned back to find Mara offering him his phaser. With a polite nod, he accepted the return of his phaser, which he put back on his hip.

She stepped forward, and the tall Vulcan moved to meet her. "I am Spock."

"Mara." She glanced at the tricorder held by a short young human man with black hair, and then she asked Spock, "You have accessed this ship's logs?"

"We have."

"Then you know about Doctor Chunvig and her forbidden experiments with the meta-genome. And why her current incarnation as 'the Godhead' must be stopped."

"We would prefer to restore Doctor Chunvig to her original form."

"I doubt the Godhead will permit that. In which case, your

Operation Vanguard would likely insist you try to capture the entity for further study, yes?"

"That is my understanding."

"That is an outcome I will not permit."

Spock gave her a nod. "Very well."

"All right then, to the task at hand. How do we deal with the Godhead?"

The question seemed to stymie Spock, if only momentarily. "Based on our observations, the entity is extremely powerful and undeniably hostile. Like other Shedai, it appears capable of inhabiting and controlling two or more bodies at once, and of coordinating their actions."

"Yes, we've seen that in the jungle. Hartür and I." She gestured at her team's pilot, who nodded in acknowledgment.

To Mara's surprise, Doctor Dolaq stepped forward. "You mentioned trying to revert Doctor Chunvig to her original form. Might that be even remotely possible?"

His question drew a response from a tall, golden-haired human woman. "To be truthful, we're not sure. I've only just started to look at what Doctor Chunvig has done, and to be blunt, I have no idea how to extract her original genetic pattern from the chimeric horror she's become. That doesn't mean it can't be done, but I'd need a lot of time and access to some serious computing power to figure it out."

That answer didn't sit well with CheboQ. "We don't have the time or the facilities for that kind of research. With all due respect, Doctor Dolaq, it will be wiser and more merciful to use the data we have to find this thing's vulnerabilities so we can kill it quickly."

"I concur," Mara said. "It is equally vital that once the Godhead is slain, Doctor Chunvig's and Doctor Verdo's research dies with it."

That request angered the blonde human woman, who seized Spock's arm. "We can't let them do that, Spock. We have orders to recover Doctor Verdo's work."

Spock remained cool and aloof in the face of the woman's protest. "We also had orders to rescue Doctor Verdo, but that objective is no longer possible. By the same token, we should consider his research equally unrecoverable."

"Saving that research is a priority-one directive, Spock."

"Stopping the Godhead is a higher-priority objective, Doctor. One that we cannot achieve without the cooperation of Mara and her fellow Klingons."

"So you're just going to let them erase the work of a man's entire lifetime?"

"In the interest of preserving the fragile state of détente that presently exists between the Federation and the Klingon Empire . . . yes. The needs of the many outweigh the needs of the few, or the one." Spock returned his attention to Mara. "In that same spirit, I will not allow you or any of your people to leave this planet with any of Doctor Chunvig's research."

Mara was impressed by the Vulcan's pragmatism. "I will agree on the condition that we jointly destroy *both* sets of data in their entirety before *either* of us leaves this world."

"Condition accepted." Spock offered Mara his hand, and she shook it.

"Our pact is made and will be honored. Now . . . let's figure out how to kill this thing."

Agreeing on an objective had been fairly simple. Finding consensus on the method for effecting that goal, however, was proving elusive. Much as Spock had suspected might be the case, the ethoses of the Klingon strike team and the Starfleet landing party could not have been more different. The task of devising an attack plan had devolved into its own clash of cultures.

Spock found the Klingons absurdly direct in their thinking, almost to the point of self-parody—a criticism he kept to himself, for the sake of preserving their tenuous alliance.

"A forward assault," D'Gol said, adjusting the positions of small rocks and other bric-a-brac the two teams had assembled to represent their forces, the enemy's forces, and the various natural obstacles and targets involved, including the river and the cave temple. "What we lack in numbers, we make up for in sheer firepower. If we fight as one, we can break the Chwii's defensive perimeter around the cave temple."

Chief Razka waved off that idea. "Charging that line won't work. We'll never pick off all their troops before they bury us in spears."

D'Gol waved his hand over the small stones that represented the Chwii. "We don't need to. We'll raze their entire fighting force from outside spear range. Several continuous beams, sweeping in a crisscross pattern, should open the way."

Mara cleared her throat, drawing a stare from D'Gol. She smiled. "Outside of spear-throwing range, in jungle like this, will mean having no line of sight to target before firing."

"We won't need one. Anyone standing between us and the caves—"

"What makes you think they'll all be standing?" Mara picked up arbitrary stones from their crude diorama. "The Chwii know how to dig in, and how to lurk in the canopy. The moment we break cover to assault the temple, they'll pop out of the ground or skewer us from above."

The Klingon first officer was growing impatient. "If we cannot depend on a surgical strike, we will use more efficient methods. High explosives. Force their ambush troops into the open. Smoke them out of the boughs." He seemed almost giddy as he flashed a broad grin. "It will be *glorious*."

Chekov's mood was souring. "I think your definition of *glorious* differs from ours."

"Agreed," said Ensign Singh. "I'm reasonably sure ours doesn't include wholesale collateral damage and mass civilian casualties."

The female warrior named Keekur cocked her head in confusion. "Why not?"

Sulu breathed a weary sigh. "This is going to take longer than we thought."

D'Gol flung his handful of stones at the planning diorama, and they bounced and rolled like dice. "I hear insults but no ideas! Tell us *your* plan, Starfleet."

Doctor Babitz shouldered her way into the inner circle. "For starters, we should try to limit our use of lethal force to the Godhead, if we can. Perhaps by developing a biological weapon tailored to its genome."

Her counterpart, Doctor Dolaq, shook his head. "We have neither the time nor the facilities to develop such a precise bioweapon. Simpler just to use munitions to implode the cave temple and bring it down on top of the creature."

Babitz rolled her eyes. "A cave-in? To kill a thing that can turn its body into smoke? So much for the myth of Klingons as tactical geniuses."

Before the conversation could degrade further into a brawl, Spock interjected, "An equally pressing concern regarding that plan is the high number of Chwii casualties it would likely inflict. If we do intend to eliminate the Godhead inside its temple, it would be preferable to find a way to first evacuate its civilian minions."

The Klingon pilot, Hartür, spit on the diorama. "Why in the name of Fek'lhr would we do that? If the little shriekers didn't want to die in battle, they shouldn't have taken up arms."

Spock found the Klingon's argument unpersuasive. "The available evidence suggests the Godhead forces these primitive beings into its service. If they are unwilling conscripts, they are more properly considered its victims than its allies. Furthermore, their status as members of a pre-warp culture entitles them to significant protections under the Prime Directive."

Mara dismissed Spock's argument with a derisive snort. "Ridiculous. What difference does it make why your enemy tries to kill you? A spear thrown by a slave kills just as well as one hurled by a champion. And their lack of technological development is certainly no defense. A stone to your skull can be as deadly as a disruptor beam. You make up so many excuses for why you cannot use your power. You talk yourselves into the jaws of defeat."

She picked up a fistful of stones and added them to the diorama, in front of the large rock that signified the cave temple. "An army stands between us and the Godhead. An army that serves it with fanatical devotion. Who cares whether that loyalty was born of love or fear? It is an armed force sworn to our destruction. It has a massive advantage in numbers and experience with the local terrain. Destroying it deprives the Godhead of one of its already numerous advantages, and brings us one step closer to completing our mission. Why is this up for debate?"

"Yeah," said Ilucci, "that darned Prime Directive is just so pesky and inconvenient, isn't it? If not for that, we could just slaughter pre-warp cultures willy-nilly, just for laughs. I mean, except for that whole 'having empathy and a conscience' thing we get hung up on."

Mara glared at the engineer. "You speak as if we are ignorant of your culture and your laws. I know the text of your Prime Directive. I'm familiar with the incidents from your history that led to its adoption, and I know from experience how Starfleet and the Federation tend to apply it in practice. Nothing in its letter or its spirit prohibits you from acting in self-defense, even against foes of greatly inferior technological ability.

"Furthermore, the principal intention of your Prime Directive is to prevent *cultural contamination* that can affect the social or technological development of a pre-warp culture. I would argue that the Chwii who have fallen under the control of the Godhead have already been hopelessly contaminated. Their social order has been upended and their way of life perverted into one of service to a mad demigod. But our past surveys of this world have shown that there are several disparate clusters of Chwii spread across this continent, and others dwelling on the islands of an archipelago chain. The majority of them have not, as of yet, been affected by the presence of the Godhead. But if the creature is allowed to grow in power, its reach will expand to encompass this entire world, and all those who dwell upon it.

"If I apply the principles of your Prime Directive, preventing the spread of the Godhead's influence, by destroying it and all those it has contaminated, would be to the benefit of those Chwii elsewhere on this planet who are not yet tainted. Therefore, eliminating the Godhead and its minions would be a step toward restoring this world's pre-contact status quo—a goal that is not only consistent with but arguably even *required* by your Prime Directive."

All of the gathered members of both teams stood, squatted, or sat in stunned silence in the wake of Mara's calmly expounded argument.

Spock favored Mara with a nod. "Logical."

Hours later, the air inside the Klingon science vessel had grown warm and heavy from a surfeit of conversation, but at long last a sketch of a plan was taking shape. Outside the ship night had fallen, bringing with it an increase in the ferocity of the rain, which rattled the crashed ship's hull with a sound like ceaseless machine-gun fire.

All Doctor Babitz wanted to do was sleep, but the group's collective need to finalize the plan of attack kept her awake and focused. She tapped the stone that signified the Godhead. "The greatest threat posed by our friend in the cave is its ability to inhabit and control multiple bodies in different locations simultaneously. Even when we're facing off with it inside the cave, part of it might be elsewhere. When we frag this thing, we need to make damned sure we get *all* of it."

The Klingon science officer, Lieutenant Mara, was taking notes. "How many bodies can these things control at once?"

"It varies. Elite Shedai can direct dozens of bodies at a time, even in distant star systems when they have an active Conduit through which to project their consciousness. The less-powerful named Shedai might be able to handle up to eight forms at a time. And their foot soldiers, the ones they call 'the Nameless,' are limited to one form at a time."

Singh asked, "Where does the Godhead fall on this spectrum?"

"No idea. But we know from Doctor Chunvig's logs that it's not a true Shedai but some kind of Klingon-Shedai hybrid. I suspect that might curtail some of its abilities, at least during this early stage of its existence. The longer it lives, the more powerful it's likely to become."

Mara grouped three black stones on the diorama. "Hartür and I have seen the Godhead moving as three different smoke-serpents, searching the jungle. It's possible it might have had more forms searching elsewhere, but for now we can set the lower end of our estimate at three."

Babitz looked over her shoulder at Spock. "Sir, do you recall how many discrete streams of vapor entered the cave temple when the Godhead reconstituted itself?"

He looked away as he searched his memory. "At least four. Possibly five."

"All right, so if we assume the Godhead was fully present when it confronted us, we can make an educated guess that the upper limit of its number of active bodies is five."

Mara placed one black stone on top of the rock denoting the caves. "Based on some of our past encounters with Shedai, I think the Godhead is also hiding a master form of some kind, inside the temple. It projects itself outward from there, but I think its core self stays behind."

This hypothesis snared Spock's interest. "Why? Is it unable to fully project itself out of the temple? Or is it afraid to do so?"

"The former, we suspect," Mara said. "A consequence of its hybrid nature."

Spock raised an eyebrow. "You've seen this before."

D'Gol interjected, "That's classified." For emphasis he shot a glare at Mara, who frowned at his rebuke but acquiesced all the same.

Babitz, however, was unable to stop thinking about what Mara's offhand comment might imply. "This is interesting. And it would match up with what we've seen of the Shedai so far. From what Lieutenant Theriault told me, the elite Shedai don't actually have true forms, only 'shapes of the moment,' as they call them. But now that you mention its limitation, the behavior of its vapor streams inside the cave temple makes more sense. They flowed out of cracks in the floors and walls, as if they were bound to that place. So it's a good bet its core consciousness resides somewhere inside that cave complex.

"But we need to make sure none of its smoke forms are off roaming the jungle when we hit it. We need to be sure it's all in one place so we can take it down in one shot."

Naq'chI tapped the cave stone with her *d'k tahg*. "Hitting it where it lives might be the best way. If this primary shape or whatever you call it is stuck in there, and we hit it hard enough, it might pull back its other shapes to protect itself. Right?"

Mara nodded. "Yes, maybe. It's equally possible that if we do enough damage to its principal form, it might lose its ability to project itself into ancillary forms. Either way, concentrating our attack on its master form is likely the key to killing it."

Hartür grinned. "So it's settled. We corner it, then we fry it 'til it smokes."

From a corner of the compartment, Razka asked, "With what?" He waited until the room turned toward him, and then he continued. "We've seen Shedai absorb phaser beams. Disruptor pulses bounce off them like they were rubber. And we've already noted we can't just bring the roof down on this thing and expect to call it a day. Small arms are not going to get this job done. What are we taking inside the cave temple that can actually do more than tick this thing off?"

D'Gol answered, "We have plasma demolition charges."

"That might work. What else?"

Singh offered, "We have plasma grenades."

The scout made a rasping sound as his forked tongue tasted the air. "We'll have better odds with the demo charges. Mister Spock, do we have spare phasers in our shuttle?"

"Negative. The secondary and tertiary arms lockers were removed as part of the refit for this mission. I presume you intend to fashion grenades from phasers set to induce a prefire-chamber feedback overload?"

"Not anymore."

Keekur spoke with the hesitant manner of someone who didn't know whether they were supposed to keep something a secret but had chosen to talk anyway. "We have some heavy-duty plasma autocannons hidden in the bush near the bridge to the temple. They pack a real punch. If we can recover them, Naq'chI and I can haul them in. They'll cut through rock like a *d'k tahg* through *juuk* fat. I'd be willing to bet they'll put a hole in that abomination."

Babitz clapped her hands together. "*That's* what I'm talking about. Let's go get those autocannons and cut the Godhead down to size!"

The Klingons roared in approval, but from behind her Babitz heard Singh grumble in her ear, "Nice plan, Doc. Let's see if it survives contact with the enemy."

21

Five down, one to go. It had been a long day on the bridge of the *Enterprise*, one of the longest Kirk had spent in some time, and it wasn't over yet. Exhausted but too keyed up to stay seated, he paced behind Benson and Waltke at the forward console, his attention fixed upon the tactical diagram superimposed over the image of Kolasi III on the main viewscreen.

His voice was sharper than he intended as he asked Scott, "Are they in position yet?"

"Not yet, sir." Scott did a better job of masking his fatigue than Kirk had, but it was clear that after nearly two full back-to-back duty shifts, the entire bridge crew was tired and on edge. Monitoring the cat-and-mouse game being played in orbit by the *Sagittarius* against the Klingon battle cruiser had been a case study in prolonged anxiety. Against all odds, the little scout ship had evaded detection for several hours, timing its deployment runs based on when Kang's ship seemed to be in one of its extended slow-cruise modes.

Kirk had expected to wait several minutes or even an hour between the launch and placement of each munition. He had not anticipated the degree to which Kang would commit to his tactic of random orbital velocity and position. Four times already the *SuvwI'* had nearly caught the *Sagittarius* in mid-deployment. Since then Nassir had become cautious nearly to the point of paralysis, a reaction that annoyed Kirk even though he understood it.

Coming that close to getting killed could spook anybody. Bad enough Nassir and his people are on such a tiny ship, but the need to do these runs without shields? It's like asking them to take six consecutive turns in a game of Russian roulette.

Benson muted an alert on the helm. "The *SuvwI'* has slowed to one-tenth impulse."

Hopeful, Kirk asked, "What's her position?"

"Far side of the planet, sir. They're also increasing their orbital distance and maneuvering to come around above the rings on their next pass."

That was the break Kirk needed. "Uhura, tell *Sagittarius* to go now!"

As she relayed his order via her improvised squelch channel, Kirk left the command well to stand behind Scott. "Now for the hard part. If they're lucky, they'll have that mine deployed in ninety seconds. Then the question becomes: Do we tell them to lie low for who-knows-how-many-more passes of the *SuvwI'*? Or do we tell them to make a run for it and hope we can regroup under cover before the Klingons spot us?"

"I'm running the numbers now," Scott said, keying in figures and formulas at the auxiliary science station. "Factoring in their best sublight speed . . . the increased distance between the deployment zone and our cover since we started this . . . and assuming the *SuvwI'* holds her current speed . . ." He frowned and looked up at Kirk. "It'll be one hell of a close shave, sir."

"I don't care, I want them out of there."

"Unless they lock down that mine in the next fifteen seconds, they won't—"

Uhura cut in, "*Sagittarius* reports the last mine is in place."

"Tell them to make a run for it, now!"

Uhura swiveled her chair back toward her console as Nanjiani called out from the science station, "Captain! Sensors read a surge of ionized gas particles on the far side of the planet! I think the Klingons are accelerating to full impulse!"

"Uhura! Belay my last! Tell Nassir to take cover!" Kirk stared at the main viewscreen, his heart pounding, sweat beading on his forehead. *Damn you, Kang.*

On the viewscreen, a tiny spark emerged from beyond the curve of the planet's northern hemisphere. It was so fast that it was almost a streak on the screen rather than a moving point. Kirk's pulse quickened, and he closed his hands into fists.

Kang is playing games with me. He knows we're here. Or at least, he suspects it. Either way, he knows we'd need to use the moon for cover, so he's timing his maneuvers based on what parts of the planet's orbit we're unable to see with our sensors at any given time. Clever bastard.

Kirk looked at Nanjiani, who continued to peer into the hooded sensor readout as if it held the secrets of life and death. *Which at this moment,* Kirk realized, *it very well might.*

"Mister Nanjiani, do you have a fix on the *Sagittarius*?"

The young Pakistani man pretended to fine-tune his station's controls, as if Kirk wouldn't recognize the telltale signs of a young officer procrastinating while searching for something they thought the commanding officer wanted to hear. "Um . . . negative, sir. They appear to have gone dark somewhere inside the rings."

"*Inside the rings?*" That was not what Kirk had expected to hear. He had assumed Nassir would make a run for the planet's southern pole, to make use of its magnetic field and the intervening sensor obstruction of the rings themselves.

As if he had heard Kirk's puzzled thoughts, Scott interjected, "It makes sense, sir. They wouldn't have reached the polar magnetic field in time."

"So what are they doing? Just drifting, dead and cold?"

Scott looked as surprised as Kirk felt. "That'd be my guess."

From the navigator's post, Waltke looked over at Scott and Kirk. "Sirs? Even powered down, the *Sagittarius* is still a big hunk of duranium floating in a field of rock and water ice. Is it really possible the Klingons won't notice them?"

What could Kirk say without harming morale? "Anything's *possible*, Ensign."

"Aye," Scott said under his breath, "but is it likely?"

A mounting dread left Kirk feeling hollow and nauseated as he pondered the myriad ways this situation could take turns for the worse. "Ask me again in an hour, Scotty."

Somewhere in the dark that filled the *Starship Sagittarius*, a sharp *crack* like the breaking of a fragile bone was followed by a swiftly brightening green luminance: an emergency chemical glow stick came to life as its binary fuel components mixed inside its now bent shell, throwing sickly light onto everything in Commander Clark Terrell's immediate vicinity.

Other members of the bridge crew ignited their own glow sticks by giving them a quick bend in the middle, producing the satisfying *snap* of cylinders fracturing inside the transparent flexible sheath. Most of the sticks were the same ugly hue of chartreuse as Terrell's, but a few had clean white light, which he knew would prove invaluable during repairs.

Maintenance would have to wait. For now, they needed to leave the ship as it was: dark and cold. On the advice of recent transfer Ensign Jamal, Captain Nassir had taken a huge risk. Knowing there was no way to get back behind the planet's moon or to its previous safe havens inside the planet's rings before being detected by the Klingon ship's sensors, he had ordered zh'Firro to dive the ship into the rings and make an emergency all-stop.

At which point he had ordered DeSalle to kill the power. All of it. Warp, impulse, batteries, the whole kaboodle. And he'd done it in a tone that made it clear he wasn't looking for a debate.

Now the *Sagittarius* was adrift in the rings of Kolasi III, a slave to its momentum, the planet's gravity, and whatever random hunks of ice or stone slammed into them. They had no propulsion. No comms or sensors. No life-support. Not even lights or artificial gravity.

Around Terrell the bridge crew floated in the dim radiance of their glow sticks. Everyone was trying to stay in the vicinity of their station, even though all the consoles were dark. At the starboard stations, Dastin and Sorak seemed to be handling the situation well. On the other side of the bridge, Ensign Jamal was doing her best to help stanch the bleeding of a head injury sustained by Ensign Taryl. In the center of the bridge, Captain Nassir hovered above his command chair, while zh'Firro, who had pressed her face into her palms, remained rooted in front of the helm by virtue of having wrapped her legs around the pedestal base of her chair.

I'd better check on her first.

Terrell pushed off a bulkhead, and then off the overhead, to set himself on a course to zh'Firro's side. He caught the edge of the helm console and halted himself beside the young Andorian *zhen.* "Sayna? You all right?"

"I'm fine," she said from behind her hands. "I just hate being blind and unable to move."

"I presume you're talking about the ship."

"When I'm flying, I *am* the ship. You know that."

"It's gonna be okay, Sayna. I promise. Hang in there." He gave her a friendly pat on her shoulder, and then he moved portside, to check on Dastin and Sorak.

When he was closer to them, Terrell realized that Dastin was hyperventilating and that Sorak was holding the young Trill man by one arm while he gently pressed a few fingers of his right hand to the man's left temple. Terrell dropped his voice to a hush as he asked, "Sorak? What're you doing?" He wasn't surprised when Sorak ignored him.

Seconds later, Dastin's breathing slowed to a normal rhythm, and Sorak removed his hands from the tactical officer. When Dastin opened his eyes, Sorak asked him, "Better?"

The Trill gave the elderly Vulcan a smile. "Much. Thank you." To their perplexed first officer Dastin explained, "I had a panic attack when the gravity went out. Sorak shared some of his *Kolinahr* discipline with me, just until I calmed down. I'm okay now, sir. I promise."

"All right, then. Carry on." A firm believer in not trying to fix what wasn't broken, Terrell took his officers at their word and headed for the other side of the bridge.

He was halfway there when someone forced open the door to the bridge: it was medical technician Tan Bao and their temporary CMO, Doctor M'Benga. The physician asked, "Does anyone here need medical help?"

Jamal raised her hand, pointed at Taryl, and replied, "Over here, sir."

M'Benga and Tan Bao pushed off from the door's jamb and soared across the bridge, one at a time, to the injured Orion woman's side. Satisfied that they had matters on the bridge well in hand, Terrell caught the back of Nassir's chair and looked up at his commanding officer. "Sir, I'd like to head aft to check on engineering."

Nassir gave him a nod. "Go."

Another push and Terrell was out the door, into the oval corridor of the main deck. He had never been fond of zero-gravity training exercises as a cadet, but he had been grateful for them more than once during his years in Starfleet. He caromed gently off the bulkheads as he proceeded aft to the ladderway, which led up to the engineering deck or down to the cargo deck. On his way he passed the open doorway to the ship's science lab, where Lieutenant Vanessa Theriault was working to make sure the lab's equipment and samples were all secure.

Terrell caught the ladder, halted himself, and with one strong pull sent himself up through the open hatchway to the engineering deck. He caught a safety handle at the top of the ladder and awkwardly swung himself around the corner to join Lieutenant

DeSalle at the ship's master systems display. "Lieutenant, status report."

DeSalle sleeved some sweat and grime from his brow. "That emergency shutdown fried a few control rods in the impulse reactor, and the warp core's gonna be a bear to restart. As for the rest? I won't know how much damage we did to the relays or the rest of the grid until we power back up and see what blows out."

"Injuries?"

The acting chief engineer picked up a palm light and swung it around the long engineering compartment, halting briefly upon each of the engineers: Threx, Torvin, and Cahow. "Negative, sir. All present and accounted for."

"Are you sure about that, Lieutenant?"

The question confused DeSalle. To help him out, Terrell dipped his chin to direct the man's attention downward. When DeSalle turned the palm light upon himself, it illuminated a pen-like metallic rod—a spare part left over from a modified torpedo—wedged into his flank, and a large bloodstain swiftly spreading away from it and down his trouser leg.

Perhaps because he was in shock, DeSalle didn't seem at all alarmed. "That's just a flesh wound, sir. Throw a little dermagen on there and I'll be good as new."

"Lieutenant, you're surrounded by a floating bubble of your own blood. About two pints' worth, I'd say. You're relieved of duty. Report to sickbay *immediately*."

"All right, sir. If you say . . ." DeSalle's eyes fluttered closed as he lost consciousness.

Terrell caught the man. "Mister Threx! You have the deck. Crewman Torvin, take the lieutenant to sickbay!"

Torvin pushed off the cold warp reactor with his feet and shot himself like a missile down the length of the deck. He wrapped his arms around DeSalle, pulled him from Terrell's grasp, and nimbly maneuvered around Terrell toward the ladderway while carrying the man.

"It's okay, sir, I've got him." The slender young Tiburonian man sent himself and DeSalle down the ladderway together, and in a blur they were gone.

Threx and Cahow floated over to Terrell's side at the master systems display. Threx wiped some of DeSalle's blood off the MSD with his sleeve. "Y'know, sir, he'd have been fine for another half hour if you hadn't said anything."

"Sure, Threx. At which point he'd have been dead instead of unconscious. Do you and Cahow need an extra set of hands up here 'til Torvin gets back?"

Threx shook his head. "No, sir. We're good." The Denobulan flashed a broad smile behind his ragged beard. "Not much we can do 'til skipper says turn the power back on."

"I suppose that's—"

A deafening boom rang the ship's hull like a hammer on a bell. Terrell and the engineers caromed off every hard surface like dice shaken inside a cup. He caught Cahow in midair and held on to her, hoping to use himself as a shield to protect her from further impacts.

As their bodies ran out of momentum, the resonance of the collision was joined by the groans of wrenching hull plates both above and below. Terrell noticed Cahow's hair smelled like reactor coolant as she trembled in his arms while looking around in terror at their shaken vessel.

Her voice was a stressed whisper: "Holy *hell* that was loud."

"It's okay, Cahow. Sound doesn't carry in space."

She scowled at him. "Then why are you whispering too?"

"Touché." He let go of Cahow and looked around for any obvious signs of serious damage. "As long as the hull wasn't breached, we should be—" He froze as he looked up through a viewport in the engineering deck's bulkhead and saw the *I.K.S. SuvwI'* cruising above them in all its predatory majesty. "Oh, no. Please, no. . . . *Damn it.*"

Cahow and Threx both looked up. She asked, "What's wrong, sir?"

Terrell's heart sank. "They're *slowing down*. Right above us."

Repetition had leeched the vitality from Kang's body and stolen the edge from his focus. Too many hours spent staring at the same stars, the same dusty rings, the same blank sensor screens. He had learned young that hunting often required patience. The ability to wait out one's prey. But at this point the mission no longer felt like a hunt. Now he was just . . . waiting.

Anticipation was among the cruelest of states. It was expectation married to hope, but all too often repaid with disappointment. His keen eyes had searched the emptiness of space and the impenetrable belt of storm clouds that ringed Kolasi III in search of a rival that refused to appear.

Damn you, Kirk. I'd hunt you properly if only my superiors would allow it.

The inaction his circumstances had imposed upon him was its own punishment. His heart yearned to race, his hands wanted to swing a *bat'leth*, his senses craved the scent of blood and the cries of his vanquished foes. Every part of him that was Klingon had to be denied, all so he could . . . just *sit here* in his command chair.

Maintaining a stoic façade taxed his patience when his blood burned to take action, any action, just to feel as if he were doing something more than watching time slip through his hands.

He wanted to tell Qovlar to hail the strike team for an update, despite the near impossibility of getting a signal through the storm, but he knew that would do more harm than good. If there was something the strike team needed to know, it might merit the effort. But just to ask them for an update?

If there was anything worth knowing, D'Gol would have con-

tacted the ship, and Qovlar would have alerted me. Pestering them can only make me look anxious. Fearful. Weak.

The stillness that surrounded Kang was maddening. He wanted to leave the command chair, stalk from one station to the next, and check each one for himself. Every ship's crew harbored at least one incompetent and likely more. Who was to say his ship's dull blades weren't on the bridge, missing the clues that would lead them to glorious victory?

But that was a fool's errand. Every gunner, every sensor officer, every warrior on his bridge knew what he wanted, and they all knew that rich rewards awaited the one who brought it to him. If any of them had even suspected they had found something of note, they would have fallen over one another in a rush to be the first to bring it to Kang's attention.

Hectoring them would only distract them and waste everyone's time. That would be the error of a novice, not the action of a seasoned starship commander.

And so Kang suffered the long seconds, the endless minutes, the interminable hours that stretched out behind and ahead of him, leaving him islanded in a sea of boredom.

At least the rings blur past more smoothly now.

Just for the sake of variety, Kang had ordered Larzal to widen the *SuvwI*'s orbit to allow for an increase in orbital velocity to twenty *qams* per second, nearly three times faster than the standard. In hours past, he had been able to discern individual rocks and hunks of ice in the planet's rings. Now it all bled together into a prismatic blur on the viewscreen.

What did I think this would yield? Did I really think a sudden leap in speed would flush out Kirk and his precious Enterprise? *That I'd catch them in orbit by surprise?*

The only satisfaction the maneuver had given Kang had been a momentary thrill of hard acceleration as the ship's inertial dampers lagged a fraction of a second behind the sudden kick of the impulse engines. A small and fleeting pleasure, to be sure, but he had reached the point of being grateful for such moments to break up the monotony of—

A *ping* of sensor contact sounded from a gunner's console to Kang's right.

He turned his chair and fixed the junior officer with a fierce stare. "Report!"

Gunner's Mate Joghur tensed like a prey animal hearing the growl of a *targ*. He double-checked his readout, and then his shoulders sagged in disappointment. "False alarm, Captain. Just a collision of ice and metallic rock inside the rings ahead of us. Nothing there."

"All stop!" Kang stood from his chair, energized. "Charge all weapons! Raise shields! Gunner's Mate, send your sensor data to tactical. Boqor, get me a visual on-screen, full magnification!" Kang's pulse pounded in his ears. This was the first hint of action he and his crew had seen in days. False alarm or not, he wasn't going to waste an opportunity for training.

The image on the viewscreen shifted to an enlarged area of the planet's rings. They scintillated in the daylight like a sea of jewels. Kang searched the rings' brilliant beauty for any sign of his enemy, but all he found were boulders and icebergs tumbling against one another in their orbit of Kolasi III. "Tactical. Any power readings?"

Boqor reviewed her console's readouts with care. "None, Captain. All cold."

Kang's instincts told him there was something there, but all of his ship's sensors told him there wasn't. Doubts darkened his thoughts and dimmed his confidence. *Am I trying to find a battle where none exists? Perhaps I should get some sleep.*

"Captain?" Boqor left the tactical console to stand in front of Kang's elevated chair. "Do you want to initiate a search-and-destroy pattern?"

It was not an unreasonable suggestion, but putting it into action would be tedious, at best. Executing a search-and-destroy operation would mean scouring the same patch of the rings for hours, bombarding it with targeted spreads of torpedoes, sweeping it with disruptor beams . . . and for what?

Kang peered at the rings. They were fairly dense, but nowhere near enough to conceal a *Constitution*-class starship. It was more likely the gunner's mate had detected a chunk of rock with trace amounts of heavy elements as it struck a ball of ice. If the *Enterprise* were anywhere inside the rings, it would be easily visible even without sensors, and that volume of duranium would be impossible to conceal at such short range.

Fek'lhr's beard, I'm chasing a nIyma.

He settled back into the command chair. "Screen to forward view. Drop shields, weapons to standby. Resume standard orbit. Continue to scan for any sign of the *Enterprise*."

Boqor returned to the tactical station without further comment, leaving Kang to reflect in peace. *You have me chasing shadows, Kirk. But I'm not done seeking your trail. Not yet.*

He imagined what his nemesis might be doing at that moment and had a flash of inspiration—one he intended to investigate during the *SuvwI'*'s next orbit.

You think you've outsmarted me, Kirk? Prepare to be proved wrong.

Silence freighted with dread reigned on the *Enterprise*'s bridge. All eyes were on the main viewscreen, which displayed a magnified image of the Klingon battle cruiser *SuvwI'*. Without apparent cause it had slowed its orbit and then halted almost directly above the last known coordinates of the *Sagittarius*.

Watching from the command chair, all Kirk could do was stew in his own anxiety. Sweat built up inside his clenched fists and waves of nausea folded over one another in his gut. If the Klingons had found the *Sagittarius*, the next move would be Kang's. The *SuvwI'* could vaporize the tiny *Archer*-class scout ship in an instant with one shot from its forward disruptor cannons or a single torpedo, long before the *Enterprise* could possibly intervene.

Or, Kirk realized, *Kang could beam up its crew and take the ship in tow.*

That was a scenario Kirk knew he could not allow. The *Sagittarius* was one of the newest ships in Starfleet, a state-of-the-art long-range reconnaissance vessel, made for speed and stealth. Kirk and his crew would be required by Starfleet regulations to destroy the *Sagittarius* rather than permit the Klingons to capture it for reverse engineering.

Let's just hope it doesn't come to that.

Scott approached Kirk's chair and kept his voice at a discreet volume. "The Klingons are running routine sensor sweeps—so far. But if they switch to an intensive search pattern—"

"We'll need to intervene. Yes, Mister Scott, I'm well aware."

There were so many steps Kirk wanted to take in preparation, but he knew most of them would intensify his ship's thermal and electromagnetic signatures and increase the risk of the *Enterprise* being detected by the Klingons. Tactically, the smart choice was to keep a low profile.

All he wanted to do was face off with Kang, consequences be damned.

He took a deep breath. *What I want isn't important. What matters is the mission, my crew, my ship, and everyone aboard the* Sagittarius. *I'm here to serve the Federation, not my ego.*

Nanjiani piped up, sounding optimistic for a change. "Captain, the Klingon ship is resuming standard orbital velocity. They've powered down their weapons and dropped shields."

Kirk exhaled in relief, and he heard others do the same around him. All the same, he kept his fists closed until the *SuvwI'* disappeared beyond the curve of the planet, and then he opened his hands and wiped them dry on his trouser legs. *That was too close.*

He turned toward Uhura. "Lieutenant, can you raise the *Sagittarius*?"

"Negative, sir. They lost comms when they shut down their power."

That posed a new wrinkle. "Mister Scott, how do we give *Sagittarius* the all clear if they have no comms? For that matter, how do we warn them if the *SuvwI'* makes another fast run?"

Scott looked at the main viewscreen with an intense expression. Apparently, he hadn't considered that question until this moment. "Aye, that's a problem."

Inspiration brightened Uhura's expression. "If we destroy the Klingons' jamming buoy, we're close enough to hail the *Sagittarius* crew via their communicators."

"Aye, lass, but we'd also be announcing our presence to the Klingons."

Kirk resigned himself to the obvious. "I think that cat's out of the bag, Scotty." He swiveled his chair toward the viewscreen. "Benson, adjust our position to give us a clean shot. Waltke, target the buoy with phasers and fire at will. Uhura, as soon as the buoy's gone, send a coded, tight-beam emergency signal to the *Sagittarius* crew's communicators. Tell them to power up and get the hell out of there."

His crew snapped into action, their efforts coordinated like clockwork. In a matter of seconds Benson maneuvered the *Enterprise* just far enough from the moon for Waltke to lock phasers onto the buoy, which he destroyed with a single full-power burst. Uhura sent the prerecorded signal to the *Sagittarius*—and then all Kirk could do was track the *SuvwI'* on a tactical readout while waiting to see if the *Sagittarius* was still operational.

Come on, Nassir. Get your people out of there . . .

Just when Kirk thought he would need to tell Uhura to belay his last order to *Sagittarius*, the tiny ship surged back to life. Rolling and yawing, it freed itself from its shallow grave in the planet's rings, pointed its nose toward the *Enterprise*, and jumped to maximum impulse. Even knowing full well what the ship could do, Kirk still felt a swell of admiration tinged with envy as the scout ship shot toward his, quite possibly setting a Starfleet speed record as it did so.

Damn, that little ship really moves.

Nanjiani crowed, "*Sagittarius* is back behind cover!"

"Helm, put us back in the moon's magnetic shadow."

"Already halfway there, sir," Benson replied.

The tactical display, which now had telemetry from the *Enterprise*'s previously deployed sensor buoy, showed the *SuvwI'* coming back around the planet for another pass.

As Kirk expected, the Klingon battle cruiser immediately slowed its orbit. "It would appear Captain Kang and his crew have just figured out we destroyed their jamming buoy."

Concern put a touch of vibrato in Ensign Waltke's voice. "Do you think they'll break orbit and come after us?"

Hoping to allay the navigator's understandable fear, Kirk said, "I wouldn't if I were him. Right now he has the advantage of controlling the orbital space, and we've betrayed our presence, so we've lost the element of surprise—not that I really think we ever had it." Kirk looked back at Uhura. "Any signal activity on their channel, Lieutenant?"

She put her hand to the transceiver in her ear, listened, and then shook her head. "None, Captain. All quiet on the Klingons' main frequencies."

"All right. Hail the *Sagittarius* via the semaphore system. Offer them help with damage control and have engineering get them what they need. Mister Scott, we've all had a long day. I think it's time we all get whatever rest we can before our landing party tries to come home."

"Aye, sir. I'll bring in the B-team."

Kirk took a moment to rub his itching eyes and massage his

throbbing temples while Scott summoned the third-shift bridge crew to relieve the weary first-shift crew who had pulled double duty. He doubted he would get much rest while knowing Spock and the landing party were still in danger, but he owed it to them to try to be at his best when they needed him.

Less than a minute after Scott had put out the call, the turbolift doors opened, and six officers poured out, all of them rested, fresh, and ready. Kirk waited until all the other officers had been relieved before he stood and faced his relief, a short man with deep brown skin and close-cut black hair wearing a gold command tunic—and froze. "Lieutenant Elliot, isn't it?"

"Aye, sir," Elliot replied in a rich baritone.

"You were part of the damage-control team on the *Constellation*."

"Yes, sir. I helped Mister Scott cross-circuit the warp and impulse controls."

Kirk nodded and clasped Elliot's upper arm. "I remember. You did good work that day. I'm glad you were with us."

"Thank you, sir."

From the turbolift, Scott cleared his throat to remind Kirk that they were holding the lift car for him. Abashed, Kirk got his mind off the planet-killer and back on his duty. "The *Sagittarius* is done deploying munitions into the planet's rings. We've had no contact with our landing party, and a lack of traffic on Klingon frequencies suggests they've had no contact with theirs. We've destroyed their comms-jamming buoy, but the Klingons might deploy another at any time, so maintain alternative communication channels. No other vessels have been detected in the system, all decks are secure, yellow alert is in effect."

"Understood, Captain. I relieve you."

"I stand relieved. Mister Elliot, you have the conn."

Kirk left the command chair to Elliot and joined the rest of the first-shift team inside the turbolift. As soon as he stepped in, Scott told the computer, "Deck three," and gave the throttle a turn, sending the lift car into a smooth, quiet descent. Within moments it arrived on deck three, and the doors slid open. Stepping out, Kirk paused to give his officers an encouraging smile.

"Sleep fast, everyone. Tomorrow's coming a lot sooner than we'd like."

22

An hour before dawn, the jungle of Kolasi III looked pretty much the same as it did an hour after midnight: pitch dark, filled with stinging rain one couldn't see from clouds that blocked out even the faintest traces of moonlight. Never in his young life had Chekov so missed seeing the stars. He knew they were still there, beyond the roiling stormhead, but they felt impossibly far away.

The mixed Klingon-Starfleet landing party spread out as it reached the edge of the jungle nearest the bridge to the cave temple. For most of the journey, Chekov had barely been able to see where he or anyone else was going. Like most of the human members of the landing party, he had been required to put his trust in the Klingons and in Senior Chief Petty Officer Razka.

Before that night, Chekov had not known that both Saurians and Klingons possessed night vision superior to that of humans, in addition to having keener auditory senses and more refined olfactory receptors. He found it hard to explain to Mister Spock why he took no comfort in knowing that both Saurians and Klingons could smell blood, fear, or smoke at distances of up to twenty kilometers, provided the source was upwind of their position.

Stop dwelling on the negative, he told himself. *If it wasn't for their heightened senses, we could not have made it back here.*

It wasn't exaggeration, Chekov knew, to credit Razka and

the Klingons with the group's safe journey through the jungle. The Klingons were experienced soldiers, but they also had been trained as hunters. They knew about tracking prey. Living off the land. Finding clean water inside vines and bowl-shaped fronds. Evading traps. And, perhaps most important of all, not wasting the entire night moving in circles. They were the best guides anyone could ask for.

Squatting in the tall greenery at the jungle's edge, the Klingons stared out across the wide, flat stretch of tall grass and broad-leafed fronds that separated them from the cave temple, with the Starfleet landing team interspersed among them. It struck Chekov as a remarkable sight, a moment worth committing to memory: Starfleet personnel and Klingon warriors united with a common purpose, shoulder to shoulder, looking in the same direction.

This isn't something I'll see every day.

D'Gol and Spock both used their own holo-binoculars to survey the terrain between their position and the cave temple. They tried to keep their voices down, but Chekov heard every word the two men said, as did every crew member from either ship, who all were eavesdropping on their superiors even while pretending that they weren't.

"We were lucky to avoid those smoke creatures," D'Gol said. "Lieutenant Mara reports they can wither or even crystallize plants."

"Indeed." Spock surveyed the quiet scene ahead of them. "I count eleven Chwii hidden in the tall plants between us and the temple's entrance."

"Fourteen. Did you miss the three lurking in the water on the riverbank?"

"I stand corrected."

Chekov suppressed the urge to shake his head. *We would know the position of every Chwii if not for the fact that their hearing can pick up subsonic and ultrasonic emanations from our tricorders, even when they are in passive mode.* Then he castigated himself for not giving credit to the Klingons, who had shared this information with them once they had agreed to join forces. *I have to stop thinking of the Klingons as "them." As of now the only "them" is the Chwii and the Godhead. We and the Klingons are all "us" now.*

Spock asked D'Gol, "Where are the siege weapons you placed earlier?"

The Klingon team leader pointed toward one spot in the grass, and then another as he said, "There and there, flanking the midpoint. We camouflaged both guns."

"So it would seem. Presuming both weapons are still there and operational, how long will it take to free them from their mounts, so we can take them inside to use against the Godhead?"

"No time at all. The mounts are made for quick release, to facilitate rapid movement."

"A most practical design." Spock looked from one side to the other, assessing the team, before he looked back at D'Gol. "How do you recommend we proceed?"

"A direct assault. Suppressing fire on the closest Chwii while Keekur and Naq'chI recover the siege guns. Once they free them from the mounts, they'll lay down covering fire while we cross the bridge and enter the temple."

Mara interrupted the two men to ask, "Will we need a rear guard?"

D'Gol shook his head. "We can't afford to split our forces. Besides, if we slay the Godhead, the Chwii will scatter. Better to commit all our strength to that objective."

Openly skeptical, Mara asked Spock, "Do you concur, Commander?"

Spock looked and sounded conflicted. "His plan is strategically and tactically sound."

"Even though it leaves us no safe path of retreat should the attack fail?"

"Historically, there is evidence to support the idea that troops fight more effectively when they are aware that there is no alternative to victory."

Sulu muttered just loud enough for Chekov to hear, "Or as some Earth general once said, 'The enemy is in front of us, the enemy is behind us, the enemy is to the right and to the left of us. They can't get away *this* time!' "

Chekov let slip a snort of laughter that he tried to bury in the crook of his elbow, but Spock, damn his Vulcan hearing, looked straight at him. "You have something to say, Ensign?"

"No, Mister Spock. Sorry, sir."

With good order restored to the ranks, Spock turned his attention back to the battlefield in front of them. "Commander D'Gol, if the Chwii summon reinforcements from the jungle, and we have no rear guard, will that have any significant impact on the likelihood of our success?"

"No. Either way we anticipate success, with fifty to seventy-five percent casualties."

"Acceptable."

The Klingon's statistics caused Chekov to pause in alarm. He looked at Sulu. "Did he just say fifty to seventy-five percent casualties?"

"Yes, he did."

"Theirs or ours?"

One of the female Klingon warriors—Keekur, Chekov recalled—overheard them and leaned in to tell Chekov and Sulu, "Both."

Chekov felt the blood drain from his face. "Both?"

The Klingon woman seemed to take pity on him. She clutched his shoulder and said in her most comforting tone of voice, "Don't worry, Starfleet. We won't hog all the glory. We'll let your team lose a few troops as well." Slapping his shoulder hard, she added, "*Qapla'*!"

Dispirited, all Chekov wanted to do was sink into the mud and let the rain drown him, right then and there. *My mother told me not to join Starfleet. I should have listened.*

Half an hour before dawn the battle was joined. In spite of the protests from D'Gol and the rest of the strike team, Mara had backed Spock's request that the Starfleet team fire the first salvos on stun settings, to at least give the Chwii a nonlethal taste of what was coming and therefore a reasonable opportunity to retreat.

Initially, it worked better than she had expected. Well-targeted shots by the Starfleeters flushed out pockets of concealed Chwii and removed defenders from key points on the upper levels of the cave temple. After less than a minute of bombardment, small units of Chwii were fleeing into the jungle carrying their stunned but still living comrades, all without a single spear or stone sent back in retaliation.

Watching the Chwii quit the field, the Starfleeters looked pleased with themselves.

Mara almost had to laugh at her new allies. *Ah, the bravery of being out of range. Let's see if your confidence survives what comes next.*

D'Gol raised his arm. "Recover the guns!" He thrust his arm forward and with one word turned potential energy into kinetic energy, anticipation into action: "*Charge!*"

Klingons and Starfleeters burst forth together, forsaking cover, and sprinted across open ground in a downpour, their weapons blazing and almost as loud as their war cries. Side by side they were kindred in arms, rushing headlong toward bloodshed and glory.

And within three running steps Mara knew something was wrong.

No enemy fire came back from the temple. No spears or stones were launched by Chwii hiding in the tall grass. From their supposed target came . . . no response at all.

From either side, blurs of motion. Mara whipped her head

left then right to see great clouds of incoming projectiles blot-
ting out the gray predawn sky to either side, and more rising
from the jungle behind each of them. Lingering in the trees'
canopy at each launch point were masses of smoky tentacles,
serpents of black vapor tracking their every movement.

Then hundreds of Chwii surged out of the jungles on either
side of the charging attack team, a pincer attack executed with
flawless, merciless precision.

It was a trap, and we just ran right into it. Qu'vatlh!

She was shouting commands seconds before the rest of the
team knew what was happening. "Incoming! Spread out! Guard
the flanks!"

Half the team broke to the left, the other half to the right.
Both laid down suppressing fire in broad sweeping arcs, and
this time no one was shooting to stun. The hundreds of Chwii
on the flanks quickly became more than a thousand—and then
sharpened stones on long wooden shafts fell from the sky like a
rain of death.

Some of the massive spears—which Mara realized must have
been launched from ballistae rather than thrown by hand—
slammed down short of their target zone, into the front ranks of
the attacking Chwii. One ripped a Chwii clean in half, another
staked a warrior's body to the ground like an insect pinned to
a collection board. More falling missiles tore arms from Chwii
footmen, severed legs, cleaved heads from bodies. In just moments the stench of blood and bowels became too great for the
wind and rain to wash away—and then the dark curtain fell
upon the advancing attack team.

Dodging the massive spears was more luck than instinct,
and it had nothing to do with skill or speed. Mara darted left
and right, zigzagged her way through the waist-high greenery,
firing her disruptor pistol to either side without aiming, just
wild shots. A spear slammed into the ground in front of her. She
tried to hurdle over it, tripped, and as she flailed for balance an-

other spear crashed down from the other side into the space she would have occupied had she not tripped. Grace recovered, she gamboled over the second spear and squeezed off several more shots in either direction, hoping that luck and the pride of her ancestors would guide her hand even from beyond the misty horizon of Sto-Vo-Kor.

A shout of pain was cut short and became a frothy gurgle—Mara glanced left to see Doctor Dolaq had been all but cut in twain by a gigantic spear. His blood and viscera spilled out like the juice and seeds of an overripe fruit as his body disappeared into the lush green fronds.

The ground shook from one giant spear after another striking down like vengeance. Stones flew past Mara's head, hurled from slings as the Chwii infantry closed in.

What I wouldn't give to be able to call in an orbital phaser strike!

D'Gol was at the front of the group, bleeding from several wounds but still upright. He looked back to shout, "We're almost at the guns! Forward!"

As if Mara needed more evidence of the universe's sick sense of humor, the guns her team sought to recover were in that moment revealed—as two teams of Chwii cast off the weapons' camouflage nets and trained the guns on the attack team.

Diving toward the ground she cried out, "Down!"

Around her the others all threw themselves into the greenery—but CheboQ the medic was half a second slow to react, and twin storms of disruptor-cannon energy ripped him to bits.

From somewhere under the fronds, Ilucci shouted, "What was that?"

Keekur hollered back, "The Godhead taught the Chwii how to pull a trigger!"

More spears crashed down from either side, quaking the ground around Mara, while sprays of disruptor fire crisscrossed above her, setting fronds ablaze even in the pouring rain. Fear told her to stay down, but her training told her that was a guaranteed ugly death. There was only one way out of this. "D'Gol! We need to take those guns! Now!"

Whooping shrieks drowned out his reply as the attacking waves of Chwii closed in. When the aliens collectively paused for breath, D'Gol called out, "Suppressing fire, flanks! Whoever's closest to the guns, take them!"

Mara got up on one knee, pulled the disruptor rifle off her back, and unleashed a barrage of disruptor pulses into the oncoming wall of Chwii. Next to her, D'Gol did the same.

Behind her she heard phasers screeching, and she knew Spock's people were holding the line.

Then, out of the corner of her eye, she saw blurs of motion—bodies throwing themselves at the gunners' nests in blind leaps of faith and courage.

On one side, the Saurian and Keekur worked in concert, leaping from the deep greenery into the nest to strike with blades in close quarters, while on the other side, Naq'chI and a human woman with black hair—Singh, they'd called her—hurdled over the front of the gun's emplacement and dropped in firing beam weapons, razing their foes with audacity and precision.

"Forward!" D'Gol bellowed. "Gunners! Suppressing fire!"

The attack team quit their positions and ran between the siege guns toward the temple, while Keekur and Naq'chI, with help from their new Starfleet friends, turned the recaptured weapons on the advancing waves of Chwii and reduced them to scorched sprays of blood and bone. As soon as the rest of the team was behind them, they detached the guns from their mounts and fell back, acting as a rear guard while the rest of the team crossed the bridge into the temple.

Clouds of spears continued to fall and clusters of stones pelted the attack team as they scrambled single file and a few at a time over the bridge into a large entrance just above the water level of the river. More sling stones ricocheted off the outer walls of the caves as Keekur and Razka, the last ones across the bridge, entered the large chamber to regroup with the others.

A wall of stone dropped from the shadows, struck the stone floor with a thunderous *boom*, and blocked the entrance. The chamber was plunged into darkness. Before anyone could activate a palm light or set something aflame, a violet glow illuminated the team from above. Mara and the others looked up toward the source of the eldritch light.

Three massive, horrifying avatars of the Godhead looked back at them.

23

Spock raised his phaser and squeezed the trigger: "Fire!"

With a high-pitched shriek his phaser's searing red beam slammed into the closest of the three avatars. The combined screeching of the entire team's weapons was painful to Spock's acute hearing, and in less than a second the broad chamber was a flurry of phaser energy and disruptor pulses, bolts of sickly green and streaks of blazing crimson crisscrossing before slamming into the three hideous forms that clung to the cave's high domed ceiling, several meters above the mixed landing party.

The monsters' dolorous wails blared like foghorns, sending out walls of sonic force so powerful that they pushed Spock and the others off balance. Then the beasts lashed out with smoky appendages that solidified and sharpened into fearsome, meter-long spikes in the moments before they struck. Spock dodged a stabbing attack, and then he ducked a slashing assault from an appendage that had solidified into a blade. After each missed attack the improvised weapons sublimated back into vapors as the creatures regrouped.

Doctor Babitz called out, "Don't let those things touch you!"

Mara added before Babitz could, "One hit and you're crystallized!"

D'Gol and the Klingons quickly spread out and put their backs to the walls, to keep the creatures in front of them and not have to worry about defending their backs. Spock, seeing the wisdom of their tactics, shouted to the landing party, "Backs to the wall, alternate your attacks!"

Spock led the way, and he and the landing party filled in the spaces in the Klingons' encircling formation. The three grotesque Shedai avatars—misshapen lumps of mottled flesh, iridescent scales, ever-changing limbs of vapor, and more eyes than Spock could easily count—appeared to be confused and slow to react to the group's changing tactics.

Then D'Gol barked, "Continual fire, close the circle! Advance!"

He, Mara, and Hartür fired steady barrages at the avatars with their disruptor rifles, while Keekur and Naq'chI hefted the siege guns and unleashed their tremendous firepower, which was bright enough to be blinding inside the confined space.

Spock added his phaser to the assault. "Steady fire! Advance!"

The landing party, moving like a second circle right behind the first, helped the Klingons corral the three massive alien horrors into the center of the chamber's domelike ceiling—

—where the trio of beings merged into one, which swelled in size and sprouted dozens of vaporous tentacles that thrashed and whipped with chaotic fury.

Ilucci paused firing just long enough to mutter, "That is *so* not good."

The monster's lashing tentacles hardened into spikes, blades, and blunt masses with terrifying speed, and within seconds the beast's erratic flailing became a stunningly effective counter-assault. One hit after another sent Klingons and Starfleeters alike flying or tumbling, and in less than ten seconds left them all broken, bruised, or bleeding.

A club-ended tentacle reared up to strike Sulu. As the smoky limb slammed down, he rolled clear—only to be stabbed through his left thigh by a spear-like appendage that had snuck behind him in the dark. Pinned in place, Sulu screamed in rage and agony, and the Shedai readied another appendage to finish him off. In a blur the black arm of vapor lunged at Sulu—

—as Razka freed Sulu with one stroke of his machete through the solidified length of tentacle in Sulu's leg, followed by a powerful slash that parried the beast's next attack.

More tentacles formed to go after the retreating Razka and Sulu, but Chekov scrambled to his feet and resumed firing his phaser into the largest of the creature's eyes.

More phaser beams and disruptor pulses flew at the monster as Chekov pushed ahead, his weapon unleashing a steady beam that would surely fry its emitter crystal in a few more seconds. Then wisps of vapor that had hugged the floor coalesced behind Chekov into a long, four-edged spike that recoiled as a prelude to stabbing the young man in his back.

Spock shouted "Chekov!" as the dark arm thrust toward the ensign—but it was Naq'chI who threw herself in front of the blow, which pierced her armor as if it had been made of paper, and plunged through her chest and out her back in a spray of fresh blood.

She dropped her siege gun and spat at the creature. "Ha'DIbaH!"

The weapon turned to mist and let her body fall to the floor.

Keekur howled in rage as she got up on one knee and resumed firing her own siege gun into the creature's center of mass. Singh holstered her phaser, grabbed Naq'chI's siege gun, and added its power to Keekur's barrage. Then more phaser beams and disruptor pulses pinned the creature against the ceiling, but stubbornly it refused to die.

Until Razka charged through the cross fire hefting in one hand the black-crystal spear tip he had pulled from Sulu's thigh. He got as close to the creature as he dared and hurled the captured length of obsidian like a javelin—and it went through the beast's hide into its fleshy core.

The creature let out a stentorian roar that rocked the ground and shook dust from the walls and ceiling. Black ichor spilled from the creature's javelin wound, and at once its plethora of smoky appendages evaporated, until only a few remained—and those it withdrew into itself as it retreated through a thin crevasse at the back of the chamber.

Spock was already in pursuit as he yelled to the others. "After it!"

The passage through which the creature had fled was claustrophobically tight. Spock had to angle his body to move through it, because it was narrower than his shoulders were wide.

The piteous groans and wails of the creature echoed in the labyrinth of the caves, but their source was clearly audible ahead of Spock. He followed the beast's moaning through the darkness, encouraged by the sound of the others following close behind him.

He rounded a curve in the passage and saw light ahead of him. Quickening his pace, he emerged into a place he had been before: the temple's main audience chamber. Spread across the dais and around the base of the giant throne was a pile of gelatinous goo dotted with eyes. Watching it with horror from the far side of the chamber, beyond the pillar of rain pouring through the skylight into the floor's sacrifice pit, was a cluster of Chwii priests and elite guards. The soldiers raised their spears as soon as they saw Spock step from the gap in the wall, but one wide-beam light-stun shot from his phaser was enough to daze them without causing serious injury, and to persuade them to retreat rather than test their luck again.

Spock circled the dais, his phaser leveled at the pile of goo, as the rest of the team arrived in the audience chamber. Razka aided the hobbled Sulu, whose left thigh was now cocooned in what resembled smoky quartz crystal. One by one the others mirrored the Chwii's expressions of horror and revulsion as they beheld the mess on the dais.

Nose wrinkled in disgust, Sulu said, "It looks like a jellyfish left in the sun."

D'Gol grimaced. "Or something I'd spit out after eating *gagh*."

Mara aimed her disruptor rifle at the goop. "Let's finish this."

She fired—and almost instantly the slime cooked off into steam. The cloud of mist gathered in the air, and seemed to be caught by a stream of air—but then Spock recognized signs of willful intention in its movement. It was no prisoner of the wind; it was going somewhere. Then he saw it bend toward and pass through the vertical seam in the wall behind the giant throne, into the dark chamber from which he had first seen the Godhead appear.

"Mister Chekov! That lever by the wall opens the doors to the chamber behind the throne. Shift the lever, please."

"Aye, Mister Spock." Chekov jogged over to the stone lever and struggled in vain to shift it from one side to the other.

After a few seconds of watching Chekov, Hartür walked over, ushered the young man out of the way, grasped the lever with one hand, and flipped it with ease. "You're welcome."

Behind the throne, the wall parted.

Spock and the rest of the team advanced with caution to peer into the dark alcove that had been revealed. At first the chamber seemed to be empty. But then Spock saw what he assumed the Klingons must already have recognized: there was someone sprawled on the floor.

Babitz asked, "Is that . . . the Godhead?"

"If it is," Chekov said, "it is greatly diminished."

Mara stepped ahead of everyone else. "Diminished doesn't begin to cover it." She raised a palm light and focused its beam on the tragic form lying facedown in the dark.

It was a humanoid. A woman with swarthy skin and black hair. Her naked body was coated in slime and filth. The woman pushed her torso up from the floor and squinted. When the palm light beam landed upon her, she quailed from its bright-

ness. Her features were Klingon; she was a smooth-headed
QuchHa' like Mara and the rest of the crew from the *SuvwI'*.

Gazing into the harsh light, she looked beaten, terrified, and
remorseful.

But Mara evinced no pity for her—just contempt.

"Doctor Chunvig, I presume."

24

Spock lowered his phaser and stepped forward to stand beside Mara. "This is Doctor Chunvig?"

Mara kept her weapon trained on Chunvig. "In the flesh. The foolish, arrogant flesh."

Outside the caves thunder growled, slow and ominous, its rumbling clearly audible through the circular skylight in the audience chamber's ceiling. But in the shadowy confines of the antechamber behind the throne, Spock was more keenly aware of Doctor Chunvig's rapid and shallow breathing, her psionic emanations of fear and shame as she tried to cover her naked body, and her overall affect of confusion and disorientation.

He returned his phaser to his belt and edged cautiously toward her. "Doctor Chunvig, do you know where you are?"

The frightened scientist didn't answer, but Mara asked, "What are you doing, Spock?"

He sidestepped, putting himself between Chunvig and Mara's disruptor. "I am attempting to ascertain if Doctor Chunvig can be saved."

"She can't. We need to finish her, right now." Mara grasped Spock's shoulder, prompting him to look back at her as she added, "It's the reason my team and I were sent here. To kill *her*."

He looked back at Chunvig, who remained huddled on the ground, wrapped only in her own arms. There was sorrow in her eyes and fear in her voice. "Please help me."

"Do you know your name? Or how you came to be on this planet?"

Chunvig shook her head. Being unable to answer Spock's questions seemed only to deepen her despair. He faced Mara. "I cannot ignore her request for aid."

Fury welled up behind Mara's cool façade. "Then you are a *fool*."

From the audience chamber D'Gol shouted, "Kill her, Mara! While we can!"

Doctor Babitz countered, "Don't let her, Spock! We have a duty to help her."

Deep thunder rolled, and on its shoulders rode strange atonal howls.

D'Gol snapped, "Someone kill Chunvig! Now!"

Keekur hefted her siege gun and aimed it toward the antechamber, only to be blocked by Singh and the other portable cannon. Half of Hartür's face was caked in blood, and he was sitting on the floor because he could barely stand, but he drew his disruptor as ordered—only to have Sulu step on the weapon with his one good leg.

Looking down at Hartür, Sulu asked, "Orders, Mister Spock?"

Ilucci and Razka took up defensive postures behind Spock, who remained locked in a battle of wills with Mara. "Violence might be the easiest choice, Mara, but that does not make it the right one."

She studied him with a quizzical look, as if she were debating a madman. "What do you think your pantomime of mercy will accomplish, Spock? Other than delaying the inevitable?"

"I want to find a solution to this crisis that isn't rooted in cold-blooded violence or wanton destruction." He regarded the sad form of Doctor Chunvig. "I want to show that there are paths to redemption, no matter how grave our mistakes."

Mara's countenance shifted from confusion and anger to sorrow and regret. "Spock . . . the resolutions you seek? Those are artifacts of *hope*, not logic. I thought Vulcans had learned not to let their emotions cloud their reason."

"And I thought Klingons believed in courage and honor. Where is the courage in killing a naked, defenseless woman? Where is the honor in that?"

"Honor is a privilege reserved for those who respect it. Doctor Chunvig is a traitor. She stole the Empire's only copy of Shedai meta-genome data and fled with it, to this backwater ball of mud, so she could defy nature and turn herself into a monster. All to serve her own warped ambitions. She forsook any claim to honor long ago." Mara moderated her tone and took half a step toward Spock. "She is a danger to both our peoples, Spock. And remember our covenant: no copies of the meta-genome research can be allowed to leave this world. That includes Doctor Chunvig's memories of her work. For the sake of peace, she must die here."

There was reason in Mara's argument. Spock faced Doctor Chunvig and raised his phaser. His finger hovered in front of the trigger. Logic told him he should do as Mara had asked, that he should fire one last shot, vaporize Doctor Chunvig, and end this fiasco.

It was what logic demanded. He heard it as clearly as he still heard his father's voice haunting him in his dreams. But when he forced his thoughts to be still, when his mind was quiet, he could also hear his mother's voice guiding him with her own gentle wisdom.

Logic could make powerful arguments for action—but it had no compassion. And it would bring him no comfort when the time came to confront his inevitable regret.

He lowered his phaser and faced Mara. "Forgive me. I cannot kill in cold blood."

She shouldered him aside. "Luckily for us all, I can."

She braced her disruptor rifle against her shoulder and lifted it to aim at Chunvig.

Then came the storm.

Rending the air with shrill cries, two massive serpents of inky vapor plunged through the skylight into the audience chamber, both racing like a river in flood. In a rush of sheer momentum they plowed through the mixed landing party, hurling Klingons and Starfleeters through the air like leaves in a gale. Spock and Mara threw themselves to the floor, and the huge tentacles of jet-black smoke hurtled past above them—

—and slammed into the frail, naked form of Doctor Chunvig.

In a flash the tentacles enveloped the female Klingon scientist—and then she absorbed them into her body, which swelled and transmogrified in the most hideous of ways, transforming her in a matter of seconds back into the terrifying grotesquerie of the Godhead.

Much too late Spock raised his phaser and fired—only to see the beam have no effect on the creature. A tentacle shot from the beast's body, ripped the phaser from Spock's hand, and crushed it into splinters as if it had been nothing but a cheap toy.

He backpedaled, pulling Mara with him. "Fall back!"

A flurry of tentacles lashed out at the wounded, weary allies, who scrambled backward before heeding an even more impassioned order from D'Gol:

"Run!"

No one cared if the retreat was orderly. All any of them cared about now was running as fast as they could go, staying more than a step ahead of those tentacles that could crystallize flesh on contact, and getting as far as they could from a horror that refused to die.

Moving with the singular purpose of self-preservation, they all ran like they had never run before in their lives—right up until the moment they turned the corner at the end of a long passageway to find a doorless, windowless dead end.

In front of them, a wall of mortared stone.

Behind them, a swiftly approaching invincible foe with the touch of Death itself.

Keekur and Singh moved to the corner, determined to hold the line as long as possible. Behind them, Mara, Hartür, Ilucci, and Razka loaded fresh power cells into their weapons. Against the far wall, Doctor Babitz did what she could to dull the pain caused by the black crystal spreading up and down Sulu's wounded left leg.

From the far end of the long passageway behind them came the bloodcurdling shrieks of the smoke-serpents hunting the landing party through the underground labyrinth.

D'Gol stood next to Spock, his anger palpable even in the dark. "What *now*, Vulcan?"

To Spock's utter consternation, he had no idea.

Keekur and Singh took turns filling the long passageway with storms of disruptor pulses from their siege guns. Each of them would push her weapon to its limit and then duck back to cover just before the emitter assembly fractured or the barrel melted, and then the other would turn the corner and unleash a fresh barrage to keep the Godhead's vaporous avatars at bay.

The members of the team who had only small arms to add to the fight darted out one or two at a time to fire past the heavy gunner. Mara had no idea whether they were really helping or just wasting their power cells, but she had a more pressing dilemma to solve.

She seized the Vulcan by his arms to compel him to train his attention on her. "Spock! Snap out of whatever mystic Vulcan trance this is and help us find a way out of here!"

His expression remained frozen in a mask of confused dismay, and his voice sounded distant and haunted. "I . . . don't know how."

D'Gol was on the verge of pointing his disruptor at the Vulcan, Mara was sure of it. Keeping hold of Spock, she shifted her position to put herself between him and D'Gol. "Spock! Talk to me!" She watched his lips tremble as if he were speaking, but no words issued from his mouth. That marked the end of her patience.

She slapped Spock's face hard enough to whip his head to his right. "Spock!"

He blinked and once again his eyes were clear, as if he had been freed of some spell. He recovered his composure and stood tall. "My apologies."

Mara shouted to be heard over the echoed screeching of the team's disruptors and phasers. "What happened back there? Why didn't you shoot?"

He averted his eyes from hers, as if in shame. "My logic became . . . uncertain."

His was the worst excuse Mara had ever heard for freezing during combat. She wanted to slap him again just on principle. "That's it? Your logic was uncertain so you decided to spare a monster from a species that we know can destroy entire planets?" She gestured toward their comrades, who were struggling to prevent the Godhead from advancing up the passageway. "How's that working out for you?"

In his eyes Mara saw both torment and conflict. When Spock glanced at D'Gol, it was with intense apprehension. The Vulcan invited her with a tilt of his head to follow him to the farthest corner of the dead end. With great reluctance, Mara did exactly that. He took hold of her left arm and pulled her intimately close to him. When he spoke, she felt the heat of his breath on her face and the pressure of his fingers digging into her bicep. "I recently experienced a profound rite of adulthood, one that Vulcans prefer not to speak of with outsiders. A marriage—"

"You mean *pon farr*?"

He was taken aback. "You know of *pon farr*?"

"It's always wise to know one's enemy. What happened?"

"A ritual challenge, initiated by my betrothed."

Mara nodded, remembering her study of Vulcan customs. "The *koon-ut-kal-if-fee.*"

"Yes. The details are irrelevant. What matters is that for a time I lost all control over my emotions. I lost myself. I thought I had recovered my discipline, restored my logic, mastered my emotions . . . but when Doctor Chunvig begged me for mercy, I was overcome by a powerful wave of empathy. Seeing her as a person, I could not also see her as a thing to be destroyed."

"There are worse things. I, for one, am glad to know you can see Klingons as *persons.* Not all Starfleeters feel as you do."

Spock shook his head and did his best to suppress a frown. "You miss my point. At a critical moment, I made an emotional decision rather than a logical one. I thought I knew my mind, Mara. But did I let my emotions mar my logic when I needed it most?"

There was tremendous regret in Spock's voice, a quality Mara heard even through the high-pitched din of phasers and disruptors firing almost nonstop. He needed to hear something that would reassure him, but giving comfort had never been a Klingon virtue.

"Logic can tell us what is advantageous, Spock. But it can't always tell us what's *right.*" Spock nodded, perhaps gleaning some insight from the only thing she could think of to say.

D'Gol stepped between Mara and Spock and forced them apart. "Are you done coddling him, Mara? Or do you think you might need to nurse him?"

"Mind your place, D'Gol! He—"

"My *place* is in command of this mission! And your Vulcan pet has led us to a dead end and our doom. To Fek'lhr with him!"

At the corner, the tempo of alternation between Keekur and Singh was accelerating as their weapons threatened to overheat due to lack of downtime between salvos. Razka and Hartür continued adding whatever firepower they could to the defense, but the monstrous roars of the Shedai avatar grew nearer by the second, and Ensign Chekov looked positively spooked as he fell back and jogged to his team leader. "Mister Spock! We can't hold the passage much longer."

Mara was embarrassed by D'Gol as he sneered at Spock, "Impress me, Vulcan! Logic your way out of a tomb of solid stone."

Spock's eyebrows climbed high on his forehead as he muttered, "Solid. Stone." He held out his open left hand to Mara. "Your light, please." Then he extended his open right hand to the ensign. "Mister Chekov, your phaser."

Chekov handed his weapon to Spock, who faced the back wall, the terminus of the dead end. Spock passed his light over its pattern of mortared stones . . . and then at the adjacent walls, which were smooth rock, carved by eons of flowing water . . . and then back at the far wall. "This was once an open passage. But this wall is new. Our phasers could not tunnel through solid rock fast enough to let us escape—but I suspect *this* wall is anything but solid."

He stepped back, raised the phaser, and fired.

It took only seconds for the mortar between the stones to crumble, causing the rocks to shift—and let in a cool, rain-washed breeze.

Spock handed Mara her light—and then he lunged at the far wall and threw himself against it, leading with his shoulder. He hit the wall with all the force he could bring, and it collapsed outward. Large stones tumbled over one another as the wall came apart in one blow. On the other side, Spock rolled clear and came up on his feet beneath a steady rain shower. Waving the phaser, he beckoned the others: "This way! Hurry!"

Doctor Babitz helped Sulu limp out of the cave. Mara, D'Gol, and Chekov were the next ones out. Spock waved everyone past him as he adjusted a setting on his phaser. "Keep going! Get as far into the jungle as you can!"

Mara followed the others to the tree line and then she looked back. Hartür, Ilucci, and Razka were behind her, and Singh and Keekur were the last ones out. Spock shouted over the rising whine of his phaser, telling them to run—and then he lobbed the overloading sidearm back into the cave tunnel before he sprinted toward the jungle behind the siege gunners.

A white-hot explosion with a resounding boom collapsed the cave entrance.

Within moments Spock had run past the rear ranks to rejoin Mara and D'Gol near the front of the ragged formation winding its way into the sodden jungle. He caught up to Doctor Babitz and helped her carry Sulu over the rough and muddy terrain.

D'Gol slapped Spock's shoulder. "Not bad, Vulcan. So what's next?"

With cool certainty, Spock replied, "Next, we destroy the Godhead, and *end* this."

25

"This is as good a place to rest as any," Doctor Babitz said to the group. "Let's stop here."

D'Gol was of a mind to keep going, to push on through the rain, fog, muck, and vines, as well as his own lingering aches and pains, but the others all halted, obviously relieved by the human physician's suggestion. He suspected her invitation to pause had been prompted by the presence of a recently fallen tree, which made for a convenient bench.

Mara sat beside him, while Babitz and Spock continued to tend to Sulu, whose left thigh and hip were cocooned in the dark crystalline substance that had taken root after he had been stabbed by one of the Godhead's solidified appendages.

Farther down the log, Hartür bandaged up some of his own wounds, as did Keekur. The Starfleeters looked as if they had been harder hit during the fight with the Godhead; their limbs, torsos, and faces were replete with scrapes, lacerations, and puncture wounds.

That's what you get for not wearing armor, qoHpu'.

Babitz used her medical tricorder to scan the mass on Sulu's leg, and then she switched off the device and looked up at Spock. "Good news: there's relatively little tissue damage under the crystal, and no broken bone. Plus, I've treated this kind of thing before, so if we can get him back to the *Kepler*, I should be able to stop the crystal before it spreads any further."

The Vulcan's response was the only dry thing on this ac-cursed planet. "Good."

Doctor Babitz moved from Sulu to D'Gol, who waved her off. "I don't need your help. See to Mara."

The blonde human fixed D'Gol with a dour look. "I already scanned you."

"So?"

"You have an internal hemorrhage. If it isn't treated right now, you'll be dead in an hour."

Damned doctors. "Fine. Do whatever it is you do." As he let Babitz set to work with her noninvasive surgical implements and hyposprays, D'Gol distracted himself by putting Spock on the spot. "Got a plan yet, Vulcan?"

"Yes."

"Well? What is it?"

"Our encounter in the passageway confirms that your siege guns are no longer powerful enough to achieve our objective. They were barely able to slow the creature's advance. If we wish to kill the Godhead, we will need to hit it with a concentrated burst of energy—one more powerful than we can create even with all of our small arms combined."

Intuition raised the hackles on the back of D'Gol's neck. The Vulcan was about to suggest something stupid. "What do you propose?"

"We must lure the Godhead out of the temple, into the open, and use your shuttle's disruptor cannons to kill it."

A growl of disapproval rattled deep in D'Gol's throat. He craned his head back and let the warm rain kiss his face for sev-eral glorious seconds. Then he glared at Spock. "Why don't we use your shuttle to kill the creature?"

"Because the *Kepler* is not armed, and carries only minimal shielding."

"Your shuttle has no weapons? How stupid are you people?"

Spock let the insult pass unchallenged. "Your shuttle, with its disruptor cannons and more robust shields, is far more likely to prevail in an attack on the Godhead."

D'Gol fished a flask of bloodwine from a leg pocket of his uniform. Took a long swig. Swallowed. "I knew you'd say something like that. But give me one good reason I should send our shuttle into harm's way while yours faces no danger."

Mara set one hand on D'Gol's arm. "It makes sense, and you know it. Besides, having our shuttle be the one to strike the killing blow will only add to our glory, D'Gol. Who wants to hear a song about brave Klingon warriors watching *someone else* slay evil incarnate?"

"You make a fair point. But I still want to know why their shuttle faces no risk."

Spock interjected, "Your assumption is mistaken. Our shuttle will be involved in the attack—just not as the primary weapon against the Godhead. Ensign Singh will board our shuttle with the borrowed siege gun and use it to provide covering fire from the air, to keep the Chwii at a distance while we lure the Godhead out of its stronghold."

"Is that all?"

"If your shuttle does not survive the killing of the Godhead, our shuttle will act as a shared evacuation vehicle, so that none of us needs to be left behind after the battle."

D'Gol felt the group's collective attention weighing upon him. He cast a probing look at Hartür. "What do you say? Feel like flying a suicide mission?"

The pilot grinned. "When do I not?"

D'Gol groaned in resignation. "Very well, Spock. I still think our shares of risk remain unequal—but even so, this is still more courage than I ever expected to see from Starfleeters." He downed another swig from his flask. "Today *is* a good day to die!"

_____

Even injured, the mixed landing party made good time in bad weather over rough terrain. In just over an hour they followed a fresh scar through the trees to arrive at the Klingons' shuttle—and as soon as Spock saw it, he wondered if he might need to reconsider his plan of attack.

He turned a skeptical look at D'Gol. "Are you sure that vessel can still fly?"

D'Gol shrugged and then asked his pilot, "Hartür?"

The landing party spread out in a semicircle behind the dented, scraped wreck of a Klingon Type-3 shuttlecraft, which sat with its starboard side brutally wedged into a cluster of huge boulders and its crumpled nose dangling over the edge of a cliff that looked down a precipitous drop to a deep jungle basin. Hartür opened the side hatch and stepped inside, apparently not concerned he might imbalance the tiny ship and send it plunging over the cliff's edge. Spock chose to err on the side of caution and stood in the rain outside the hatchway.

Inside the shuttle, Hartür settled into his seat in the cockpit and powered up the ship's engines, which came to life with a dramatic thrumming sound that quickly abated to a purr. "We've got primary power," he hollered to Spock. "But about twenty microfractures in the starboard hull. I can patch them, but it'll take time."

"A resource we do not have in abundance, Mister Hartür. Can your shuttle mount an attack without those repairs?"

The pilot flipped some switches, checked some gauges. "The *QInqul* is ready to fight. She might not be spaceworthy, but she's airworthy at low altitude. For now, that's good enough."

"Agreed." Spock faced D'Gol. "We should retrieve arms and gear now, while we can."

D'Gol gave a short, shrill whistle, and then he pointed at the outer hatch for the shuttle's aft compartment. "Keekur! Lend me a hand."

A brisk wind bent the falling rain almost sideways for several seconds as Keekur and D'Gol opened the hatch. Then he beckoned Mara and the Starfleet team—minus Babitz and Sulu—to step closer. "We'll do our best to distribute the firepower evenly. If you don't recognize something, speak up. There won't be time for questions once the fighting starts."

With speed and efficiency, the Klingon team leader and his gunner handed out small arms and assorted munitions, describing items as they went along.

D'Gol pushed a weapon into Chekov's hands. "Heavy disruptor rifle. Two power cells."

Keekur handed Ilucci a satchel. "Plasma grenades. Blast radius ten *qam*s. Five-second fuses. You good?"

"*Pfft*. I'm *great*. Used to pitch for my platoon's softball team when I was a boot."

The Klingon woman stared blankly at him. "I don't know what that means."

"It means I can throw." Ilucci slung the satchel's strap across his chest and moved on.

Keekur passed Razka a bandolier lined with small explosives. "Smoke charges. You know what to do with these?"

Razka slung the bandolier over his camouflage poncho. "Cover movement and indicate positions when calling in supporting fire."

She handed him an extra disruptor rifle. "I knew I liked you, Saurian."

Ensign Singh stepped up. D'Gol handed her a small backpack with a protruding cable. "Heavy-combat power pack. Patch it into your siege gun."

Singh connected the cable at the charging port, and her weapon's readouts all surged back to maximum. She noted the improvement and gave D'Gol a nod and smile. "Rock on."

Keekur beckoned Spock, who had refrained from joining the group. "You lost your phaser in the caves. Take one of our disruptors."

Reluctantly, Spock approached the *QInqul* and accepted the Klingon sidearm from Keekur. "Thank you." He looked at D'Gol. "We should get Doctor Babitz and Mister Sulu aboard now. Time is a factor."

"Of course. Keekur, take the *mek'leth* and the rest of the grenades. Give me the *bat'leth*." While his gunner pulled the last of their munitions and a massive, curved, double-bladed Klingon sword from the cargo area, D'Gol beckoned Sulu and Doctor Babitz. "Get on board."

Babitz helped Sulu stand and hobble inside the *QInqul*. D'Gol followed them inside and leaned into the cockpit to speak with Hartür while Babitz and Sulu strapped into seats in the passenger compartment. "Waste no time coming back. We scared off a few of the Chwii, but that monster still has an army guarding his gate—and we can't hold them off forever. Understand?"

"Understood, Commander."

"Good. The one called Sulu doesn't have much time, so fly like lightning, my brother." D'Gol slapped Hartür's shoulder and left the shuttlecraft. As soon as he stepped outside, the hatch closed behind him. He walked back to stand with Spock and the others as the *QInqul* powered up its thrusters, lifted itself off the rocks with unexpected grace, and shot away to vanish beyond curtains of fog and rain that lingered above the jungle basin below.

Spock turned to address the group. "Now we must make our way back to the temple."

Ilucci winced. "Do we really have to?"

"There is no other way," D'Gol said to the engineer. "The Godhead must be destroyed, and it falls upon us to do it."

"I'm surprised you wouldn't rather just bug out and vaporize the temple with a few volleys of torpedoes from your ship."

D'Gol and the remaining Klingons traded bewildered looks before he replied to Ilucci, "Where would be the honor in that? Orbital bombardment is a last resort. A true warrior faces their enemy. Risks their life in open combat. No one writes songs about those who run away and hurl missiles from a distance."

Chekov, Singh, and Razka shot disapproving looks at Ilucci, who raised his hands in a gesture of surrender. "Fine, I'm a schmuck. Sorry I asked."

"We should start moving," Spock said, leading the way back up the *QInqul*'s scar through the jungle. "We need to be in position to attack the temple before the shuttles return."

Falling in behind Spock, Razka asked, "What if the Chwii army finds us first?"

"Then we shall need to fight our way through them and return to the temple at all costs, *before* the Godhead recovers its full strength and brings the fight to us."

"Great," Razka said, not bothering to hide his sarcasm. "No pressure."

It felt like an ice pick was jammed into his left hip socket and some sadist was grinding it against the bone while a thousand stinging insects burrowed through the meat of his thigh, but Sulu refused to scream. Squeeze his eyes shut and roar through gritted teeth? Sure. But he wouldn't scream. Not even when the smoky crystalline sheath on his leg felt like it was made of cold fire.

Sprawled on a bucket seat in the *QInqul*'s passenger compartment, he tried to focus on anything except the pain of the Shedai-inflicted wound. The Klingon shuttle shivered as Hartür pushed it to its limits. The whine of its engines was almost as loud as the shrieks of wind slicing through the cracks in its hull and the rapid-fire patter of rain on the overhead.

It was impossible for Sulu to see any details through the forward viewport, which had been reduced to a blurry wash of wind-whipped rain. But he was lucid enough to catch the dark blurs of treetops silhouetted against lightning-riddled clouds—

split seconds before Hartür slammed the *QInqul* through them, shearing off one treetop after another without losing speed.

Thud-crack! Another tree's crown was shaved off and flew up and over the shuttle. Babitz frowned at the arboreal carnage, then shook her head at Sulu. "Heaven help us, he's a daredevil just like you." She ran another scan of Sulu's leg with her tricorder. "It's spreading faster than I expected. How's the pain?"

"Nothing I can't handle, Doc," Sulu lied, his voice as taut as the head of a snare drum. Sweat beaded on his forehead and ran like tears from under his hair.

A jolt of impact shook the *QInqul* as another treetop was launched to its doom.

Sulu was secretly impressed. *This guy really knows how to haul ass.*

He leaned to his right so he could get a better look at the flight controls of the shuttle and see how Hartür operated them. Their markings were all in Klingon script or numerals, but Sulu was pretty sure he recognized most of the controls by context alone. As for the rest of them, that was why he found it fascinating to watch Hartür at work.

Never know. This might be useful knowledge someday.

For a moment Sulu was able to focus, to think about something other than—

Unholy, white-hot pain! Like a lava corkscrew twisting into his gut.

Sulu gasped in shock, then groaned as he doubled over. If not for his seat's safety harness, he would have landed on the deck.

Babitz freed herself from her seat's harness and moved in front of Sulu to help him sit up and then lean back. "Breathe, Lieutenant. Slowly. Deep breaths. In. Out."

"I know how to breathe, Doc. I can't inhale twice in a row, can I?"

"I'll chalk up that outburst to the pain." She loaded an ampoule of something blue into her hypospray and pressed the device to his carotid. With a hiss and a momentary tingling sensation, the medicine passed through his skin and into the artery. Sulu felt the drug move through his system, and when it reached his gut the excruciating pain dulled just a bit. Babitz scanned him with her medical tricorder. "Pulse rate slowing. Feeling better?"

Sulu felt a touch loopy. "Better than what? Getting kicked in the groin? Maybe. Having a slab of cedar-planked salmon for dinner? Not even close."

Hartür looked back from the cockpit as the *QInqul* shaved another tree down to size. "He sounds a bit blunted. Will he be able to fly?"

"Sure." She knocked on the crystal cocoon. "After I get *this* thing off him."

Her tricorder beeped rapidly. She muted it.

Hartür's concern deepened. "What did that mean?"

Babitz checked the tricorder's readout. "The crystalline substance is starting to invade his torso. If it reaches vital organs, this could get dicey."

"How much time does he *really* have?"

The fearful look in Babitz's eyes and her refusal to answer told Sulu and Hartür all either of them really needed to know.

The Klingon pilot mumbled a few curses, and then he banked the shuttle to port and poured on the speed. "I was taking a slightly roundabout route to avoid some complications, but it sounds as if your man doesn't have the time to spare. You'd better strap back in, Doctor."

Alarmed, Babitz quickly got back in her chair and secured its safety harness. "What did you mean by 'avoid some complications'? What kind of complications?"

"The kind that has a wingspan three times ours and looks at us like we're food." He threw more switches and a burst of acceleration pushed her and Sulu hard against their seatbacks. Then the pilot pointed toward one of the shuttle's starboard viewports. "*That* kind."

Babitz snapped her head to the right, but it took Sulu a few seconds to roll his head in that direction so he could see out the viewport. Once he did, he wished he hadn't.

The creature was like something out of a myth, like the Aztecs' fabled winged-serpent deity Quetzalcoatl, except this horror had spines instead of feathers, a mouth full of fangs, and vast leathery wings. Just as Hartür had warned, the beast dwarfed the *QInqul*—and was in the midst of making a wide turn to charge straight at it.

Oh, that's really not good.

"Hang on," Hartür shouted over the rising whine of the engines. "This is—"

A deafening *bang* and a sickening screech of wrenched duranium: the dragon—what else was Sulu supposed to call this thing?—raced over the top of the *QInqul*, but lashed the shuttle's nose with its spiked tail, tearing off part of the forward hull. The shuttle bucked upward and stalled for half a second until the engines kicked back on.

Outside the shuttle, countless bolts of lightning split the cloudbanks. Thunder rolled like a harbinger of the apocalypse. And audible above it all was a fierce roar of primal hunger and fury that echoed off the landscape below.

Through a portside viewport, Sulu caught another dark smear of motion between the clouds as the monster banked into a wide turn to set up its next attack run.

Smoke streamed out of the damaged bow of the shuttle.

The engines' tone dropped in pitch and volume. They were losing speed.

Grinning like a maniac, Hartür looked back again at Sulu and Babitz.

"As I was saying? This is where it gets rough."

26

The mixed team made good time until they were just a kilometer from the temple.

Then the ambushes began.

Razka was on point with Keekur. They were slashing a fresh trail through the jungle with his machete and her *mek'leth* when a spear materialized like a phantom from behind a ragged veil of fog, sailing toward them on a shallow arc through the mist.

"Heads up!" He dodged left, and Keekur darted right. The spear flew past between them and slammed into the muddy path they had left in their wake.

Shouts of alarm filled the sultry air behind them. Spears and stones were converging on the landing party from every direction. Next came war whoops from the Chwii, who moved swiftly to close their formation around the team like a noose around a neck. In the gray half-light that reached the jungle's floor, Razka caught glimpses of Chwii sprinting or scurrying from one tree to another, or scuttling through the waist-high greenery.

With a hard blink, Razka engaged his inner eyelids, enabling his thermal vision. Then he almost wished he hadn't. Clusters of alien heat signatures were closing in from every direction.

Great Bird help us. He drew his phaser in his left hand. "Mister Spock! Enemy contact on all vectors. Hundreds of hostiles, closing fast."

Keekur sniffed the air. "A trap."

"You don't know the half of it." Razka pointed into the hazy distance until he knew she saw what he did: three serpentine twists of black vapor, racing around trees and heading toward the landing party at terrifying speed. "Shedai smoke serpents, right flank!"

Spock raised his voice but kept his tone steady and calm: "Forward, double-quick time! Weapons free!"

Razka hefted his blade and looked at Keekur. "Let's do this." She gave him a nod, and then she sheathed her blade and pulled her siege gun off her back and braced it on her hip.

She opened fire and ripped holes in the jungle as if she were the fist of God. Fiery pulses pulverized tree trunks and Chwii soldiers, vaporized curtains of moss, and churned the waist-height ground cover into smoking mulch—along with any Chwii hiding in it.

As one, she and Razka charged, him hacking and her firing as they ran, obliterating everything in their path with fire and steel.

Spears and stones appeared by the battalion, bending through the steam-filled air toward the two of them. Some of the primitive projectiles disintegrated in the furious barrage of the siege gun, but enough made it past the fire curtain that Razka had to let himself take hit after hit to protect Keekur, because she was the only reason they weren't sitting ducks.

Harried by a storm of rocks and spears, Razka and Keekur fought shoulder to shoulder, pushing forward against impossible odds as if they were an unstoppable force of nature.

And for just a few dizzying minutes . . . they were.

Spock wanted to move more quickly to make himself a harder target to hit, but he could go only as fast as Razka and Keekur could blaze a path. He and D'Gol kept finding themselves too close together, and they alternated falling back to make sure they weren't offering some Chwii spearman a two-for-one kill on a lucky throw.

A stone struck a glancing blow across Spock's forehead. He turned with the blow to reduce the impact, but bright green blood sheeted down his forehead and pooled in his eyebrows.

D'Gol howled like a wounded *le-matya* as a Chwii spear nicked the back of his right calf. "*Ha'DIbaH!*" He reached down, grabbed the spear that had cut him, and hurled it back the way it had come—straight into the chest of a frontline Chwii infantryman. "And there's more where that came from, you filthy *yIntaghpu'*!"

Not far from the other side of the trail, a Chwii popped up from the lush ground cover and raised a spear—only to have Spock blast it from his hand with a precision phaser shot.

They are too close—at this range they could put a spear straight through any of us. He adjusted his weapon's setting as he shouted orders to his people over the enemy's war cries. "The enemy has closed to point-blank! Set phasers wide-beam, heavy stun! Sweep the flanks!"

He unleashed a broad arc of phaser energy on the left flank and swept from the front of the formation toward the middle. Within seconds, half a dozen Chwii he hadn't even seen staggered forward out of the rain-soaked greenery and collapsed.

This fight will hinge on what runs out first: our power cells, or the Godhead's pawns.

———————

Mara had no time to tell Spock that Klingon disruptor rifles had no wide-beam setting. Instead she let Chekov strafe the ground cover with his rifle to flush out the Chwii on the right flank, and then she picked off the *novpu'* with ruthless precision.

But the smoke-serpents were moving faster now, heading right for the landing party. She made her best guess as to how fast Razka and Keekur were making progress. Then she estimated how soon the serpents would slam into the strike team and kill them all.

The trail blazers were fast, but nowhere near fast enough.

We aren't going to make it. Time to change the plan.

She sprayed the right flank with another flurry of kill-setting disruptor pulses, and then she looked toward the rear guard.

Ensign Singh made the most of her siege gun, leveling swaths of the jungle to deprive the Chwii of cover while neutralizing their hidden infantry several bodies at a time. Master Chief Ilucci lobbed plasma grenades into the hollows of the jungle Singh's barrages couldn't reach. Each blast launched broken, smoldering Chwii bodies into the air.

Mara shouted over the piercing screech of the siege gun firing on automatic. "Singh!" The ensign looked over her shoulder at Mara, who pointed at the Shedai serpents closing on the right flank. "Target the serpents! Defend the flank!" She fell back to take Singh's place in the rear guard. "I'll take over back here. Put the firepower where we need it!"

Singh jogged forward to the middle of the formation and unleashed a nightmarish broadside of siege-gun pulses into the trio of smoke-serpents. The beasts shrieked and recoiled, and then they split up. Singh kept her fire trained on the one that had chosen to charge straight into her continuing barrage. As the beast closed to less than ten meters, she called out "Chekov!"

Chekov spun from the left flank, saw the serpent, and scrambled to aim his weapon. The beast reached point-blank range before he fired—and sent a full-power disruptor-rifle kill shot down the creature's roaring maw. The smoky fiend flashed white—and then evaporated, leaving behind a cloud of dust that quickly dispersed in the wind and rain.

"One down, two to go," Singh said, in search of a target. "Where are they?"

It was too late to act when Mara saw the beast's terrifying

blur—as it lunged from a drifting cloud of battlefield smoke into the front of the landing party.

––––––––––––––

Curtains of smoke impervious to the rain hung over the land laid waste by the siege guns. Razka was ready for a Chwii to leap through one at any second, or for another salvo of spears and slingshot stones to fly his way—but he wasn't ready for the billowing wall of smoke to come alive in the space of a breath. By the time he realized the smoke was changing shape, it was too late: the serpent manifested and struck like a Terran cobra, obliterating Keekur's siege gun as it plunged like an enormous obsidian blade through her gut.

The broken siege weapon fell in pieces from Keekur's hands and pattered into the mud at her feet. Frothy blood spilled from her mouth, which gaped open in shock and horror. Then, in the time it took Razka to overcome his own shock and reset his phaser, a dark, smoky crystalline substance metastasized from her impaling wound and cocooned her entire body.

Then the serpent recoiled and withdrew from Keekur, its solidified portion sublimating instantly into smoke—and Keekur's crystalline shroud exploded into glassy shrapnel, leaving nothing of her to be found.

Backpedaling, Razka realized he was next on the serpent's hit list. He fired his phaser at the beast, for whatever good that would do, as he yelled out, "Little help?"

A maelstrom of disruptor pulses from behind him flew over his head and shredded the smoke-serpent. Just as the creature seemed ready to evaporate, it retreated a few hundred meters upriver toward the cave temple, which now was in sight thanks to the violent landscaping inflicted by Keekur's siege gun.

Also in sight was the next wave of charging Chwii infantry and spearmen—who broke through the nearest wall of smoke in a line thirty soldiers wide, all of them screaming like maniacs as they descended on Razka, who was still alone several meters in front of the rest of the team. He reset his phaser for pulsed fire to conserve energy and started shooting, but the Chwii refused to slow their charge. The front rank leveled their spears for a skewering assault.

Razka raised his machete to a parrying position and prepared to die.

D'Gol sprinted past him, with nothing but his traditional Klingon *bat'leth* in his hands and a crazy grin on his face. "C'mon, Saurian! Don't tell me you want to live forever!"

What am I supposed to say to that?

At a loss for words, Razka charged into battle beside the Klingon commander, who turned spears into kindling and Chwii into corpses with one merciless swing after another of his crescent-shaped sword. Beside him, Razka cleaved off spearheads with his machete, and then severed arms and heads to join them. By the time he and D'Gol had finished off the Chwii's first rank of attackers, they both looked as if they had been baptized in a river of alien blood.

The only difference was that D'Gol was enjoying the carnage, laughing like a madman, a butcher in love with the stench of the abattoir.

Cutting down another Chwii, all Razka felt was shame.

This is not what I joined Starfleet to do.

I came to discover, not destroy.

Chekov and Singh charged past him and D'Gol on either flank and, with two sweeps of a disruptor rifle set to kill and a siege gun on full automatic pulse fire, they obliterated more than half of the Chwii troops in front of them. When the remaining Chwii abandoned their assault and fled into the jungle, Spock shouted, "Cease fire!"

Bereft of weapons fire, the battlefield fell eerily quiet. All the sounds of animals in the jungle had gone silent. The only sounds were the crackling of small fires, the patter of hard rain on the smoking ground, and the soft burbling of the river passing by.

In the distance, the smoke-serpents retreated into the cave temple.

Bloodied, tattered, bruised, and short of breath, all the surviving members of the mixed landing party except for Spock dropped to the blood-mudded ground.

Chekov muttered, "I thought we were goners."

"We might yet be, sir," Razka rasped. "The Chwii aren't in full retreat. I can see their heat signatures on a nearby hillside. They're regrouping. Gathering reinforcements."

Spock moved to Razka's side. "How many, Chief?"

"Enough to make what just happened look like a warm-up."

"Then we'd best keep moving. If the Chwii cut us off from the temple, our mission will fail—and we will most likely all die."

D'Gol snorted in amusement. "Such optimism. We all die *someday*, Vulcan. That's not important. What matters is *how* you die—and what you do while you're *alive*."

"An interesting philosophy. *If* we die, how do you propose we do so?"

The Klingon commander smirked. "Taking these *petaQpu'* down with us."

Sulu had no idea what kind of technology Doctor Babitz had used to reverse the spread of the crystalline substance that had enveloped his leg and invaded his abdomen, but he didn't need to know. What mattered was that the top-secret gizmos she had brought along on the *Kepler* worked as promised, and now he was back at the shuttle's controls, trying to keep the *Kepler* steady in the face of tempestuous headwinds while also keeping up with Hartür, who continued to fly the *QInqul* like some kind of lunatic.

"Stay still," Babitz chided while treating the puncture wound to his leg, "unless you want to have a six-inch scar on your thigh."

"Some folks like scars. Some people find them *sexy*."

The doctor shot him a sour look. "You done?"

"Sorry, Doc."

Sulu leaned forward and tried to peer upward through the forward viewport. The winged predator that had hectored the *QInqul* was still lurking somewhere nearby. He felt it. It had circled the *Kepler*'s landing site after the *QInqul* had set down to discharge Babitz and Sulu, and he was sure he had caught a glimpse or two of the creature in the minutes since taking off for the return to the landing party.

A hundred meters ahead, the *QInqul* disappeared inside a thick wall of low-altitude clouds. Tracking the Klingon shuttle with the *Kepler*'s sensors, Sulu made certain nothing was forcing the *QInqul* to change course or fall out of the sky.

The *Kepler* passed through the cloud bank like a bullet, and as soon as Sulu had a clear view of the river, he knew the plan had taken a turn for the FUBAR. Thick smoke rose from a swath of razed jungle dozens of meters wide and a few hundred meters long. It led out of the jungle, almost all the way to the cave temple at the river's head. Within moments the shuttle was close enough to the carnage for Sulu to see hundreds of corpses littering the ground.

"My God." He opened a comm channel and hoped it worked. "*Kepler* to Spock. Come in, Mister Spock. Do you read me?"

To Sulu's relief, Spock replied, *"Affirmative, Mister Sulu. What is your status?"*

"Airborne and inbound, ETA sixty seconds."

"Be advised, we are taking heavy fire from the east. We need immediate air support."

"Understood. Patching in the *QInqul*." Sulu switched to a multichannel setting. "*Kepler* to *QInqul*, do you copy?"

Hartür answered, *"Affirmative, Kepler. Go ahead."*

"Our people on the ground are taking fire from the east and need support. I can swing in to pick up Singh, but it looks like the landing party is pinned down on a narrow strip of riverbank. Space is tight, and we'll be vulnerable on the ground. Can you cover us?"

"*Consider it done. I'll make a pass, push the hostiles back with some strafing. That should buy you the time you need to set down for Singh. Once you dust off I'll come back around for another pass to cover the strike team. QInqul to D'Gol, do you copy?*"

"*D'Gol here. Speak, Hartür.*"

"*Dig in and stay low. First attack run starts in thirty seconds, attack direction north. After* Kepler *loads and clears off, second pass will follow, attack direction south. Acknowledge.*"

"*Understood. Good hunting, QInqul. Qapla'!*"

Sulu made sure the channel was still open. "Did you copy all that, Mister Spock?"

"*Affirmative, Mister Sulu. Exercise caution when you set down. The enemy appears to be exceptionally motivated.*"

"Understood, sir."

"*Chief Razka is setting smoke to mark your LZ.*"

Along the skinniest strip of the riverbank, along a thick stretch of untrammeled jungle, a small flash of detonation was followed by a quick-rising plume of bright green smoke.

"Visual confirmation, green smoke. On approach, ETA twenty seconds." Sulu fired the thrusters to quickly decelerate, in order to keep the *Kepler* clear of the *QInqul*'s suppressing fire.

The rapid slowdown knocked Doctor Babitz against the center navigation console and made her fumble her medical instruments. As she gathered the tools off the deck, she glared up at Sulu. "Do that again and I might amputate your leg by mistake. Or maybe on purpose."

Sulu didn't feel the least bit guilty, but he offered the doctor a sheepish smile just to smooth things over. "Sorry, Doc." He set his eyes on the LZ. "You'd better go strap in. This next part might get ugly."

Babitz rolled her eyes and strapped herself into the command chair. "What else is new?"

The bridge to the cave temple was close enough that Chekov was sure he could throw a rock and hit it. He was just as sure that if he or any other member of the landing party raised their head from the muddy ground, the Chwii would put a spear through it.

Muddy water splashed against the toes of Chekov's boots as he lay prone on the riverbank. The landing party had been jogging along the riverside, heading toward the temple, when the Chwii sprang their latest ambush. There was little between the riverbank and the tree line that deserved to be called concealment, never mind hard cover, so when a maelstrom of spears and stones had flown from the shadows between the trees, the group's only option was to stand and be impaled or use the shallow slope of the riverbank as a meager defilade.

Stones splashed down in front of him, spattering his face with warm mud. He winced and then risked lifting his disruptor rifle a few centimeters, just enough to squeeze off a shot or two through the drifting green smoke and into the trees, at enemies he couldn't see but heard whooping like wild men. Then a spear would arc toward him and he'd bury his face in the muck until he was sure it had missed.

Lying next to him on the shallow grade was Ilucci. The engineer had taken a slingstone to the right side of his face, which was swelling and turning shades of red, yellow, and violet. He winced as another stone skipped off the mud and bounded over him and Chekov into the river. "I thought phasers versus sticks and stones didn't sound like a fair fight. Now I'm not so sure."

Chekov flinched as a spear passed over him and sank into

the river. "I am! Sticks and stones seem to have a definite advantage!"

From upriver Mara called out, "Look sharp! Smoke-serpent on the move!"

Chekov stole a look and saw the vaporous serpent winding through the jungle, just inside the tree line. Close enough to see, but too concealed to target.

Spock shouted, "Singh! Can you get a shot?"

The young woman was pinned in the mud with everyone else, unable to risk standing up to use her borrowed siege gun. "Negative! I'm under fire and my power cell's running low!"

Down the line, D'Gol, Razka, Mara, and Spock loosed random sprays of disruptor pulses or phaser fire into the trees, if only to discourage the Chwii from committing to a full-scale charge of the riverbank. Even Chekov knew what that would mean.

We wouldn't last half a minute. He nudged his rifle over the shallow edge and peppered the jungle foliage with several seconds of pulsed disruptor fire. *They'd either cut us down or force us into the river. Either would be a death sentence.*

Over the white noise of rain splattering into mud came the high-pitched whine of shuttlecraft engines. There were two distinct pitches of engine sound, which meant both shuttlecraft were on their way. Chekov looked up and struggled to see past leaden curtains of rain—and then the two spacecraft appeared, the *QInqul* in front, the *Kepler* close behind. The *QInqul* accelerated into a shallow descent as it fell into position above the riverbank.

Too excited to stay silent, Chekov shouted, "Shuttles inbound!"

"Stay down," Spock said. "Don't move until I—"

A hundred bodies burst forth from the jungle, sprinting with mad abandon toward the river—and the smoke-serpent attacked with them.

Hartür's voice crackled over the landing party's comms: "*QInqul to landing party! Nobody move! I got this!*"

The jungle army was on its third charging stride, and just three strides more from overrunning the landing party, when the *QInqul*'s ship-grade disruptor cannons strafed the Chwii's entire front rank in a single northward sweep. Chwii bodies erupted by the dozen into steaming clouds of viscera and pulverized bone, or vanished in white-hot flashes. In the wink of an eye, their first rank of attackers was swept off the battlefield.

The *QInqul* raced past overhead and climbed into a wide banking turn.

On the riverbank, the smoke-serpent's form turned tenuous for several seconds. Chekov hoped the creature would retreat into the jungle and take the rest of its Chwii minions with it.

Instead the monster let out a terrifying shriek-howl and surged back to full strength. Its cry was still resounding through the jungle when another fifty Chwii broke from cover and charged toward the river, every last one of them roaring like a berserker.

A spear dropped between Chekov and Ilucci, but it was close enough to the engineer that it shaved some stubble off his cheek. For half a second Ilucci stared in wide-eyed horror at the spearhead next to his face—and then his rage took over: "Screw this!"

He grabbed the spear's shaft, pulled himself up, yanked the weapon from the mud, and hurled it back at the Chwii who'd thrown it. It sank into the alien warrior's chest.

Ilucci reached into his satchel and pulled out two plasma grenades. Juggled one into his free hand. Armed them both. And lobbed them with a flourish into the next wave of Chwii.

They detonated with retina-searing flashes and ear-splitting bangs. Orange flames and a shock wave shredded a dozen Chwii footmen along the jungle's perimeter.

Another spear soared over the blast and slammed down into Ilucci's left foot, staking him to the muddy ground. The master chief screamed out an ancient Earth vulgarity. It was just one word, but he made it last for several seconds and put it through a few key changes before he collapsed onto his back and hyperventilated with his foot still inescapably impaled.

Somewhere upriver the *QInqul* was coming around for another pass, and downriver the *Kepler* was looking for a safe place to set down—but in the middle of the fray, there was nowhere to run and another wave of bodies bounding out of the jungle hell-bent for blood.

Spock got up on one knee and steadied his aim with a Klingon disruptor pistol. "Fire at will!" He unleashed a furious storm of disruptor pulses into the attacking Chwii, and beside him D'Gol and Mara did the same. Within half a second Singh and Razka were up and shooting, and Chekov, defying every urge for survival that told him to stay down, got up and opened fire.

Lethal disruptor pulses and heavy-stun phaser beams crisscrossed, catching the Chwii in pincerlike traps. Chekov's heart slammed in his chest and he felt sick to his stomach, but he kept firing, picking off one target after another, his reflexes faster than he'd ever remembered them being. His hands shook from adrenaline overload but he fought on, his breaths short and shallow, his throat as dry as a funeral drum, his vision blurred by rain and steam and tears.

Mere meters in front of him, sentient beings fell in clusters, cut down by forces they could never have hoped to match— some slain by Chekov, or with his participation at least.

Six more Chwii fighters burst into view, but these were different—larger, almost twice the size of their comrades. Ogrelike, these Chwii were festooned in garments made of reptilian scales and colorful feathers, and flowers covered their chests, held in place by the fact that their stems were embedded into the warriors' flesh. Unlike their peers who came wielding spears or stones, these giants toted double-headed stone axes with handles as large as Chekov's legs.

They bellowed throaty war cries as they charged.

Down the line, Spock, D'Gol, and Mara unleashed kill shots and vaporized their gargantuan attackers. Singh and Razka reset their phasers and took down two more.

The last one barreled toward Chekov with his axe raised to strike.

Chekov loaded a fresh power cell into his rifle—and froze.

He saw the Chwii giant's red eyes. The pupils were dilated, as if the ogre were under the influence of a stimulant or a hallucinogen, or perhaps both. He was running flat out, screaming at the top of his lungs, clearly pushed to the brink of madness.

There was no doubt in Chekov's mind that this goliath meant to kill him.

But his finger refused to squeeze the rifle's trigger.

The ogre-Chwii raised his axe over his head and leapt into the air.

Chekov kept his rifle aimed at the giant but couldn't fire.

The mountain of Chwii dropped toward Chekov, swinging his axe to bring the killing blow, when a phaser beam slammed into the titan's chest and vaporized him in a pulse of light.

Shaking uncontrollably, Chekov looked left toward the source of the beam. Chief Razka was already resetting his phaser to heavy stun, to prepare for the next wave of Chwii.

Chekov's mind felt blank, but when he caught Razka's eye he said in a flat voice, "Thank you, Chief." The Saurian nodded but said nothing. Looking into his large eyes, Chekov was overcome by a nauseating wave of shame that compelled him to add, "Sorry, Chief."

Razka unleashed a volley of suppressing fire toward the tree line, forcing several Chwii to abandon their charge and duck back under cover. Then he moved to stand beside Chekov. "No need to apologize, sir. Trust me: being able to kill is *nothing* to be proud of—and *not* being able to kill a person is no cause for shame."

The Saurian kneeled next to Ilucci and without any preamble pulled the spear from the man's foot. Ilucci hollered a blue streak as bright red blood surged from his boot. Razka pulled off Ilucci's shredded boot and said to Chekov, "Can you get the medkit from my pack, sir?"

"Of course." Chekov retrieved the medkit and handed it to Razka.

"Thank you, sir." With the efficiency of a trained medic, Razka began treating Ilucci's injury. "I'd be grateful for some covering fire while I stop the master chief's bleeding."

"Yes, Chief." Chekov kneeled next to Razka and Ilucci and took over peppering the tree line with blasts of disruptor fire. To his surprise, the more he fired, the calmer he became.

Down in the mud at his side, Razka wrapped a watertight bandage around Ilucci's foot, and then he tucked away the medkit, raised his phaser, and fell in next to Chekov.

"Hang tough, sir. I've got your back, and you've got mine. Right?"

Chekov mustered the ghost of a smile and nodded. "Aye, Chief."

"Then we've got nothing to fear, sir." He clapped a scaly hand on Chekov's shoulder. "Field scout's honor."

27

Making a fresh pass over the riverbank, Sulu saw that the fighting appeared to be tapering off. The team on the ground had repelled a major assault from the jungle, thanks to a strafing run by the *QInqul* and a whole lot of luck. Spirals of smoke twisted up from the canopy, and dark clouds drifted between the trees at ground level, cloaking the forest's interior in near-total darkness.

The comm crackled. *"Spock to Kepler. Mister Sulu, do you read me?"*

"Affirmative, Mister Spock. Go ahead."

"The fighting here seems to have abated. However, all our tricorders have been either damaged or lost. Can you confirm the status of the Chwii soldiers?"

"Aye, sir. Give me a moment." Sulu checked the sensors. "I read several dozen Chwii within a five-kilometer radius, but they're scattered and their movements suggest they've lost unit cohesion. The only concentrated pocket left in your vicinity appears to be a group of two dozen Chwii defending the bridge to the cave temple."

"Acknowledged. Set down near the green smoke and take Ensign Singh aboard. She'll use her siege gun to cover us from the air."

"Copy that, Mister Spock. Setting down now. Clear the LZ."

As Sulu guided the shuttlecraft into a gentle descent, Doctor Babitz reached over from the command seat and reopened the comm channel. "Doctor Babitz to Mister Spock. Do any of the landing party need medical help?"

"*Affirmative, Doctor. Master Chief Ilucci is unable to continue. Please prepare to take him aboard the* Kepler."

"Understood. We'll be ready. *Kepler* out." She closed the channel and freed herself from the seat's restraints. As she stood she said, "I'd better get the surgical kit back out."

"Sounds like it," Sulu said, easing the shuttlecraft toward the ground.

Through the forward viewports, he saw the riverbank strewn with the bodies of dozens of Chwii, all of them scorched or blasted apart. The steady rain washed vast pools of blood into the river. Mara and D'Gol walked toward the LZ, and behind them Razka and Chekov carried Master Chief Ilucci, whose left foot was bare and wrapped in bandages. Trailing them was Singh, who looked as if she ought to be too small to tote a siege gun but did it anyway.

The *Kepler*'s landing gear was less than a meter from touchdown when a breeze blew the column of green smoke across the shuttlecraft's bow, obscuring Sulu's vision for half a second.

When the smoke cleared, it was already too late for him to shout a warning.

A Shedai smoke-tentacle shot out of the jungle and slammed into Mara.

The blow threw Mara into the air—and into the river.

On the riverbank, Singh dashed clear of the others and unleashed hell with her siege gun. She shredded the smoke-serpent into wispy bits, forcing it to retreat and vanish into the jungle just as quickly as it had struck.

Babitz ran to the portside hatch and opened it to get a clear view of the river. Sulu looked out the door and saw the same thing she did: Mara being swept away in the swift, unrelenting current of filthy water.

Sulu opened the comm. "Mister Spock! Permission to—"

"GO, Mister Sulu!"

Sulu powered up the engines and looked back at Babitz. "Hang on, Doc!"

She grabbed a handhold beside the open hatchway and gave him a thumbs-up. "Go!"

He swung the *Kepler* hard about and punched the accelerator. *Hang on, Mara, we're coming.*

D'Gol pointed downriver. "Are you crazy, Vulcan? You just sent away half our air cover!" The Klingon's temper was as hot as his breath in Spock's face, and just as repellent.

"I released the *Kepler* to save *your* science officer."

"If Mara can't swim, that's her problem." D'Gol gesticulated toward the temple. "Now we've got to fight that *thing* with only half the air support."

"A single gunner on the *Kepler* will not make a significant difference in the battle to come. And as it happens, the power cells for Ensign Singh's siege gun are depleted, rendering that discussion moot." Spock wiped fresh pools of his own green blood from his eyes and raised one hand to his wounded forehead to block the pounding rain so he could take a clearer look at the cave temple just a few dozen meters away. "There are only two dozen Chwii defenders left in front of the temple, and none inside. We should be able to break their morale and scare them off with a wide-field, low-power sustained barrage."

The Klingon commander's anger boiled over. "I did not come all this way just to *scare them off*! They challenged us. Ambushed us. Killed my men. They deserve to die."

"Be that as it may, I command the majority of our remaining personnel, and Starfleet's rules of engagement require us to at least *attempt* to achieve our mission objectives through the use of nonlethal tactics *before* resorting to greater force."

D'Gol shook his head as he pulled out his communicator.

"What a tragic waste of firepower." He flipped open his communicator and adjusted its transmission strength. "D'Gol to Hartür. Do you copy?"

The pilot's voice came back crackling with static. *"I copy. Go ahead, Commander."*

"Mister Spock has decided we will use *nonlethal* tactics to drive off the Chwii defenders at the temple's bridge. We'll attack from the east. Set the *QInqul's* disruptors to minimum power, widest field, and come in low, attack direction north."

"Understood. Banking into my attack vector now. Ten seconds to contact."

"Acknowledged. Starting our assault. D'Gol out." The brawny Klingon dialed down the power on his disruptor rifle to its lowest setting, and then he widened its beam to its fullest. "Ready, Vulcan?"

Spock looked down the line to confirm his people were in position. Ilucci had given Spock his phaser and been taken to cover now that he was effectively immobilized, but Singh, Razka, and Chekov all stood ready at Spock's side, weapons set for minimum power. They nodded at him to signal they were set, and Spock nodded at D'Gol. "Ready."

"Then let's not keep Sto-Vo-Kor waiting."

D'Gol charged toward the bridge, firing his disruptor in regular pulses. Spock and his three remaining personnel sprinted toward the cave temple, blanketing the area ahead with overlapping waves of stunning energy.

As Spock had hoped, the Chwii who had been hiding in the riverbank's tall grasses and fronds quit their hiding places and scattered in confusion. A few stumbled toward the attacking landing party, but those unlucky ones quickly realized their mistake and changed direction.

The rear rank of Chwii defenders held their ground long enough to stand and bend back with spears ready to launch, only to be pummeled by the *QInqul's* twin disruptor cannons.

The crimson energy pulses, even at minimum strength, were enough to hurl Chwii through the air like leaves caught in a storm. The Chwii who could still stand dragged away their comrades who could not, and in less than half a minute the riverbank and the cave temple were empty of Chwii.

Spock noted the results with satisfaction, and then he adjusted his phaser's settings. "Well done, everyone. Now we must finish what we came to do. All weapons to maximum power, tight beam. Chief Razka, do you have Master Chief Ilucci's last plasma grenade?"

"Aye, sir."

"Please have it ready." To the Klingon, Spock added, "If you would do the honors, Commander."

D'Gol opened his communicator. "Hartür! Kill the Shedai!"

"Gladly."

A shrill whine of charging disruptor coils sliced through the breathy voice of rainfall. The humid air was cut by a sharp infusion of ozone—and then Hartür fired the *QInqul's* disruptor cannons at maximum power. Blinding white pulses of energy hotter than the surface of a Class-A main-sequence star transformed the misting rain into walls of steam and blasted an edifice of rock, packed mud, and vines into an expanding cloud of hot dust and motes of molten glass.

Within seconds, the façade of the cave temple collapsed and slid into the river. The interior passageways and fortifications of the temple were pushed into the hillside, drilled into red-hot slag by the *QInqul's* merciless fusillade. For a moment it looked to Spock as if the entire temple might sink into the depths without giving up the Godhead.

Then the wound in the ground exploded like a volcano.

A shock wave threw the landing party backward several meters to just short of the tree line, and sent the *QInqul* tumbling and yawing until its nose kissed the muddy river.

Countless tons of glowing-hot stone, steaming mud, and

freshly made glass shot into the sky, peppering the bellies of storm clouds with fiery debris trailing thick smoke. Lava oozed from the pit behind the river's head. The orange-white flow rolled into the water with a hiss.

From beneath the lava . . . from between the steam and the smoke . . . from behind the veil of the incessant rain . . . something colossal and monstrous rose from the pit.

The Godhead's form resembled nothing else Spock had ever seen. It defied simple taxonomical classification. It was not crustacean or reptilian, neither cephalopod nor insect, but it manifested features of all those phyla and others for which Spock had no names. It had a spiky, misshapen thorax and a bulbous head littered asymmetrically with eyes of many different shapes, sizes, and kinds; it hovered as if in defiance of gravity, and beneath its enormous scaled-and-plated abdomen it trailed seven black tentacles, each over twenty meters long and lined with thousands of suction cups and countless undulating cilia.

And though Spock was loath to admit it, the creature must have possessed formidable psionic power—because the mere sight of the abomination drove his logic into remission and tendered his conscious will to his human half, which was all but paralyzed by horror. . . .

—but he retained enough self-control to give one clear order: "FIRE!"

Spock fired first, and then the rest of the landing party unleashed their weapons on the titanic alien.

Razka pitched the last plasma grenade almost directly into the creature's face, where it exploded with a brilliant orange cloud of fire.

Then the *QInqul* hit the beast with everything it had.

Disruptor pulses shredded the tentacles, punched holes in the scaly abdomen, tore off pieces of its spike-armored thorax, and cooked dozens of its unblinking eyes into charred paste.

The creature shrieked louder than the thunder that rolled

across the sky. Its movements seemed to call down fearsome bolts of lightning that slammed into the *QInqul* and left the shuttlecraft wobbling and smoldering, but the shuttle's guns kept on firing.

Smoke-serpents climbed from the pit of destruction and bent toward the *QInqul*. Spock pointed at them. "Landing party, target the smoke-serpents!"

The ground team trained their firepower on the vaporous tentacles, tattering them with phaser beams and disruptor pulses until the Godhead's misty ancillary forms dissipated and collapsed back into the churning pit of molten rock.

Hartür pivoted the *QInqul* back and forth to slash the Godhead's form from head to tail with steady bursts of disruptor energy. With his latest sweep he severed the last of the monster's tentacles and ignited some kind of reaction inside the creature's abdomen. Cracks spread through the creature's exoskeleton, and fiery light blazed through the fissures.

D'Gol shouted into his communicator, "Finish it, Hartür!"

The *QInqul* ceased firing for just long enough to let the guns fully recharge, and for Hartür to target his shot.

Then the shuttle fired a massive burst of disruptor energy at the monster's head.

An explosion turned the dreary gray of the storm into a retina-searing glare.

Spock and the others all looked away. When the glow abated and they turned back, Spock was the first to be able to see, thanks to the protection of inner eyelids he had inherited from his father, an adaptation that had proved vital in the sunbaked deserts of Vulcan.

Where the monster had towered over the Kolasi jungle, nothing remained but a yawning pit of radiant glass belching heavy smoke. Several dozen meters away, hovering above the river with its hull scorched and cracked but its spirit unbroken, was the *QInqul*.

D'Gol shouted into his communicator, "Good shooting, Hartür!" Then he let out a triumphant laugh as he slapped Spock's back. "*Qapla'*, Vulcan!"

Seeing the devastation of the killing field, Spock knew he would never take pride in what he and his team had done this day, as necessary as it might have been. "*Qapla'*, indeed."

———————

Sulu pushed the *Kepler* as fast as he dared, and he feared it still wasn't fast enough. Sheeting rain against the viewports left him almost blind, so he was flying on instruments, but the storm's interference meant the shuttle's sensors weren't as precise as he would have liked—especially when it came to the heights of trees in his path.

Snap-crack!—and another tree's crown was torn off, this time by the *Kepler*'s port nacelle. The impact juddered the small craft and sent Doctor Babitz stumbling against a bulkhead. "What the hell's wrong with you? I thought you knew how to fly!"

"I fly in space. I don't deal with wind. Or rain, or trees, or"—a bang of impact from above accompanied the appearance of a new dent in the shuttle's overhead—"dragons."

He banked to starboard and pushed the *Kepler* into a brief dive followed by a sharp climb, in a desperate attempt to shake off the flying reptile hounding his spacecraft. Then he fired the thrusters in a bid to make up for more time he had just lost.

Babitz stumbled forward and fell into the command chair. "That thing is still on us! Try getting closer to the river."

Was she out of her mind? "Closer to the river? You mean below the jungle canopy?"

"Did I stutter? Yes!"

She *was* crazy. "Space is too tight down there, and the turns are too sharp. I'd have to slow down so much we couldn't catch Mara."

"Well, we can't—" A collision from starboard sent the *Kepler* into a half roll to port. Babitz held on to her seat and the forward console until Sulu righted the shuttle. "We can't stay up here! This thing's gonna have us for lunch!"

"We have to stay up here until we get ahead of Mara."

"Then gun it! Let that thing out there taste our impulse!"

"You can't use impulse power this close to the surface!"

"Says who? And before you answer: Were they trying to escape a dragon when they said it? Because if not, I don't give a damn."

He couldn't believe what he was hearing. "I suggest you strap in, Doc. 'Cause if you didn't like the ride down on thrusters, you're definitely not gonna like this."

Babitz scrambled to secure herself into her seat's harness. "I'm set! Do it!"

"Hang on!"

Against regulations and his better judgment, Sulu programmed the *Kepler* to make a one-tenth-of-a-second quarter-impulse burst—and then he pressed ENGAGE.

Everything outside the viewports became a wash of gray.

The inertial dampers were a fraction of a second slow to compensate for the impulse jump, and Sulu wondered if the five-hundredths of a second his body spent experiencing twenty g's would crack his spine or give him a stroke.

Then the view outside the *Kepler* reverted to something resembling a sloppy watercolor painting of a jungle besieged by endless storms, and though his head was swimming and his vision was populated by dozens of floating violet dots, he was still conscious and not paralyzed.

Next to him, Babitz looked like she was in shock—and then she pressed her hand to her mouth and started to retch toward the starboard bulkhead without producing anything.

Sulu checked the sensors, adjusted course toward the river, and smiled at the airsick doctor. "I warned you."

In between agonized dry heaves she grumbled, "Just shut up and fly."

_____

The river tasted like dirt. One mouthful of filthy water after another choked Mara as the current pulled her along like a piece of flotsam, and the more desperately she kicked and flailed to keep her head above water, the harder the river pulled her down.

With every passing second the river seemed to get faster, and the rocks in her path got larger. The waterway was packed with threats hiding beneath the waterline: boulders, fallen trees, tangles of thorny vines. Always just enough to hurt her, never enough to stop her.

Predators nipped at her as she raced past, a slave to the elements.

A few times she thought she heard the whine of a shuttlecraft's engines, but when she tried to look up, the river used that moment to slam her into something and force her back under the surface. When she broke through to open air once more, there was no sign of a shuttle above.

No one is coming.

She considered pulling off her tunic and turning it into some kind of air bladder, to use as a flotation device. Anything to keep her head above water.

When she touched the front of her tunic, she felt the cold scar of crystalline rock spreading across her torso, and the ache of the wound beneath it. She remembered the smoky tentacle racing out of the trees and slamming into her, its tip solidified into a killing edge.

Even if I don't drown, this poison will reach my hearts in minutes. The river or the Shedai wound—they were both death sentences. She knew it. *A lesser spirit would take the easy way out. Surrender to the water or succumb to the poison.*

Despair tried to embrace Mara and drag her down into its black abyss.

She kicked her legs, broke through the river's frothy white-caps, and filled her lungs with another breath. *If death wants me, let it break me—but I won't defeat myself.*

I do not surrender! I do not yield! I am Klingon!

The last thing Sulu needed while skimming the jungle's canopy was Babitz shouting in his ear, "We're gonna miss her!"

"No, we're not." He had one eye on the sensor display, which showed the river's twisting path beneath the *Kepler*, and the other eye looking out the viewport to peer through the rain. "We're almost there. Just a few more seconds . . ."

"She's coming up fast, Sulu! If we don't get under the canopy—"

"I know the mission, Doc." He pointed at a shadowy break in the endless green sprawl of the jungle's treetops, dead ahead of the shuttle. "A gap above the river, right there!" He hooked his thumb over his shoulder. "Prep the spare climbing harness."

Babitz hurried aft to get the extra harness and a hundred meters of climbing rope from the cargo compartment. Sulu poured on the speed and then halted the *Kepler* directly above the gap in the canopy. He angled its nose to match the direction of the river's current, gently lowered the shuttlecraft through the broad opening in the jungle's treetops, and parked it fifteen meters above the wild rush of the muddy river. Another look at the sensors confirmed they were ahead of Mara, but she was soon to catch up to them.

The doctor stumbled back to the front of the shuttle, her arms loaded with gear, and shot a confused look at Sulu. "Now what?"

"Anchor the rope to the command seat's base. Can you tie a double half hitch?"

"Of course I can, I all but grew up on my father's sailboat." She kneeled beside the shuttle's other front seat and secured the working end of the rope to the seat's base with fast, practiced motions. In the time it took Sulu to check Mara's position on the sensors again, Babitz had threaded the other end of the rope through the rings of the orange climbing harness. "Set."

"Okay, she's almost here, get ready at the hatch."

Babitz hauled the harness and coiled rope to the open hatchway. Gripping the handhold for dear life, she looked down at the river. "My God, it's like a flood of sewage."

"It's just muddy, Doc."

"I assure you, it's more than just muddy. It—" She squinted upriver. "I see her!"

"Lower the harness. Try to keep it above water so she'll see it."

Gusts of wind buffeted the shuttle. Sulu fired the thrusters to compensate and hold the small craft steady. "Just a few more seconds . . ."

Worry colored Babitz's voice. "Something's wrong. She's barely afloat." The doctor strained to see what was happening in the river below. "Dammit, she's *drowning*. She won't be able to grab the harness!"

"Give her a chance, Doc! Let it drag in the water ahead of her, maybe we can snag her with it." Sulu eased the shuttle into a slow vertical descent. "I'll get us a bit closer."

Babitz gripped the climbing rope with one hand and a safety handhold on the bulkhead with the other. Rain-driven wind surged through the open hatchway, slicking the deck and almost knocking her off her feet. She recovered her balance and looked down. "She's got a crystalline mass on her torso! Even if she's awake, she's in no shape to aid her own rescue."

The moving blip on the sensor display told Sulu the bad news.

"She passed us, Doc! If she can't grab the harness there's nothing we—"

"Follow her, now!" Babitz hauled up the rope, hand over hand, towing the orange harness back up to the open hatchway as fast as she could. "Move it, Lieutenant! That's an order!"

"Aye, sir." He initiated a vertical ascent toward the gap in the canopy.

Babitz snapped, "No! There's no time! Catch up to her down here! GO!"

"All right, but remember—*you asked for it.*"

He punched the throttle and pushed his skills to the edge, tracking the hairpin turns in the wild river. Great sheets of moss and vast tangles of vines filled the open air above the water, bridging the different sides of the canopy. More than obstacles, they were barriers, walls of vegetation suspended above the madly coursing flood.

Sulu gunned the *Kepler*'s thrusters and ripped right through them.

The snapping of vines came in such rapid sequence that they reminded Sulu of the sound of corn kernels popping in an oiled pan over an open flame.

He banked hard to port, yawing the shuttle almost onto its side as he navigated another turn, and then he forced the *Kepler* the other way, hard to starboard, yawing with enough force to make the shuttle's spaceframe groan in protest.

Behind him, Babitz swore under her breath while shimmying awkwardly into the harness as his maneuvers threw her side to side. She bounced off the starboard bulkhead, and when he punched the accelerator, she was launched aft, into the narrow aisle between the seats. Then he bashed through another dense cluster of vines as she was standing up, and the sudden deceleration knocked her flat onto her stomach.

He dipped the shuttle under a vine cluster, made a rolling turn through a gap in the next one, and then poured on the speed to shred through another like a katana through cobwebs.

The dots and numbers on the sensor display showed good news for a change. "Heads up, Doc! We've almost caught up to Mara! We're thirty meters behind her, closing fast."

The doctor struggled to her feet. "Steady as she goes, Lieutenant." She adjusted the straps and coils on the harness until it was snug on her torso. "Let me know when we're ten meters out."

A large object appeared on the sensors—as an ear-splitting shriek preceded a bone-jarring jolt of impact that made the shuttle's control panel go dark for a fraction of a second.

The same dragon that had been chasing them that entire morning swooped in front of the *Kepler* from above and slammed its spiked tail against the shuttle's nose as it passed.

Babitz glared through the viewport as the beast arced downward—toward Mara. "Stop that thing before it reaches her!"

"How? We don't have any weapons."

"We have thrusters and shields. *Ramming speed*, Lieutenant!"

28

"This isn't over until I know every last speck of that thing is dead," D'Gol had said to Spock. It was a sentiment with which Spock had strongly concurred.

The two of them stood together at the edge of the crater that now yawned where only minutes earlier the cave temple had stood. Infernal heat emanated in waves from the smoldering pit, turning the Kolasi jungle's despised rain into a welcome comfort. Above and behind them hovered the *QInqul*. Hartür was using the shuttle's sensors to search for any surviving traces of the Shedai meta-genome. As thorough as Hartür's destruction of the temple had been, Spock and D'Gol both had pledged not to let any data about the Shedai leave this planet, nor to leave behind any samples of the bizarre alien genetic material for others to find and exploit.

A thin facsimile of Hartür's voice issued from D'Gol's communicator. *"Grid eight clear. Starting deep scan of grid nine."*

"Acknowledged." D'Gol surveyed the field of destruction. "What of the Chwii?"

"Still in retreat, Commander."

"Good." The Klingon lowered his communicator and turned a bemused look at Spock. "When I heard the tales of Gamma Tauri IV, I thought they were lies. Even now, having seen it myself, I still find it hard to believe."

Spock understood the man's reaction. "Witnessing something

as profoundly alien in its form and consciousness as the Shedai can be a most disquieting experience."

Amusement, confusion, and contempt collided on D'Gol's furrowed brow. "I was talking about Klingons and Starfleeters fighting on the same side, acting with common purpose." He spit, as if to expel a foul taste from his tongue. "That's the part my captain will never believe."

"Indeed. I expect a similar degree of resistance from mine."

Hartür interrupted via the communicator, *"Sensors have something in grid nine."*

D'Gol drew his disruptor pistol. "Guide us to it."

"Sixteen qams *from your current position, relative bearing two one point four, z-minus two point two* qams."

Spock drew his phaser but let D'Gol lead the way. They descended into the pit. Each step they took closer to its nadir, the hotter the ground became beneath their boots. The heat was uncomfortable within three steps. After five it reminded Spock of the coming-of-age ritual in which he had been required to traverse the rocky plain of Vulcan's Forge barefoot. After ten steps he had to marshal his hard-won psionic discipline to block out the pain.

If D'Gol was in any discomfort, he hid it with superb aplomb. They arrived at a large stone, roughly sixty centimeters wide and half as tall. It was radiant with heat, but D'Gol reached down and with gauntleted hands flipped it over as if it weren't as hot as glass from a furnace.

Embedded in the searing-hot dust beneath where the rock had been was a smear of something biological. A bit of half-cooked flesh, perhaps. Maybe a crushed eyeball. It was difficult to identify what it once had been, other than organic in nature.

D'Gol kneeled beside it and looked up over his shoulder toward Hartür on the *QInqul.* "Is this what we're looking for?"

"Maybe. Readings are garbled. Signal is weak."

"Weak sounds about right." D'Gol stood and took a step back from the charred mess. He looked at Spock. "Together?"

"Together." Spock and D'Gol aimed their weapons at the smeared tissue. D'Gol counted to three, at which point they both opened fire—continuous full-power shots that lasted over five seconds.

When they ceased fire, there was nothing left of the smear. Just molten rock. Spock lowered his weapon. "Détente."

D'Gol nodded. "Détente."

Hartür's tone turned to one of alarm. *"Commander? I'm not sure that was the only—"*

A long shaft of sharp smoky crystal exploded from D'Gol's chest.

Klingon blood sprayed into Spock's face. He staggered backward and only then saw the tentacle of black vapors that had risen from a fissure a few meters farther down the pit. And crawling out of that fissure was a grotesque chimera—Doctor Chunvig's head, shoulders, and arms mounted on a crustacean-like thorax, which was being pushed upward by a mangled insectoid abdomen with tentacles instead of legs.

Next to Spock, D'Gol's body slid off the crystalline spike. A shroud of black crystal formed around the corpse as it rolled down the pit's slope into its fiery center.

Retreating out of the pit, Spock fired at the abomination pursuing him. At the top of the crater, Singh, Razka, and Chekov all had come running at the sound of his weapon. He continued to shoot at the monster as he yelled to the others, "It's the God-head! Shoot to kill!"

The trio spread out to get clear shots at the creature. Spock had almost reached them when his communicator beeped twice on his belt. He pulled it free and opened its grille with a turn of his wrist. "Spock here!"

"This is Hartür! Get your people to cover! NOW!"

Overhead, the *QInqul*'s impulse engines whined as Hartür powered them up.

There was no time to argue tactics. The situation was out of

Spock's hands, and he knew it. He closed his communicator and shouted to his team, "Fall back! Find cover!"

Chekov and Singh retreated, but Razka held his ground at the crater's edge until Spock got to him. The Saurian reached down, took Spock's hand, and hefted him out of the pit with one powerful motion. Even as they sprinted away from the pit, Spock felt compelled to look back.

The creature's tentacles flailed in the air and its hideous cries resounded through the jungle, all as Hartür pushed the *QInqul* into an almost vertical climb, directly above the pit.

Razka and Spock caught up to Chekov and Singh, and together they huddled behind a cluster of large boulders inside the jungle, over a hundred meters from the pit.

In the sky, the *QInqul* vanished into the storm clouds.

Seconds later the Klingon shuttle reappeared, its forward disruptor cannons blazing, the craft now in a full-power nose dive toward the pit—and the creature.

Tumbling down after the *QInqul* were its ejected antimatter pods.

The Shedai Godhead pulled its damaged, nightmarish body over the edge of the crater, only to be knocked back into the pit by a merciless rain of disruptor pulses. The creature tried to retreat but the hail of wild energy pursued its every step—until the *QInqul* slammed into the creature at nearly the speed of sound.

A flash of fire filled the jungle with white light and bone-breaking thunder.

And for one shining instant, it stopped raining.

Sulu's maneuvers had Babitz pinballing against the bulkheads and clutching the anchored portion of the climbing rope for dear life. She watched the dragon's flank swing toward the open hatchway as Sulu banked to port to ram the creature again. He had hit the beast several times in the past minute, but it continued to follow Mara down the river, apparently unwilling to give up an easy meal bobbing on the surface.

The creature dipped under a dense mesh of vines, and Sulu followed it, nicking the lowest-hanging vines as the *Kepler* sped beneath them. A kick of acceleration sent Babitz stumbling aft, while outside the hatchway the wall of jungle trees melted into a green blur.

She regained her balance and staggered forward to ask Sulu what was happening when a portion of the dragon's head bashed through the open hatchway just an arm's length from her. She fell against the starboard bulkhead as the creature shrieked, filling the shuttlecraft with its carrion-stench breath and lapping the overhead with its forked tongue. Then it broke free and swung wide, apparently to build up speed for another lunge at the shuttle.

Sulu looked back at Babitz. "I think we got its attention!"

"You don't say." She glanced out the forward viewport and her jaw went slack. "No. Tell me that's not—"

"The waterfall," Sulu said, finishing her sentence. "Thirty seconds out." He winced and fought to retain control as the dragon slammed against the rear port quarter of the shuttle. "If you've got any bright ideas, Doc, now's the time."

Twenty-five seconds until Mara goes over the waterfall.

Babitz faced the hatchway, drew her phaser, and put her back to the starboard bulkhead. "Sulu! When I fire, yaw ninety degrees to port!"

"When you what? What're you—?"

She leapt from the hatchway with her harness's anchored climbing rope's slack paying out behind her before he realized she was gone.

At the apex of her jump, in that microsecond before gravity took hold, as the dragon was swooping toward her and the shuttle, she fired her phaser on heavy stun and hit the beast square in the face. And then she and the monster both were falling, plunging like stones toward the river.

Babitz had just enough time to tuck her phaser under her poncho, put her feet together, and cross her arms against her chest before she struck the muddy rapids. She arrowed through the surface into its cloudy, roiling depths, and was shocked by how cold the water was. Kicking as hard as she could, she fought to get back to the surface—and then the climbing rope went taut and towed her out of the dark, back into the rain-swept morning air.

Above her was the *Kepler*, rolled ninety degrees to port as she'd ordered. Sulu struggled to keep the shuttle steady as he piloted the craft on its side, but at least now he could see Babitz in the water directly beneath him. Whether he could hear her, she was about to find out.

She pointed at an obstacle jutting from the river ahead of her. "Rock! Steer left!" Sulu stretched back and craned his neck to look down at Babitz through the open hatch. He pointed at his ear and shook his head. Babitz pointed with her whole arm as she repeated, "LEFT!"

The line went taut as Sulu adjusted the shuttle's position—and towed Babitz straight into the massive, water-smoothed boulder. Over the rush of the river and the whine of the shuttle's engine she didn't hear her two lower ribs cracking, but she damned sure felt it. She glared up at Sulu. "Your *other* left!" But cursing him was a waste of time as the *Kepler* slammed through another pocket of vines, raining fragments into the river behind Babitz.

She fished for her communicator under the water and pulled it from her belt. *I sure hope this thing's waterproof.* Pushing it above the water, she opened its grille with a flick of her wrist. "Babitz to *Kepler*! Do you read me, Sulu?"

A garbled voice answered, *"Go ahead, Doc!"*

"Watch the rocks! Shift me left, then—"

The rope snapped tight and dragged her half out of the water as it pulled her left.

"Easy! Too high!" The rocks shot past on her right. Up ahead she saw the foaming churn that defined the top of the waterfall—and she saw Mara being pulled inexorably toward it, all but powerless to save herself. "Get me right of center! Line me up with Mara!"

I can't see you both at the same time!

"Just do as I say! A nudge to the right!" The rope went from loose to tourniquet in an instant and pulled Babitz rightward. "Almost there! A little more!"

Ahead of her, Mara was just a dozen meters from the edge.

The *Kepler* drifted by such a small degree that Babitz could barely see the difference, but she watched as Mara shifted closer to being in front of her—and then she was there.

"PUNCH IT!"

The shuttle's thrusters roared, and at the end of the rope Babitz sliced like a knife through the rapids. Under the water, hidden rocks, thorny vines, and unseen predators nipped at her, each taking its bit of flesh as she raced past, while ahead of her Mara drew closer to the edge—three meters . . . two meters . . .

"SULU!"

From above, a *bang* like thunder as Sulu fired the *Kepler's* impulse engine. Icy water stung Babitz's face as she rocketed through the river's last meters of froth.

A thud of collision with something else in the water—and hoping against hope, Babitz clutched whatever she had just struck, wrapping her arms and legs around it.

A split-second submerged in the great spume at the waterfall's crest—

—and Babitz broke free into open air, dangling at the end of the climbing rope, with the barely conscious Mara locked in her full-body embrace. Babitz grinned at her. "Gotcha!"

Stunned and perplexed, Mara took in the rain-swept landscape spread out beneath them. Then she stared up the rope at the shuttlecraft towing them through the air. "Are you *insane*?"

"Probably. But I'm an officer, so who can tell?"

Spock and the rest of the landing party emerged from the jungle. Razka and Chekov were on either side of Master Chief Ilucci, helping the engineer limp along while keeping his weight off his wounded left foot. Ensign Singh, once more wielding only her Starfleet-issued phaser, walked several paces ahead, scouting the area for any signs of Chwii activity—or surviving Shedai biomass. A few dozen meters out from the tree line she continued to signal all clear.

There was nothing left of the temple. Its previous modest crater had been widened to a much larger one. This new pit's sides were smooth slopes of blackened glass littered with jagged chunks of scorched duranium from the hull of the *QInqul*, and the heat from the shuttlecraft's fiery sacrifice meant no one from the landing party could risk getting within twenty meters of its precipice. Waves of heat radiation rippled above the crater, and the rain—which had returned with a vengeance just as swiftly as it had been dispelled—sizzled when it struck the black glass.

Singh regarded the devastation with a sad expression. "Not one of our finest hours."

Stopping beside her, Spock replied, "I regret that I must concur."

The others hobbled to a stop a few meters behind Spock and Singh. Ilucci asked, "Any chance that monster's still alive?"

"It seems unlikely, but few things are ever truly impossible, Master Chief."

Spock's communicator beeped. He raised it and opened its grille. "Spock here."

Sulu replied, "*Shuttlecraft* Kepler *inbound to your position. ETA twenty seconds.*"

"Acknowledged, Mister Sulu. Were you able to rescue Lieutenant Mara?"

"*Affirmative. Doctor Babitz is treating her wounds right now. She'll be fine.*"

"Good work. Before you land, make a sensor sweep of the area for Chwii activity, and then make a second scan of the crater, to confirm there are no traces of Shedai meta-genome."

"Scanning now. Stand by."

Spock looked south and saw the *Kepler* appear above the treetops, cruising toward the landing party's position on the eastern riverbank. "Ensign Singh, please guide Mister Sulu in."

"Aye, sir." Singh jogged several meters away from the landing party to an open patch of level ground. As soon as she had a clear line of sight to the *Kepler*, she raised her arms to signal Sulu that she was directing him to a safe landing zone.

Sulu's voice returned over Spock's communicator. *"Both sensor sweeps are clear, sir. The nearest Chwii are twenty-one kilometers northwest and continuing to move away, and scans of the crater show no organic matter in it, around it, or under it."*

"Very good. Land, but do not power down. Stand by for immediate takeoff once the landing party is aboard."

"Understood, sir."

Guided by Ensign Singh, the *Kepler* slowed until it arrived above the landing area, and then Sulu initiated a slow, smooth vertical descent that culminated in the landing gear sinking several centimeters deep into the mud.

As soon as the shuttlecraft was securely on the ground, its portside hatch slid open. Doctor Babitz was the first person to exit the shuttle. She was covered in half-dried mud, from her matted blond hair to her river grass–entangled boots. Once on the ground, she turned and helped Mara out of the shuttle. The Klingon woman was just as mud caked, and where the middle of her uniform had been cut away, a prominent scar was visible on her abdomen.

Ilucci seemed amused by the women's disheveled state. "Damn, Doc. You look like the air-dried winner of an Argelian mud-wrestling match. And *she* looks like the loser."

Babitz glared at him, visibly in no mood for his brand of juvenile banter. "I can still choose to *amputate* your foot, Master Chief."

Duly chastised, he gave her a nod of contrition. "Copy that, sir."

Sulu remained inside the shuttlecraft, at its controls. Through the open hatchway Spock noted the tangled mess of wet climbing rope and a water-logged orange climbing harness on the deck between the pilot's and commander's seats.

Mara beckoned Spock toward the shuttle with a tilt of her head. They met far enough away from the others that they could speak confidentially, thanks to the shuttle's engine noise.

"Are you all right, Lieutenant?"

She nodded. "Yes. Thanks to your pilot and doctor." She touched the scar on her belly. "I don't know how she was able to remove the parasitic crystal, but I am grateful she did." Her mood turned somber as she regarded the black crater. "Where are D'Gol and Hartür?"

"Your commander was slain by the Shedai Godhead. Your pilot sacrificed your shuttle and his life to kill the creature. Both fought with dignity and valor." He glanced at his landing party. "They, and the rest of your team, saved our lives."

Mara lifted her chin slightly, a gesture of pride. "We stood together against a shared enemy. Honor demanded no less." Her pride turned quickly to melancholy. "And the Shedai meta-genome data?"

"Destroyed. The last sensor logs of the meta-genome were lost with the *QInqul*."

"Then our pact is fulfilled."

"It is." Spock gestured toward the *Kepler*. "If you wish, you are welcome to leave with us."

She refused with an ironic smile and a shake of her head. "I fear that would raise more questions than I am prepared to answer. But if you would be so kind as to inform Captain Kang that his wife Mara is alive and in need of a ride back to the ship?"

A small nod. "I shall do so." He faced the landing party. "Everyone aboard."

Chekov and Razka carried Ilucci past Spock and Mara, and helped the portly noncom to his seat inside the shuttlecraft. Singh escorted Babitz back to the *Kepler*'s hatchway, where Mara stopped Babitz with a gentle hold on her arm. "Before you go?"

Singh gave the two women a look. The doctor nodded her assurance, and Singh boarded the shuttle, followed by Spock, who lingered near the hatchway.

Alone outside the hatchway with Babitz, Mara seemed almost apologetic. "It can be difficult for Klingons to express gratitude. I am . . . thankful to you and Lieutenant Sulu for saving my life—but especially to you, for coming into the river to get me."

Babitz shrugged. "I'm sure you'd have done the same for me."

"No. I wouldn't have. . . . At least, not before today."

The doctor smiled. "And what about tomorrow?"

"Tomorrow, we shall see."

Babitz shook Mara's hand, and then she climbed inside the shuttlecraft. Spock stepped in front of the open hatchway as he prepared to close it for takeoff, and he paused as Mara stepped back, stood at attention, and smiled at him.

"Strength and honor, Spock."

He raised his hand in the traditional Vulcan salute. "Live long and prosper, Mara."

He closed the hatch and secured it as Sulu began the shuttle's lift-off.

From his place in the commander's chair, Spock saw Mara through the forward viewport as Sulu steered the hovering *Kepler* onto its departure vector. As the shuttlecraft made a smooth vertical ascent to clear the jungle's canopy, ragged veils of mist and rain swept over the riverbank below and stole Mara from sight.

Then Sulu fired the shuttle's thrusters and sent it racing skyward into black banks of lightning-laced clouds, toward an uncertain and likely perilous rendezvous in orbit.

Assuming we survive our return through the storm, Spock mused, keeping his thoughts to himself for once.

Kirk rushed onto the bridge of the *Enterprise* as soon as the turbolift doors opened. He bounded down the steps into the command well, straight to his command chair. As he arrived, Lieutenant Commander Scott was already vacating the center seat. "Report, Mister Scott."

"Seventeen minutes ago sensors picked up a major explosion on the planet's surface, near the center of the landing party's assigned mission area."

Taking his chair, Kirk asked, "What kind of explosion?"

Scott's expression turned grave. "Hydrox and deuterium."

A yeoman approached Kirk's chair with a cup of coffee on a tray, but he waved her off. Alarm was enough to quicken Kirk's mind this morning. "As in, the fuels from our shuttle?"

"That was my first thought, as well. But thirty seconds ago we picked up a heat bloom in the lower atmosphere, over the mission area. Ionizing particles and chemical traces consistent with a prolonged hydrox burn by a modified Class-F shuttlecraft."

Kirk looked at the image of Kolasi III on the main viewscreen. The bluish-white orb with its iridescent rings looked so placid, but the belt of black storms around its equator was anything but peaceful. "If that burn was the *Kepler*, she'll be flying blind into the Klingons' patrol route."

"Aye, sir. That she will."

Keenly aware of the seconds elapsing on the ship's chrono, Kirk pondered an ever-growing set of variables with mounting concern. The shuttle. The *Sagittarius*. The Klingons. And whatever classified findings the landing party might have made on the surface. "Mister Nanjiani, has there been any sign of the Klingons' shuttle in pursuit of the *Kepler*?"

The science officer looked up from the hooded display. "None, sir. No indications of other contacts in the planet's atmosphere. Also, I've just confirmed that the explosion we detected earlier contained trace elements consistent with Klingon starship-hull alloys, and was of a magnitude consistent with the volume of hydrox fuel and deuterium I estimate the Klingon shuttle would have had left after making a flight from orbit to the surface."

Alarmed, Kirk looked back at his acting first officer. "Scotty, if that explosion was the Klingons' shuttle being destroyed, then regardless of the cause . . ."

"Aye. We might have an interstellar crisis on our hands."

"What are the odds the Klingons detected the explosion?"

Scott's worries were plain to see on his face and hear in his voice. "Better than fair, sir. And I'd lay even odds they've registered the heat bloom and identified it as one of ours."

Kirk reflexively curled his hands into fists. "So. Kang's guard will be up, and he'll be looking for payback. Not the news I was hoping for this morning, Mister Scott."

"No, sir. But like it or not, our shuttle is still on its way."

"Yes, it is. Which means it's time for us to bring our landing party home." Kirk deftly swiveled his chair as he doled out orders around the bridge. "Uhura, hail the *Sagittarius*. Tell Captain Nassir I'm initiating our emergency retrieval operation. Lieutenant Benson, plot a course to take us into orbit at full impulse. Put us between Kang's ship and the shuttle's recovery point inside the rings. We can't let Kang have a clear shot at the *Kepler*."

"Aye, sir," Benson replied as she entered the new course into the helm.

From the comms console, Uhura replied, "Captain Nassir signals ready, sir."

"Very good. Mister Waltke: arm all weapons, and raise shields." Kirk used the control pad on the armrest of his command chair to open an intraship channel. "All decks, this is the captain. Red alert. All hands to battle stations. This is not a drill." With another push he closed the channel and shot an apprehensive look at Scott. "Time for the fun part. Lieutenant Benson, take us into orbit. It's time I had a talk with Captain Kang."

The sensor readings of the storm's interior were constantly in flux, but Spock was starting to suss out patterns and predicates, enough that he was able to predict the worst of the storm's lightning strikes and thunder. "Helm, shift two point seven degrees starboard, nose up four degrees, and engage auxiliary impulse power."

"Adjusting," Sulu confirmed as he turned Spock's orders into actions.

The *Kepler*'s forward viewports were again protected by their closed blast shutters, which meant Sulu was once more piloting by instruments alone. Without seeing the maelstrom outside, Spock felt it, just as he had during the shuttle's descent days earlier. In spite of his efforts to steer the *Kepler* away from the storm's most violent zones, it continued to be rattled by thunder, buffeted by hurricane-force winds, and jolted by lightning that made interior panels vomit sparks.

A telltale null spot in the sensor readings rippled toward the shuttle.

"Ionic disruption in three seconds. Full thrusters."

The disruption wave rolled through the shuttle, leaving nauseated stomachs and dizzy heads in its wake. Inside the *Kepler* lights flickered and went out, along with half the command console, but the shielded reserve batteries kept the helm online, and Sulu managed the transition from impulse power to thrusters without losing any of the shuttle's acceleration toward orbit.

"Expertly done, Mister Sulu. Impulse drive back online in five seconds."

"Acknowledged, Mister Spock." When perhaps he thought Spock wasn't looking, Sulu blinked hard and gave his head a mild shake.

"Mister Sulu? Are you experiencing a reaction to the distortion field?"

Sulu feigned nonchalance. "It was nothing, sir. I'm fine."

"Perhaps we should get a medical opinion." Spock swiveled his chair to look back at Doctor Babitz—only to find the exhausted medical officer fast asleep in her chair's harness, snoring softly, and seemingly oblivious of the mayhem rocking the tiny spacecraft.

Razka looked at Babitz from his seat across the aisle, and then he shrugged at Spock. "I think it would be a shame to wake her, sir."

With a genial smile Sulu added, "Really, sir. I'm *fine.*"

"Very well. Continue on this heading. We should clear the storm in ten seconds."

"Looking forward to it."

Spock tracked their progress on the sensor display. Right on time they broke free of the storm and shot upward through the tenuous higher altitudes of the planet's atmosphere.

"Ten seconds to vacuum. Adjust heading to bearing three-one-five mark two-seven."

"Aye, sir. Course laid in for recovery rendezvous point."

After the wild ride through the stormhead and the days of continuous rain and thunder that had preceded it, the abrupt blissful silence felt peculiar, verging on eerie. There was nothing more than the thrum of the engines, the soft purr of the ventilation system, and the gentle feedback tones from the flight and command console. In some ways it reminded Spock of going to the library as a child, in the Vulcan capital city of ShiKahr. Blissful, sacred quiet.

Shattered by a rapid, shrill alert beeping from the console in front of him.

He silenced the alarm and checked the sensors. "Contact. A large vessel on an intercept course for our position." He paused for a second to verify the sensor reading. "A Klingon D4 battle cruiser." Reasoning there was nothing to lose by verifying the enemy vessel's presence with his own eyes, he lowered the blast shutters.

Outside the viewports, beyond the multichromatic beauty of the planet's rings, loomed the dark-gray-meets-olive-drab hulking mass of Kang's ship, the *I.K.S. SuvwI'*. It was parked directly on top of the *Kepler*'s predetermined rendezvous point for recovery by the *Enterprise*—which was arriving at that same moment with the *Sagittarius* by its side.

A light flashed on Spock's command console. It denoted an incoming comm signal—from the *SuvwI'*. For a moment Spock considered first checking in with Captain Kirk on the *Enterprise*, but he reasoned that Captain Kang might not be the sort of person to exhibit patience under circumstances such as these.

Spock opened the channel and a dramatic masculine voice issued from the *Kepler*'s console speakers: "*Attention, Starfleet shuttlecraft. This is Captain Kang of the Klingon battle cruiser* SuvwI'. *Your presence in the Neutral Zone is a violation of the Treaty of Organia. Cut power to your engines and prepare to be towed by tractor beam into our shuttlebay, where your vessel will be boarded and you will be taken into custody. Any attempt you make to flee or resist will be taken as an act of war and met with lethal force. You have thirty seconds to confirm your receipt of and intention to comply with these orders. If you fail to do so, you will be destroyed without further warning. Acknowledge.*"

Sulu looked at Spock. "Kang sure likes the sound of his own voice, doesn't he?"

"So it would appear." Spock noted the *Enterprise* and the *Sag-*

ittarius taking up attack positions relative to the *SuvwI'*, and he decided that the most logical course of action would be to give Captains Kirk and Nassir as much time as possible to deal with Kang, an outcome that would be best served by not provoking Kang into prematurely destroying the *Kepler*.

He opened a response channel. "Captain Kang, this is the Starfleet shuttlecraft *Kepler*. We confirm receipt of your transmission and will comply without resistance. Cutting our engines now." He nodded at Sulu, who powered down the shuttle's impulse drive. "Our shields are down, and we stand ready to be towed by your tractor beam. *Kepler* out."

From the back of the shuttle, Chekov sounded shocked. "Mister Spock, you're not serious? We're just giving up without a fight?"

Spock found the question almost amusing. "I suspect the captain has spent our time away preparing for this moment, and that the best way we can help is to do *nothing at all.*"

Kirk listened to Kang's lengthy transmission to the shuttlecraft *Kepler*, and then to Spock's terse reply. *Well done, Spock. Keep him on the hook, right where we want him.*

Around the bridge of the *Enterprise*, everyone was calm but fully alert. Benson was preparing evasive-action plans at the helm. Waltke was precalculating firing solutions to force the *SuvwI'* away from the shuttlecraft. Nanjiani was monitoring every energy emission he could detect from the Klingon battle cruiser, ready to warn Kirk of any hint of Kang's next move.

At the communications console, Uhura monitored their now-restored coded frequency with the *Sagittarius*. "Sir? Captain Nassir confirms he has a phaser lock on the *SuvwI'*."

"Good. Tell him to hold steady, Lieutenant." Kirk straightened his posture and struck a proud pose before he added, "Hail the Klingon ship. Tell Kang I want to speak with him."

It took only a few seconds before Uhura replied, "I have Kang on ship-to-ship."

"On-screen."

The image of the *SuvwI'* with its tractor beam locked onto the *Kepler* was replaced by the visage of Captain Kang. Swarthy and bearded, the Klingon starship captain had a piercing stare and an almost noble bearing that Kirk secretly found admirable. But Kang's demeanor took a turn for the smug. *"What do you want, Kirk? To plead for the lives of your shuttle crew? Or maybe you wish to surrender and spare yourself the shame of defeat?"*

"Far from it, Kang. I'm giving you thirty seconds to release my shuttlecraft, stand down, and let us depart in peace."

" 'Us'? Ah, yes. Of course." Kang smiled like someone who finally had figured out the punch line to a joke. *"Unless I'm mistaken, that's an* Archer-*class scout ship off your starboard bow. Has Starfleet finally assigned you a chaperone, Kirk?"*

"You now have *ten* seconds to release the shuttle."

Kang smirked. *"Or else . . . what?"*

"Five seconds, Kang."

The Klingon was unfazed. *"Four. Three. Two. One. Zero."* He looked up. Around. To either side. Then back at Kirk. *"Well? I'm waiting."* He adopted a mocking tone of feigned pity. *"Was something supposed to happen, Kirk? Maybe you thought you'd detonate a cluster of improvised gravitic mines you so carefully hid in the planet's rings."* He called up an image of his ship's cargo bay as an inset frame; in the middle of that image was a pallet stacked with the devices improvised and deployed by the crew of the *Sagittarius*. *"Perhaps these six gravitic mines? All of which my crew found and disarmed an hour ago."*

Kirk squinted at the inset image. "Well, that's odd. I count only *five* gravitic mines."

Kang snapped, *"Look again! There are clearly* six!*"*

After studying the image for a few more seconds, Kirk

frowned and shook his head. "No, I don't think so. But let me get a second opinion. Mister Scott?"

His chief engineer and acting first officer left his station and descended into the command well to stand next to Kirk's chair. "Aye, sir?"

"Scotty, have a look at that inset image. How many gravitic mines do you count?"

A quick glance, and then Scott answered with confidence, "Five, sir."

On the viewscreen, Kang was furious. *"There are* six! *Why do you waste my time, Kirk?"*

"What do you want me to say, Kang? When I look at the feed from your cargo bay, I see five gravitic mines—and one isolitic pulse device *disguised* as a gravitic mine, with a sixty-second trigger linked to the detection of stray graviton particles from a Klingon tractor beam."

Fury and pride faded from Kang's face, leaving only a slack stare of horror. *"No!"*

Spock interjected over the open channel, *"Captain Kang: before you lose comms, I bring a message from your wife, Mara. Send her another shuttle at your next opportunity. Spock out."*

Kang lost any semblance of composure. *"Damn you, Kirk! You and your whole crew of* yIntaghpu'! ghe'torDaq luSpet 'oH DaqlIje'! Sop—!"

A brilliant flash of white light washed out the inset vid frame, and then the entire comm signal from the *SuvwI'* distorted before collapsing into a hiss of static followed by silence.

Kirk felt pleased with himself. "Lieutenant Uhura, I didn't catch the last part of Kang's message. Did the universal translator fail?"

"No, sir. Our database for *tlhIngan Hol* remains limited. Apparently, it wasn't able to translate Kang's last remarks before we lost contact."

"No matter. I'm sure he'll be happy to repeat them the next

time we meet." He looked at the main viewscreen and smiled at the image of the *SuvwI'* floating derelict and powerless. "Fine work, Mister Scott. That ought to keep them busy for the next hour or so."

"Aye, sir, but I can't take the credit. The IPD was Mister De-Salle's idea."

"I see. I admire your honesty, Mister Scott, though you did just talk yourself out of a very good bottle of bourbon." Kirk sat back and let his shoulders relax. "Mister Waltke, bring the shuttle aboard ASAP, and have the *Sagittarius* take station to starboard. Lieutenant Benson, set a course for Federation space. Five minutes from now, I want us all to be anywhere but here."

Adrift. No shields. No weapons. No power, propulsion, or comms. Nothing but silence and the shame of defeat. Kang's only solace was the darkness that hid him from the eyes of his crew.

Around him, the bridge of the *SuvwI'* stirred with muted curses and the clatter of tools. His officers' repair efforts were empty theatrics; they had to know as well as Kang did that there would be nothing they could do to reverse the damage of the isolitic pulse weapon. That burden rested on the shoulders of Chief Engineer Qurag and his legion of grime-covered tool-pushers.

It won't matter anyway. By the time Qurag gets main power back online, the Enterprise *and her little friend* Sagittarius *will be long gone. Revenge will need to wait for some other day.*

He reflected on the last few reports his crew had made before their failed attempt to capture the Starfleet shuttle. In retrospect, the explosion that Boqor had detected on the planet's surface before the altercation in orbit was most likely the destruction of the *QInqul.*

What could have happened to it? It was a question Kang knew would be impossible to answer without further information.

How many of the strike team had been aboard? For that matter, how many were still alive? The one named Spock had made a point of telling Kang that Mara was alive, but he hadn't mentioned anyone else. Did that mean Mara was the sole survivor? Or just that he hadn't thought the others worthy of mention?

Too many questions. No answers. Just time wasted, sitting in the dark.

Kang felt as if his impatience was burning a hole in his stomach. There was so much he wanted to know about the strike team's mission outcome. Did they find Doctor Chunvig? Were they able to neutralize her and purge her illegal research? And what was the Starfleet team doing down there? Had they also been seeking Chunvig? Did the strike team engage the Starfleeters in battle? If they had, this encounter would be only the beginning of a long and bloody debacle.

The notion of renewed hostilities with the Federation would once have pleased Kang. On some level, it still did. But he had seen enough of war to know that as with any good thing, it was possible to have too much of it. Conquest was always glorious, but so was a bountiful harvest. There were times for celebration, and times for remembrance. For strengthening the Empire's foundations before once again expanding its boundaries.

Isolated in his command chair atop its dais, Kang wondered if there would be anything resembling victory to be wrung from this seemingly ill-fated encounter. It would be at least another hour or maybe even twice as long before he would know anything for certain. He would have no answers to his litany of questions until he could send another shuttlecraft to the planet's surface to pick up Mara and bring her back to the *SuvwI'*.

If nothing else, I am thankful Mara did not go to Sto-Vo-Kor without me. But unless I think of a way to frame this fiasco for the High Command that does not make me look like an utter petaQ, *they might well decide to take my command and deliver me to Fek'lhr.*

It was a skill every commanding officer of the Klingon Imperial Fleet needed to cultivate if they wanted their careers to last longer than the life cycle of a *zeet*-fly: reframing a disastrous encounter to resemble a successful one. Part of what made the task challenging was that it would be accompanied by a copy of the ship's sensor logs. Which meant it was necessary to persuade the generals of the High Command and the members of the High Council that what they clearly saw in sensor recordings was not in fact what actually occurred.

I can say the SuvwI' *is outdated. Too old to face off with a relatively new Starfleet battle cruiser like the* Enterprise. *And then take into account that the* Enterprise *had help from a second starship* . . . He vacillated on how to describe the *Sagittarius*. It needed to sound threatening but also not directly contradict the sensor data. Then he had a flash of inspiration. *Yes! A second starship, a special high-velocity stealth vessel, one with a tremendous tactical advantage that I can argue we should nullify by making a treaty with the Romulans for their cloaking technology.*

He wondered if his superiors would believe any of that. Then he decided he didn't care.

I have come too far to concern myself about the opinions of others. As long as Chunvig is dead and her research destroyed, the High Command will call me a hero, as will the Council.

But that would come later. For the next few hours all Kang would have were his regrets and his hobbled starship. Alone in the center seat, shrouded in shadow, there was nothing for him to do but rage in silence at the one soul who deserved to suffer for all of this.

Damn you, Kirk. Damn you straight to Gre'thor.

29

Federation Ambassador Akeylah Karumé dreaded official parley conferences with her Klingon counterpart. Such meetings were as mannered as Japanese kabuki and as pointless as a vegan barbecue. Regardless, the terms of the recently negotiated Treaty of Organia obligated her to sit in her office on an upper level of Starbase Vanguard, endure a tirade of verbal abuse via subspace comm, and pretend it didn't infuriate her almost to the verge of homicide.

It didn't help that Ambassador G'jar of the Klingon Empire was in rare form today. The skinny, pale, ridge-headed bloviator had entered the meeting shouting, and he hadn't relented or even moderated his volume for over fifteen minutes, in spite of the fact that frothy spittle flew from his mouth whenever he uttered hard consonants.

"Lies and perfidy! It was no accident two Starfleet vessels were in the Kolasi system at the exact moment the Empire needed to effect a vital rescue operation! It was sabotage! I—"

"Permit me to interrupt," Karumé said in a tone that made clear she wasn't even remotely asking for permission. "Rescue operation? My understanding is that Captain Kang sent a strike team to the surface of Kolasi III. They were there only to kill and destroy, not to rescue."

"Irrelevant! They had valid orders, but your Starfleet landing

party interfered and got them all killed! Or maybe even murdered them all themselves!"

"No one who was actually there has said any such thing."

"I'm *saying it, you* petaQ*! Your people were there to obstruct our mission!"*

It took great self-control for Karumé to resist the urge to raise her voice or massage the pounding ache from her temples. Instead, she mustered the ghost of a smile. "Your strike team's sole survivor, Lieutenant Mara, insists that she and her team willingly allied themselves with the Starfleet landing party in order to destroy a Shedai threat. Commander Spock of the *Enterprise* filed a report that is nearly identical in its account of events after the two teams met."

"*So you admit your people were on the planet!*"

Karumé sighed. *His stupidity is magnifying my headache, I'm sure of it.* "We've never denied it, G'jar. Are you sure you got enough sleep last night? Because you don't quite seem to grasp the details of the matter, despite having the after-action report open in front of you."

"*There's nothing to grasp, Earther! Your ships breached the Neutral Zone without receiving advance permission from the Klingon Empire, as required by the Treaty of Organia!*"

"So did yours. Based on your own people's field reports, Doctor Chunvig was the first to do so, by more than a week." Karumé picked up her data slate and skimmed the report from Commander Spock. "Both our team and yours reported nearly identical accounts of what transpired on Kolasi III. So tell me again: What *are* we arguing about?"

"*How quickly you forget! Your people attacked the* SuvwI', *a military vessel in the service of the Klingon Empire!*"

Given no choice but to feign ignorance, Karumé looked again at her data slate, and then she shook her head. "Hm. No, sorry. Official logs from the *Enterprise* and the *Sagittarius* make no mention of any direct hostile action against the *SuvwI'.*"

"Liar! Treacherous HaDIbaH*! They set a trap for Captain Kang's ship! He found their trap and captured it, not knowing that was part of their elaborate deception!"*

She pantomimed taking another look at the data slate for confirmation. "No, sorry. The logs say nothing about any traps being set by either ship."

"Choke on your lies, yIntagh*! Your people modified five photon torpedoes into gravitic mines, and transformed a sixth into an isolitic pulse device disguised as a gravitic mine!"*

"That sounds familiar. Hang on a second." She ran her fingertip down the slate's edge, as if she were speed-reading. "Captain Kirk did report seeing objects in a vid feed from the cargo hold of Kang's ship that resembled the devices you describe. But he denies creating them."

"You know *he did!"*

"Do you have proof? As in, hard incontrovertible evidence you'd be willing to present to a Starfleet tribunal to call for Captain Kirk's court-martial?"

G'jar squirmed in his seat, and finally some of the fire went out of his rhetoric. *"No, not exactly. The jury-rigged devices were all too badly damaged by the pulse device for Kang's crew to make a positive identification of their provenance."*

"So for all you or they know, those devices could have been left behind by smugglers. Or even abandoned there by some other Klingon vessel that illegally entered the Neutral Zone."

The Klingon's forehead creased and his eyebrows knitted in a show of annoyance. *"Stop insulting my intelligence."*

"I'm not sure that's actually *possible*, G'jar." She put the data slate on her desk and pushed it aside. "Do you have any other baseless accusations you'd like to make without having a shred of evidentiary support? Because it's getting late and I'm getting bored."

He slammed his fist down onto his desktop's control pad as he shouted "Qu'vatlh*!"*

To Karumé's great relief, the screen went dark, and a small error code appeared that confirmed G'jar had terminated the conversation from his side. She switched the viewscreen to standby mode and buried her face in her umber-brown hands. *Goddess, how he vexes me.*

Hoping a kick of caffeine would banish some of her mental fatigue, Karumé picked up her mug and took a sip, only to find her black coffee had gone tepid during her session of verbal abuse by G'jar. *Well, isn't that just perfect.*

She put down the mug, reclined her chair, and took a moment to adjust the drape of her brightly colored robes. It had been a long day before G'jar had drained the sense out of it, and judging by the proliferation of demands from the Federation Council and the office of the Federation president for updates and analyses of the Kolasi III situation, it was far from over.

Ambassador Jetanien made this all look so easy.

Karumé recalled with a smile the pompous mannerisms of her former superior in the Federation Diplomatic Corps, a Rigellian Chelon who to her resembled a gigantic bipedal turtle with exquisite fashion sense and a majestic bass-rich voice. After a near-total breakdown of Federation-Klingon diplomatic relations the previous year, Jetanien had announced that he was taking an indefinite leave of absence and departing for worlds unknown.

It had been several months since Jetanien's departure from Vanguard, and no one had heard from him since. In his absence, and very much against her wishes, Karumé had been promoted to take his place as the Federation's senior diplomatic officer on Starbase Vanguard.

Jetanien used to move through this station like a king, and when he spoke he pontificated like a university professor. He had a speech for damned near everything and made a million obscure references I never understood. His perfectionism, his micro-

management, his oxygen-stealing ego—I shall never forget how they constantly enraged me.

How I wish he were still here.

————————

He had listened intently, minded every word of every question and every answer, and had waited for Admiral Nogura to ask follow-up questions and Captain Nassir to answer them, but when the two superior officers were done talking, Lieutenant Ming Xiong remained discomfited.

"Sirs? I have questions, if I may."

From either side of Nogura's desk in his office above the operations center of Starbase Vanguard, Nassir and the admiral regarded the trim, thirtyish anthropology-and-archeology officer with waning patience. Nogura, whose salt-and-pepper eyebrows matched his charcoal-and-steel buzzcut, spoke first. "About *what*, Xiong?"

Suddenly on the spot, Xiong cast a sideways look up at Starfleet Intelligence liaison Commander ch'Nayla, only to find the lanky Andorian *chan* studiously avoiding all eye contact. Xiong drew a breath and pressed onward. "Why wasn't a sample of the modified Shedai meta-genome recovered for analysis? Something like that might have advanced our understanding of how the meta-genome interacts with other genetic strings."

An overhead light cast a bright reflection off the top of Nassir's bald head as he faced Xiong. "As I explained to the admiral, Lieutenant, our landing party had to make certain compromises to secure the cooperation of the Klingon strike team from the *SuvwI'*." As if to prolong Xiong's discomfort, the captain sipped his coffee. "That, plus the subsequent damage to the party's tricorders, rendered any data from the landing mission unusable."

"What about the shuttle's sensors?"

"By the time they were in range of the area known to serve as the creature's lair, the last traces of the meta-genome had been sterilized by the sacrifice of the Klingon shuttle *QInqul*."

"Couldn't data have been recovered from Doctor Chunvig's ship?"

Nassir shook his head. "According to Doctor Babitz, there wasn't much to find. And what little our people found, the Klingons vaporized."

"And I presume the same was true of Doctor Verdo's research?"

"No, *that* they recovered. But it was all subsequently lost when their tricorders were damaged in combat against the natives and the Shedai."

The scope of the landing party's failure seemed almost farcical to Xiong. "Did they bring back *any* new intelligence about the Shedai?"

"None of any note. At least, none that they logged."

Finally, ch'Nayla joined the conversation by cutting in to ask, "How much new intel about the Shedai did the Klingons acquire during their operation on Kolasi III?"

The question made Nassir think a moment before answering. "Doctor Babitz and the *Enterprise*'s first officer, Commander Spock, both insist the last survivor of the Klingon strike team left the planet with no more knowledge of the Shedai than that with which she arrived."

Xiong checked his notes from the earlier portion of the briefing. "That would be science officer Lieutenant Mara of the *I.K.S. SuvwI'*? Captain Kang's *wife*?"

"I think that's correct, yes."

"And just how much knowledge of the Shedai did Lieutenant Mara possess when she arrived on Kolasi III, Captain?"

"There's no way I can know that, Lieutenant. Based on statements she made to the landing party, Doctor Babitz thinks Lieutenant Mara has been privy to as much classified intel about the Shedai as either you or I might be right now."

That was the second-worst news Xiong could have expected

to hear. He had to wonder: How much more did Mara know, and from whom had she learned it? "Captain, did your people on the landing party report any statements or actions by Lieutenant Mara, or by any member of her strike team, that would suggest the Klingons know of the Vault on Starbase Vanguard, or the true purpose of Operation Vanguard itself?"

Nassir ceased pretending to be patient and surrendered to his exhaustion and frustration. "No, dammit. My people heard nothing of the sort. They were too busy fighting for their lives."

"My apologies, Captain. It's just that after some recent breaches in Starbase 47's security, I've been compelled to seek out any possible lingering weaknesses in our OpSec."

The Deltan man gave Xiong a polite half nod. "Of course."

Nogura leaned forward and folded his hands atop his desk. "For all its setbacks and losses, it sounds as if the mission to Kolasi III went as well as we could have expected. Perhaps better, if we take into account Babitz's and Spock's after-action reports, both of which described a new spirit of cooperation with the Klingons. I'm no fan of their empire, but even I would have to think that the possibility of an armistice and maybe even one day an alliance with the Klingons would pay tremendous dividends for the cause of galactic peace."

Commander ch'Nayla seemed less excited by that notion. "It might be too soon to make such prognostications, Admiral. Future relations between the Federation and the Klingon Empire will likely be strained and politically delicate for decades to come."

"No doubt. But progress has to start somewhere, Commander. It might as well be here." Just as quickly as Nogura's optimism had manifested, it slipped away, surrendering the admiral to a black mood. "The problems are the Tholians, who have no interest in peace, and the Shedai, who seem hell-bent on either subjugating us or annihilating us. Either one could disrupt our mission in the Taurus Reach, and bring about the deaths of millions in the process."

Weighing those words, ch'Nayla asked, "Is that an argument for caution, Admiral?"

"Maybe. Maybe not. The truth is, I don't know. My fear is that it's only going to be a matter of time before someone stuck inside this political pressure cooker explodes, and once that happens, the time for talking will be over, and the only language left will be bloodshed. Once we cross that line, there won't be any more chances for cooler heads to prevail." He turned a worried look to the star map on his office's viewscreen. "The stakes of our mission only go up from here."

Kirk heard Spock's voice from the speaker next to the door: *"Come."*

The door slid open with a soft *whish*, and Kirk stepped inside Spock's quarters. The lighting had been dimmed, and Spock apparently had increased his cabin's temperature and reduced its humidity to levels that better suited the Vulcan half of his physiology. Feeling the hot, dry air wash over him, Kirk flashed back to the *Enterprise*'s recent visit to Vulcan—and to the horrifying sensation of Spock's hands around his throat, crushing the life out of him.

Here's hoping his adjustments to the climate controls are purely nostalgic.

He moved past the small alcove that contained Spock's desk and books as well as several assorted bits of memorabilia, and found his first officer sitting on the end of his bunk, his hands folded in front of his face, his index fingers steepled and pressed against his lips. The half Vulcan was dressed in his regular duty uniform of black trousers, boots, and blue tunic. Though his stare seemed to be peering through the blue-gray bulkhead in front of him, he acknowledged Kirk's arrival with a perfunctory salutation of "Captain."

"Spock? Are you feeling all right?"

The Vulcan remained eerily still as he replied, "Physically, yes."

His answer troubled Kirk. "It's not like you to request a day of medical leave without even visiting sickbay. Which is a breach of regulations, by the way."

"I am aware."

Kirk stepped cautiously past Spock, as if seeing his friend from the other side would somehow shed any light on his unusual behavior. "Unless you want Doctor McCoy to order you into sickbay for a full work-up, you might want to try talking to me, Spock."

Spock lowered his hands and set them palms down on his thighs. "My apologies, Captain. I did not mean to create an issue with which you would be asked to contend."

"Spock, it's fine. What I'm trying to say is, if there's something you need to talk about, you can trust me to keep your secrets. I'm here to help, not to judge."

The first officer looked at the deck, then he closed his eyes for a few seconds. When he opened them, he looked at Kirk. "Forgive me, Captain. I have been troubled by many things since our encounter with the planet-killer."

"I understand, Spock, believe me. That's been on my mind, as well." For a moment Kirk considered sharing his misgivings about the suicide of Commodore Matt Decker, but he elected to keep those thoughts to himself, at least for now. "Why has it troubled *you*?"

Spock folded his hands in his lap and shifted to face Kirk. "When I consider the immense technological prowess and manufacturing capability required to engineer and produce something as horrific as the planet-killer, I am compelled to think of the Shedai, and the fearsome technologies they unleashed upon our own galaxy. I wonder what gave rise to their brutal, domineering mastery of forces great and minuscule, their control over sciences so arcane and occult that they have become lost to time. And when I realize the scales of destruction of which both were and are capable . . . I cannot help but wonder, Captain: Is it possible that there are some forms of knowledge that should not be allowed to propagate? Could it be that there are concepts that are intrinsically *evil*?"

The question was not what Kirk had expected. During their years of shared service, his first officer had asked him many questions of a logical nature. This was one of only a few times Spock had posed a question within a moral frame of reference.

"I'm not sure, Spock. The Academy taught us not to think in absolutes, to reject such binary concepts as good and evil. I've always found that advice useful. But is that what you're talking about? Or is there some other dimension to your question?"

Spock seemed to turn his focus inward. "I have tried to replicate the thought processes of the Shedai as they lorded their power over their vassal worlds, and those of the Romulans and the Klingons as they have so cruelly oppressed theirs. I have tried to understand how they rationalized their tyranny by embracing their perspective on galactic politics.

"But I cannot accept their outcomes. They are *not* logical."

He looked up at Kirk and was visibly distraught. In a being who had less-than-complete control over their emotions, what followed might have devolved into anguish. But for Spock the cost of confronting reality's abject cruelty was confusion and alienation. Kirk imagined he could almost see tears welling in Spock's eyes as the first officer continued.

"What were they *thinking*, Jim? What must be lacking in a species that would even conceive of something so terrible as the planet-killer, never mind be so morally bankrupt as to actually build it and unleash it upon the universe? What tragic flaw would account for such evil? A dearth of imagination? The absence of empathy? The lack of a conscience?"

Kirk didn't want to play devil's advocate for the planet-killer, but he wanted to offer his best friend something that might feel like hope. "Maybe they were scared, Spock. Desperate."

"Perhaps. But I'm not sure that absolves them of the sin of releasing those atrocities. Nor will history forgive us if we fail to halt the proliferation of Shedai-based technologies."

"What do you mean, Spock?"

"All the mistakes I see in the origin of the planet-killer. I see the same technological and biological recklessness in the creation and replication of the Shedai meta-genome."

It was a damning allegation, and one that Kirk was ill-equipped to refute. "I see what you're saying, Spock. But I'm still not sure there's any such thing as an intrinsically evil idea. The moral ramifications of any technology, great or small, lie in what is done to acquire and develop it, and then what is done *with* it."

"Exactly my point, Captain. Look at how many lives have already been lost in a futile effort to monopolize the Shedai meta-genome. See how many worlds have been made to suffer. I once thought as you do, that knowledge for its own sake was an absolute good. But my own experience with the diabolical secrets of the Shedai compels me to reconsider my position."

Kirk found it unnerving to hear Spock, an avowed man of science, accuse any form of knowledge of being morally corrupt. His inner optimist drove him to try to steer Spock back toward the shores of hope, however distant they might presently seem. "Have faith, Spock. Some good might yet come of this research, however flawed it might be."

His first officer did not sound persuaded.

"We shall see, Captain. We shall see."

Kang lay awake in his bed, propped up on one elbow, watching his beloved Mara sleep. Their quarters aboard the *SuvwI'* were dark and quiet, and his crew knew well from experience that to disturb him or Mara for anything less than an existential danger to the ship or to the Klingon Empire would result in the offender being expelled from an airlock without a pressure suit.

Faint service lights along the bulkheads limned Mara's profile with an amber glow. Kang admired his wife's elegant, angular features. Her exquisite nose; her delicate chin; her sharp cheekbones. Though she was a *QuchHa'*, she was twice the woman of any other Klingon, Kang was certain of it.

How perfect you are. You are my world. My life. More than honor, I treasure you. And I will never forget how close I came to losing you.

Her words haunted him. Upon first hearing them he had found them hard to believe. Now he found them impossible to forget. From anyone else he would have denounced them as lies and collected the mendicant's head. But how could he doubt Mara?

She insisted the Starfleeters had saved her life. At great risk to their own. That they could easily have left her to her fate, but that they had fought monsters and nature itself to rescue her.

Humans risked themselves to save my Mara.

Was it possible the High Council and the High Command both were wrong about humans? About Starfleet? About the Federation? The villains Kang had been trained to fight would never have acted so nobly. Was it possible that everything the Empire had told Kang about the people of the Federation was nothing more than . . . *propaganda*?

They tell us our enemy has no honor. Yet what is honor if not courage free of the expectation of reward? What is honor if not the willingness to sacrifice all for a principle?

More troubling to his thoughts was Mara's after-action report. She had reported in gruesome detail the abomination that Doctor Chunvig had made of herself, and the tremendous acts of violence and destruction of which even a debased Shedai was capable.

Worst of all, she had documented just how difficult the mutated Doctor Chunvig—who had adopted the sobriquet Shedai Godhead—had been to kill. After less than three weeks of absorbing power from the primitive inhabitants of a stone-age planet, the Godhead had made itself nearly impervious to small-arms fire, and by the end of its battle with the combined Starfleet-Klingon strike team, even the siege-gun disruptors had not been enough to subdue the monster. Only the brutal sacrifice of a shuttle crashing directly into it had slain the thing.

If that is what a false Shedai can do, how fearsome must the real ones be? And if they are so terrible, what kind of fools must the Federation be to tempt their wrath?

Eldritch terrors from before the dawn of history . . . that was not the enemy Kang had joined the Imperial Fleet to fight. Whatever the Federation had set in motion in the unclaimed sectors of interstellar space that separated the Klingon Empire from the Tholian Assembly, he wanted no part of it. Not unless there was some way to turn it to his advantage.

In the name of Kahless, what kind of nightmare has Starfleet awoken in the Gonmog Sector? And how can I use it to persuade the High Command to give me a bigger ship?

30

Ensconced in his command chair on the bridge of the *Enterprise*, James Kirk reveled in the return of familiar ambient sounds. After weeks of repairs his ship was starting to sound like itself again. The pitch of air moving through its ventilation systems, the low steady hum of the impulse-power system resonating through the plasma conduits, the soft feedback tones of bridge consoles once again operating at peak efficiency: this sounded like home.

Equally comforting to Kirk were the familiar faces and voices that surrounded him. Though his years of service had taught him that change was the only true constant in Starfleet, and that it was best not to get too attached to one's crew, he had realized how much he missed the banter of Lieutenant Sulu and Ensign Chekov at the forward console only after it became absent. How much he had missed *them*, these brave, noble young officers.

Spock had resumed his post at the sciences console, but Scott remained at the bridge's engineering station, coordinating the ship's last few repairs. When the chief engineer happened to glance in Kirk's direction, the captain beckoned him with a tilt of his head.

Scott wrapped up his current conversation over the intraship comm and left his post to stand beside Kirk's chair. "Sir?"

"How are we doing, Mister Scott?"

"The old girl's in grand form, sir. Hale and able, and ready for warp speed."

"Splendid news. Speaking of which, have you told Mister De-Salle that I've put him up for a commendation?"

"The Star Cross, aye! He couldn't be vogier, sir."

Having no idea what *vogier* meant, Kirk smiled. "Glad to hear it." Scott returned to his post as Kirk swiveled his chair to look at Uhura. "Lieutenant, any response from Starfleet?"

"We're to set course for the frontier, any uncharted sector. Your discretion, sir."

Her news put a smile on Kirk's face. "That's what I like to hear!" He let his chair turn back toward the main viewscreen. "Mister Spock? Is the crew ready to get underway?"

His half-Vulcan first officer looked up from the hooded sensor display. "Affirmative, Captain. All hands accounted for, and the ship is ready for service."

Behind Kirk, the turbolift doors parted with a soft hiss, and Doctor McCoy strode onto the bridge in a rare good mood. "Call me a miracle worker, Jim! For the first time in months, sickbay is completely clear of patients. Not even a sniffle. Ask me how I did it."

Unable to resist taking the bait, Kirk asked with a straight face, "How'd you do it?"

"I announced it was time to start this year's round of mandatory physical exams."

Kirk chuckled. "You're a cruel man, Bones." He set his eyes on the main viewscreen and its tableau of a cosmos awaiting discovery. "Mister Sulu, set a course: *thataway*. Warp four."

Sulu beamed with excitement at Kirk's open-ended command. "Aye, sir." Then he smiled at Chekov, who brightened as well. Working in tandem, the helmsman and navigator set the *Enterprise* in motion toward stars unknown but shining with possibilities.

As warp speed stretched the stars on the viewscreen into

streaks, Spock and McCoy settled in on either side of Kirk's command chair. McCoy gazed wistfully at the bent starlight. "Once more into the unknown. Maybe I'm getting soft in my middle age, but I think I'm starting to enjoy this."

"That makes two of us, Bones. Deep space, the unexplored sectors of the frontier . . . this is what I joined Starfleet to see. And if it means leaving behind Operation Vanguard and its classified catastrophes, so much the better."

Spock lifted an eyebrow but kept his true feelings hidden. "Though some of its methods are questionable, I would have expected you to embrace its mission to uncover the unknown."

"Vanguard's methods aren't just questionable, Spock. They're downright suicidal. Mark my words: if I never see Starbase 47 again, it'll be too soon."

His denunciation seemed to put Spock in a pensive mood. The first officer joined the doctor in focusing upon the main viewscreen's panorama of stars. "Be that as it may, Captain, I suspect we have not seen the last of Starbase Vanguard."

Acknowledgments

As always I wish to thank first my wife, Kara, for her unwavering support and encouragement; my agent Lucienne Diver for handling the fine print; my editors Ed Schlesinger and Margaret Clark for continuing to hire me after more than twenty years of my tomfoolery; my copy editor and compañero Scott Pearson for making my prose the best it can be (short of it being written by someone else); and my pals Glenn Hauman, Aaron Rosenberg, Dayton Ward, James Swallow, Robert Greenberger, and John Van Citters for listening when I needed to vent.

Special shout-outs are due to Marco Palmieri, with whom I created the *Star Trek: Vanguard* saga back in 2004; Kevin Dilmore, who, with his writing partner Dayton Ward, shared the saga's writing privileges with yours truly; and visual artist Doug Drexler, whose exquisite CGI renderings gave the *Vanguard* book covers their signature style.

Last but not least, thank you, readers, for having bought so much of my *Star Trek* scribblings over the last twenty years (and thirty novels). Live long and prosper!

About the Author

If you've got a problem with bunnies,
you've got a problem with David Mack,
and he suggests you let that marinate.

Learn more on his official website:
davidmack.pro
Or follow him on Twitter:
@DavidAlanMack